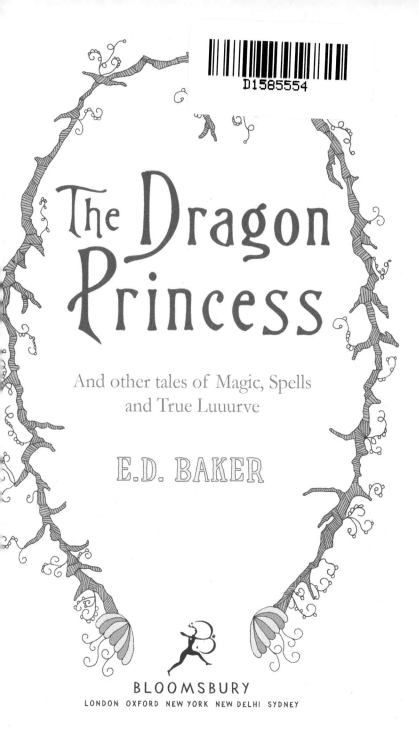

The Dragon Princess

And other tales of Magic, Spells
and True Luuurve

E.D. BAKER

BLOOMSBURY

LONDON OXFORD NEW YORK NEW DELHI SYDNEY

Bloomsbury Publishing, London, Oxford, New York, New Delhi and Sydney

This omnibus edition first published in Great Britain in October 2011
by Bloomsbury Publishing Plc
50 Bedford Square, London WC1B 3DP

www.bloomsbury.com
www.edbakerbooks.com

No Place for Magic first published in Great Britain
by Bloomsbury Publishing Plc in 2008
First published in the USA
by Bloomsbury USA Children's Books in 2006
Text copyright © E.D. Baker 2006

The Salamander Spell first published in the USA
by Bloomsbury USA Children's Books in 2007
Text copyright © E.D. Baker 2007

The Dragon Princess first published in the USA
by Bloomsbury USA Children's Books in 2008
Text copyright © E.D. Baker 2008

The moral right of the author has been asserted

Illustration of dragon and title page art by Sinem Erkas

A CIP catalogue record for this book is available from the British Library

ISBN 978 1 4088 1474 1

Printed in Great Britain by CPI Group (UK) Ltd, Croydon, CR0 4YY

5 7 9 10 8 6 4

This book is dedicated to Ellie for being my sounding board, to Kimmy for laughing at all the right places, to Victoria for her insight, to Nate and Emiko for their support and enthusiasm, and to all my wonderful fans who wrote to me wanting to know what happens next.

Contents

Contents

No Place
for Magic

One

A tendril brushed my face, tickling me on the nose. I jerked my head back and whacked it on the table leg behind me. "Wretched plant!" I said, rubbing my head with one hand as I pushed the vine away with the other.

Ever since my aunt had returned to her normal self, she hadn't been able to keep her mind on anything but her beloved Haywood. Her magic had suffered for it, becoming muddled and not quite as she'd intended. The flowering vines she'd planted in the Great Hall to celebrate their reunion had spread across the walls, engulfed the table legs, and threatened to cover the doors and windows. Because they were too tough for an ordinary knife to cut, it was up to me, the Green Witch, to keep them under control. Once again I was on my hands and knees, bumping my head and banging my elbows as I used magic clippers to trim the ever-growing vines.

Being the Green Witch meant that I had a lot of extra

1

responsibilities. Although I was the most powerful witch in Greater Greensward, as well as its only princess, most of the things I had to do as its protector were neither glamorous nor exciting. At least I didn't have to clean out the moat very often, a job I really hated.

I was reaching for the next curling vine when a bright yellow butterfly landed on my finger and fluttered its wings as if trying to get my attention. "What do you want?" I asked.

The butterfly stomped its feet with impatience. I raised my finger to my ear and tried to listen, but couldn't hear anything over the usual early morning bustle of the Great Hall. Squires were cleaning their knights' weapons while flirting with passing maids. My father's hounds were scuffling over a bone in the corner. The steward was directing the hanging of new banners along the walls.

I could hardly hear the tiny insect, but then I remembered that their voices were extremely soft. Hearing them requires a magic spell, undivided attention, and a very keen ear. I'd had enough practice creating my own spells that coming up with one to hear the butterfly was easy.

Although I'd never spoken with a butterfly before, I expected its voice to be sweet. Instead it sounded like an old man who was hoarse from shouting. "Take your time, lady," said the butterfly. "I don't have anything better to do—just flit from flower to flower until I've inspected every one in that garden. It shouldn't take me much longer than, say . . . my entire life! So, what's it going to be? Are you going to see the old lady or not?"

"Who are you talking about?"

"I knew you weren't paying attention. I could be back at work doing something important, but no, I had to carry a message to someone who can't even be bothered to listen!"

"I'm sorry. I couldn't hear you. What was your message?"

"I don't have time for this! The old lady with the roses wants me to tell you that she's going to work on her house today. She wants to know if you're going to come help. That's it. That's all I know. If you'll answer her question, I'll be on my way. I have a lot of flying ahead of me, so if you don't mind . . ."

"Yes, I'll be there. You have your answer—now go."

A shadow loomed over me as the butterfly zigzagged across the Great Hall and up to one of the windows. "What was that all about?" demanded my mother, who had slipped up behind me.

I sighed and turned around. Although the removal of the family curse had made my grandmother and aunt sweet and kind again, it hadn't done a thing for my mother. She hadn't been affected by the curse, so she was the same as she'd always been. It didn't matter to her that I was the Green Witch and sixteen years old; she still treated me as if I were five. The only time she listened to

3

what I had to say was when I turned into a dragon, and then *everyone* paid attention to me. Most of the time, she tried to tell me what to do while I tried to avoid her.

If I'd been thinking clearly, I might have given her some excuse, but instead I made the mistake of telling her the truth. "I told Grandmother to let me know when she was going to work on her cottage. She sent word that she's about to start."

"So you're going to the Old Witches' Retirement Community? Then we can ride in my carriage together. I was planning to go see her today anyway."

"Ride?" I said, adding the vine clippings to the pile I'd already started. I hadn't ridden in a carriage for months, because I hated the jostling and bumping and now had other ways to get around. As the Green Witch I toured Greater Greensward on my magic carpet every few weeks. When I wasn't using the carpet, I generally flew another way, as a bird, a bat, or a dragon, although being a dragon was the most fun.

"I was just about to leave," I said. "If you have something to do first, you can come when you're ready." I was still hoping that I could go by myself. The Old Witches' Retirement Community was only a few minutes away if I went as a dragon, leaving me enough time to stretch my wings and soar above the clouds and . . .

"I'm ready now," said Mother. "You won't get out of it that easily."

It had been almost two months since I'd learned how to turn myself into a dragon. I'd done it out of necessity at the end of the tournament held to celebrate my sixteenth birthday. My grandmother and aunt had gotten into a magical argument, and I'd had to turn myself into the biggest, fiercest creature that I could think of to get them to listen. Since then I'd taken to saying the spell so often that the people of Greater Greensward had grown used to seeing a green dragon soaring overhead. I liked being a dragon because it made me feel stronger and freer than I'd ever felt before. As a dragon, I could also fly farther and faster than in any other form I'd ever tried.

Unfortunately, traveling with my mother meant that I wasn't going to get a chance to be anything but my human self. She never had wanted me to do magic, although she had gotten used to it after I proved that I had the talent. Recently, we'd formed a sort of unspoken truce; she wouldn't tell me how awful magic was and I wouldn't use it around her unless it was absolutely necessary, but there was always the chance that one of us might forget and slip. Because this made our relationship even more strained and uncomfortable than it had been already, being in a confined space with her for any length of time was one of the last things I wanted to do.

The ride was worse than I'd feared; a heavy rain the night before had scoured large ruts in the roads, and of course my mother refused to let me use my magic to do anything about them. She and I both knew that I would eventually be the one to fix them, just not while she was there. We were well inside the enchanted forest on the road to Grandmother's cottage when we hit a bad bump and I thumped my head against the side of the carriage.

Mother clicked her tongue and said, "I suppose you're going to tell me that you'd rather be flying. Don't bother," she added when I opened my mouth to speak. "I know you don't like spending time with me. You never have. You always preferred my sister's company over mine, and who could blame you? Her responsibilities were exciting, whereas I had the boring and thankless job of supervising the running of a castle. And now that you're safeguarding the kingdom with your magic, you have even less time for me."

"I didn't know that you . . ."

"Of course you didn't," she snapped. "You never think about how I feel. I just hope that when you have a daughter, she considers your feelings more than you have mine and shows you more respect as well. I know you think I'm foolish and don't know what I'm talking about, but I'm right far more often than you think I am."

"I never . . ."

"It would serve you well to start listening to me. Ah, here we are," she said, leaning forward to peer out the window. "I hope your grandmother has the presence of

6

mind to let me choose the candy for those shutters. Oh, dear, is that my father? I thought he was still at the castle."

"He is moving in with her," I reminded my mother.

She sighed and sat back in her seat. "I know and there isn't a thing I can do about it. It's a very bad idea, if you ask me. She'll catch her death of cold if he stays in her cottage, mark my word!"

My grandmother's cottage was one of the more traditional styles of candy-decorated gingerbread. Since the curse had ended, she often invited the family to visit, and Eadric had grown fond of the icing on her roof. I thought it was only right that I help her patch her house, considering how much of it Eadric had eaten.

Grandmother was waiting by her gate when the carriage rolled to a stop. "Where's my favorite young man?" she asked, craning her neck to look around me as I stepped down. "I made some extra gingerbread for him."

"If you mean Eadric, he went hunting with Emma's father," Mother declared, appearing in the door of the carriage. My mother had long feared that no one would ever ask for my hand, and even though Eadric wanted to marry me, she seemed to resent him, perhaps because she hadn't chosen him herself.

"I'll save it for him then," Grandmother said. "Come see what I've done so far, Emma. I've decided to build an addition. Your grandfather should have some space he can call his own. Oh, good. Here he is now."

A blue haze drifted toward us from the direction of the rosebushes, taking on the vague outline of a man. As it drew closer, it became more distinct until I was able to recognize the ghost of my grandfather King Aldrid. Even so, the sunlight kept him from looking as nearly solid as he did when indoors.

"Hello, my dears," he said in a whispery voice. "It's a pleasure to see you."

We shivered at his approach. Grandmother pulled her shawl more closely around her shoulders and smiled up at him. "I'll go see about the candy," Mother said, backing away. Glancing at her father's ghost, she hurried around the corner.

"I'm sorry I disturb her so," said Grandfather.

Grandmother shook her head. "It isn't your fault, dearest. Chartreuse was the first to hear about your death from the banshee and took it very hard. It was difficult for her to accept that you'd come back as a ghost."

Everyone knew that my mother was afraid of ghosts. For years she had claimed that she didn't believe in them, a convenient reason for not visiting her own father, who spent most of his time in the dungeon. However, everyone had seen him kiss my grandmother, thereby ending the family curse. Mother could no longer pretend that he didn't exist. Even so, she tried to avoid his company, claiming that the chill of his ghostly presence gave her the sniffles.

8

Once the curse had ended and Grandmother was once again her sweet self, Mother visited her more often. "Making up for lost time," she called it. I wondered if she would still come around after Grandfather moved in.

While Grandmother and I fetched the cooled slabs of gingerbread, my mother stayed inside the cottage, collecting the candy. One of the community rules stated that the occupants had to repair their cottages themselves without the use of magic or hired hands, although they could get friends or relatives to help. This seemed odd in a community where many of the cottages walked around on chicken legs and the magic was so thick at times that the air seemed alive with it. I think it was meant to promote community spirit, but whatever the reason, it meant that even the older witches residing there remained active.

We were setting the first slab of gingerbread in place when Grandfather said, "Has Eadric heard from his parents? They were so angry when they left."

Grandmother shook her head. "I still can't believe that woman said those things. She had a lot of nerve, calling Emma a horrid little witch and all those other awful names. They suited me, not you," she said, glancing in my direction.

"Those names don't suit you anymore," I said. "And I hope that isn't how she feels about me now. After his parents left, Eadric wrote to her, telling her how much he loves me. She's my future mother-in-law—at least I want her to be."

Grandmother gave me a sharp look. "You're not going to let her stand in the way of your marriage, are you? The women in our family have more spine than that!"

"I'm still going to marry Eadric. It's just that I'd rather do it with his parents' blessing. I don't think his father hates me like his mother does, but he didn't seem too happy that I'm a witch. And didn't you hear Queen Frazzela say that they'd pass Eadric over and give his brother, Bradston, the crown if Eadric married me?"

"Do you really think they'd do that?"

"I don't know, but I'd rather not take the chance. His whole life Eadric has been planning to rule Upper Montevista. I don't want to be the one to stand in his way. And can you imagine what an awful king Bradston would make?"

My mother had returned carrying a basket of gumdrops, but I noticed that she was careful to stay as far as possible from my grandfather. "I told you that taking an interest in magic was a bad idea," she said. "If you hadn't started practicing, she wouldn't have had anything to complain about."

"Don't be silly, Chartreuse," said Grandmother. "I didn't raise you to be so shortsighted. If Emma hadn't shown an interest in magic, your sister, Grassina, and I would still be under the influence of that awful curse and

I wouldn't have my Aldrid back. Frazzela is just too muzzy-headed to recognize a gem when she sees it. Our little Emma would make anyone proud."

"I couldn't agree more," said Grandfather. "Why, I remember when Emma was trying to find Hubert's medallion and . . ."

A sparrow darted through the garden, skimming the tops of Grandmother's roses. It landed on the rock-candy sundial and twittered a greeting. Herald, Grandmother's orange tabby, licked his lips and wiggled his back end as he prepared to pounce. As the sparrow opened his beak, Herald twitched his tail and leaped.

"Not so fast," said Grandfather, thrusting out his arm and waving his fingers. A wind sprang up that only the cat could feel, blowing him midleap into the rosebushes. Yowling, Herald clawed his way out of the roses and took off across the yard. Grandfather chuckled. "I don't think that cat likes me."

The sparrow bobbed its head. "Your Highnesses," it said. "Lady Grassina requests the pleasure of your company in the swamp behind the castle. She says that Princess Emeralda will know where to go." Having delivered its message, the sparrow took off, going back the way it had come. Grassina must have used a spell on the bird to make it speak the human tongue, because even my mother had looked as if she could understand what it was saying.

11

Grandmother had been smoothing icing with her hand before attaching the first gumdrop. "What do you suppose she wants?" she said, wiping her fingers on her apron.

When I saw that they were all looking my way, I shrugged. "I have no idea. She hasn't told me a thing."

"Does she expect us to go now?" asked my mother. "She can't order us around. We're in the middle of this."

"Well, I'm going," announced Grandmother. "I want to see what this is about. Herald, you keep an eye on the house."

An orange-striped tail dangled from the leafy branch of a crab-apple tree at the edge of the yard. The only sign that Herald had heard her was the angry twitch of the tip of his tail.

My mother dropped the gumdrops she was holding back into the basket. "If you're going, there's no use in the rest of us staying here. We'll take my carriage."

"I prefer to fly," said Grandmother.

"And leave me to ride by myself? I thought you liked my company, Mother."

Grandmother sighed. "Of course I do, Chartreuse."

"Then that's settled. We'll all take the carriage, except, er, Father, if you don't mind . . ."

"Don't worry, Chartreuse. I know there isn't room for me."

Two

The ride to the swamp was only slightly less unpleasant than the ride to the cottage had been. The driver of the coach was more familiar with the changes in the road and was able to miss some of the deeper ruts. Although my mother didn't say anything at first, I knew that the spots of color on her normally pale cheeks meant that she was angry.

"Doesn't it bother you that Grassina is being so inconsiderate?" she finally blurted.

My grandmother had looked composed with her hands folded in her lap as she gazed out the window. When she turned to face us, she seemed surprised at the question. "Why, no, not at all. I'm sure that your sister wouldn't have asked us to come on a whim. I don't know why she wants us there, but whatever it is, it must be important."

The spots on Mother's cheeks flamed as she bit her lip. "You're taking her side, just the way you did when we were girls."

Grandmother nodded. "Yes, I am, but I take your side when you aren't around and your sister questions something that you do. I always give my girls the benefit of the doubt. I'm sorry the curse turned me into a horrible mother for all those years."

"You take my side, too?" my mother said as if that was all she'd heard.

"Of course," said Grandmother. "You just aren't there to hear it."

"Oh," Mother said. Although she didn't speak again until we reached the swamp, the bright spots faded from her cheeks.

I understood why Grassina had said that I would know the place she meant. My aunt and I were the only people from the castle who visited the swamp, and we'd been exploring it for years. But if this was as important as her summons made it seem, there was only one place we'd find her. She'd be at the pond where I'd first met Eadric and where she had changed Haywood from an otter back into a human.

We left the coach at the road as close as we could get to the swamp and walked the rest of the way. My mother was horrified, of course, because it meant getting her shoes dirty. She tried to keep her hem out of the muck

14

when we reached soggier ground, but she didn't have much luck and finally gave up altogether, letting her hem drag wherever it would.

I was pleased to see that I was right about Grassina's choice. She was waiting where I'd thought she'd be, with Haywood at her side. Eadric and my father were there, as well as another man I'd never seen before. It wasn't until I saw that he was wearing priest's robes that I began to understand why we'd been summoned.

The ceremony was lovely. Grassina and Haywood stood before Father Alphonse at the edge of the water while the rest of us watched from farther up the bank. Although she wore one of her ordinary moss-green gowns, had a simple wreath of ivy in her hair, and carried a plain bouquet of daisies, the glow of happiness that lit Grassina's face made her as lovely as any bride had ever looked. Haywood was wearing one of the tunics my aunt had embroidered for him. It was decorated with oak leaves and acorns in dark greens and warm browns that seemed remarkably lifelike. He looked proud and happy standing beside Grassina, reminding me of the expression he'd worn when he was an enchanted otter and they had just found each other again.

As far as I was concerned, only one thing marred the ceremony: my mother wouldn't stop complaining. Although she stood on the other side of Eadric and my grandparents, I could hear every word she said, and none of it was nice. I glanced at the rest of my family. From their expressions, my father seemed to be the only other person who could hear my mother's tirade. Unfortunately, I could hear her as clearly as the grasshoppers chirping in the field behind us, the birds calling in the trees across the river, the fish burbling in the river, and . . . It occurred to me that I hadn't undone the spell allowing me to hear the butterfly. Maybe that was why everything seemed so loud.

"She's so inconsiderate—having her wedding in a swamp!" said my mother as the priest talked about love and marriage. "What a deplorable site for a wedding ceremony! Demanding we go to this godforsaken place just because . . . Do you smell that? I just know this is a breeding ground for the plague. What is that on my shoe? Ooh, I think it's moving!"

I saw my father lower his head toward hers. "It's a slug, my dear. It won't hurt you."

"And do you, Haywood, take Grassina as your lawfully wedded wife?" said Father Alphonse.

"And calling us here at the very last minute! She had to have known how much planning her wedding would have meant to me. If she'd given me fair warning, I could have had a dress made for her and a feast prepared. I could have sent out invitations, had the castle cleaned, gotten her a gift. . . . It's her fault that no one will have

16

presents for her. If she'd waited a few days, although a week or two would have been better . . ."

"There, there, Chartreuse," said my father. "I'm sure she'll understand."

"*. . . as long as you both shall live,*" said the priest.

Glancing pointedly at Queen Olivene and the ghost of my grandfather, my mother added, "And after they die, too, if they're anything like my parents."

At least they have a good marriage, I thought, remembering how often my parents had refused to talk to each other when I was growing up.

Eadric squeezed my hand. "What a great wedding," he whispered to me as Grassina and Haywood exchanged rings. "I'd like a simple wedding like this. I could talk to the priest after the ceremony and ask him to stick around to do ours. We could even have it here in the swamp, if that's what you really want."

"We can't," I said, although I would have liked nothing better. "I want to get your parents' blessing first. If we're going to get married, I want to do it right."

"I don't think they're going to give it," said Eadric. "You know what they were like when they left, and they never did reply to my letter."

"That's why I want to get their blessing. I don't want to cause a rift between you and your parents."

"If there's any rift, they were the ones who made it."

"Eadric, I mean it. Blessing first, then the wedding."

"All right, if we have to," he said, but he didn't look happy about it. "We'll go see them as soon as we can. I don't want to put off our wedding any longer."

"*. . . man and wife,*" said Father Alphonse.

Grassina and Haywood kissed and everyone watched in silence. When they pulled away to look into each other's eyes, someone sobbed softly. I realized that my mother was crying.

We were starting to line up to congratulate the bride and groom when I heard splashing behind us in the swamp. Whoever it was seemed to be having a terrible time, tripping and falling, then swearing when he tried to get up. When I turned to see who it was, Eadric's eyes followed mine and his hand immediately flew to Ferdy, his singing sword. It was one of my father's guards slogging through the taller grass with his sodden hat in one hand and a mud-covered shoe in the other. He was pouring water out of the shoe when he stopped in front of my father, but he must have forgotten about it because he slapped himself in the face with it when he tried to salute. Sputtering, he used his sleeve to wipe muddy water from his eyes, then said, "Your Majesty, I've come to report that Prince Jorge has escaped from the dungeon. He was there when the guard last checked, but he's gone now and the door is still locked from the outside. I was stationed by the dungeon door, and I swear no one got past me."

"He must have bribed someone in the castle to let

18

him out," growled my father. "When I find out who it was, I'll . . ."

"Actually, he could have gotten out any number of ways," said my grandmother. "And before you start threatening to lop off someone's head, why don't you let Emma and me take a look. I'm sure that between the two of us we can learn what actually happened."

Father nodded, aware of how useful a little magic might be, but from the look in his eyes I knew that if we couldn't find the answer, someone was bound to pay the price.

Eadric, too, looked grim. It was because of him that Jorge was in the dungeon. The prince hadn't been pleased that I'd preferred to be in the swamp rather than with him. Because I wouldn't marry Jorge, his father, King Beltran, had led his army into war against Greater Greensward. With Eadric's help, I'd used my magic to end the war, but Jorge still wasn't satisfied. When my father held the tournament for my sixteenth birthday, the prince had shown up disguised as one of the contestants and had done his best to kill Eadric. Fortunately, a health and safety spell had foiled his plan, and Jorge had been thrown into my father's dungeon.

Of course, the dungeon wasn't quite like it used to be. My mother had had it cleaned out when she married my father and had used it for storage since then. The guards had scrambled to get a cell ready for a prisoner, finally settling on one with a tiny window. The cell had been used to house old furniture in need of repair and was cluttered, but dry and relatively clean. Rather than make him wait while they emptied it completely, they'd left a few pieces behind. A cracked washtub, a rickety table, and my old bed with the broken leg weren't much, but they were more than most prisoners had.

We'd never intended to keep him there for long because custom decreed that the prince be released as soon as his ransom was paid. Although my father sent word to King Beltran that his son was in our dungeon, the old king was too stingy to send his ransom. Two months later the prince was still in the cell, gaining weight from Cook's good food and taunting the ghosts who dared stop in.

Although Father and Eadric both looked upset, I almost welcomed the news that Jorge had escaped. I'd been avoiding the dungeon for as long as he was in residence, and I missed my forays down there to visit my ghostly friends. Unfortunately, I knew that if Jorge were loose, he'd be up to no good as soon as he got the chance.

While my parents stayed to talk to the newlyweds, Grandmother and I went to the dungeon. Eadric and my grandfather insisted on going, too, which was just as well, because some of the shyer ghosts wouldn't talk to anyone except another ghost. We found the dungeon just as the guard had described. The door was locked from the outside, the straw mattress rumpled but unoccupied. While Eadric checked under the bed and in the washtub to make sure that Jorge wasn't hiding, I looked around for magical clues. Like most other things, magic leaves a kind of residue for those who know how to find it. Holding my hand out to feel for the energy, I wasn't surprised to find that magic had been used there in the very recent past.

"I found someone to talk to us," said my grandfather, floating back through the door.

Two ghosts followed him into the cell, making the space unbearably cold. I shivered and moved closer to Eadric's warmth while my grandmother pulled her wrap tight around her shoulders. I recognized both of the ghosts as acquaintances of my grandfather's to whom he had introduced me before. One was Hubert, the ghost of an elderly servant who had been thrown into the oubliette to die. He still wore the ghostly chain around his neck, less tarnished than the real one that had been buried along with his bones after the skeletons in the dungeon helped us. His companion was Sir Jarvis, a gentleman of the court from some century past whose noble bearing offset Hubert's aged stoop. The difference in their status would have kept them apart when they were alive, but as ghosts they had become the closest of friends.

"Do I know you?" Hubert said, peering up at me through his straggly hair.

21

"Of course you do, old man," said Sir Jarvis, patting Hubert's arm. "It's King Aldrid's granddaughter, Princess Emma. You met her a few months back, don't you remember?"

"No!" snapped Hubert. "Never met her before. Nor any of these other people. Although I'd like to meet this one," he said, winking at my white-haired grandmother.

My grandfather's outline seemed to grow until his head looked like it was about to touch the ceiling. "That is my wife, Queen Olivene!"

"Beg pardon, sir," said Hubert, cowering as he probably had when he was alive. "Didn't mean to offend."

"And no offense will be taken as long as you can provide us with some answers," said my grandmother. "Tell us, were either of you near this cell earlier today?"

"I wasn't, Your Majesty," said Sir Jarvis, "but Hubert might have been."

"Maybe I was," Hubert said, suddenly shifty-eyed. "Why do you want to know?"

Grandfather loomed over Hubert, making the servant's ghost shrink back. "The prisoner in this cell escaped a short time ago. We want to find out how he did it."

"Don't know anything about that," Hubert said, sounding defensive. "Didn't see any man leave."

"This isn't getting us anywhere," said Eadric.

"Just what did you see?" I asked the ghost.

Hubert shrugged. "Saw one man arrive in a puff of

smoke, he did. A bit later two birds flew out the window, *fft,* right between the bars like that!" he said, brushing his hands together.

"And did you hear what they said?" asked my grandfather.

"I don't know! I guess they chirped like most birds do. What kind of question is that? I want to go now. Asking questions about chirping birds!" Muttering to himself, Hubert drifted from the room, leaving Sir Jarvis to apologize.

"So they left as birds," said Eadric. "At least that's something."

I nodded. "I just wish we knew who came to help Jorge."

"There's a hamster," said Grandfather, pointing at a furry little creature scurrying along a narrow ledge. "Maybe it knows what happened."

The dungeon was overrun with hamsters that had been spiders until Grassina cast a spell to change every one of them. They were shy and skittish, so I didn't hold much hope that the hamster would talk to me. When I bent down to talk to this one, it gave a high-pitched squeal and fell off the ledge. Thinking that it might be hurt, I reached down to pick it up, but it limped away before I could catch it.

"I'd leave it alone if I were you," said my grandmother from the doorway. "You'll only frighten it more. Look who I found," she said, holding out her cupped hands and opening them to reveal a fuzzy rat. It was Blister, Grassina's rat from when she'd made her home in the dungeon. My aunt's magic dust had made its fur grow long and silky. My suggestion along with one of her spells had made it unable to speak unless it had something nice to say. The rat didn't usually say much anymore.

"Oh, you found *him*," I said.

Blister turned his head my way only after hearing my voice. "You would be here, wouldn't you?" he muttered.

"We want to ask you a question," I said. "Did you see what happened in this cell today?"

"You're asking me?" said the rat. "I can't see a thing through all this hair. And it's your fault. If you weren't such a . . ." Blister stopped talking.

"Don't bother with him," I told Grandmother when she glared at the rat. "He wouldn't help us even if he could. I wish there were someone else we could ask. I'd love to know what Jorge said."

"If only walls had ears," said Eadric to himself.

He grunted when I turned and flung my arms around him. "That's it!" I said. "You are so brilliant! You've given me the best idea. How about this . . ."

> If walls had ears to hear,
> And also mouths to speak,
> Imagine what they'd say
> If they weren't quite so meek.

24

Please give this wall a chance
To tell us what it heard
When Jorge left this room.
(We know he was a bird.)

We all waited, half expecting the wall to say something profound. When it didn't say anything at all, I tapped it with my finger and said, "Well, don't you have anything to say?"

"No," said the wall. "Leave me alone."

I couldn't have been more surprised. "Really? You finally have the opportunity to talk and you don't want to?"

"That's right," it said. "Now go away."

"All right," I said. "We will, just as soon as you answer our questions."

"What if I don't want to?"

"Then we'll stay right here until you do."

"What do you want to know?" it asked in a grudging kind of voice.

"We want to know who you saw in this room today," said Eadric.

"That's easy. I saw a human with yellow hair and blue eyes. He was here most of the day. . . . He has been every day since I first saw him. Then there was this funny crackling sound, and a shorter human appeared with lots of hair on his face and none on the top of his head. The first human shouted at him, 'It took you long enough.' Then the hairy-faced human said, 'I'm sorry, Your Majesty. I just got off the island. I came here as soon as I heard what had happened.' The yellow-haired human stomped his foot and shouted, 'Well, don't just stand there, fool. Get me out of this dung heap!' Then the hairy-faced man waved his hand and they both turned into birds."

Eadric turned to look at me. "It was Olebald, wasn't it?"

"It must have been," I said. "That means he finally got off the island where I sent him. This can't be good."

"They were interesting," said the wall, "but not nearly as much fun to watch as the man who thought he was a bat. He was here for years before he got the idea that he could hang upside down from the ceiling. I don't know how many times he landed on his head."

Eadric's eyes looked grim and his jaw had tightened the way it does when he's really angry. "If Jorge's loose, we're leaving tomorrow morning for Upper Montevista. We'll go see my parents and get their blessing so we can get married before Jorge can do anything else. If I know him, all he can think about now is what rotten thing he can do to prevent our wedding."

"You can't leave now!" said the wall. "I have so much I want to tell you. Why just the other year . . ."

Grabbing my arm, Eadric hustled me out of the cell. We could still hear the wall talking as we left the dungeon. I considered staying behind to undo the spell, but I didn't quite have the heart.

26

Three

fter eating a breakfast of bread and cheese with Eadric, I returned to my tower to get ready for our flight to Upper Montevista. We would be leaving as soon as Eadric came back from seeing his horse. Although we planned to be gone only a few days, Eadric was too fond of Bright Country to leave without saying good-bye.

I spread my magic carpet in front of the window and was watching a broom sweep it clean when I heard a knock on the door and an unmistakable voice said, "I know you're in there, Emeralda. Open the door this instant."

I ground my teeth, irritated that my mother could still make me feel like a child. Although I would have loved to pretend that I wasn't there, I decided to be mature and let her in. Hating myself already, I opened the door and stepped aside.

"There you are," she said, pushing past me into the room. "I heard that you intend to . . ."

I knew when her eyes fell on the sweeping broom

that it was all she would need to set her off. Kicking myself inwardly, I twitched my fingers, sending the broom into the storage room.

"You can't resist, can you?" she said, her eyes narrowing. "You use magic for even a simple task like sweeping. I'm so disappointed, Emeralda. You always have to take the easy way out. Would it really have been that much more difficult to summon a maid to do it?"

I dug my nails into the palm of my hand, trying not to answer the way I really wanted to. Arguing with her only made things worse. "Did you want to talk to me about something?" I said, my voice as even as I could make it.

"As I was saying, I heard that you intend to go to Upper Montevista to visit Eadric's parents. Am I correct in assuming that you're going to talk to them about your wedding plans?"

I nodded. "Eadric and I hope to receive their blessing before we get married."

"And you want to take that," she said, glaring at the magic carpet before turning to me with a disgusted look on her face. "Don't be a fool! That should be the last thing you'd want to do. If Eadric's parents are as appalled that you're a witch as I believe they are, don't you think it might be wise to travel in a more traditional manner? Rubbing their noses in the very thing that they dislike about you is not a good way to win their favor."

I hated that she was right. "I suppose," I said.

28

"Then put that *thing* away and decide what you want to take with you. You'll be traveling with the best carriages and a full retinue. I'll see to the arrangements. You'll have to inform Eadric, of course, and choose enough clothes to last at least a week on the road. You'll also want to take your nicer gowns so you can make a good impression when you arrive. I'll send a maid up to help you."

"You don't need to do that," I said, but she had already disappeared down the stairs.

I always cleaned my tower myself because I didn't like the idea of anyone touching my magical possessions. The same held true for packing, so it didn't matter if my mother sent someone to help me; I wouldn't be letting her in.

I was rolling up the carpet when Li'l fluttered out of the storage room and landed on my worktable. "Your mother is just the same as ever, isn't she? Are you going to do what she said?"

"I guess I have to. She was right about Eadric's parents, so I really don't have much choice."

"Can I go with you?" the little bat asked. "Garrid is going to be gone for a while, and I don't have anyplace else to go." Garrid, a vampire, was her mate.

"You could stay here if you want to. The door will be locked and no one will bother you."

Li'l's head drooped and her voice grew soft. "But I'll be all alone. I've never been all alone before."

29

"You might find that you like it," I said. Then she heaved an enormous sigh and I couldn't help myself. "But you can come if you want to." After all, I was supposed to go with an entourage, and I really didn't have that many people I wanted to take.

"Oh, goody!" said Li'l, flapping her wings and rising into the air to circle around my head. "Goody, goody, goody, I get to go! I've never been in a carriage before. Your mother said that you should take clothes. Should I take something, too? I could take my string, or some nice bugs. Will we sleep in the carriage or under a tree? Does the carriage have rafters? Will I have to stay awake while the carriage is moving? We're going to have so much fun!"

I was getting dizzy from watching her. "You won't need to bring a thing," I said, laughing. "I'm sure you'll find plenty of nice bugs along the way."

"Along the way where?" said Eadric. I'd changed the spell on the door lock so it would let him in, although he usually knocked first.

"It looks like we're going to have to change our plans," I began.

Eadric scowled. "Yes, I know. Your mother told me."

"I'm going, too!" said Li'l. "Emma said I could."

"Huh," said Eadric. "At least someone is excited about this trip."

"Here," I said, handing him the rolled-up carpet. "Could you put this away for me?"

Eadric grinned. "As long as you pay the fee."

"All right. I'll even pay in advance." Hooking my finger into the neck of Eadric's tunic, I pulled him toward me and kissed him squarely on the lips.

"Yuck! Do you two have to do that in front of me?" asked Li'l, landing on the table and covering her eyes with her wings.

"You mean bats don't kiss?" Eadric asked.

"Not like that!" said Li'l, turning her back to us.

Suddenly, I heard a sloshing sound. A light like a shooting star whooshed from the bowl of salt water I kept by the door, hitting the floor on the other side of the room and depositing a beautiful, full-sized mermaid with slanted dark blue eyes and pale skin tinged with green.

"*Oof!*" said the mermaid, landing on her tail. "I never can get used to that."

"Coral!" I said. "Is that you?"

"Hi, Emma!" she replied, flinging her mass of blue-streaked silver hair over her shoulder and scattering droplets of water everywhere.

Coral was one of Grassina's friends whom I'd once visited. A tiny castle rested in the bottom of the bowl, but it wasn't until I had swum in the salt water myself that I'd known it was the mermaid's home and part of the ocean. I didn't know that she could come visit us as well. "It's good to see you," I said, not sure why she was here.

"You, too, but I really can't stay. I've come to ask you for a favor."

"Of course," I said. "I'll do whatever I can." She'd helped Eadric and me when we needed her, and I couldn't say no.

Her eyes lit up as she thrust a hand into her hair. "I was hoping you'd say that," she said, pulling out something green and squirmy. "I'm on my way to visit my friend and she's allergic to shellfish, so I was wondering if Shelton could stay with you until I get back. I'd leave him with Octavius, but they can't seem to get along."

"That's because he's a pinheaded nitwit," said the little green crab as he scuttled down the mermaid's arm to the floor. "He keeps threatening to rip off my shell and feed me to the sharks."

Coral sighed. "You did tie his arms in knots."

"Only after he wrapped me in seaweed and stuffed me in the trash!"

"See what I mean?" Coral said, shaking her head.

"Actually, we were about to go on a trip ourselves," said Eadric. "So maybe this isn't the best time for . . ."

"We'd be delighted to have Shelton stay with us," I interrupted. Magical beings were easily offended, and it was always better to stay on their good side. Unfortunately, Octavius, Coral's octopus butler, wasn't the only one who found Shelton annoying. The little crab had bickered with Eadric from the moment they'd met.

"Then it's all settled!" exclaimed the mermaid. Blowing a kiss to Shelton, she drew a silver comb from her hair and pulled it through the strands. "Thank you!" she called as she began to glow. A moment later, she was so bright that we couldn't look at her, and with a whoosh and a splash, she was back in the tank.

"Hey," said Eadric. "We had to stick our hand in the water before we could go into the bowl!"

I shrugged. "Maybe it was easier for her because she was already wet."

"So Princess," said Shelton, "how have you been? I'm doing fine, in case you want to know." Shelton swiveled his eyestalks toward Eadric. "Better than you, I guess, since *he's* still around. Say, that otter isn't here, is he? I've been having bad dreams about him."

"Grassina turned him back into a human," I said.

Eadric chuckled. "Too bad, huh?"

"Please don't get started, you two." The trip was already going to be too long. If I was going to have any peace at all, I'd have to keep the two of them separated, but that might not always be possible if we were traveling together. And Eadric was already unhappy about our change of plans. . . .

"Shelton," I said when Eadric had left the room to get his things. "Perhaps you should stay here while we're gone. We'll be away only a few days. We're going to travel by coach, which you probably wouldn't like anyway."

The little crab's eyestalks drooped. "You mean you don't want me to go with you? I thought you liked me, Princess."

"I do, Shelton, but that isn't the point. We're going to be very busy, and I won't always be able to spend time with you."

"I understand," said Shelton, looking even more dejected.

I tried not to look at him while I chose the things that I would take with me. Space wasn't a problem because I'd recently purchased an acorn trunk at the magic marketplace. Although it looked like a regular acorn, it could hold just about anything. I had yet to learn if it had any limits.

It took me only a few minutes to pack my clothes. When I was ready, I stuffed my acorn in the pouch I wear on my hip and headed for the stairs.

Li'l had never liked my mother and always tried to stay out of sight when she was around. Instead of going through the castle with me, the little bat flew out the window and went straight to the first carriage waiting in the courtyard. When I arrived, Eadric was there with Bright Country saddled and ready.

"Let's get going before my mother makes us take everybody in the castle," I told Eadric.

"Do you want to ride with me?" he asked. The few times we'd gone anywhere on horseback, we'd ridden Bright Country together. The stallion was a destrier, bred

34

for carrying knights in full suits of armor, so carrying Eadric and me in ordinary clothes was easy for him.

"I'd love to," I said, taking his hand. Eadric hauled me up behind him, turning Brighty toward the gate. "We're ready to go now," I called to the coachman, who was watching us open-mouthed. Although my mother had a row of coaches ready and waiting, I hoped we could take just one and still avoid a large entourage.

"Very good, Your Highness," he said, although I noticed that he'd raised an eyebrow.

Brighty hadn't taken more than a few steps when my mother came rushing out the castle door followed by a dozen knights, a flock of servants, and two ladies-in-waiting. "Stop right there," she commanded, glowering at me. "I knew you'd do something like this! I told you that you needed a full retinue and I'm going to see that you get one, even if you don't think it's necessary."

My mother had been right about the carpet, but I hated traveling with large groups of people. I'd done it, of course, when I'd gone places with my parents. My mother never traveled any distance without taking half the court. With so many people, however, we couldn't travel very fast or far in one day, and we had to take so many extra carriages and food and luggage that it felt as if we were moving an army. And forget about being spontaneous. My mother always planned everything in advance, so if it wasn't already scheduled, we didn't do it.

Mother hurried across the courtyard to where we still sat astride Bright Country. "So, you weren't even going to take a carriage?"

"Actually, one was supposed to follow us," I said, feeling sheepish.

Mother sniffed. "You have your own palfrey to ride if you want to enjoy the fresh air. I expect you to conduct yourself with decorum, which is why I selected two ladies-in-waiting to travel with you." She nodded toward the women waiting behind her. I knew both of them, of course, although not very well.

The older woman curtseyed first. "Your Highness," she said. It was Hortense, one of my mother's older ladies-in-waiting. Everyone knew better than to do anything unseemly when Hortense was around for fear of receiving one of her famous tongue-lashings. I'd always suspected that one of Hortense's duties was to act as my mother's spy.

The other lady-in-waiting curtseyed so low that she had a hard time getting back up. Her name was Lucy, and she was the plumpest of my mother's ladies as well as the best at doing my mother's hair. My mother never traveled without Lucy, so I was surprised she was sending her with me. "Your Highness," Lucy said, panting from exertion.

"These ladies will accompany you. Even so," Mother said, looking thoughtful, "I don't think this is enough. To make the right impression, one must be impressive."

"Mother, I'm not waiting for anyone else. Eadric and I want to get started today."

"And you will. The rest will leave tomorrow. Your father is busy or he'd have come to see you off. Be careful on the road and listen to your ladies. They can advise you on etiquette in foreign courts."

"Of course, Mother," I said. *Why hadn't Eadric and I left sooner?* "But if I have to have more people along, I'll take an extra carriage. I'd prefer to ride alone in mine."

"If you must," my mother conceded.

Hortense and Lucy climbed into the second carriage while I slipped off Bright Country's back. The horse whuffled my hair as I patted his neck, knowing that no matter how uncomfortable riding him might have been, the carriage was going to be much worse.

I glanced at the palfrey my mother had mentioned. She was tethered to another horse that one of the servants was riding and seemed like a nice enough mare, but I didn't know her and didn't feel like getting acquainted just then. Instead, I climbed into the first carriage and sat back with a sigh.

"Hi!" said Li'l once the door was shut. Carriages don't have rafters as she'd hoped they would, but the little bat had found purchase for her claws and was hanging upside down in the corner. "Isn't this exciting! I can't wait to get started."

The carriage moved with a jolt, making Li'l sway

back and forth. "Then it looks like you got your wish," I said, feeling glum. My mother wasn't happy because I didn't have a full complement of escorts. I wasn't happy because my mother had been right about one thing and now I was stuck with so many people. And as for Eadric, well, at least he had a horse he liked and didn't have to ride in a carriage.

We hadn't quite reached the gate when someone shouted and the carriage rolled to a stop. "Now what?" I said, sticking my head out the window.

"When you get back, we'll plan a lovely wedding for you," my mother called from the steps to the castle. "Your father still has to arrange the wedding contract, so we'll have plenty of time to make all the necessary arrangements."

"Great," I said, waving good-bye. Settling back in my seat, I closed my eyes and sighed.

Four

We made good time the first day, partly because I refused to make the frequent stops that my mother usually demanded. At least I was the only human in my carriage and didn't have to talk to my mother's hand-picked ladies. Li'l slept most of the morning, dangling from the roof of the carriage like a little black tassel. We had gone only a few miles past the farms surrounding the castle grounds when I felt something crawl onto my lap.

"Oh!" I said when I realized that it was Shelton. He must have hidden in the folds of my gown just as he had on the day that we met. "What are you doing here?"

"I was thinking about what you said. I won't mind if you don't spend all your time with me. I like to travel and see the sights, so you go right ahead and do whatever it is you need to do. If you're going on a long trip, you need me to go with you. You never know when these might prove useful," he said, clacking his claws. "Where are we going anyway?"

I sighed, knowing that I wasn't about to take him back and risk having my mother add to my entourage. "To visit Eadric's parents. They live in Upper Montevista, the kingdom just to the north of Greater Greensward. I've never been there myself, but I hear it's very beautiful."

"Are there any oceans?" asked the little crab.

I shook my head. "No oceans, but there are a lot of mountains."

"That's too bad," he said, and then he scuttled up the wall to the window ledge. "Wow, this thing goes fast!" Grabbing hold with his claws, he fought to keep his balance until I put my hand up to help him.

"I suppose," I said, although a moment before, I'd been thinking how slowly we were moving.

"Where are we now?"

I leaned forward to look out the window. "We're in the enchanted forest. This is the only road that will take us where we want to go. These trees are hundreds of years old."

"Do they have coconuts?" he asked, swiveling his eyestalks toward the tops of the trees. The only trees growing on the island where we'd met had been surrounded by fallen coconuts that the green crabs seemed to love.

"No," I said. "Sorry."

"What are those?" he asked, pointing at a doe and her fawn.

Shelton was interested in everything. After growing up on a tropical island, he had lived on the ocean floor with Coral, so all the things I was used to were new and exciting for him. He was full of questions about the animals, the size of the forest, the way some of the trees pulled up their roots and moved around, and why all the horses screamed and the ladies-in-waiting shrieked when a griffin flew by and I had to say a spell to send it on its way. When we passed a waterfall and saw a green-skinned nymph swimming in the pool at its base, his eyestalks twirled as he asked, "Is that a mermaid?" He was disappointed when I pointed out that she had legs instead of a tail, but he seemed pleased to have seen her at all.

By midafternoon I was already sore from the jolting of the carriage and tired of the stuffy air. Casting a spell on a leather pouch to make it leak-proof, I filled it with water for Shelton and wedged it in the corner of the carriage. The little crab was happily bobbing in the cool water when I had my coachman stop and went to meet the palfrey I'd been given. The dappled gray had been tethered behind the last carriage and left saddled and ready. I introduced myself before climbing onto her back, but she didn't seem interested in me or in the fact that we could talk to each other. I asked her name and learned that it was Gwynnie. She grunted as I settled myself in the saddle, but seemed eager when I asked her to trot toward the front of the line.

"He's so handsome," she said, nodding her head toward Eadric. "All the girls have been talking about him."

Of course I thought Eadric was handsome, but I didn't know that horses looked at people that way, too.

"I've seen you with him around the stables. Do you think you could introduce me?"

"Sure, if that's what you really want."

We trotted past my carriage to where Eadric was riding with some of the knights. He'd stayed in the front most of the day, dropping back only long enough to talk to me or to see how everyone else was doing. I was proud of the way he had taken charge of our expedition, even though traveling this way hadn't been his idea.

When I reached Eadric's side, I smiled at him and said, "I have someone I'd like you to meet. This is Gwynnie."

Gwynnie laid her ears flat against her skull. "I don't want to meet *him*. I meant that good-looking stud the human is riding."

I had to admit, in his silver-trimmed bridle and matching saddle, Eadric's stallion did look very nice. Bright Country pricked his ears at Gwynnie and whinnied hello. She whinnied back, so I knew they'd get along just fine.

"How far are we from Upper Montevista?" I asked Eadric.

"If we keep going at this rate, we'll be there in two or three days. I can't wait for you to see it. It's one of the most beautiful kingdoms in the world. You'll love the mountains. We have the highest peaks and the deepest valleys."

"What about swamps?" I asked. "You know how much I like swamps." I still wanted to get married in one, although I hoped it would be the one back home.

Eadric glanced at me as if I should have known better. "There aren't any swamps in Upper Montevista. That's why I came to Greater Greensward to find the meadwort and happened to meet that witch."

"You mean that when Bradston made up the story about seeing your true love's face in the bottom of a cup of meadwort tea, you came all the way to my kingdom? I didn't know you were gullible enough to go that far."

Eadric gave me a disgusted look. "I prefer to think of it as trusting."

"I've met your little brother. I can't imagine why you'd trust him about something like that."

"Brad can be very convincing when he wants to be," Eadric said, shrugging. "It's how he gets away with so much."

"So what else can you tell me about your kingdom aside from its deplorable lack of swamps? Do you have any enchanted forests?"

"No, but we do have griffins and rocs and trolls in the mountains. On the higher slopes there are other creatures that no one has seen but we know are there by their giant footprints."

"Uh-huh. Are there any other differences that I should know about?"

"We like our food a little spicier in Upper Montevista than in Greater Greensward."

"Oh, really? You never seemed to think that there was anything wrong with our food."

"There isn't," he said, patting his nicely rounded stomach. I don't think Eadric ever met a dish he didn't like.

"Anything else?" I asked.

"Well, yes. I probably should have told you this before: the people of my kingdom aren't as comfortable with magic as the citizens of Greater Greensward are. A lot of my parents' subjects don't like witches."

"You must be extremely open-minded for someone from Upper Montevista."

"I am," he said, looking smug. "But then you've always known that I'm extraordinary."

Gwynnie flicked her ears when I shifted my weight in the saddle. "If your people don't like witches, I'd better not do any magic while I'm there," I said. "I don't want to turn them against me before we even meet."

Eadric frowned. "Are you sure that you can do it? You're used to using magic to take care of things."

"Now you sound like my mother! I don't have to do magic all the time. You'll see."

We rode in silence after that, involved in our own thoughts. I was irritated that no one seemed to think that I could get along without my magic. It was true that it had become an important part of my life, but it wasn't all there was to me. I was a lot more confident than I used to be and more capable and . . . I realized that most of what I valued about myself was tied to my magic one way or another. If I couldn't use it, would I be as confident or as capable?

By late afternoon the enchanted forest had given way to the more normal kind, with trees that didn't move around and no creature more frightening than a bear. I was slapping at the flies that couldn't seem to leave Gwynnie alone when a voice shouted, "Hellooo!" and a group of riders appeared through the trees. The man in front was oddly dressed in a leather jerkin and little pointed hat. His beard was trimmed in the middle so that it formed two long curls on either side of his chin. Although the knights who were my escort drew their swords and urged their horses into a protective circle around us, Eadric seemed delighted to see the man.

"He's from Upper Montevista!" said Eadric. "We must be near the border."

Reluctant to sheathe their swords, the knights sat watching the stranger's approach with wary eyes. "Hellooo!" he said again as his horse stopped in the center of the road, forcing us to stop as well. Sweeping his hat from his head, he bowed low in the saddle while smiling broadly at Eadric. "I'm Broadnik Bentwin from Chancewold. We heard that our prince was returning home and hoped that you and your party would honor us by dining in our fair town tonight. It's good to see you back, Your Highness."

Eadric nodded graciously and replied, "We'd be delighted to take you up on your offer, Goodman Bentwin. I've missed a good Montevistian meal these last few months."

I heard a knight chuckle behind me. Apparently my family and the kitchen staff weren't the only ones in the castle who knew about Eadric's appetite.

"That you'll have, Your Highness," said Broadnik. "Along with some excellent entertainment the likes of which you won't get anywhere but our kingdom. Now, if you'll excuse us, we'll be heading home to tell everyone to prepare for your arrival." Twirling his cap on one finger, he set it on his head and turned his horse to face back the way he'd come. With a signal from Broadnik, the other riders turned as well and trotted off into the forest.

"Wasn't that nice?" said Eadric, looking as pleased as if he'd just won a round in a tournament.

"Very," I said, although I wasn't nearly as happy about it. When the knights returned to their places and we could talk without being disturbed, I leaned closer to Eadric. "You could have discussed it with me before telling that man that we'd eat in their town. Do you even know how far away it is? What if we want to stop before then or keep going past it?"

Eadric frowned. "You didn't ask me about changing our plans. You just let your mother tell us what to do."

"But she was right, especially if it's true that the people of Upper Montevista don't like magic. Flying there on a magic carpet would have been a big mistake."

"Maybe," said Eadric. "But you could have talked to me about it before you made up your mind."

I tightened my fingers on the reins, making Gwynnie toss her head and snort. "If you didn't want to do this," I said, "you should have told me."

"I didn't say that I didn't want to do it," said Eadric. "I just meant . . . Never mind."

Eadric and I didn't have much to talk about for a while after that, although Bright Country and Gwynnie continued to nicker as if they'd known each other for years. I listened to them for a time, but soon grew tired of hearing about their favorite grains and what pastures they liked best. The sky was graying when we finally left the trees behind and the road curved to meet a river. With the ground rising and falling in rock-strewn swells ahead of us, it wasn't until we topped one of the hills that we saw a town nestled in the sweeping curve of the riverbank. A new-looking stone wall stood between it and the river.

"That," said Eadric, "is Chancewold."

"You mean you've been there before?" I asked.

"Once, before I met you. Look, there's Goodman Bentwin now."

The sun was setting as we reached the town and met the crowd that had come to greet us. At Broadnik's suggestion, a small group of men accompanied some of my knights and servants to a site downriver large enough to accommodate all of our tents while the rest of our welcoming party led the way through the narrow streets to the town square.

The air was rich with the smell of roasting meat and the garlands of flowers that draped the fronts of the surrounding buildings. Although the cobblestones had been swept clean, the overlooked feathers and bits of straw proved that the farmers had held their market there, probably that very day. Tables and long benches had been set up in the square, and women wearing their best gowns bustled around bringing platters of food and flagons of ale. The whole place had a festive air as if they were celebrating some sort of holiday. From the way they looked at Eadric, I guessed they were.

I listened as the men greeted him like a long-lost friend while the women smiled and curtseyed. A few maidens actually fluttered their eyelashes at him, something I thought no one really did. Eadric treated them all with equal respect, even calling many of the men by name.

The tables had been set up to form a square with a narrow aisle leading to the center. We took our seats at the head table along with Broadnik and the other local notables. Those townsfolk who weren't serving also went to their benches, where they remained standing, watching Eadric expectantly. I could tell that he hadn't noticed, because his attention was already on the food set before us.

"Eadric," I whispered. He dipped his hands in the water offered by a little boy with damp hair and a missing front tooth.

"Eadric," I said a little more loudly while he dried his hands and eyed a roasted goose on the platter closest to his plate.

"Eadric!" I said again, jabbing him with my elbow as inconspicuously as I could when he leaned across me to reach for the bread.

"What?" he said, nearly dropping it.

"I think they want you to say something," I whispered, nodding toward the townspeople.

"Hmm?" Eadric's mouth was already full. He looked up and saw everyone watching him. Swallowing hastily, he wiped his mouth with the back of his hand and stood. "Good folk of Chancewold, it is wonderful to be back in Upper Montevista among my own people. It is even better that you invited my beloved, Princess Emeralda of Greater Greensward, and myself to eat with you tonight.

Thank you for offering us your gracious hospitality and all of this marvelous food. Now, since I'm sure you are all hungry, and I know I am, let's dispense with any more formality and enjoy this delightful meal!"

While Eadric spoke, the townspeople smiled and nodded, studying me with interest when he called me his beloved and laughing when he said that he was hungry, as if indulging a favorite son or nephew. Apparently, Eadric's habits were as well known in Chancewold as they'd become at my castle.

The meal was a feast with roast poultry and game, a full side of beef, and a stew made of fish cut into chunks in a peppery sauce. Even the vegetables were hotter than I was used to, but only a few things were so spicy that I couldn't eat them.

Eadric, however, ate everything, no matter how hot. He smacked his lips and groaned with pleasure more than once, although he did reach for his flagon of ale to wash down each bite of the fish. We were nearly through the meal when five young couples dressed in brightly colored clothes filed into the center of the square and a musician strummed his first note. A drum and a pipe soon joined in as the couples began to dance. Having nearly eaten his fill, Eadric looked up to watch the dancers whirl past.

"That's marvelous!" I said as a male dancer tossed his partner into the air and caught her.

"It's a traditional folk dance," said Eadric. "Every movement, every color, every note has a special meaning."

"So tell me, what do they mean?" I asked.

Eadric shrugged. "Don't ask me. I never can remember all that stuff."

"They certainly seem to like you here," I said as yet another maiden flashed him a very warm smile.

Eadric shrugged again. "I killed a dragon for them when it came down out of the mountains to eat the farmers' cattle."

"A dragon!" I said, horrified. We'd come to know quite a few dragons, some of whom had become very close friends.

Eadric patted my hand. "That was before I knew how to talk to them. Before I knew any personally."

"You wouldn't kill one now, would you?" I asked, shivering.

"Of course not," he said, giving me a half smile. "I'd have you talk to him until he flew away."

The dancing wasn't the only entertainment we had that night. After the young couples left the square, a score of older men and women took their places and engaged in a contest of high-pitched warbling that they said was the way mountain folk talked to their neighbors. When an older man with a barrel chest won the contest, a tiny red-headed woman came out to demonstrate local birdcalls. She started with a few songbirds, then moved on to the calls of bigger birds such as the eagle, the phoenix, and the roc, the biggest bird of all. Each time she paused to take a breath between roc screeches, we could hear horses screaming in terror just outside the town square. I'm sure I wasn't the only one who was relieved when she sat down.

The tables had been cleared, the last of the ale poured when a maiden with silvery braids (and probably more than a little fairy blood) approached our table and flashed a smug grin at me, then gave Eadric a saucy wink. "When you were here before, Prince Eadric, we had a different sort of contest," she said. "My friends and I were wondering if you'd like to do it again."

"Yes," called a maiden from one of the tables. "Let's have another kissing contest!"

Eadric turned a deep red and his eyes flicked nervously toward me. "I don't think that's such a good idea," he said, and then he very pointedly gazed up at the stars. "Look at that—it's gotten very late. I think it's time we go to our tents. You wanted an early start in the morning, didn't you, Emma?"

"Of course," I said, and then I turned to the girl leaning against the table. "Prince Eadric doesn't need a contest. He already knows who the best kisser is."

"I do indeed," he said, sounding relieved. Taking my hand, he leaned toward me for a kiss. It wasn't long, but it was warm and tender.

The silver-haired girl turned on her heel and flounced off to her seat while the other maidens glared at me.

When Eadric had eaten his last bite and taken his last sip, Broadnik said, "We'll escort you to your tents. Your men have pitched them farther away from the river in a level spot nestled between the hills. We'll have to pass a bend in the river to get to it, so stay close together. It isn't safe by the river at night." Clearing his throat, he glanced at the men seated nearby before turning back to Eadric. "That's something we wanted to talk to you about, but we wanted you to have the chance to enjoy your dinner first. We've been having a problem with sea monsters the last year or so. It's why we built the wall. We were hoping you might be able to help us."

Eadric stood and patted Ferdy, whom he rarely took off anymore. "Don't worry," he said. "A sea monster that could make it this far upriver won't be any problem for my singing sword."

"You have a singing sword?" asked the boy who was missing a tooth. "Can I see it?"

While an admiring crowd of men and boys gathered around Eadric and Ferdy to escort them to the river, I was left to follow with my ladies-in-waiting. Some of the local maidens stayed behind to help clear the square; the rest tagged along as we filed through the streets. From the venomous glances they gave me, I was sure they were hoping that I'd trip and fall into the river headfirst, leaving Eadric available again.

Although enough townsfolk carried torches to fend off the darkness, they couldn't block the night's sounds as we entered the rugged terrain surrounding the town. Unseen birds called warnings at our approach, and deep-throated insects thrummed in the rocks nearby. A howling in the distance was plaintive, with an oddly human quality. Eadric had told me that werewolves plagued his kingdom off and on; they must have come back.

As we passed the end of the wall and drew closer to the river, the rushing water nearly drowned out the cries of the birds, and I could smell the pungent odor of freshwater and dead fish. The women from town who had gone this far left us, some of the torch-bearing men hurrying them back. The rest of the men became more vigilant, breaking off their conversation with Eadric to study the river. I noticed that the men around me were armed with pitchforks and stout sticks, as if they could be of any use against a sea monster.

"The river looks so peaceful," I said to the young man closest to me.

"It looks peaceful because it's deep," he said, holding his torch high. "This is the Yaloo River. Its headwaters are in the mountains north of here. By the time it gets this far, it's very deep and stays that way as far as the sea. You wouldn't believe what we've seen in these waters this past year. Some monsters have started going upriver to spawn, but the real horrors are the ones that come here to eat them. We used to enjoy walking by the river, but now it isn't safe for man nor b—"

Something enormous splashed in the middle of the river, sending wavelets over the bank almost to our feet. Torches were held higher, their light reflecting off the water where ripples continued to arrow in our direction. Whatever was out there was coming our way. Their swords drawn, my knights ran to join Eadric on the riverbank.

"Get back, Your Highness!" said the young man as others hustled me behind an outcropping of rock. I could hear the cries of the ladies-in-waiting as they huddled together close by. The men hovered around me for a moment, but when one of the villagers near the water called out, they ran back to join their companions, shouting, "Stay there!" to me and taking their torches with them. I tried to follow them, only to have the one man who had been left to guard me block my way. Retracing my steps, I strained to hear what was going on while trying to think of how I could help without it being obvious that I was using magic.

I heard running feet, the slap of something large and wet on stone, a man crying out, then Ferdy's familiar voice. "Slash, hack, chop and whack . . . ," he sang, which meant that Eadric was fighting the sea monster.

Hiking up the hem of my gown, I was trying to climb

the rock to see if I could help when there was a high-pitched keening and the rush of wings, and something hit me in the chest, knocking me back the few feet I had climbed. I landed on the ground with an *Oof!* then struggled to sit up, realizing when I couldn't that something heavy was weighing me down and had started to lick my face. My hands met scales when I tried to push it off.

"Emma," said the voice of an adolescent dragon, "I've been looking all over for you. See what I won!"

I rubbed my eyes and tried to see my assailant in the near dark. From the sound of his voice I knew it was my friend Ralf, but I couldn't make out what he was doing. "Ralfie," I said, "you shouldn't be here!"

Ralf backed out of the shadow of the rock and into the moonlight. "I had to come, Emma. I've been looking all over for you and then I heard you were here and I had to show you my award! See," he said, using his claws to hold up a ribbon that dangled from his neck. Some sort of oddly shaped stone hung suspended from the ribbon, twirling in the dim light.

"How did you win it?" I asked, peering at the stone.

"I graduated from dragon geography class with top honors," he said. "We're going to have a big feast to celebrate, and my parents and I want you to come. It's tomorrow night and . . ."

The sea monster roared and it must have been fairly

close, because water splattered down on us from above, drenching us both. Then the sound receded as if the monster were moving off.

"Thank you for inviting me, Ralf, but you shouldn't be here. If those men see you, you'll be in big trouble. Please go back to your parents' cave. I'll come see you as soon as I get home."

"But Emma," Ralf whined, thrashing his tail. "I really want you to come! It won't be the same unless . . ."

"Over here!" someone shouted. "It's a dragon!" I glanced up to see the man who had been guarding me standing only a few yards away, hefting a pitchfork in his hand.

"Ralf," I whispered, "please go!"

"That man has a poky thing, Emma!" said Ralf. "I can't go; he might hurt you! Where's Eadric? Why isn't he here to keep you safe?"

"That man isn't going to hurt me, Ralf, but he will hurt you if you don't go! Please, Ralf, just . . ."

"Back away from it, Your Highness!" shouted the man. "Even the small ones are deadly." Other men had begun to gather behind him, including some of my knights.

Ralf began taking deep breaths to stoke the fire in his belly. He had only recently begun eating gunga beans and hot flami-peppers to get his fire going. Although his flame was feeble compared with what it would be someday, it was enough to injure someone. I didn't have any choice. If I didn't use my magic, someone was bound to get hurt.

The man with the pitchfork was edging around Ralf, with the little dragon turning to face him. "Prince Eadric!" called the townsman. "Here's another dragon for you to kill!"

Eadric shouted, but I couldn't make out his words. It was Ferdy's voice that rang out loud and true above the noise around me.

> Take that, you monster from the deep!
> It's time for your eternal sleep.
> With one more slice and one more whack
> I'll see that you cannot come back!

I shrieked and froze where I was, pretending to be frightened. Holding my hand over my mouth as if I were terrified, I whispered the beginning of a spell.

> Hide this dragon—scale and claw,
> Tooth and fiery breath—

The sea monster roared, and a huge chunk of bloody flesh flew over the boulder and slammed into my legs, sending me sprawling. The rest of the spell I was about to say flew out of my head.

Ralf had built up a good flame. Nearly five feet long, it kept the men from getting too close. Unfortunately, maintaining such a big flame while dodging the jabbing pitchfork made him a little light-headed and confused. By the time I was able to sit up and saw that Ralf had began to fade from sight, he was whimpering and his flame was sputtering.

"That dragon's wearing a magic charm!" shouted another townsman when Ralf had nearly faded away. "Look, he's disappearing!"

"Get him before he's gone altogether!" yelled another voice.

I groaned when I saw that the incomplete spell hadn't been enough. Only parts of the little dragon had disappeared. Everything covered with scales had faded away, which meant that his body, wings, tail and head were gone. His claws were gone, too, as were his teeth and the last of his flame. Unfortunately, his eyes were still visible, as were the pads of his feet and the tip of his nose. His award still dangled from his invisible neck, and when he ran toward me, I could see his damp footprints in the torchlight.

"Ralf," I said under my breath. "Go home!"

"Not until I know you're safe," he told me.

The men rushed me, pushing me away from Ralf so they could form a circle around him. Happy that I'd been forgotten once again, I took the opportunity to whisper a new spell.

Murky fog, come to this place.
Of this dragon leave no trace.
Neither print nor sound nor scale.
Of this dragon leave no trail.

A thick fog rolled in off the river, enveloping everyone and everything. It was a strangely silent fog, absorbing all the sounds Ralf made and some of the men's as well. While the men floundered around, trying to find Ralf without hurting each other, I backed away and called his name. A moment later, the little dragon bumped into me. Nudging me with his nose, he pushed me away from the men. When we had gone far enough that they couldn't hear us, I bent down and wrapped my arms around Ralf's neck.

"You're very brave, Ralf," I said. "Thank you for protecting me."

Ralf may have tried to say something, but the fog still absorbed his voice.

"I need to take the spells off you, but we have to be very quiet. Those men are awfully close. As soon as you're back to normal, you'll have to go home. And don't worry. I'll be fine. No one is going to do anything to me. Understand?" With my arms around him, I could feel the little dragon nod. I said the spell quickly before anyone could interrupt us and was still hugging him when he reappeared.

"Remember, you're going to come see me when you go home again," said Ralf.

"I won't forget," I said.

The little dragon licked my face with his hot, rasping tongue before slipping away into the night. Although I was relieved to see him go, my nerves still jangled. I hated the way doing magic in secret made me feel. When Eadric and I were wed, if he became king of Upper Montevista, I'd be queen of this country. I didn't like the thought of lying to my future subjects, now or ever.

The fog had dissipated into the night, leaving the air cold and clammy. The men soon found me and assumed that I'd wandered off while trying to get away from the dragon. Eadric was with them, having dispatched the sea monster with Ferdy's help, but I could tell that he was not as jubilant about it as he would have been only a few years earlier. Getting to know dragons had made it harder for him to kill monsters, even when he didn't have a choice. Eadric didn't tell me any details other than that he'd be sending some of his men to protect the villagers from passing sea monsters. He did, however, seem concerned about me.

"Are you sure you're all right?" he asked. "The men said you were in real danger."

I patted his arm. "I was fine. Ralf came looking for us, which wouldn't have been a problem if your friends from Chancewold hadn't seen him. He's gone now, but I promised we'd go for a visit as soon as we could." Yawning, I leaned against him and rested my head on his shoulder.

"Let's go find our tents," Eadric said, hugging me to his side. "It's been a very long day."

I was fighting to keep my eyes open when he lifted the flap to my tent. Swaying on my feet, I gazed bleary-eyed through the opening, too tired to take another step. Eadric swung me into his arms and kissed me on the cheek as he carried me inside, setting me on the bed in the corner.

He was straightening up when Hortense stormed into the tent. "Have you no sense of decency?" she hissed at him. "You shouldn't come anywhere near her tent at night. And you!" she said, rounding on me. "You should be ashamed of yourself, letting him in."

"We weren't doing anything," I mumbled sleepily, feeling like a small child.

"That doesn't matter. You two should never be alone in here, especially not at night. Do you know what you're doing to her reputation?" Hortense said, turning back to Eadric.

"But we're getting married as soon as we can arrange it!" said Eadric.

"Hmph!" said Hortense. "As if that mattered! Queen Chartreuse was right to send me. Who knows what you two would be up to if I weren't here!"

Having a lovely kiss good night, I thought as Hortense ushered Eadric out of my tent. Too tired to change into my nightclothes, I stretched out on the bed and fell asleep.

Five

E adric woke everyone before the sun was fully up the next morning. He said he wanted to get an early start, but I had the feeling that he was afraid the maidens from the town might embarrass him again if we stayed longer.

I was still tired, so I chose to ride in the carriage with Li'l and Shelton. Maybe I'd be able to sleep a little longer.

"Li'l told me about the sea monster," Shelton announced once the carriage was under way.

"I heard the noise and went to investigate," said Li'l. "That thing was big! Eadric was brave to fight it the way he did. When it dragged him into the water, I was sure we'd never see him again, but then he popped up like a cork and climbed out."

I could feel a knot form in my stomach. "Eadric was in the river?"

"For a really long time," she said.

"I wish I'd been there," said Shelton. "I could have

64

shown him how to fight a sea monster. Remember when the three of us climbed into that sea monster's mouth and . . ."

"I remember," I said, not wanting to think about Eadric facing something like that alone.

No longer sleepy, I signaled for my carriage to stop long enough for me to get out and reach Gwynnie. Eadric was happy to see me and just as tired as I was. We rode together, enjoying each other's company without needing to say a word. After a time I dozed in the saddle, and Eadric may have as well. When my head nodded sharply, waking me with a start, we were in the foothills and could see the snowcapped mountains in the distance.

By noon we'd entered a pine forest so dark that it seemed as if night had fallen. I was wondering how much farther we'd have to go when Eadric said, as if reading my thoughts, "My parents' castle isn't far once we get out of this forest."

"So we'll reach it tonight?" I asked, looking forward to a nice soft bed.

"No, but at the rate we're going, we'll be there tomorrow. We're making really good time. If I didn't know better, I'd say that it was almost magical." Eadric smiled when he said it, but I thought he looked a little wistful.

"It would have been a lot faster if some people had more understanding subjects in their kingdoms," I muttered.

"Isn't it almost time to eat?" Eadric asked, patting his stomach.

I glanced up, but the trees blocked my view of the sky. When I started to look away, something dark darted past at the edge of sight. "What was that?" I asked.

"I didn't see anything," said Eadric.

Another dark shape shot through the trees, squawking. "Did you see that?"

Eadric shrugged. "It was probably just a crow."

"It was too big to be a crow," I said, shaking my head.

And then they were all around us, landing beside the horses like a small noisy flock. If Bright Country hadn't stayed so calm, I'm sure Gwynnie wouldn't have either, but she only snorted and pranced a few paces, letting me calm her with my hand and a few soft words. The knights behind us had a more difficult time with their mounts, who bucked and fought the reins while the carriage horses screamed and tried to rear up.

Although it seemed like more at first, only four witches hopped off their broomsticks, cackling and talking all at once. "Hello there, lovebirds!" called a familiar voice. It was Oculura, the witch who had moved into the old cottage in the enchanted forest near my castle. Her sister, Dyspepsia, was there as well, looking as sour-faced as ever. I'd never seen the other witches before.

"Why don't you introduce us?" said the shorter of the two, a woman with curiously pale skin.

"Princess Emeralda, Prince Eadric," said Oculura, "I'd like you to meet my friends Klorine and Ratinki. Klorine is the pushy one." The witch who had asked for an introduction had come forward with her hand extended. It took me a moment to realize that she wanted to shake mine.

"Pleased to meet you," she shouted, pumping my hand up and down until my shoulder ached. "I've heard so much about you two. When we learned that you were going to pass through our woods, I made sure we came out to greet you." I nodded, slightly dumbfounded. Klorine had a very odd way of talking. Not only did she speak loudly, enunciating each word distinctly, but she paused after each sentence as if waiting for someone else to speak, although it was obvious that she hadn't finished what she was going to say.

I waited for her to say something else until she looked at me expectantly and smiled. "Um, yes, well, it's nice to meet you," I said, turning to Eadric for help when the woman wouldn't let go of my hand. He didn't notice, however, because he was squirming under the unyielding gaze of the other witch, Ratinki. Skinny and wrinkled like an old apple, she had to be one of the oldest women I had ever met. With the dirt on her clothes and skin and the odor wafting toward us, she also had to be the smelliest.

"Let go of her hand," said Oculura to Klorine, prying the little witch's fingers from mine. My hand had gone numb, so I shook it while they both looked at me apologetically.

"Sorry," Klorine nearly shouted. "I'm not used to talking to real people. I live in a cave with an echo for company."

"You remember me, of course," said Dyspepsia, looking grumpy. As I'd invited them to visit us at the castle only the week before, I thought it was a very odd question.

"Hello, Dyspepsia," I said. "It's nice to see you again."

Apparently mollified, she grunted and rubbed the small of her back. "Back's paining me again. Broom riding does it every time."

"Got anything to eat around here?" interrupted Klorine.

Eadric perked right up, turning away from Ratinki for the first time since her arrival. He grinned when I said, "I'll see what I can do."

While the servants tended to the horses and the knights stood guard, Eadric and I joined the witches at the base of a tree. I'd invited the ladies-in-waiting to sit with us, but after seeing our guests, Lucy claimed that she'd rather eat our normal travel fare in the shelter of the carriage. Hortense made a point of sitting between me and Ratinki, who spit onto her palm and used the moisture to wash her hands. Although Hortense looked horrified, she didn't say anything to the witch.

We were making ourselves comfortable on the blanket when Ratinki spoke for the first time. In a rough and gravelly voice, she turned to Hortense and said, "I saw the way you looked at me. I'm going to turn you into a slug for that."

Pointing a wavering finger, the old woman said,

> That young woman sitting there
> Didn't have to stop and stare.
> Make her be a slimy slug,
> A slippery, gooey, squishy bug.

"No, wait," I said, throwing up my hand as I recited a quick blocking spell. There was a soft fizzling sound and . . . nothing happened. Hortense continued to sit there looking as prim and proper as always. When it was obvious that she wasn't going to change, I turned to Ratinki and said, "Please don't cast spells on anyone in my party. I need to get them back to my kingdom just as they left it."

"You are good!" the old witch growled. "Oculura said that you were powerful, but I didn't believe her until now. I've never seen anyone block one of my spells before. And that was fast, too!" She scowled and rubbed her mottled scalp under her wispy white hair.

"You'll have to excuse them," said Oculura. "Ratinki and Klorine live deep in the woods and don't talk to people very often."

"Do you live in a cave, too?" I asked Ratinki.

"Wouldn't dream of it!" she exclaimed. "Damp, nasty things! I have a nice little one-room hovel with a good rebuilding spell. Every time the villagers burn it down, it's back three days later, good as new."

Even Eadric looked horrified. "The villagers burn your home?"

Ratinki nodded. "Every few years. I don't mind too much—gets rid of the vermin."

"Why don't you move away?" I asked.

"Why should I? They aren't bad folk. Aside from pelting me with rotten vegetables and setting their dogs on me and stealing my food and . . ."

"Burning your hovel?" Klorine said helpfully.

"Yeah, that, too," said Ratinki. "Aside from those things, they leave me alone and I leave them alone and that's the way it should be. Besides, if I moved away, who would I spy on when I got bored?"

Eadric's stomach rumbled, reminding me of why we were sitting there. The food we'd brought with us was bland and none too plentiful, so after casting a quick searching spell to make sure that no one else from Upper Montevista was around, I pointed at the center of the blanket and said,

Pies and cakes and hot eel stew,
Tarts and breads and berries new.

Bring us lots of tasty food.
We're in a hungry kind of mood.

"Wow!" said Klorine when the food appeared on the blanket. "You can do that? I wish I could! Then I'd never go hungry again!"

"I don't do it very often," I hurried to say when I saw Eadric's expression. He looked as if he'd just won the biggest prize in the biggest tournament. Actually, I'd never made food purely through magic before, so I was a little apprehensive about how it would taste. I needn't have worried.

"This is good!" said Ratinki through a mouthful of fresh bread.

Sampling the eel stew, Klorine exclaimed, "This is better than good! This is the best food I've ever eaten."

"I'm glad you like it," I said, watching Eadric take an entire rhubarb pie.

I sat back, eating very little while enjoying the blissful looks on our guests' faces. I was curious, though—was Ratinki's treatment at the hands of the townspeople typical? When Klorine began to slow down, I asked her, "And how well do you get along with your neighbors?"

"Who, me?" she replied. "Just fine. My closest neighbor is a nymph who lives in the bottom of a lake in my cave. I don't see her very often, but when I do, she's always friendly."

"I meant your nonmagical neighbors."

Klorine shrugged. "None of them lives very close. The ones who come by don't know I'm there."

"You did have that one run-in, though," said Oculura.

"That was years ago. I was young and foolish then. I helped a girl find her soul mate, but he didn't like her when she found him. She was disappointed and told her whole village that I'd ruined her life. They came after me and I had to hide in the woods. That's when I found my cave, so it was a good thing after all. Any more of those tarts? I really like the ones with blueberries."

Even Eadric finished before Klorine and Ratinki, who ate until the very last crumb was gone. When it was time for them to leave, they had eaten so much that they had to struggle to get their brooms off the ground while Oculura and Dyspepsia circled impatiently above them.

I was climbing back into my carriage when Hortense came running over. "I didn't want to say anything in front of those women, but their manners are atrocious. And the stories they tell . . . I shudder to think about it. I hope you aren't going to let yourself be unduly influenced by them. Your mother would never approve if she knew you were keeping company with women like that."

I sighed and paused with my foot on the step. "I'm sure you're right. She doesn't approve of most of the things I do."

I'd started to pull myself into the carriage when Hortense placed her hand on my arm. "That's not all," she said. "I wanted to thank you for what you did back there. Thank you for stopping that horrid woman from . . . from . . ."

"Turning you into a slug?"

"Yes," she said, cringing. "Precisely."

"You're welcome," I said. "Although may I suggest that the next time you encounter someone you find disagreeable you not let it show on your face. I may not always be around to stop them."

Hortense nodded. "Yes," she said, her expression serious. "I'll have to work on that."

It wasn't until we stopped for the night that Eadric and I discussed what the witches had told us. Li'l had already left for her nightly excursion and wouldn't be back until morning. Everyone else except the guards and Hortense had gone to their tents. The senior lady-in-waiting was not about to shirk her duty, and I knew she wouldn't go to bed until I did. With our backs to the fire, Eadric and I shared a large rock while we watched the dancing shapes that the flames cast on the trees around us.

"I didn't know life was so awful for witches here," I said. "Poor Ratinki seems to think that living the way she does is normal."

"I had no idea," said Eadric.

I reached for his hand and squeezed it. "You have to do something. Make some sort of decree or law or something."

Eadric picked up a pebble and chucked it into the woods. "I can when I'm king, but there's not much I can do about it now. Even then I don't know if it would do much good. I can't make people like someone."

"Witches in Greater Greensward are treated with respect, but it's different here. I don't understand why these witches stay in Upper Montevista if they're so obviously hated."

Eadric shrugged. "It's where they've always lived. They don't know that it doesn't have to be this way. Besides, having a Green Witch is why witches are respected in Greater Greensward. You help keep it safe to live there. The witches here don't help at all."

"Why should they? People get angry with them when they try. You heard Klorine. When the girl she helped wasn't happy with the results, she turned on the witch who had helped her."

"Maybe that isn't the kind of help the people of Upper Montevista really need," he said, swatting at a mosquito tickling his cheek.

I opened my mouth to reply, then closed it with a snap. Maybe Eadric was right. Maybe they needed help, but only of a certain kind. I wished there was something I could do about it.

While Eadric and I shared a long and pleasant kiss, Hortense cleared her throat and muttered to herself, letting us know that she disapproved. She was still watching us when we said good night and retired to our tents. I was almost asleep when the werewolves started to howl. They sounded awfully close, certainly close enough to make everyone nervous. I heard the guards talking and the jangle of metal as the men who were supposed to be off duty joined them. Voices from the other tents told me that nearly everyone else was awake as well, although I thought I heard Eadric snoring.

Back home I would have chased away the werewolves long before this, but I'd been so conscious of not upsetting the Upper Montevistans that I'd done nothing, hoping that the creatures would leave us alone. But lying there in the dark, listening to the worried voices of the people around me, I knew that I'd have to take some sort of action or spend the night waiting for the first step of a stealthy paw, the first ragged scream cut short. Slipping out of my tent, I told the closest guard to let the others know that I would take care of it and that they needn't worry. Jumpy people shoot at anything that moves, and a stray arrow in my back was the last thing I needed.

I made my way only a short distance into the woods, then took on the most effective form I knew, the one that had become second nature to me over the last few months—a dragon.

The change was fast now—so fast that it happened between one breath and the next, but with great speed came great pain. When I could breathe again, I was iridescent peridot green with dark emerald claws and pale green translucent wings, more than fifteen feet long and able to breathe fire. Like Ralf's mother, I had acquired a taste for gunga beans and flami-peppers.

Raising my wings above my head, I brought them down in a mighty sweep that brushed the boughs on either side and lifted me above the tops of the trees. I'd been facing the direction of the werewolves' voices, but they'd moved and I moved with them. Dragons can see perfectly well in the dark, and can switch from normal vision to the kind that sees the heat that warm bodies give off. I used both, noting the doe and her twin fawns asleep side by side, the squirrels curled up in their nests, and the paler warmth of the turtle losing the heat it had absorbed during the day.

Wolves were easy to find, but I was hunting werewolves, who were smarter than their nonmagical counterparts and far more malicious. The first time I'd encountered them, I'd hoped that I could talk them into leaving my kingdom, but werewolves are devious and won't listen to logic. I'd had to singe their tails with flame to drive them out then and every time after that. I already knew that I'd have to do the same now.

Following their trail, I circled around toward our camp. I was in no mood for conversation, certainly not with hairy ruffians who liked ripping throats out and would be more than happy to lap the blood of my entourage. With a roar that shook the pine trees until needles rained from the boughs, I swept down on them, breathing a long pinpoint of flame that stopped just short of their furry backs, herding them ahead of me.

I was congratulating myself on a job well done when the pack split in two, leaving me to choose which faction to follow. Picking the smaller group, I tried to herd them back to their fellows, but found that I had to chase each werewolf when they went their separate ways. Because I had no desire to start a fire that could engulf a dry pine forest and knew that flaming too often might do just that, I decided to use a talent other than fire. Twisting and turning between the trees, I flew just above werewolf height, following the biggest beast. Dragons can fly faster than the swiftest horse can gallop, so I had no problem catching up with the werewolf and snatching its tail with my claws. The werewolf writhed in my grasp, snapping and snarling, but it weighed too much to turn back on its own tail and reach me.

Hauling the werewolf into the air, I carried it to the top of the tallest tree and deposited it on one of the sturdier branches. A regular wolf might have squirmed and fallen to its death, but a werewolf possessed human cunning as well as the animal kind. Crying pitifully, the werewolf held on to the swaying branch while I collected its pack-mates one at a time. When I'd gathered the entire pack, I grasped a tail in each of my clawed feet and carried them out of the woods and up the side of a mountain, depositing them on the shores of an isolated island surrounded by near-freezing water before flying back down the mountain for more. If it had been my kingdom, I would have carried them even farther. Since it wasn't, I just wanted them to stay away until we had left their territory.

When I'd moved the last of them, I turned and headed toward our camp. Before landing, however, I checked to make sure that everyone was all right, then flew on, not wanting to stop being a dragon just yet.

There were only two drawbacks to being a dragon. First, it made me feel fearless, and sometimes a little fear was a very good thing. I took risks when I was a dragon that I never would have considered as a human. Second, being a dragon was so much fun, so exciting, so *enticing*, that it was tempting to stay that way a little bit longer each time. My greatest fear, however, was that if I did, I might want to stay that way forever.

Turning back into my human self was particularly difficult that night. Chasing down the werewolves had taken most of the night, making me remain in my dragon form longer than I ever had before. Being a dragon felt so right, so perfect for me that I began to wonder if I really had to go back. Physically I felt wonderful; my blood coursed hotter, my muscles were stronger, I could fill my lungs with one deep breath and hold it for minutes at a time. My reflexes were faster, too, and my mind seemed sharper. And there were so many things that a dragon could do that a human could scarcely imagine. I could fly, swooping low or soaring high, pivoting on a wing tip or gliding for endless miles. I could bathe in lava or burrow through mountains of ice, and all the while feel as comfortable as a human on a warm spring day. A whole world waited to be explored in a way only dragons could manage. If I remained a dragon, I could see sights no human had ever seen, go places no human had ever gone. I'd never have to put up with people like Frazzela or my mother or . . .

And then I thought about my dear, sweet Eadric, who never failed to hold my hand when he thought I might be frightened, who always tried to come between me and danger even when I didn't need him to, and who cared how I felt about nearly everything. Eadric was kind and strong and brave and honorable—the kind of knight that other knights only claimed to be. He was also the love of my life, no matter what form I happened to take.

Although staying a dragon meant that I'd be free to do whatever I wanted to for the rest of my life, I already had something even better waiting for me in a tent, snoring so loudly that I could almost believe I heard him from far away. I could be a dragon now and then, but I knew that I could never leave Eadric for long.

Dipping one wing, I turned around again, heading back to camp and the far more ordinary life of a human witch.

Six

As a dragon I'd seen that we had almost reached the edge of the forest, so I wasn't surprised when the trees thinned out, giving way to a rocky slope. Eadric assured me that his parents' castle was only half a day's ride away. I'd been hoping it would be much closer.

The road we were on wound around the mountainside. Although it afforded us fantastic views, the steep incline tired the horses and made our travel slower. We hadn't gone far beyond the tree line when the ground began to shake and pebbles shifted under the horses' hooves, making them skittish and hard to control.

"Are earthquakes common here?" I asked Eadric.

"Not at all," he said. "I don't think this is an earthquake. Notice how rhythmic it is? I think it's probably a . . ."

"Giant!" shouted Lucy, pointing wildly as she hung out of the carriage window. The curve of the mountainside prevented us from seeing more than the giant's head

81

and shoulders, although it was enough to tell that he wasn't in very good shape. His coarse brown hair stuck out from his head like straw, and his tunic was rumpled and dirty, unlike most of the giants I'd seen who kept themselves very well groomed. From the way he was moving he looked as if he were staggering, his head lolling with every step.

"This is bad," said Eadric. "There's a village just a few miles farther in that direction."

"I can't imagine why a giant would want to go so close to a village unless he wants to make trouble," I said. "He has to know how much damage he can do just by walking down the street." A giant this big could do even more damage than most. His head was higher than my father's tallest tower and broader than that of any giant I'd seen before.

"He's either sick or drunk," said Eadric. "Look at the way he's walking. I'll go see which it is. You stay here with the carriages, Emma. It's safer here. There's no telling what he'll do when he sees me."

"Then you shouldn't go by yourself," I said, turning Gwynnie to join him. "I can use my magic to stop him if he's really out of control."

Eadric looked exasperated when he shook his head and said, "If you won't stay here because I ask you to, consider how many people there are in the village who could see your magic. Do you really want to risk it?"

"But . . . ," I began, then realized that he was right.

82

Unlike Greater Greensward, where my father's subjects expected me to confront trouble, the people of Upper Montevista would be horrified to see a princess facing a giant and even more so when they realized that I was a witch.

I watched helplessly from Gwynnie's back as Eadric and my knights picked their way across the rocky ground. "I can't just sit here," I muttered to myself. After what had happened with the sea monster, I wasn't about to let Eadric face the giant without me. Biting my lip, I tried to decide what to do. Without any trees or shrubs to hide behind, I couldn't very well change without anyone seeing me, unless . . .

I was all fumble fingers as I tied Gwynnie behind my carriage, although the mare was the only one to notice. Li'l was asleep, hanging upside down from the carriage roof. Shelton, however, was wide awake, clutching the window frame and waving his eyestalks with excitement as he watched the giant's progress.

"Is that a real person?" he asked as I swung the door open and climbed in. "He's ever so much bigger than you."

"He's a giant," I said. "They're all bigger than me. He isn't acting right, so I'm going to go see why."

"But I heard Eadric," said Shelton. "He said you should stay here. I admit he's a bossy know-it-all, but I think he's right this time. If that giant is real, no one should go near him, least of all you. What would happen to me if something happened to you? Eadric would probably cook me or feed me to some wild beast."

"Thanks for being so caring," I said. "I'll be fine and so will you. Now stand back."

It took only a moment for me to turn into a hawk. Not only was the bird fast, but it had marvelous eyesight, and right now that was what I needed most. I didn't dare get too close since I didn't want to be seen, so I'd have to watch from a distance. Springing from the carriage window, I took to the air, spiraling upward until I had almost reached the high, puffy clouds. I glanced down and saw Eadric and the knights approaching the giant, who was only a few strides from the outermost building in the village. He looked drunk to me, and I was certain of it when I heard him start to sing.

> Oh, give me an ale, a stout-hearted ale
> In a bottomless, endless mug.
> I'll do my best to drain it dry.
> You know I'll give it a good try.
> And if I can't, I'll be coming back
> To try it again tomorrow.

The giant ended his song with a hiccup that shook the village and crumbled chimneys. Looking as if his eyes couldn't quite focus, he was about to set his foot on a wagon loaded with firewood when Eadric and his knights arrived. "Ho there, Giant!" Eadric called. The giant turned, staggering. Closing one eye, he peered down at Eadric and Bright Country.

"Look!" the giant said with a foolish grin on his face. "A puppy!" Reaching for Eadric, he tripped over his own feet and landed on his knees, shaking the ground so that the carriages rattled. "Ouch!" he said. "That wasn't very nice. Bad puppy!"

"This way, Giant," Eadric shouted as the giant crawled to his feet with difficulty, shaking his head and moaning. Spinning Bright Country around, Eadric kicked him into a gallop, taking the rocky terrain far too fast. The other knights ran with him, but the giant seemed interested only in Eadric and the silver-maned Bright Country.

"Come back here, puppy," he shouted loudly enough to start rockslides on the next mountain over. Lurching after Brighty, he followed Eadric away from the village and far across the rock-strewn slope. Although I'd been sure that the destrier would outrun him, the giant was catching up. Eadric must have heard him, because he began turning Brighty in a zigzag pattern, but even that didn't slow the giant.

It was time that someone did something, and that someone was going to have to be me. The giant had given me the idea himself. Because witches' magic doesn't have much effect on beings that exist through magic, I couldn't cast a spell on him. I'd have to cast it on something else without using obvious magic. Pointing a claw at the ground between Eadric and the giant, I said,

> Move the rocks to form a bump—
> Not too high, more like a hump.
> All we want the bump to do
> Is catch the giant by his shoe.

Eadric was still racing away when the ridge rose up, tripping the giant. I held my breath until the giant hit the ground with a splat so loud that Bright Country was blown over and avalanches started on every mountain in the chain. The knights cheered when the giant didn't get up. I began to breathe again when Eadric stood and stepped aside so Bright Country could scramble to his hooves.

When the giant continued to lie there unmoving, I wondered if he'd been injured in his fall. Then, with a snort and a gargle, he began to snore, and I knew that he'd done just what he was supposed to do. The giant had fallen down, and fallen asleep.

I flew back to my carriage when a group of exultant villagers threw open their doors and hurried out to thank Eadric. By the time he returned, I was waiting impatiently astride Gwynnie. "How did it go?" I asked.

"Very well," he said, wiping the sweat from his brow. "I had the giant follow me until he collapsed, exhausted.

I told the villagers to make a lot of noise when he wakes up. That should drive him away."

"Why would noise drive him away?" I asked.

"Because he's going to have a very bad headache when he wakes, and loud noise will only make it worse. He'll leave, all right, as quietly as he can."

"It sounds like you thought of everything," I said.

"I try," Eadric replied, looking very pleased with himself.

I didn't mind that Eadric believed he'd taken care of the giant on his own. He'd been very brave to lead the giant from the village the way he did, and if anyone deserved the credit it was Eadric. However, having to be secretive bothered me enough to put me in a bad mood, which hadn't improved by the time we finally saw the royal castle of Upper Montevista.

It was a forbidding-looking castle, not airy and light like my home. Thick-walled, with few windows and four dull gray towers, it was perched on a jagged pinnacle of rock called Castle Peak with only one route to its gate across a narrow, steep-sided ridge. Although it commanded breathtaking views of the valley far below and much of the mountainside, the castle itself wasn't at all pretty. At least Eadric was happy to see it.

I sat up straighter in my saddle, sorry that I hadn't taken the time to fix my hair and change into a clean gown. The castle guards had already spotted us, and we could see the flurry of activity on the walls. Their prince was coming home.

At Eadric's command, the knights who'd been in front fell back, and the two of us led the way across the ridge. With the ground falling in sheer drops on either side of the road, I could see that the castle would be easy to defend. A drawbridge before the castle gate made unwanted visitors even less likely. As our horses clattered across the wood and we entered the passageway beyond the portcullis, I looked up to see the murder hole from which defenders could drop boulders or pour boiling oil from above. I was glad that we were welcome.

Eadric's parents must have been alerted to our arrival, because they were waiting for us as we entered the courtyard. It was obvious that his mother was upset. Her eyes were red, her face mottled and tear-streaked. Eadric's normally amiable father, King Bodamin, looked angry and very, very worried. At first I thought it was because I was there, but then the queen rushed to Eadric's side, exclaiming, "My darling boy! You've come just when we need you most!"

"Indeed," said his father. "Tell me, son, did you see anything unusual on your way here?"

Eadric and I exchanged glances. "Well," he began. "There was a drunken giant . . ."

Queen Frazzela glanced at the king. "You don't suppose that giant was involved?"

The king shook his head. "I don't know what to think."

"What's going on?" asked Eadric, frowning. "What aren't you telling me?"

The queen sighed and dabbed at fresh tears. "Your brother has been kidnapped."

Her husband looked annoyed. "Now, we don't know that, my dear," he said before turning to Eadric. "The scamp has been ill and tucked in his bed for the past week. Last night he became restive and sneaked out of the castle, something I strongly discourage, I might add. He's been looking for dragon eggs, and he may have thought he'd have better luck at night. Bradston is only ten years old! He knows I don't approve of his solitary forays even when he's healthy, as I've told him . . ."

"Bodamin, you're rambling!" said the queen.

"Ahem, well, yes, I suppose I am. As I was saying, he sneaked out, but wasn't missed for hours because we thought he was in his bed. A stable boy admits to having seen him go. Everyone has been looking for him, except no one can find hide or hair of the rascal. I was afraid that he might have taken a bad fall, so my men have been searching the cliffs and er . . . rocks below."

"He wouldn't have fallen," said Eadric, shaking his head. "Bradston is more agile than a mountain goat. I've never seen him miss a step."

"That's what I said!" wailed the queen. "I know he's

still alive, because the banshee hasn't come to tell us that he isn't. And I would have sensed it if my little darling were hurt." A lady-in-waiting offered her a clean cloth to wipe her eyes. The queen took it, handing the woman her soggy one in return as new tears dripped down her pale cheeks. "I just wish I knew where he was. He's still not well and I'm sure he must be terrified."

Eadric looked grim. "Bradston isn't afraid of anything, although he'll have reason to be when I get through with him if this is another of his tricks. Mother," he said, reaching for my hand, "I've brought Emma for a visit. I'd appreciate it if you'd welcome her and make her comfortable while I organize a search party. I'll find Bradston for you."

Queen Frazzela looked at me as if she hadn't realized that I was there, although she couldn't have missed seeing me sitting on my palfrey right next to Eadric. "Ah," she said. "You brought *her*. I suppose it can't be helped, but this is a very bad time to have a visitor, especially one with her inclinations."

"Mother," said Eadric, with iron in his voice. "You can't talk about Emma that way. I want you to remember that this is the girl I'm going to marry. And you can hardly blame her for coming at a bad time. We had no way of knowing about Bradston."

"*She* might have," his mother said with obvious distaste. "You forget that I've seen her true nature. Go, organize your search party. I'll see that the girl is suitably housed." The queen turned to gesture to one of her waiting servants.

"Suitably housed for a princess, you mean," said Eadric.

The queen's back stiffened. "For a princess," she added, although I could tell from her voice that it pained her to say it.

After Eadric took my knights to confer with his father's, I had to wait in the courtyard for someone to show me to my room while Lucy fussed over me. After she'd tidied my hair and straightened my gown, I'd had enough. "You can help me more by seeing to our rooms," I said, trying to shoo her into the castle. Although she went easily enough, Hortense refused to go until I told her that I was exhausted and was relying on her to find a place for me to rest. Satisfied that she had an even greater mission than to wait with me, Hortense bustled off into the castle, determined to set things right.

I was finally free to find my friends. Slipping into my carriage, I fetched a sleepy little bat and a skittery crab, tucking them into my sleeves. Because there was still no sign of anyone coming to get me, I sat down on a step to wait. "Why did the queen leave you out here?" Shelton asked, his voice muffled by fabric. "Coral would never be so rude. Why don't we just go in and have a look around?"

"Because that wouldn't be polite either. As my old nurse used to say, 'Two wrongs don't make a right.'"

Shelton giggled, tickling my arm with his eyestalks. "And two rights don't make a left. That would take three, wouldn't it?"

I laughed for the first time in days, and said into my sleeve, "That's true. I hadn't thought of that."

"Pardon me, Your Highness, are you all right?" someone asked from the steps behind me.

I turned, holding my sleeve to keep Shelton inside. A scullery maid stood at the top of the steps smelling of fresh baked bread.

"I'm fine," I said. "Why do you ask?"

Giving my sleeve a funny look, she curtseyed and said, "No reason. The queen says I'm to take you to your room. Come this way, if you please." I hurried to keep up with the little maid as she took me through a door and up a winding set of stairs. "I can't take long because Cook doesn't know I'm gone and won't be happy if I'm not there to turn the spit." We turned down a corridor lit only by a few narrow arrow slits. "Ah, here we are. It isn't much, but it's better than some. Now, I'd best be off or Cook'll box my ears again."

The maid shut the door behind her, leaving me in a small room with a tiny unglazed window and a pallet on the floor. When I saw that the trunk that stood in one corner was filled with someone else's clothes, I wondered who had been made to give up her room for me.

"Is she gone?" Shelton asked.

"She's gone," I said, pulling him out of my sleeve and setting him on the trunk.

The crab scuttled across the wooden surface, waving his claws in the air. "So this is where they put us? This is disgraceful! It looks like a closet. Even the butler has a better room in Coral's palace. I would, too, if I had a room."

"We'll be fine here," I said, setting Li'l on the trunk beside Shelton. The little bat fell over, murmuring something about drafty caves, and went back to sleep.

The room was dark, depressing, and as drafty as the rest of the castle, but at least it was clean. I didn't think anyone, including the room's usual occupant, would mind if I made it a bit more pleasant. Using some simple spells, I added a bright-colored tapestry to the wall to keep out the draft and turned the pallet into a regular bed, adding feather pillows and a warm blanket. The rest would have to do.

Shelton was trying to peek inside the trunk when I lifted the chain from around my neck and held my farseeing ball to the light coming through the window, saying,

> Find the prince who lives here, too.
> Find Eadric's younger brother.

93

Show me where he is right now
Despite his nasty mother.

"You're going to help that awful woman?" asked
Shelton, waving his eyestalks at me. "I know I wouldn't if
I were you."

"If you were me, we wouldn't be here," I said. "And
just because his mother was rude to me doesn't mean
that I won't help find the boy. I'm doing this for Eadric,
not for her."

I had to wait a while for the spell to work, which surprised me because my magic is usually much faster than
that. When an image finally began to appear in the
farseeing ball, it was dim, with lights flickering at the
edges, and I had to concentrate before I could understand what I was seeing. It was a narrow, stone-walled
passage embedded with some kind of shiny pebbles
and . . . The passage seemed to move as I watched, but it
wasn't the walls that were moving, it was the prince.
Striding along as if he owned the place, Bradston was
following some sort of creature carrying a torch that . . .
I squinted at the farseeing ball. It was a four-headed troll,
which meant that, in the troll world, it was a being to be
reckoned with. Other trolls followed behind the prince,
one with two heads, the rest with only one.

I was peering at the ball, trying to make out where
they might be, when the troll in the lead stopped

abruptly. One of the heads glanced down; suddenly my perspective changed and all four heads were looking directly at me. Startled, I nearly let go of the farseeing ball.

"I know what you doing," croaked a head with a bad overbite and fiery red hair that had been chopped into short spikes.

"You not do that here," a brunette head spat at me.

My hand shook. I'd never heard voices or any kind of sound from my farseeing ball before. Every time I'd used it, the ball had shown me an image and nothing more. Even worse was the fact that the troll could see me, too. Some new magic was being worked here, and not through anything that I had done. I looked more closely, hoping to get a clue about what was going on. The troll was wearing an ornate golden chain around all four of her necks and was looking into something connected to the chain. From the way she was holding it I wondered if she might have a kind of farseeing ball of her own. But that didn't make sense. Only magic users could see into farseeing balls, yet I'd never heard of a troll having magic.

"You try use magic here, I kill boy in worst way," said the red-haired head. "Go now, unless want me show what can do."

A wavering light approached the troll from behind, resolving into a one-headed troll carrying another torch. "Your Majesties," he said, bowing. "Cave behind treasure room ready."

The four-headed troll whipped around to face him. All of the heads shouted at once, but one head seemed the loudest. "Quiet, numbskull!" she shrilled. "Not now! Can not see I . . ." The image in my farseeing ball went fuzzy, then disappeared altogether, something that had never happened before. I frowned and shook the ball, but no other picture appeared. Sighing, I slipped the farseeing ball back under my neckline. At least I knew what had happened to him and where he had gone. The queen of the trolls had kidnapped Prince Bradston and taken him to her underground home.

"I'll be right back," I told Shelton on my way out the door.

The little crab darted to the edge of the trunk. "Where are you going?" he asked.

"To find Eadric," I said. "I have to tell him what I learned."

Armed with my newfound knowledge, I went in search of Eadric. It didn't take long to find him with a discreet tracer spell, but I had to wait outside the door until he'd finished talking to the assembled knights.

"I know who took Bradston," I said as the last knight left the room. "The troll queen has him."

Eadric rubbed his chin, frowning. "The troll queen, huh? I was sure you were going to say that Jorge and Olebald took him."

"How do you know where Bradston is?" asked

Queen Frazzela. She'd been standing in the corner, and I hadn't seen her when I'd come in.

"I'm sorry you don't like magic, but it was the only way I knew of to find Bradston."

The woman's face turned crimson, and her voice shook as she said, "I knew you would do magic here. You witches are all alike—coming where you aren't wanted to ply your wicked trade. Well, I won't have you casting spells in my castle! I forbid it, do you understand?"

"You forbid it at the cost of your younger son's safety?" I asked, my own voice as steady as I could make it. "Do you really hate magic that much?"

"I . . ." I could tell that the woman had a scathing retort on her lips, but then she seemed to deflate as her maternal side won out. In half-strangled tones she asked, "Where is he? Is he all right?"

"He looked fine, for now. He's in an underground tunnel, wherever the queen makes her home." Turning to Eadric, I asked, "Are there any mines around here? Somewhere you might find precious gems?"

Eadric frowned as he thought. "I remember hearing rumors about Roc Mountain. . . . But that's all they are—rumors. No one who has gone there has ever come back."

"They wouldn't if the trolls lived there, would they? See what you can find out about that mountain. I think that's where we'll find him."

"What do you mean *we*?" demanded Queen Frazzela.

"Who do you think you are to invite yourself along? Eadric will lead the search party, and they won't need you or your horrid magic!"

"I'll have to go with them if either of your sons is to come back. Eadric is the bravest man I've ever known, but even he is no match for a mountain full of trolls. Just who do you think would have the advantage in the queen's own mountain? He won't have a chance without me, so I'm going whether you want me to or not!"

Eadric put his arm around me and pulled me closer to kiss my cheek. "I'd rather you stayed here," he whispered in my ear. "Trolls are horrible creatures, and I may not be able to protect you the way I'd like."

"I'm going with you, Eadric. Don't you know me well enough to know that I can protect myself?"

"With my help," he said. "But I'll be busy helping Bradston."

"And so will I," I said, looking into his eyes so he'd know that I meant it.

Eadric sighed and turned back to his mother. "Emma is the Green Witch—the most powerful witch in her kingdom and probably in ours as well. I'd rather not take her into danger, but if she's willing to go, we stand a much better chance of getting Bradston out safe and sound."

"I see you're siding with her!" the queen said, looking as if she'd been slapped.

"It's not a matter of taking sides. I love Emma,

Mother. I'm marrying her, with or without your permission, and I believe she's right about this."

Queen Frazzela drew herself up to her full height, which was still shorter than either of us. "Just bring Bradston back," she said, her eyes blazing. "And keep your nasty little witch and her horrid magic away from me!"

And this woman is going to be my mother-in-law? I thought, then bit my lip as I wondered how I'd ever be able to spend part of each year living in a castle with her.

Seven

The rest of the day was spent preparing for our expedition. Gathering food and weapons takes time, as does readying horses and men. Later I was told it was amazing that everything was ready to go so quickly. I didn't use any magic where anyone could notice, but if swords were sharpened more easily and food was more plentiful than expected just because I happened to be around, no one seemed to mind. If we had to take an army with us, I wanted to make sure that it didn't hold us back.

Hortense was upset that I was going, but not enough to want to join us. Once Queen Frazzela understood that I was going no matter what, she ignored me until we were about to leave. After a tearful good-bye to Eadric, she turned to me and said, "Take good care of my boys." It wasn't much, but at least it was something.

We were riding through the ranks of soldiers that were waiting to follow us when I noticed the way that some of them were looking at me. As far as I knew I had done nothing to warrant it, but their eyes showed how little they liked me. It made me wonder if they had seen me at the tournament or had simply heard rumors about me. Either way, it left me feeling unsettled and edgy.

The sun was rising over the mountaintop when we crossed the narrow causeway. Because we had to move as quickly and silently as possible, I'd left my carriage behind and rode Gwynnie, who was under strict instructions to be quiet. Both Li'l and Shelton were in my sleeve again, partly because they wanted to go and partly because I didn't want to leave them with Eadric's mother. Although King Bodamin had wanted to accompany us, his leg had swollen with gout and he wasn't in any condition to ride. I felt sorry for him because he was obviously in pain, but pleased that it meant Eadric and I could ride together.

We had scarcely left the causeway when Eadric's second-in-command rode his horse up to ours. "I suggest we take the northern route off the mountain," he said, opening a map drawn on a square of hide. "The trail is steeper, but it would take us to the valley only a few miles from Griffin Pass. There shouldn't be any griffins there this time of year, and it leads east to the foot of Roc Mountain."

Eadric traced the pass with his finger. "That route would add nearly a day to the ride. Wouldn't it be better to approach the mountain from the south?"

"I'd advise against it, Your Highness. A basilisk has moved into these caves," the soldier said, tapping the map. "And there are rumors of other beasts killing travelers here and here. No one has passed that way successfully in two or three years. Whatever is there isn't letting anyone through. And as for the woods beyond . . ."

"We'll take the northern route then," said Eadric. "If we ride harder and faster, we should be able to cut back on any extra time it would take."

"Very good, Your Highness," said his officer, letting his mount drop back as we rode on.

He had been right about the trail being steeper. Eadric and I spoke in muted voices until we reached an area where the slope was angled too sharply for all but the most sure-footed of horses. The trail changed at that point, snaking across the slope, then switching back on itself in a slightly less perilous descent. A small group of soldiers preceded us down the trail while the rest followed behind. We grew quiet, talking only to our horses to reassure them when they balked at the more difficult spots. As we zigzagged across the mountain's face, we could hear the men behind us, out of sight behind the rocks and the spindly trees that grew on that part of the mountain. Gwynnie was nervous, so I still had to give her most of my attention, but I did catch a few words here and there.

". . . a witch, I tell you."

"Where I come from, we drive witches out."

". . . might not be true . . .

". . . hear the queen?"

". . . after that tournament . . ."

Although I tried not to let their conversation bother me, I couldn't help but remember the way some of them had looked at me in the courtyard. Back home in Greater Greensward I was respected more for being the Green Witch than I'd been for being a princess. Here I had the feeling that being a princess was the only thing that kept them from throwing stones at me. When I turned to say something to Eadric, his jaw was set and he looked angry. It seemed he had heard them, too.

When our horses were on more normal footing again, I tried to distract Eadric by telling him what had happened when I saw the troll queen. We talked about trolls, sharing what we knew. I'd heard that they liked to brag. He'd heard that they were vicious fighters who ate their defeated enemies. We'd both heard that they weren't very smart and that they avoided sunlight, preferring to live in caves and deep forests. It was rumored that the touch of sunlight on their skin could turn them to stone, but neither of us knew anyone who had actually seen that happen. Neither of us knew much about the troll queen either, other than what I'd seen. As we entered another section of the pine forest, we grew silent, not sure who or what might be listening.

We stopped that night in a valley, setting up camp on

both sides of a brush-lined brook that was fed from snow-chilled mountain streams. We were traveling light, so the men were going to sleep out in the open on one side of the brook near the tethered horses. Eadric insisted that I have a tent set up on the far side. I think he was remembering what he'd overheard as well as the way his men had looked at me the few times we'd stopped, because he wouldn't let any of them come near me.

I went to bed as soon as the tent was ready, but the thin fabric didn't prevent me from hearing the cries of unfamiliar birds and night-hunting animals, as well as other creatures that I didn't normally notice. My hearing was still sensitive from the spell I'd used to talk to the butterfly. I hadn't undone it yet because I wasn't sure that I wanted to; I could hear so many interesting things now. But as I lay awake, listening to the mice in the ground under my tent and the aphids on the leaves nearby, and a lot of other creatures that I couldn't identify, I wondered if I might not be better off without it. At least then I might be able to get some sleep.

Suddenly I heard the *whump* of huge wings cutting through the night sky. When the horses started screaming, and I heard the distinctive screech of a griffin, I couldn't just lie there and do nothing. Knowing that griffins were very territorial and wouldn't be able to resist the cry of another of their kind, I sat up in the dark and said a simple spell to have a griffin distress call lead the approaching griffin far into the forest. It was something that *could* have happened on its own, so it shouldn't raise anyone's suspicions.

When I heard the call of the false griffin, its strident notes sounded all too close. As the real griffin responded, the call moved away, leading the griffin farther and farther from our camp. It took a while for the horses to settle down, but when they did, I finally drifted off to sleep . . . and woke up soon after as Li'l popped back into the tent, making the smallest of sounds. After spending most of the day cramped and stiff inside my sleeve, she had gone off to explore when it grew dark. I was surprised that she was back so soon.

"*Psst*, Emma!" she said. "Wake up!"

"Li'l," I said. "It's the middle of the night! What are you . . ."

"Shh! Don't talk, just listen!"

I did then, waiting for her to explain, but it wasn't her voice that she wanted me to hear. Someone or something was coming through the woods and trying to be quiet about it. I listened harder. Whatever they were, there was more than one out there. I tried to shut out the other sounds and focus on the new arrivals. There were a lot of them, and they were coming our way.

"Who are they?" I whispered.

"I don't know," said Li'l. "They're big and ugly and smell bad, and you wouldn't believe it, but some have more than one head and . . ."

"Trolls!" I said, throwing off my blanket. Grabbing Shelton, my shoes, and my cloak, I slipped under the tent flap and would have stumbled over Eadric if there hadn't been a full moon that night to light up the clearing. He was sleeping on the ground in front of my tent, his hand on Ferdy's scabbard. Knowing him, he was probably there to guard me. I clapped my hand over his mouth and shook him by the shoulder. "Eadric, be very quiet and listen to me," I said when his breathing changed and I could tell that he was awake. "Trolls are coming through the woods. We have to warn the others."

I could feel Eadric nod under my hand. "Stay behind me," he whispered when I'd uncovered his mouth. After he'd belted Ferdy's scabbard on his hip, Eadric and I crept toward the brook. We had nearly reached the water's edge when the first troll appeared, bringing with him the smell of rotten eggs. Crouching behind a shrub, we watched as he swung his club in an arc and smashed my tent flat. The ground beneath us vibrated as the troll raised his club over and over again, beating the tent into the soil.

Eadric set his hand on Ferdy and was about to draw him from the scabbard when other trolls appeared, no longer making any effort to be quiet. The smell grew stronger the closer they came, until it was almost overwhelming. I placed my hand on Eadric's to prevent him from waking his sword, then pushed him farther into the brush while the trolls milled around, bellowing so loudly that it hurt my ears.

As other trolls converged on my campsite, I wondered why they had attacked my tent first and seemed to be ignoring Eadric's men. It was only after they began crashing around that the knights and soldiers had noticed them, taking up their weapons before the trolls had even looked their way. The first trolls to see the men now jumped from stone to stone to cross the water, and the fighting began. Men shouted, trolls bellowed, horses screamed while swords flashed in the light of the campfires, and clubs thudded against fragile bones. Roaring so loudly that my heart jumped in my chest, the trolls ripped up saplings and used them to knock men flying into the night air, only to land in silent, broken heaps. It was obvious that the men were outmatched. One man fell for every swing of a troll's club, yet the men's swords seemed to have little effect on the trolls.

As more trolls entered the clearing, trampling the remains of my tent into the dirt, we could hear others coming through the woods behind us. Eadric and I were still crouched behind the shrubs when Li'l came back. "You wouldn't believe how many are out there!" she said, fluttering her wings in agitation. "The woods are full of them!"

"Your men don't stand a chance!" I whispered to Eadric.

"I have to go help them," he said, trying to pull Ferdy out as he rose from a crouch.

I pulled him back down, saying, "No, you don't. Even Ferdy would be useless in a fight like that. If you go now, you'll be killed. Then where would I be without my Eadric? And what would your brother do without you there to rescue him? Look, your men are retreating."

Eadric looked over in time to see his men leaping onto their horses' backs and tearing up the slope, away from the trolls and us. Instead of following, the trolls lumbered back to the water's edge. "What we do now, Headbonker?" hollered one.

"Follow them, idiots!" shouted a troll with two heads sprouting from his stocky body. He was dressed in a tunic edged with silver and seemed to have an air of authority about him. Gesturing to the rest of his army, he shouted, "All you trolls, hunt humans down!"

"That's not good," I said. "We can't have all these trolls marching on the castle. If I can just keep the other trolls from crossing the . . . I know what I'll do. Keep your head down and Ferdy in his scabbard so I can concentrate."

"What do you have in mind?" Eadric asked.

"You'll see," I said, and began my spell.

This brook sleeps in its graveled bed
As it has since ages past.
Please wake it now and make it grow
To a river deep and vast.

Even in the moonlight I could see the brook changing. Once a yards-wide flow of water only a foot deep,
the brook swelled, overflowing its banks as if flood-
waters from upstream were just now reaching it. The water that had been so clean when we'd stopped for the
night became murky with silt and the plant life it carried
away. It reached the brush where Eadric and I were hiding, forcing us out into the open, but the trolls had gathered by the water and were too intent on what it was
doing to notice us.

The trolls who had been midstream when the water
swelled were swept off their stepping-stones and carried
away, splashing and choking. Those who had been about
to cross turned around and began shoving the trolls behind them. A brawl broke out as the river rose around
their ankles, then up to their knees.

I was wondering what I should do next when I saw
the troll leader coming our way. For the first time I noticed a chain with a ball around his neck that reminded
me of the one I'd seen on the troll queen. "Quiet!" he
bellowed, and the fighting trolls froze in place. While one

head stared at the ball, telling the other head what it saw, the second head looked around as if trying to find whatever the first head was describing. The troll took another step, then another, until the second head glanced our way and saw Eadric and me crouched behind a too-small rock. "She there!" the troll roared, raising his arm to point. The gathered trolls turned to gape. Brandishing their clubs and shouting, the closest ones started lumbering toward me.

As the trolls drew nearer, a dozen spells flew through my mind; I rejected them one after another. I almost turned us into bats, but there was Shelton to consider. Still in my pocket, the little crab wouldn't know how to fly and might be too confused to learn quickly enough. I rejected other animal forms as well, then decided to try a spell I'd never used before. The advancing trolls were only a few club-lengths away when I blurted an invisibility spell. We disappeared a moment later.

The troll closest to us was slow to notice and swung his club anyway, narrowly missing us as Eadric dragged me aside. "Hunh!" the troll grunted when his club thumped the ground. "Where they go?" Raising his club, he examined the underside as if expecting to see us impaled on its pointy spikes. When he saw that we weren't there, he turned to the troll behind him and asked, "Humans get past you, Nortle?"

"Not me!" said the other troll. "Maybe Flart."

"Not past me!" said a shaggy-headed troll with pro-truding teeth. Flart poked the other troll in the stomach with his club. Nortle responded with a gentle tap to Flart's skull.

While the trolls passed the blame for our disappear-ance, Eadric and I tried to slip away, but the poking and tapping quickly turned into fighting, and Eadric and I were caught in the middle where flailing clubs whistled past our heads. When a troll fell against us, Shelton scut-tled out of my sleeve and pulled his hair, hard. The troll yelped and looked wildly around. Shelton lost his balance and was about to fall from my sleeve when I let go of Eadric's hand to grab the little crab. As long as Eadric and I were in contact we could see each other, but the moment I let go, he was as invisible to me as he was to everyone else.

"Eadric!" I whispered loudly, reaching out for him.

"I'm right here," he said, but I held my breath until our probing hands found each other again.

The fighting had spread to the rest of the army. Careful to hold on to each other, Eadric and I crept away while the two-headed leader tried to pull a pile of his sol-diers off each other. When we were safely past the last of the trolls, Eadric helped me climb onto a large flat-topped rock that projected into the current. We stood side by side, gazing back upriver to where the soldiers had camped. The site was abandoned except for a pair of trolls who were pacing back and forth, demanding that their friends come get them, and threatening them if they didn't.

"My men took the horses, so they should be able to outrun the trolls," said Eadric. "They'll be safe once they reach the castle. I want you to go back to the castle now. The quickest way would probably be for you to turn yourself into a bird and fly there. You can stay invisible until you're safely inside."

"I'm not leaving you! You can't be serious if you think I'm going to let you go all the way to Roc Mountain by yourself."

Eadric set his hands on my shoulders and met my eyes with his. "You're not going with me. You mean too much to me to risk taking you there. This expedition has gotten too dangerous, and it's only just begun."

I took half a step back, stopping only because I'd reached the edge of the rock. "Is this what you think our marriage is going to be like? You'll make all the major decisions and tell me what to do? Grassina and Haywood have made all their decisions together for the past few months, and they weren't even married yet. I thought married people were partners who helped each other. If we're going to get married, you'll have to understand that I love you and I'll never let you walk into danger alone. I want you to be safe just as much as you want me to be. I'm going to help you in any way I can, and if that means going into a troll mountain, so be it. Now, you know that we don't have time to argue about this. Bradston needs us as soon as we can get there. This may not be the way you'd originally planned, but we're still Bradston's only hope."

"You can be so stubborn!"

"Only when I have to be," I said. "Like when someone is trying to make me do something that I know is wrong."

Eadric sighed and shook his head. "Then I guess we'd better get started." He held my hand while he hopped off the rock, then helped me down after him. "So," he said as we started to walk, "do you have any idea how that troll with the two heads was able to find us?"

"I think that ball he wore could show him where I'd worked magic. He used it to find us after I changed the brook into a river, and again when I made us invisible. It was probably how he found us in the first place. He must have known where I was by the magic I used in my tent."

"What magic was that?"

"I lured a griffin away from camp. It wasn't a very big spell, but I guess it doesn't have to be for that ball to pick it up. I think it must be a magic-seeing ball. I've heard about them, although there aren't very many around. They're generally made to keep an eye on a troublesome witch or wizard. A farseeing ball can locate just about anyone, but the person who uses it has to have some ability with magic. Magic-seeing balls are different. Although a magic user has to make it, anyone can use it, even someone who has no magic of his own. It locates the witch it was meant to find as soon as she uses her magic. I wondered how the troll queen could see me. It makes sense if she had a magic-seeing ball that was focused on me. Do you suppose the two-headed troll was using the queen's or had one of his own?"

"Let me see if I understand this," said Eadric. "Someone who has no magic can look into that ball and see someone using magic? Does that mean that every time you use magic, that ball is going to tell the trolls where you are?"

"Or at least where I was when I used the magic. I guess I won't be able to say any spells for a while if we don't want the trolls to find us. It will be a lot easier to rescue Bradston if their army doesn't know where we are." I rubbed my temples, trying to massage away the headache that was just beginning. "There's something *I* don't understand. Someone made a magic-seeing ball to see *me*. To focus the ball, you have to include something that belongs to the person you're focusing it on. What could they have used that was mine?"

Eadric nodded. "That's a good question, but I have a better one. If you can't use magic, how are you going to turn us back? We can't hold hands all the way to Roc Mountain."

"Yeah," said Shelton. "And I want to go for a swim. Even freshwater is better than nothing."

"Don't worry," I said with more confidence than I felt. "I'll think of something."

Eight

"Would you look at this!" Eadric said, emerging ahead of me from a stand of trees that extended all the way to the water's edge. It had probably gone farther, but the bank had been washed away, carrying the trees that had been growing there with it. The sun had finally reached down into the valley while we were stumbling along the riverbank, making it possible to see the extent to which the river had grown during the night.

"What's wrong?" I asked, coming up behind him. Then I saw the river ahead and he didn't have to answer. An enormous pile of boulders that had long ago tumbled as far as the new riverbed blocked our way. Although it would have been easy to pass the day before, the river had continued to widen and now almost filled the valley from one side to the other.

Eadric used his free hand to gesture up ahead. "The best way to get to Roc Mountain is to follow this valley, but as it is now we can't walk along the river unless we turn into mountain goats. Flying would be better, but we'd have to use magic then, too. And since we can't use magic because the only way we'll get Bradston back is if we have surprise on our side . . ."

I let go of Eadric's hand and sat down abruptly, leaning against the trunk of a tree.

"Hey!" said Eadric. "Why'd you do that?"

I didn't want Eadric to see me looking as discouraged as I felt. Sometimes being invisible can be handy. "I need some time to think," I said, which was true as far as it went. I also needed some time to myself. The mess we were in was all my fault. If I had said a different spell to keep the trolls away from the men, or even one to limit the size of the river, we could have walked the length of the valley in half a day.

"Emma!" Eadric sounded alarmed. I glanced up but couldn't see him until he bumped my head with his hand. "Ah, there you are!" My distress must have shown on my face, because he dropped down beside me and took my hand in his. "What's wrong?" he asked.

"I've let you down," I said. "I feel terrible about it. I was supposed to get us to Bradston. Now I can't even get us to the end of the valley. I can't use my magic and there's no way else to . . ."

"Of course there's another way!" said Eadric. "That brook went through the valley and out the other end, which means that the river does, too. The ride might be rough, but I'm sure we can cobble together some sort of raft and let the river carry us there."

"That's a brilliant idea!" I said, and I kissed him full on the lips. "I don't know why I didn't think of it."

Eadric stood up, still holding my hand. "Because you've gotten in the habit of using your magic to solve our problems. But not every problem needs a magical solution."

It didn't take Eadric long to find fallen trees to form the floor of our raft. He lashed them together with vines, then made a makeshift rudder so we could steer it. The raft came apart twice as we dragged it to the water's edge, but he put it back together each time without complaining. After that, I didn't have the heart to tell him that it still didn't look very sturdy.

Once we had the raft by the water, it slipped in easily enough and we had to scramble to get on board. The logs started separating almost immediately, so we set to work tightening the lashing as best we could while trying to stay in physical contact with each other. Shelton didn't help much. He kept disappearing, and each time I was afraid he'd fallen overboard. Eadric finally got tired of my fretting and said, "If you're so worried about him, why don't you just make us visible again? I wish you would anyway. It's safe now—the trolls can't reach us here."

"We talked about this. If I use my magic, they'll see

that we're on the river and will know that we're headed toward the mountain. At least now they don't know where to look for us. And if we stay invisible, we might have a better chance of sneaking into the mountain and finding Bradston."

Eadric shrugged. "Suit yourself, but you're going to have to do it sooner or later."

The water had been smooth at first, but as the valley narrowed, the river coursed over rocks and boulders that had fallen in ages past. White water foamed around us as we rushed past plumes of spray and boulders too big for a giant to lift. We were fortunate at first because the raft hit a partly submerged rock and spun around, but didn't tip or come apart. The next time, however, it caught on something we couldn't see under the water, and we lost one of the logs. After that, we had to fight to hold the raft together. When it hit the next rock, the whole thing came apart, and I tumbled into the water headfirst.

Over the previous year and a half I'd become a very good swimmer—as a frog or a fish or even as a turtle. I hadn't done much swimming as a human, however, so I floundered in the water, trying to turn myself around and find Eadric and the remains of the raft before I was too far away to reach them. As my skirts weighed me down and caught on wedged branches and jagged rocks, I was tempted to turn myself into something, anything, that could fly or swim or . . .

"Emma!" Eadric shouted. "Where are you?"

"Over . . . here!" I spluttered as water washed over me. I looked wildly around, trying to find him in the foam, forgetting that he was still invisible, too.

"You have to turn us back now!" he shouted from a direction entirely different from where I'd been looking. "It's the only way I'll find you." Even if he'd been visible, the water was so rough that I might not have been able to see him in the churning waves.

"But . . . ," I began.

"No *buts*!" he shouted. "Just do it bef—"

When Eadric stopped talking, I nearly panicked. He must be underwater. What if he was seriously hurt? Forgetting the trolls and Bradston and everything but Eadric, I said the first visibility spell that I could think of.

"There you are!" said Eadric as we all became visible again. He was holding on to a log from our destroyed raft and was only a few yards away. Shelton was already climbing onto the log when Eadric towed it toward me. Grabbing the back of my gown in one fist, he dragged me to the log and held me until I'd draped myself over it.

"Thank you!" I gasped. "You don't know how happy I am to see you."

"About as happy as I am to see you," he said, and he kissed me.

"Don't you two ever let up?" grumbled Shelton from his perch atop the log.

We rode down the river holding on to the log while trying to stay in the channel and away from the rocks. Shelton strolled up and down, chattering and enjoying the spray. I saw Li'l overhead now and then, coming back to check on us before taking off again. When the river left the valley, the water spread out over a greater distance, becoming shallower in the process until our feet touched the ground. Eadric and I climbed out, abandoning our log. Shelton had crawled onto my shoulder, snagging my hair with his claws, but I didn't mind. I was too happy to be out of the river with Eadric to let anything bother me.

"That was fun!" said Shelton. "Can we do it again?"

Eadric snorted and sat on the ground to dump the water out of his boots. I wrung out my clothes as best I could, wishing that I could dry us both with a little magic.

"Now we head due north," Eadric said, patting Ferdy to make sure he was still there.

"I thought we were going east through Griffin Pass," I said.

"We were, but the rapids carried us past before I knew it. We don't have any choice now. We'll go north. I saw where the basilisks' caves were on the map, so we can avoid them altogether. As for the other beasts . . . I'm sure Ferdy and I can handle them, whatever they are."

For the first few miles the landscape seemed normal enough, with scattered trees and scrub. Then the land abruptly changed as if we'd crossed a line and entered a completely different kingdom. The ground was dry and hard, and where there were rocks, they were shattered as if a giant had beaten them with a mighty club. There was evidence that wildflowers had once grown there as well as trees, but they were withered now, their leaves so dry that they rattled when the wind blew. From where we walked I could see small brown and white hills dotting the ground at uneven intervals. There was no sign of life, although I thought I heard a rooster crow.

We were approaching the first hill when I started to smell something awful. Eadric smelled it at the same time. "Where is that stench coming from?" he asked, making a face.

"I don't know, unless . . ." What had looked like a small hill from a distance was actually a dung heap nearly as high as my waist. The smell was so terrible that we had to hold our noses.

Shelton turned his eyestalks to examine it as we hurried past. "I'd hate to meet whatever did that!"

We continued on and soon saw a stone spire rising above the land. Perched on top was an enormous nest built from trees piled one on top of another. The nest sagged in places as if it were on the verge of falling apart. Shading his eyes against the glare of the sun, Eadric looked up and grunted. "Looks like a roc's nest, which explains the dung heaps. I've never been here before, but I've heard about this place. That pointy rock has been here for as long as anyone can remember, although the stories say that it wasn't always here. A witch planted it a long time ago, intending to build her home on the peak, then left when the people of Upper Montevista turned against her. Some say she was the reason that people in this kingdom don't like anyone who wields magic."

"I wonder what she did that was so awful," I said.

"I have no idea, but if you ask me, she couldn't have been a very smart witch. If she had been, she would have chosen a better spot to put her home—like on top of a mountain."

"Or in a swamp," I said.

"Or on the bottom of the ocean like Coral's palace," said Shelton, sounding wistful.

I patted the little crab with one finger. "Shelton, I think you're homesick."

"Who, me? Never!" said Shelton. "What's *homesick* mean?"

"It means you miss your home, like Emma misses Greater Greensward," said Eadric.

I smiled at him, pleased that he knew me so well.

Although the nest looked abandoned, we gave it a wide berth while trying to keep our bearings. Unfortunately, our path took us past more roc droppings and the awful smell.

123

We were passing another one when we saw toads using their front feet to roll eggs toward the dung heap.

"I don't know much about this kind of thing," said Shelton, "but is that normal?"

I gasped as the pieces of the puzzle came together. "Eadric," I said, "remember how your officer mentioned some other beasts that killed anyone who tried to pass through here? He didn't know what they were, but I think I do. If you see anything moving, don't look at it. And if you get a glimpse of something that looks like a snake or a rooster, look the other way. We're in a cockatrice breeding ground and we . . ."

"A what?" asked Shelton.

"I've never seen any before, but I've read about them in one of Grassina's bestiaries. That's a book that tells about different kinds of animals, Shelton," I told the little crab. "Cockatrices come from yolkless eggs that roosters have laid."

"I don't understand how a rooster can lay an egg, let alone one without a yolk," said Eadric.

"I don't either," I said. "I'm just telling you what I read. Anyway, toads take the eggs into dung heaps to hatch. And don't ask me why toads would care about the eggs, because I have no idea."

"And out comes one of those things you mentioned?" said Shelton.

Eadric nodded. "That's right. They have the head,

legs, and wings of a rooster and the body and tail of a snake. They're so ugly that you'll turn to stone if you look one in the eye. They can even shatter rock and wither plants with their ugliness."

"You're pulling my claw!" said Shelton. "There's no such thing . . . Is there?"

Eadric seemed to enjoy making Shelton nervous. "They're real, all right. I've heard that in some places people won't travel without a weasel. That's the only kind of animal cockatrices are afraid of, because weasels are immune to their gaze."

"I wish we had a weasel with us now," said Shelton, shifting from leg to leg.

"So do I," I said. Better yet, I wished I could turn us into weasels or maybe birds so we could fly away. But I couldn't risk any magic again. It was bad enough that I'd had to make us visible on the river. Not only had I used magic that could tell the trolls where we were, but I'd taken away whatever advantage we might have had by being invisible when there were cockatrices around. I could only hope that the trolls would think we had drowned.

"Just keep your eyes open," I told Eadric. "But don't look at anything."

We walked more carefully then, letting our eyes flick from one thing to the next without looking at anything for too long. There were more dung heaps beyond the spire, although only a few had toads near them. When

I saw movement out of the corner of my eye, I looked away, afraid of what I might see. "Look straight ahead," I told Eadric. "I think there's a cockatrice to our left."

I should have known better than to tell him, because the first thing he did was turn his head to look. "That's no cockatrice. It's just a big toad."

"I told you not to look!"

Eadric shrugged. "I won't when it's a cockatrice, but I can look at toads, can't I?"

He was so exasperating. "And how will you . . . Oh, never mind. Just keep your eyes straight ahead," I told him, missing my magic more than ever.

We came across our first cockatrice only a few minutes later. It was sunning itself on a pile of gravel, and I looked away as soon as I realized what it was. The creature was smaller than I'd expected and had a head more like a chick than a rooster. I hurried Eadric past it without telling him that it was there.

The cockatrice had seen us and wasn't about to let us go. "Yoo-hoo! I'm over here. Look at me!" it called in a high-pitched voice. "I can't believe it! You're acting as if I don't exist! You should see how beautiful I am. It isn't every day that someone gets to admire such magnificent plumage!"

"Keep going and pretend you didn't hear it," I whispered to Eadric.

I could hear the clack of tumbling gravel behind us,

but I didn't dare turn around. It stopped after we'd gone a few dozen feet.

As we continued on, we began to see previous cockatrice victims scattered across the barren ground. Men and trolls had been frozen in stone in various positions, some running, others raising their swords or clubs, a few even reaching to cover their eyes. We saw birds frozen with their wings spread, about to take off, while others lay broken on the ground, having frozen and fallen from the sky. It was an eerie setting, made more dangerous by the stone mice and insects that could trip the unwary.

The next cockatrice was waiting for us and had planted itself directly in our path. I looked away immediately, clapping my hand over Eadric's eyes. "Keep going!" I said. Turning aside, I tried to hustle him away from the little beast.

"I just wanted to say hello!" it cried in a plaintive voice. "You're missing a marvelous opportunity! I'm perfectly lovely and have so much to offer!"

"Most humans couldn't understand what it was saying," Eadric muttered.

"Exactly," I said. "And we have to pretend that we can't either."

That cockatrice followed us, too, although not as far as the first. We kept going, encountering one cockatrice after another, each one claiming to be beautiful. I was beginning to wonder if we would ever escape them entirely when Li'l found us again. "Hi, guys!" she said, startling me so that I let out a tiny shriek. "Sorry," she said. "I just came to see what you're doing."

"We're trying to get away from the cockatrices," said Shelton, sounding impatient.

"Then why are you running in circles?" asked Li'l. "Wouldn't it be better if you went straight ahead?"

"Circles?" I said in disbelief.

"Yeah. See, you're headed toward that pointy thing with the nest on top. Did you want to go back to the river?" Li'l tilted her wing in the direction we were going. The spire lay straight ahead, with the river running behind it in the distance.

"No," I said, and I pointed back the way we'd just come. "We want to go that way."

"So why aren't you?" Li'l asked.

"Good question," Eadric mumbled, but he stopped when I frowned at him.

"We want to, but we have to avoid the cockatrices. Give me a minute to think," I said. I considered asking Li'l to lead us out, but she shouldn't look at a cockatrice any more than we should. Eadric had mentioned a weasel, but we didn't have one, so that was out. I'd heard that a cockatrice would freeze if it saw its own reflection. Unfortunately, we didn't have a mirror with us. I thought about the cockatrices we'd come across. None of them was very big or very fearsome, maybe because they all seemed to be young. Each one had followed us for a time, although not for very long. Maybe, like a lot of other animals, they were territorial. *And maybe,* I thought, tapping my cheek with my finger, *they have a reason to be.*

"I want to try something," I said. "You three stay here with your eyes shut. No matter what you hear, don't open them until I tell you to, understand?"

Eadric frowned. "What are you going to do?"

"Nothing any more dangerous than what we've already been doing. Remember what I said. No matter what you hear . . ."

"We know," said Eadric, "although I should be the one to lead us out of here."

I left Shelton and Li'l perched on Eadric's shoulders, something none of them was happy about, and walked a short distance toward the spire. Keeping my eyes shut, I called out in a loud voice, "I wish I could see that really beautiful cockatrice. The one I passed a little while ago. I think it was the most beautiful cockatrice in the world, but I have to see it again to be sure."

From every direction there came the scratching of claws on gravel as the cockatrices overcame their natural reluctance to leave their territory. Bragging about their beauty, they kept coming until I could hear that they were only a few feet away. "Now stop!" I said, holding up my hand. "There are so many of you that I'm going to need your help in deciding. Please turn to your neighbor and take a good long look, then tell me which one of you is the most beautiful."

I heard the sound of feathers rustling, and then the cockatrices all began to talk at once. "She must mean me!"

"No, I'm sure I'm—"

"Anyone can tell that I—"

The chorus of excited voices was loud at first, but as one cockatrice after another looked at its neighbor and turned to stone, the voices dwindled into silence. I never did hear which was the most beautiful, but by keeping my eyes straight ahead I was able to find Eadric and finally leave the cockatrice breeding ground for good. My only regret was that we couldn't take one of the little monsters with us to use against the trolls.

Nine

We left the shattered land just as abruptly as we'd entered it. With one step we went from gravel and sand to lush grass that felt soft beneath our feet. Ahead of us lay a mixed forest of spruce and leaf-bearing trees, with Roc Mountain rising in the distance. It was an oddly shaped mountain, which, according to Eadric, people thought looked like a roc, although no one had ever seen any of the giant birds on it. The forest lapping at its base looked welcoming in the late afternoon heat. Like a thirsty man who sees an oasis in the desert, we hurried toward the trees and the shade they offered. Cool air washed over us as we stepped beneath the green canopy. Eadric and I sighed with relief and sat down in the shade to rest while Li'l settled on the branch of a tree.

We hadn't gotten much sleep the night before, and I couldn't make myself go any farther. Although our stomachs rumbled with hunger, we fell asleep, dozing against a tree's rough bark. We would have slept longer than we did, but Shelton grew tired of waiting for us. "Get up!" he said, pinching me hard enough to raise a welt on the back of my hand. "We have places to go and a prince to rescue."

"You didn't have to do that," I said, rubbing my hand.

Eadric was rubbing a similar welt on the arm he'd had around my shoulder. "I'm hungry," he said. "Why don't I start a fire and cook a crab for supper?"

"Ha, ha! Very funny," Shelton said, not sounding at all amused. He skittered down my leg, then turned to face Eadric with his claws clacking. "You can't eat me!" he said. "I'd pinch you really hard if you tried. And if you did . . . why, I'd be all stringy and taste really bad and . . ."

I scooped up the little crab and set him on my shoulder. "Don't worry. I won't let him eat you."

"I wouldn't be so sure about that," Eadric told Shelton while helping me to my feet. "She has to sleep sometime."

"Stop it, you two," I said, losing my patience. "We have enough to worry about without you fighting."

"You heard her," said Shelton, but he quieted down when I poked him.

Li'l flew overhead to keep us on course while Eadric and I made our way through the forest. We were both hungry, so we stopped to look for berries in the few likely spots we came across, but didn't find anything edible.

When I heard the first rumble of thunder, I thought it was Eadric's stomach. It wasn't until the wind picked up, waving the branches overhead and making the leaves rustle like rushing water, that I knew a storm was approaching.

"Li'l!" I called into the darkening sky. "Can you look for some kind of shelter? A cave or hut would be fine."

"I'll see what I can find!" she called back, as she disappeared into the gloom.

When she finally met up with us again, she led us through the woods in a new direction. We covered our heads and ran as the wind grew stronger and loose leaves and twigs fell on us like hail. The rain had just started to pelt us when we came to the clearing she had found and saw the remains of a long-deserted castle. Lightning ripped the sky, lighting up the clearing, then thunder boomed, and a tree cracked, splitting in the forest behind us. The smell of sulfur soured the air, and I could feel my hair stand on end as Eadric grabbed my hand and ran.

Lightning blazed again. I stumbled and would have fallen if Eadric hadn't been holding my hand. He pulled me through the gateway, over the ruined portcullis, and across the cracked and broken paving stones of the courtyard. The wind was whipping my hair into stinging strands that bit my cheeks when Eadric dragged me up the steps and past a sagging door. It was dark inside, lit only by the lightning flashes showing through the doorway and the narrow windows set high on the walls. We had stepped directly into the Great Hall, empty except for some old, rickety tables and a massive fireplace too crumbled to use.

While Eadric tried to find a torch with enough oil left to burn, Li'l took off to explore on her own and I began to look around the Hall. Shelton rode my shoulder like my own miniature knight ready to protect me with his claws.

The storm moved on, but we were fortunate that Eadric had found a torch and some candle stubs that smelled of rancid fat. He lit the torch easily enough with a flint he always carried, and we began to explore together. The castle was in a terrible state, its walls crumbling and even missing in some sections where the roots of trees had forced their way in. The few pieces of furniture that we saw were broken or rotting, the scraps of tapestries black with mold. Rats had taken over the kitchen, gnawing everything that wasn't stone or metal and fouling the rest. Certain that we wouldn't find anything to eat, we didn't look for food. Instead we headed upstairs to find a place to sleep.

We were in a hallway on the second floor when Li'l stopped by to make sure that we were all right, then left in search of her own dinner, an easy task for an insect-eating bat. I remembered my days as a bat and thought of all the meals I'd enjoyed that I couldn't stomach as a human. Eadric had been thinking about food as well. "When we get Bradston home to my parents, I'm going to insist that they have a feast. We'll have roast venison, eel stew, fruit tarts, and aged cheese . . ."

"That isn't helping," I said. "You're just making me hungrier."

Eadric sighed. "I don't think I could get any hungrier than I am now."

Although the castle had been so silent after the storm that we could hear each other breathe, the wind began to howl again, coming closer as if it were inside the castle itself. I was reaching for Eadric's hand for comfort when an apparition dressed in gray flew into the corridor, her long, white hair streaming behind her. Eadric's hand met mine and I gripped it so tightly that it probably hurt. Whatever she was, this creature terrified me just by being there. It wasn't so much her red, sunken eyes and gaunt features that made her frightening; there was an air about her of great sorrow and hopelessness that turned my knees to jelly while making me want to flee. I was hoping that she would pass us by, but she saw us and stopped to float above our heads. Eadric shoved me behind him, and I could feel that his skin had turned cold and clammy.

"Oh, woe is me!" she wailed. "What evil has come to pass on this most dreadful of days? Invaders have come to this forsaken castle, here to disturb the peaceful slumber of . . ."

Eadric stuck out his chin and said in as brave a voice as he could manage, "What are you going on about, banshee? If you mean us, we're not invaders. We came here to get out of the storm."

Of course she's a banshee, I thought, mentally kicking myself for not recognizing her from the descriptions I'd heard. Only someone with the power of a banshee could have made me feel such overwhelming despair.

When the banshee smiled, her eyes sparkled, and she didn't look nearly as scary. "You mean you aren't here for some nefarious reason?" she said. "Then welcome, you poor things! I'm so glad you're here! I never get to talk to anyone except when I'm working, and then I'm supposed to say things like, 'Woe is me' and 'Beware' and 'Uncle Rupert is going to die.' And then they look at me like I have two heads, which I don't because I'm not a troll, and they always say, 'Oh, no, the banshee is here!' Do you know how that makes me feel? Every time I show up, people run screaming and warn everybody else that I'm around. Believe me, I've thought about staying home and sleeping late, but I can't because I care about people. Without me to warn them, people would die unexpectedly, and then where would their relatives be? When I tell them, they have time to make arrangements, say good-bye . . . you know—important things. I'm actually a very nice person; it's just that no one gives me a chance to prove it."

"Sorry to hear that," I said, not knowing what else to say.

"Thanks," she said, her smile becoming even more brilliant. I began to wonder why I'd found her so frightening.

She glanced at Eadric and blinked. "You're looking at my teeth, aren't you? Pardon me," she said, and she stuck her finger in her mouth. "Darn bugs! But that's what I get for flying around with my mouth open." Raking the fingers of her other hand through her hair, she frowned when she found a snarl. "I must look a fright. Do you know what flying all day does to your hair? It's going to take hours to get all the knots out. Say, you don't have a cucumber on you, do you? I've heard that cucumber slices feel refreshing on your eyes." The banshee yawned until her jaw made a cracking sound. "I am *so* tired! I've got to go to bed. Choose whatever rooms you'd like and I'll see you in the morning." Rubbing her already red eyes, she drifted past us down the hall.

When Eadric pulled me into his arms and held me tight, I could feel that he was shaking. "That's such a relief!" he murmured into my hair. "I thought she was here to make one of her announcements. The last time I saw a banshee was the day my grandfather died from a hunting accident. A banshee came before we knew that his injuries were serious. When I saw her tonight, I thought it meant that I was going to lose you. I couldn't bear that, Emma." He kissed me on the lips before I could reply, a tender kiss that banished the last of any despair I'd felt from the banshee.

"At least this banshee turned out to be nice," I said when I could talk again. "I didn't really want to go looking for someplace else to sleep."

Shelton tickled my neck with his eyestalks. "Are you going to stand around all night and talk about sleeping, or are you actually going to do something about it? I'm so tired I can hardly hold up my eyes."

"All right then," said Eadric. "Let's see what these rooms look like."

Exhausted, we chose the first two rooms we could find that had solid walls and no holes in the floors or ceilings. From the ragged bed curtains and the rotting tapestries on the walls we could tell that they had once belonged to members of a noble family. Eadric left a sputtering candle on the floor, then went to his room while I set Shelton beside the candle.

"Wow!" he said. "The floor in here is soft. What is this stuff?"

I touched the floor, then rubbed my fingers together. "It's just dust."

"Ick!" he said, picking his legs up one at a time and shaking them. "This place is worse than the room Eadric's mother stuck you in. At least that one was clean."

I blew out the candle and crawled across the

musty-smelling bed. "Yes, but the banshee's nicer than Eadric's mother." The little crab was still puttering around the floor when I lay down and pulled the blanket scraps over me.

Although most castles were cold and damp, the banshee's castle was the worst I'd ever visited. It had been years since fires had heated the fireplaces, and the cold clung to every surface. I lay shivering under threadbare blankets that wouldn't have been fit for my father's hounds, waiting for my body heat to warm the mildew-stained fabric. When I finally drifted off, I slept fitfully and woke at every little sound. I didn't succumb to a restful sleep until the sun came up, heating the air through the one narrow window.

The next time I woke, Eadric was sitting on the edge of my bed, gazing at me. "I didn't want to wake you. You looked so peaceful lying there."

"Have you seen Li'l?" I asked, rubbing my eyes.

Eadric reached down to brush a lock of hair from my cheek. "She stopped by to check on us, then went outside to look around. She says this castle is too creepy even for her. It is pretty bad," he said, looking around the room. "We shouldn't stay any longer than we have to. We'll say good-bye if we see the banshee, then be on our way."

I felt a slight tug on the blanket and looked down to

see Shelton clambering up the side of the bed. "The sooner we're out of here, the better," he said. "I think I'm allergic to dust."

My stomach rumbled loudly enough for everyone to hear. "Maybe the banshee has some food," I said.

"Would you really want to eat whatever a banshee eats?" asked Eadric.

"Maybe," said Shelton. "But I won't know until I see it. Why are we wasting our time here?"

We found the banshee in the Great Hall sipping from a mug. She looked much better than she had the night before. Although her skin was still pale and her cheeks were gaunt, her eyes were a nice shade of brown instead of blood red, her hair was braided and covered with a light veil like my mother often wore, and her voice wasn't nearly as screechy as it had been the night before.

"I want to thank you for your hospitality," I told the banshee. "That was a terrible storm last night. I don't know what we would have done if we hadn't come across your castle."

"Pah!" she said. "Don't thank me. Having you here is such a treat. It's nice to talk to someone who isn't blubbering in her sleeve." The banshee set her mug on the table with a click. "That's something I don't understand. Why do they have to be so gloomy? If I were about to die, I wouldn't want to spend my last hours around people who were moaning and tearing their hair out. I'd want to laugh and have a good time." She sighed and ran her fingertip around the rim of her mug. "But that's just me. Maybe some people like being mournful. I do it because I have to. It's part of my job."

Shelton had taken refuge in my sleeve when I'd come down the stairs. Trying to get my attention, he pinched me, hard. "Ow!" I said, more startled than hurt. When the banshee looked at me quizzically, I pulled the little crab out of my sleeve and set him on the table. "This is Shelton. He's a friend of ours."

"Aren't you the dearest little thing!" said the banshee, bending down for a closer look. "I've never seen anything like you before. You must be very special."

"Oh, I am," he said, raising his eyestalks to look at her. "I normally live in the ocean with a mermaid named Coral, but she had to go away, so I'm visiting Princess Emma and Prince Eadric. We went to visit Upper Montevista, but Eadric's brother had been kidnapped. I'm helping them find the boy now."

"Your brother is missing?" she asked, turning to Eadric. "Is that why you're here?"

I glanced at Eadric, not wanting to tell the banshee more than he was willing to share. He shrugged as if to say, "why not?" so I told her about the trolls kidnapping Bradston. "We're on our way to the troll queen's home," I said. "It isn't far from here, is it?"

"No," said the banshee. "Not if you know where

you're headed. Follow the row of pine trees to the village, then go straight through to the edge of the forest. The entrance is easy to see. I've never been inside, but I've seen it with my mirror. I check my mirror every day so I'll know who's about to die. Sometimes when I look at it, I hear people talking about the troll queen. They say that she's evil and enjoys destroying whatever she touches. She tortures her victims before eating them." The banshee glanced at Eadric. "And you say she has your little brother? That poor defenseless boy. You must feel so sorry for him, living his last hours in the hands of that horrible monster."

"That's why we're in a hurry," said Eadric. "We want to get him out of there as soon as we can."

The banshee bit her lip, then said, "I know what we should do! We'll ask my magic mirror to show us what your brother is doing. Although in all good conscience, I have to tell you that no one who isn't a troll has ever gone into the queen's caverns and come out alive. But we'll take a look and then we'll know for sure."

The banshee kept the mirror in her bedchamber, an even gloomier room than the ones in which we'd slept. The bed hangings were tattered shreds, as faded a gray as her gown. There were no tapestries on the cold, stone walls, and the draft was much worse because of the gaping hole where the ceiling had partially collapsed. I didn't see any sign of torches or candles, so perhaps she didn't need them.

Eadric didn't seem to have noticed any of this, having gone straight to the mirror. "How does it work?" he asked, prodding the mirror's frame.

"You don't need to touch it," the banshee hurried to say when it wobbled on its stand. "Step back and you'll see."

Eadric and I stayed off to one side while the banshee stood in front of the mirror and announced loudly, "I want to see Prince Bradston of Upper Montevista."

The surface of the mirror rippled and the banshee's reflection disappeared. A boy came into view, lying on a bier surrounded by gibbering, prancing trolls. Blood dripped from the bier, and it was obvious that the child no longer lived. It was very convincing, but something about it was not quite right. Although the boy looked like Bradston, he looked too sweet, too innocent, too different from the Bradston I'd met. I'd been around him only briefly, but I knew with a certainty that the Bradston in the mirror was not the real one.

Eadric gasped. "No!" he said. "That can't be possible!" I put my arms around him and held him close.

"You see, Eadric," said the banshee, her voice filled with pain. "There's no hope for him. Your brother is already gone. It's no use trying to rescue him."

"That can't be right," I said, shaking my head. "I don't think that's really Bradston. Ask the mirror again, but tell it to show you the truth. I don't use magic mirrors myself, but I've been told that they aren't always reliable, especially when they get older."

"Oh, I'm sure this mirror is right," said the banshee. "It was given to me when I became a banshee. It has to be right every time."

"How old is it?" I asked.

The banshee shrugged. "At least a few hundred years, I expect."

"Then it may not be accurate anymore. Please try it again," I said. "We really need to know about Bradston."

The banshee looked from me to the mirror and back. "I suppose it won't hurt to try, although it's just going to show us the same thing again. Mirror, show us the truth about Prince Bradston of Upper Montevista. As he actually is this very minute."

The image of the boy and the dancing trolls disappeared and a gray fog swirled in its place, fading away to show three figures seated on the floor of a small cave. The picture grew larger as if we were moving closer to them until they looked as though they were in the room with us.

"There's Bradston," I said, "and those must be some of his captors." Two trolls sat beside the boy, who was laughing so hard that he had to hold his sides. The trolls seemed uncomfortable, as if they didn't understand what was going on but didn't like it nonetheless.

Eadric laughed out loud. "Now *that's* Bradston. He's making fun of the trolls. He's probably teasing them about something they've done. I should know. He's acted that way around me often enough."

"How is that possible?" asked the banshee. "He was dead in the other image. How do I know which one is right?"

"I'm sure the second one is. The boy in it is acting like the real Bradston," said Eadric.

The banshee wrung her hands. "Yes, but what about all the images I've seen over the years? Those people were about to die. I went to warn their families and they did die, just like I'd foreseen. But if there are two images . . . Is it possible that they wouldn't have died if they hadn't been expecting to because of what I'd said? This is terrible! What am I going to do now? If they died because of something that I did . . ." Wailing and tearing at her hair, the banshee fled down the hall as the image faded from the mirror.

Eadric took my hand in his and turned it over to kiss my palm. "Thank you for showing me the real Bradston. That first image had me convinced that he was dead."

"I know," I said. "I almost believed it myself. Those poor people, if what she said was true . . ."

Eadric shuddered. "Let's get out of here before she comes back. I shouldn't have believed her, but lies are harder to discount coming from a magic mirror. I prefer fighting trolls to listening to a banshee. Ferdy and I can handle trolls just fine," he said, patting his sword again.

"I'm sure you can," I said, and I turned my head so he wouldn't see my smile.

Ten

It was nearly noon when we left the banshee's castle. We started out by following the row of pine trees that she'd mentioned. Stone markers showed that an old road had once run beside them, but it had long since fallen into disuse and was mostly overgrown. Because we still couldn't find anything to eat, we continued walking long after we normally would have stopped. When darkness fell and the pine trees melted into the rest of the forest, we asked Li'l for help. She was happy to lead us and flew off to look around.

The night was well along when we reached the village that Li'l had found, making the few candles still burning in the windows a welcome sight. Grouped around a small central field, a cluster of narrow houses with steeply pitched roofs had been built so close to each other that they seemed to present a united front to the surrounding forest. Only a narrow gap separated the houses, leaving barely enough room for two people to walk side by side.

"I hope there's an inn here," said Eadric. "And I hope they're still serving supper."

I yawned and brushed my hair out of my eyes. "And I hope they have some rooms available after we've eaten."

"I hope they have a nice bucket of water," Shelton said from inside my sleeve. "And maybe a little salt to add to it."

"I'll see you later," said Li'l. "I don't like inns. There are always too many people there who like to hit bats."

After walking the length of the path that led between the houses without seeing an inn or anyone to talk to, Eadric declared, "We're not sleeping outside tonight. This village is too close to the troll's mountain. Anything could be in these woods." Picking the closest house, he rapped on the door with his knuckles. The thump was so loud in the otherwise silent night that I was sure everyone in the village must have heard it.

I gasped when a man stepped out of the shadows only a few feet away. "May I help you?" he asked with an odd accent to his words. The light from the windows did little more than outline his shape in the gloom, and I couldn't help but feel uneasy.

"We're seeking lodging for the night," said Eadric, stepping between me and the man. "Is there an inn close by?"

The man chuckled, but it wasn't a pleasant sound. "No inns that you could reach tonight. However, I have some empty rooms that I let out to travelers. Will it be just the two of you?"

"Yes," said Eadric, placing his hand on Ferdy's hilt. Apparently I wasn't the only one who felt ill at ease around the stranger. "And if we could arrange for supper as well . . ."

"Of course," said the man. "I'm sure my wife can come up with something."

I took Eadric's hand as the man led us to the largest house in the village. As narrow as the others, it was two stories tall with a pair of windows on the upper floor that looked out over the street. Despite the candles flickering in the windows, it didn't look as if anyone were home. I drew back when the door opened to a dank, earthy smell that seemed out of place indoors. "Are you all right?" whispered Eadric as he tucked my arm in his.

"Yes," I said, "but this house—"

"Right this way," said the man, leading us into the large front room. A table had been set with two trenchers and two mugs as if we'd been expected. I looked around, thinking we were alone in the silent house, and was surprised to see a grizzled old man watching us from the corner by the hearth. "My neighbor, Humphrey," said our host, who I could now see was fair-haired with pale skin and piercing blue eyes. There was a whisper of sound, and a young woman with the same coloring stepped into the

149

doorway of another room. "And this is my wife, Sulie. She'll see to your needs. My name is Corbin. Please sit. Sulie will have your supper ready soon." With a nod to his wife, the man disappeared out the front door.

We took our seats as the woman set a pitcher of ale on the table. "I'll have the food ready in just a minute," she said. "Drink plenty of this nice stout ale. It builds up the blood."

"Aye, that it does," said Humphrey as Sulie left the room. "That ale is good for you. I've had my fair share over the years and I'm still here." He laughed when he said this as if at a private joke. "Where do you hail from?" he asked, wiping his eyes.

"I'm from Greater Greensward." Wondering if I should tell him about Eadric, I glanced across the table and knew right away that my prince wasn't going to be any help. He was downing his ale as if he hadn't had anything to drink in days, and didn't seem to be paying attention to anything else.

It wasn't until the young woman set clay bowls in front of us that Eadric looked up. "Here you go," said Sulie. "This'll put meat on your bones and thicken your blood."

"Looks good, doesn't it?" said Humphrey, but he was looking at me, not the food.

The bowls held a thick stew filled with some kind of meat and chunks of vegetables. I'd given up eating meat after I'd turned into an animal the first time, but I was too hungry to go without eating anything. Swallowing the chunks of carrots and potatoes as fast as I could, I tried not to think about their meat-soaked flavor. Eadric, however, had no such problem. After finishing his stew, he reached for what remained of mine. While he ate, I chanced to look around the room and caught the old man watching me. I fidgeted under his gaze until Eadric had scraped my bowl clean.

"Eadric," I said under my breath. "Perhaps we could see about those bedchambers now."

Sulie had already left the room, but Humphrey must have heard me, because he called to the young woman, saying, "They want to go to bed!"

"Of course you do," she said to us, wiping her hands on her apron as she came out of the room in the back. "You must be tired after such a long walk. I'm sure you won't have any problem falling asleep."

"How do you know we walked a long way?" Eadric asked, quirking an eyebrow.

"Because everywhere is a long way from here," Sulie replied, laughing. "Now, if you'll follow me . . ."

Eadric glanced at the empty bowls. "I wasn't finished eating."

Sulie shrugged, saying "I'm sorry, but that's all there is. We weren't expecting company." Then turning to me, she added, "Your lad has a hearty appetite! I like that in a man."

Humphrey laughed again, and I could feel his gaze

151

on my back as I started up the creaky stairs. He'd made me uncomfortable, although I couldn't say why, so I was relieved when we reached the landing and the old man could no longer see us.

There were four doors on the second floor and Sulie showed us to two of them. Neither of the rooms was very big. Eadric gave me the larger one, but was soon back, knocking on my door. I let him in, wondering what he could have to say now when he hadn't spoken a word during supper.

"I think you should come to the other room," he said. "Its window is small and has a shutter on it. The bed will be easier to move, too."

"Do you want to trade rooms?" I asked, not sure what he was saying.

"Not at all. I'll stay there, too. I think I can defend it better if it comes to that."

"Defend?" I said. "What makes you think you'll need to?"

"Because something's not quite right about this place. Did you notice that there are no roads going in or out? And I think it's odd that ordinary people would want to live so close to the trolls' mountain. I wouldn't be surprised if they have some sort of agreement worked out with the troll queen. Maybe they tell her about everyone who's passing through, or maybe they turn them over to the trolls in exchange for their own safety. Those stories about trolls killing travelers are true, you know."

"And you think shutters would keep us safe?" I asked.

Eadric shrugged. "They're better than nothing."

"Fine," I said. "But I get the bed. All I want is a good night's sleep."

We were about to leave the room when Li'l flew in through the open window. "There you are!" she said, landing on my shoulder. She was out of breath and I could feel her little heart pounding.

"What have you been up to?" I asked, following Eadric from the room.

"I was looking for bats," said Li'l. "I just wanted to meet them and ask if they knew anything about the troll queen. The whole village smells like them, but I couldn't find a single one."

"That's odd," I said. "Where do you think they went?"

"I don't know. That's why I was looking for so long. This is a nice room," she said as we stepped into the other chamber. "It reminds me of a cave."

"Yeah," said Eadric. "Me, too." The room was small and dark, with one tiny window and a narrow bed. It was situated over the room where we'd eaten, and I could hear people talking below us. "I closed the shutters," Eadric continued. "I'm going to push the bed in front of the door to block it."

"Why?" asked Li'l. "What are you afraid of?"

"Eadric thinks the people in the village might have told the trolls about us," I replied.

"Really?" Li'l fluttered to the window and landed on the sill. "Then we should take turns watching." The little bat shuffled from one side to the other, peering through the cracks in the shutters.

I helped Eadric move the bed. We were shoving it against the door when a clock somewhere in the village chimed midnight. "Did you hear that?" I asked.

"You mean the clock?" said Eadric.

"No, what came after it. They were talking downstairs, but they stopped when the clock chimed. They didn't stop when it chimed before. Wait!" I held up one finger to silence him, listened for a moment, and said, "Humphrey just said, 'It's time,' but he didn't say what it was time for."

Eadric looked puzzled. "How can you hear that?"

"I needed to talk to a butterfly a few days ago, so I had to have extra-sharp hearing."

"Uh-huh," said Eadric. "I believe that, coming from you. Maybe when he said, 'It's time,' he meant it was time to go to bed."

I cocked my head to listen. The stairs creaked as someone climbed them, just as they had for us. "Maybe, except . . ." The creaking grew louder and I could hear a difference. "There are more people now. At least five or six."

154

"Would you look at that," Li'l said, peering out the window again. "All those people are coming this way."

I edged past the bed to peek out the crack in the shutters. It was true. The doors of the village had been thrown open, and everyone was heading toward the house where we were staying.

"*Psst*, Emma," whispered Eadric. "Look at that."

I turned away from the window. Someone was on the other side of the door trying to push it open, but it barely moved an inch before smacking into the bed.

"Whatever you do," I told Eadric, "don't open the door. I have a bad feeling about this."

Whoever was on the other side hesitated, then tapped on the door and said in a pleasant voice, "It's me. Corbin. I've come to see if you need more blankets. Just ask me in and I'll give them to you."

"We're fine," I said. "The night is warm."

"I've brought you another candle as well."

"We don't need another candle. We'll be going to sleep soon," I said.

"Then open the door and we can have a nice chat about what you'd like for breakfast."

"Maybe we should . . . ," said Eadric.

"Don't you dare move!" I spat at him, then called to our host, "There's no need. Whatever you normally make would be fine."

Something scrabbled at the shutters, sounding like a

mouse in the walls. "Emma," said Li'l. "I think you'd better see this."

"What is it now?" I muttered, bending down to peer out the crack again. I couldn't see at first, because something was in the way. Then it moved and the moonlight showed me a man floating in midair, poking ineffectually at the shutters. There were other people there as well, people who would have seemed normal if they hadn't been floating outside a second-floor window.

"Are those people supposed to have teeth like that?" Li'l whispered, peering out the shutter beside me.

"Only if they're vampires," I whispered back. They were fangs, not teeth really, and they looked out of place on the middle-aged woman and the little girl who leered at the shutters as if they knew we were watching from inside.

"Come join us," called the woman. "We'll have a party and you'll be the guests of honor!"

"I bet," I muttered, and then I turned to my friends. "Don't worry. We're safe in here. Garrid told me that vampires can't come in unless they're invited. Just don't open the door or the window. We'll be able to leave in the morning when they go to sleep."

"Some of them are bats," Li'l said. "Or at least they are now."

A cool, dank vapor filtered into the room through the shutters. I peeked out again. Sure enough, there were bats outside flying side by side with the floating vampires. I was still watching when there was another puff of cool, dank air and a little old lady with a kindly face turned into a bat.

Corbin, or whoever was on the other side of the door, started knocking loudly, demanding to be invited in. Eadric faced the door with his arms crossed and his legs braced as if awaiting the onslaught of an army. Convinced that no one was about to come through that door, I turned back to the window in time to see Li'l struggling to open it.

"What are you doing?" I said, slapping the shutter closed again.

"Didn't you see him? Garrid has come looking for me. I have to go to him!"

I shook my head and bent down to take a peek. "That's not possible. How could he be here?"

"Did she say that Garrid's here?" asked Eadric. "We could use another strong arm. Maybe we should let him in."

I turned back to Eadric in disbelief. "Another strong arm that happens to belong to a vampire? I don't think so. He may be Li'l's mate, but do you really think he'd side against a village full of . . . Li'l, wait! What are you doing?"

In the moment that I'd had my back turned, Li'l had pulled the shutter open enough that she could squeeze her tiny body through. As I watched in horror, she darted into the night sky and was lost in a flurry of bat wings and jubilant voices.

"Li'll!" I cried out, but she was gone . . . and back again in an instant with a familiar bat in tow. It *was* Garrid. If I hadn't been a bat before myself, I never would have recognized him, but I'd learned to tell the difference on more than one frosty night excursion. Garrid was a particularly handsome bat, just as he was an exceedingly handsome man.

"Emma, quick!" shouted Li'l. "Let us in!"

I couldn't lose my little friend, not after all we'd been through together, so I opened the window just wide enough to let her in and . . . in came a flood of bats, all of them vampires except one.

Two bats whispered sweet nothings into each other's ears. The rest came straight for Eadric and me.

"What the . . . !" shouted Eadric as a cloud of bats covered him from head to toe. I could see him fighting them off as a similar wave knocked me away from the window, against the bed, then down to the floor. My first thought was that Garrid had betrayed us. The second was that I'd have to use magic to save my Eadric. I was holding my arms in front of my throat, trying to fend off their fangs while furiously working on a spell, when a voice shouted, "Off them! They're my friends!" and all the bats fell away.

It was suddenly so quiet in the room that I could hear Eadric's ragged breath as I tried to catch my own. I sat up, jerking my hand away when it touched the leathery skin of a bat. Then a firm grip enclosed my fingers, and Garrid the man was helping me to my feet. "Sorry about that," he said before turning to Eadric. "It didn't occur to me that they'd follow me, but you know how it goes. Invite one vampire in and they think it means everyone's welcome."

"Then it wasn't a trick?" I asked.

"Emma, how could you?" cried Li'l. "Garrid would never do such a thing. He came looking for me."

"Uh, Li'l," Garrid said, scratching his head and looking sheepish. "I didn't know you were here. It wasn't until I heard your voice that I knew it was you."

"Then why are you here?" she asked, fluttering to the bed. "I bet I know! You were visiting friends and heard my voice and came to protect me. That was it, wasn't it?"

"Actually, I arrived only a few minutes ago. I was delayed at my last stop. That was family business, too, just like this. As the oldest member of the family, I have to give my permission before anyone can marry, so I stop by every few months to see if anyone is engaged. It's a tradition, you understand, but tradition is very important when you live as long as we do."

"You mean these people are your relatives?" I asked.

Garrid nodded. "On my mother's side. Second cousins six times removed, that kind of thing."

"Why didn't you tell me?" Li'l asked. "I would have loved to have come with you."

Garrid looked even more sheepish than before. "It didn't occur to me. I've been making the rounds for hundreds of years and I've never had a wife to bring before."

"A wife!" shouted one of the bats. There was another puff of dank air and the bat turned into the grizzled old man who had sat beside us at supper. "Why didn't you send word that you had married! We'd about given up hope that you ever would! And what is your name, young lady?" he asked, extending his hand to Li'l.

Li'l looked flustered at first, then pulled her wings close to her body. I could tell she was upset. "I'm not a young lady. I'm a bat," she said in a tiny voice.

The old man looked surprised at first, but he quickly recovered himself and smiled down at where she sat on the bed. "And a beautiful bat, too," he told Li'l. "I must say, Garrid, you've found yourself a lovely wife."

"I know I have," said Garrid. "But thank you for saying so. And now I'd like to invite you all to an unexpectedly joyous celebration. I want you to have the chance to meet my wife and our dear friends Prince Eadric and Princess Emeralda." All the vampires in the room began to talk at once, excited at the prospect of a party even if it didn't involve drinking our blood. "You'll have to tell me later why you're here," he told me. "I know it wasn't because you were looking for me."

"I will," I said, "although you'll have to excuse us from your celebration. You're used to staying up, but we have to leave in the morning. All I want to do now is sleep for the rest of the night, undisturbed."

"We'll see what we can arrange," he said, smiling down at me.

A short time later, Eadric and I were in the room that was supposed to have been mine. While he slept on the floor with Ferdy by his side, I lay curled up in the bed sleeping peacefully with Shelton keeping watch from my pillow. Boards had been nailed over the window and on the door hung a sign that read,

NO ONE IS WELCOME,

SO DO NOT DISTURB!

Eleven

Li'l was unusually quiet when we started out the next morning. She had celebrated with Garrid and his relatives all night, but she usually stayed up until dawn, so I knew she wasn't acting that way because she was extra tired. When Garrid offered to accompany us after hearing about our mission, she looked more upset than pleased.

The two of them took turns flying above the trees to make sure we were headed in the right direction and to tell us how to get around obstacles such as bottomless pits and werewolf dens. The first time Li'l left and came back, she landed on my shoulder and stayed there until it was her turn again. She sat with her wings covering her head, another sign that she wasn't happy. Garrid, on the other hand, laughed and joked when he wasn't flying, alternating between riding on Eadric's shoulder and mine. I knew that he was aware of Li'l's bad mood, however, because he kept trying to get her to talk to him and told funny stories to try to make her laugh. After a while he gave up and sat in puzzled silence, glancing at her now and then.

Garrid wasn't the only one who was worried. We'd been walking for a few hours when something occurred to me. "Eadric," I said. "What if the troll queen guessed that we're in the forest? She could be surrounding it right now, waiting for us to come out."

Eadric snorted. "I doubt it. Haven't you seen how big this forest is? More likely they'd figure out where we were going and wait by the entrance."

"Is that supposed to make me feel better? Because it doesn't."

"Don't worry," he said, patting Ferdy. "Between the two of us, we can take care of anything. I wish you'd have a little faith."

"I would," I muttered under my breath, "if we weren't talking about trolls. I've seen what they can do."

"Bradston looked good when we saw the truth in the mirror, didn't he? That boy can even give trolls a hard time," Eadric said with a hint of pride in his voice.

"He looked fine, although his skin seemed a little odd. Your mother said that he was sick. Did she ever tell you what was wrong with him?" I asked.

Eadric shrugged. "I assumed she meant that he had a cold. My mother makes a fuss over the smallest sniffle."

"He didn't look like they hurt him or anything," I said.

"They'd better not," growled Eadric. "He's my little brother, and if anyone is going to hurt him because he was stupid enough to fall into the hands of trolls, it's going to be me."

✧

It hadn't taken long for Li'l and Garrid to find the entrance to the trolls' caves, but then, they were bats, after all. As we neared the edge of the woods, it was Li'l's turn to check our position, and she came back only a few minutes after leaving. "There are trolls up ahead, lurking in the underbrush. Wait here. I'll tell you when it's safe to go on."

Garrid waved his wings to stretch them. "I'll do that, Li'l."

"Don't bother," said Li'l. "Even a bat like me can handle this."

"What was that supposed to mean?" he said, settling back on my shoulder as Li'l flew away. "She's not acting like herself at all. I wish I knew what was bothering her."

"That's a woman for you," said Eadric. "One little mistake and they're mad at you for days."

"What mistake? I don't even know what I did wrong!" wailed Garrid. "She was fine at the party last night. My relatives are all crazy about her."

When Li'l finally returned, we followed her through the trees to a patch of underbrush that had been trampled flat. The rotten-egg smell of troll was so strong that we had to hold our noses before we reached it and long after we'd passed by.

"I think we would have known they were here," I said.

"Anything with a nose would know they were here," said Eadric. "There's nothing subtle about trolls."

"The entrance is up ahead," said Li'l. "There are two trolls playing a game with bones just inside. You can't see them until you go in.'

"Sentries," said Eadric. "Ferdy and I'll take care of them."

"Save your blade," said Garrid. "There's no need to let the trolls know you're here if they don't already. I'll distract them and . . ."

"*We'll* distract them, you mean," Li'l said with a bite to her voice.

Garrid glanced at her, then nodded. "Li'l and I will distract them and let you know when you can come in. Be ready. This won't take long."

While Eadric and I hid among the boulders and loose rocks edging the entrance to the caves, Li'l and Garrid flew toward the opening, flitting around each other in what I would have thought was a friendly way if I hadn't been able to hear them.

"What other relatives haven't you told me about, Garrid?" asked Li'l. "Are your parents still alive, or any brothers or sisters?"

"I was an only child, Li'l. I told you that. And both of

my parents were killed in the vampire-werewolf wars. Why do you ask? Look, the trolls are behind that rock. The big hairy one has a club."

"I'm not stupid or blind. I can see them and they both have clubs," said Li'l. "I just wondered who else you hadn't told about me because you were too embarrassed. Ooh! Watch out! The hairy one almost got you!"

Garrid grunted, then said, "Embarrassed? Because of you? You can't possibly think that!" The vampire huffed, panting with exertion. "Take that! And that! Look out, Li'l! That one's going for his club!"

"Garrid, watch out! Garrid? Don't worry! I'm coming! Squeeze my mate, will you, you rotten, scum-sucking, dirt-licking ... Ha! How'd you like that! Want another one? One good bite deserves another and ... there! Good! Garrid, are you all right?"

"I'm fine! It takes more than a clout on the head and a ham-fisted squeeze to hurt me. Uh-oh. They're not giving up, Li'l. It looks as if a bat attack isn't enough to get rid of these dimwits. Watch out. I'm going to ..."

"Garrid! Why'd you do that?" shrieked Li'l.

"Good day, gentlemen," Garrid said in his man voice. Although I couldn't see him, I knew he'd changed from a bat into his human-looking self. "I've never tasted troll blood before, but I like it now that I have. I'll give you a choice: which one of you wants to join us for all eternity and which one wants to die this very minute?"

"Aagh!" bellowed the two trolls, kicking up gravel as they ran past Eadric and me. I giggled when I saw that they kept their hands covering their beefy necks as they ran into the forest, because I could hear Garrid saying, "I knew they couldn't tell one of us from the other. Thank you for biting that one, Li'l. I couldn't bring myself to do it. Blood that foul would have curdled in my stomach and made me ill for days."

"The funny thing is that I couldn't actually bite him. His skin was too thick," said Li'l.

"Then his head must be thick, too," said Garrid. "Because he thought you had!"

"What happened to the trolls?" Eadric asked when I nudged him. "I couldn't hear a thing."

"They thought that Li'l and Garrid were vampires out for their blood," I said. "Let's go before the trolls stop running and decide to come back."

A bat once again, Garrid was waiting for us at the tunnel entrance. He must have heard what I'd told Eadric because he said, "They won't be back here any time soon. Li'l and I made a big impression."

"I wish I'd seen it," said Eadric.

"Maybe next time," said Garrid. "But only if Li'l . . . Where did she go? She can't be mad at me *again*!" Turning on a wing tip, he flew into the cave after his wife.

"He means she can't *still* be mad, doesn't he?" said Eadric.

"Now what did you mean when you accused me of being embarrassed?" I heard Garrid say to Li'l.

"What am I supposed to think when you don't introduce me to anyone? I didn't even know you had any living relatives until last night. It must be hard to say, 'I'd like you to meet my wife. She's a real bat.'"

"Don't be ridiculous!" said Garrid. "I love you. I'll announce it to the whole world if you want me to. World, this is my wife, Li'l. She's a real bat! See—I wasn't embarrassed at all."

"You wouldn't be—here inside a mountain where no one can hear you except me. And don't you dare tell me that my feelings are ridiculous. You have no right to . . ."

"Is everything all right?" Eadric asked, taking my hand in his. "You look worried."

"Everything is fine," I said, giving his hand a squeeze, but I was wondering if Eadric and I were going to argue like Li'l and Garrid once we were married.

Although we'd packed special torches to take into the caverns, we'd lost them along with everything else when we'd escaped the trolls at the river. Learning of this, Garrid had asked his relatives to make torches for us, something vampires rarely needed. We were happy enough to have them when we started out, but they soon became a nuisance, because they bled dark smoke that stank even more than the ever-present rotten-egg smell of the caves and were sure to give us away. When we came to a deserted sentry post in the tunnel and found some of the trolls' torches, we were delighted to exchange them for ours.

"At least these smell like the rest of the torches around here," Eadric said as he lit them.

"That's true," I said. "But don't you think it's odd that no one is here? Two tunnels merge at this very spot. It seems like an important place for a sentry."

"Maybe they're taking a dinner break," said Shelton, who was riding on my shoulder again. "I know I would if I could."

"And abandon their posts? A real soldier wouldn't do that," scoffed Eadric.

"These are trolls," I said. "Who knows what they do. Still, I think it's odd."

"Hmm," said Eadric, kneeling down to study the other objects the trolls had abandoned.

"There you are," sang out Li'l as she and Garrid flew into sight.

"There's another abandoned sentry post up ahead," said Garrid.

Lil flew closer, making her shadow loom large on the passage wall behind her. "What do you think it means?"

"I'm not sure," said Eadric. "It looks as if the trolls took off in a hurry, leaving nearly everything behind." He poked something with the toe of his boot, turning it over. "See, here's a club, and this was probably someone's meal." A bloody haunch of some kind of animal lay in the dust, covered with soft, wormlike insects.

"Keep your eyes open," said Garrid. "There's something strange about this. It isn't normal for trolls to abandon food."

"Maybe it's a trap," said Shelton. "Crabs know all about traps."

"Then why do so many get caught in them?" asked Eadric.

Shelton waved his eyestalks in irritation. "I said we know about them. That doesn't mean we understand them."

This time when Li'l and Garrid flew ahead, they waited for us at the next abandoned sentry post. Eadric found bone fragments like the ones the first trolls had been using to play a game as well as a note written in some strange lettering. "I might be able to read that," said Garrid. "You pick up all sorts of things when you live as long as I have. Let me see . . . Ah, yes. It says, 'Take two blister beetles and call me in the morning.'"

"It sounds like someone wasn't feeling well," I said.

"Maybe," said Eadric. "I just wish I knew what was going on."

Li'l and Garrid took off again, but were back a few minutes later with news to share. "There's a troll up ahead," said Li'l. "He's lying on the ground moaning."

We started to hurry. "Ferdy and I can get him to tell us what's going on," Eadric said, tapping his sword's hilt for emphasis.

"Don't take Ferdy out unless it's absolutely necessary," I told Eadric. "You know how loud he is."

Eadric looked annoyed. "He can be quiet when he has to be."

"Uh-huh," I said. "I've heard him hum. Just keep him in his scabbard if you can."

"Say," said Shelton. "You do know where you're going, don't you? There could be miles of passages in here. Do you know which one we want?"

"Of course we do," Eadric said, turning to me. "We do, don't we?"

I shook my head. "Not exactly. All I know is that he's being held in a room near the troll queen's treasure chamber."

"You mean we have to search this entire mountain?" asked Li'l.

I felt defensive when I said, "At least I picked the right mountain. This is where the trolls live, so he has to be around here somewhere."

"We'll find him," said Eadric. "We just have to start thinking like trolls."

"As long as you don't start acting like one," muttered Shelton.

"If anyone asked me," said Garrid, "I'd say that we're heading in the right direction. Li'l and I explored some of the side passages. Most of them looked like no one has set foot in there for years. The passage we're in is the most traveled. I think that if we look for the more heavily guarded passageways, we're bound to find him."

"You're so smart," Li'l told Garrid, gazing at him with love in her eyes. Apparently their conversation had taken a different turn when we could no longer hear them.

"Gick! Not you, too! It's bad enough when *they're* all mushy," Shelton said, pointing at Eadric and me. "I thought bats were smarter than that."

Eadric grinned. "I guess not."

Shelton almost fell off my shoulder when I jabbed Eadric in the side with my elbow.

We found the sick troll lying in the entrance to a large cavern. He was alone, although there were enough weapons and food scattered around him for two or three trolls. He moaned when he saw us, then fell back and closed his eyes. After glancing at me, Eadric approached the troll with his hand on Ferdy's hilt, but without pulling the sword from its scabbard. Keeping a cautious distance, he poked the troll with his foot, saying, "Sit up and answer some questions."

The troll rolled his head from side to side and moaned. "Go 'way," he mumbled. "Not want now. Eat later when feel better."

"I think he's sick," I said, going to stand beside Eadric. "Look at his face."

Blotchy and covered with deep purple spots, the troll did look terrible. He was sweating profusely, and his long dark hair was plastered to his head. Looking down from his perch on my shoulder, Shelton said, "That's a troll? They looked scarier at night."

The troll opened his eyes again, only this time his gaze fell on Shelton. "Ohhh, I seeing things," he moaned, and he covered his eyes with his hand. I'd never really noticed a troll's hands before. They were big and meaty with thick nails at least four inches long that looked like formidable weapons.

"Let's go," said Eadric. "We're not going to get anything out of him."

Although we kept to the most traveled passages, it was a while before we encountered any more trolls. We had passed through one cavern after another, all of them without sentries, when we came to an exceptionally large space where water covered most of the floor. Standing at its edge, it was impossible to tell how deep it was, but when we held up our torches, we could see sinuous shapes gliding along the bottom.

Eadric had warned everyone to be careful to avoid making noise that might echo, but Shelton was too excited at seeing so much water to keep quiet any longer. "Would you look at that!" he said, scrambling down from my shoulder to the ground. "A crab could enjoy a place like this!"

173

"Stay with us, Shelton!" I said.

My words bounced back, reminding me that I shouldn't have spoken. I was reaching to snatch the little crab from the water's edge when a voice croaked, "Who there?" from the far side of the pool. Shelton skittered away from my grasp as a torch flared, revealing a shaggy-headed troll. The troll must have been unsteady on his feet, because the torch dipped and swayed.

"Hurry!" Eadric said, turning to Garrid. "Stop that troll before he can raise an alarm."

Garrid darted over the water, turning into the shape of a man when he reached the other side. There was a shout and a splash, then the troll collapsed and Garrid was beckoning to us. Li'l had already joined him by then, so Eadric and I hurried around the pool.

"What did you do to him?" I asked Garrid. The troll lay sprawled on the ground, his arms thrown over his head.

"Nothing," said Garrid. "Look at his face."

I saw what he meant right away. The troll was sick, his face covered with purple spots just like the other troll we'd seen. His eyes were closed and his breathing was labored. He wasn't going to be warning anyone of anything for a while.

"What fell in the water?" Eadric asked, holding the torch out over the pool.

"He had a key in his hand and threw it in when he

174

saw me. I'm sorry I wasn't fast enough," Garrid said, shaking his head.

"A key to what?" I wondered aloud.

Garrid took the torch from Eadric and held it so that its light fell on the wall of the cavern where a metal-studded door blocked the passage. "I don't think he wanted us to open this," said Garrid. "Which means that it's probably the way we need to go."

Eadric crossed to the door and tried to open it. Nothing happened and he turned to face us, saying, "We need that key. Did anyone see where it went in?"

When no one had, Garrid held the torch over the pool so we could look for it. Li'l flew low over the water and was the first to spot the key resting on a yellow rock at the bottom. It was so far from the edge that someone was going to have to wade in to get it. Before Eadric could step into the pool, however, I knelt down beside it and reached my hand in to see how deep it was. The moment my fingers broke the surface, the water began to churn, and the fin of some sort of monster rose above the foam. I lurched backward, sitting down hard.

"What is that?" asked Li'l, frantically flapping her wings to get away from the water.

"Whatever it is, we can't go in," I told Eadric.

A round, scaly face surrounded by writhing tentacles

rose above the water, turning its catlike eyes on us. Its neck was long and slender like a snake, and as the water calmed, we could see the thickening of its body below it. Water bubbled at opposite sides of the pool. The monster wasn't alone.

"Clive," said the first monster. "Look at this!"

Another monster rose out of the water and swiveled its head to examine us. This monster didn't look anything like the first. It was all sharp angles and points with a narrow, pointed head, pointy, fan-shaped ears that stuck out to the sides, and a sharp crest that started just above its eyes and zigzagged down its back.

"They funny-looking trolls," said Clive.

A shapeless, jellylike sack that was mostly transparent floated across the water, rising and falling as it gulped or expelled air. While its friends talked, it raised a cluster of eyestalks from one of its bulges and waved them in our direction. "They not trolls," burbled the monster.

"What else they be, Edgar?" said the first monster.

"Don't know," said Edgar. "Look tasty, though."

"If not trolls, maybe can eat them," said Clive. "What you think, Churtle? Fatlippia make us promise not eat trolls, but she not say about those things."

"Can eat them, if not trolls," said Churtle, the first monster.

I took Eadric aside and said, "No one is going in after that key. Do you think we can talk them into giving it to us?"

"Perhaps they'll do it if we give them something in return," Eadric said, scratching his chin.

"That rude, talking secretlike," said Clive.

"Maybe are trolls," burbled Edgar. "Trolls always rude."

"What could we possibly have that they would want?" I asked Eadric, trying to keep my voice soft enough that the monsters couldn't hear me.

"That's a good point," said Eadric. "Could you use your magic here? I remember how good you were at taking care of the monsters Grassina put in the moat during her nasty days."

I shook my head. "We're in the troll queen's own mountain, at her very doorstep. Using magic now would be like knocking on the door to announce that we're here. This is no place for magic! No, we're going to have to think of something else."

"We ask them," said Clive. "They know if trolls or not."

"Is there anything I can do to help?" Li'l asked, landing on my shoulder.

"I'll do whatever I can," said Garrid. "But I must warn you that I don't know how to swim."

"Then I'm the best swimmer here," said Eadric. "If you three could distract them, maybe I could slip into the water and . . ."

"Get eaten?" I said, hating the idea. "I'd use magic before I'd let you do that."

177

"Hey you! You trolls?" called Clive. "You tell us. We hungry. You look yummy."

"Pretend you don't understand what they're saying," I whispered to my friends.

"We hear you!" said Churtle. "Why trolls pretend can't understand?"

"Maybe proves them not trolls," said Clive.

"But can understand, so must be trolls," said Churtle.

"This too hard," moaned Edgar. "Edgar not understand."

"Hey!" said Clive. "What that? Something move at bottom."

"I not see anything," said Churtle. "Maybe piece of Edgar. Edgar, you lose piece again? Pull self together. Churtle hate when Edgar let self go."

"It not Edgar!" said Edgar, sounding as if his feelings had been hurt. "Edgar all here."

"How you tell?" said Clive. "Clive not know where Edgar is until swim into Edgar. It disgusting!"

"Edgar not disgusting! Clive disgusting! Clive poke Edgar for fun! Laugh when Edgar leak. Clive mean. Edgar not like Clive." Raising one of his jellylike bulges out of the water, Edgar swatted Clive on his snout.

Clive spluttered and coughed, then said, "Edgar runny glob of snot! I not like Edgar either. See how Edgar like be poked." His crest rose as Clive lunged for Edgar. The jellylike monster gave a high-pitched shriek as he let all his air out at once, sinking to the bottom like a stone. Clive followed, appearing to shrink as he swam farther and farther down.

"Must see this! Wait for Churtle!" shouted Churtle. He plunged into the water, his smooth back arching above the surface, then disappeared with a flick of his tail flukes.

"Yoo-hoo, over here! Is this what you were looking for?" It was Shelton, holding the key with both front claws.

"You got it!" I said, reaching down to pick up the little crab.

"Here, you take it," he said, dropping it into my hand. "That thing is heavy!"

"When you ran off that way, I thought we'd lost you for good," I said.

"Naw, I just wanted to wet my shell. But I don't like that water. Tastes funny. Too many minerals, I guess. So," he said, his eyestalks perking up. "Anything interesting happen while I was gone?"

Twelve

I held my breath as Eadric put the key in the lock and didn't exhale until he'd pushed the door open. Li'l fluttered beside me, too nervous to hold still. We were both disappointed when the passage beyond didn't look like anything special. Then Garrid stepped over the threshold and raised the torch high. "Oh," we breathed, for the stone walls were studded with gems of every color. Although the light from the torch wasn't very bright, it reflected off the gems, making them sparkle and wink until our eyes ached and we had to look away.

"This is the passage I saw in my farseeing ball," I said. "They took Bradston this way."

"No wonder they keep that door locked," said Shelton. "I wonder how hard it would be to pry off those stones. I bet Coral would like one!"

"We're not thieves," said Eadric. "We're here to get my brother back and nothing more."

"Spoilsport," grumbled Shelton. Before I could stop

him, he'd scrambled from my shoulder to the ground and was poking at one of the gems. I was surprised when he snapped it off with his claw. "Did you see that?" asked Shelton. "They were stuck on. Someone put them there to make the walls look pretty."

"And it worked, too," said Li'l. "This is beautiful." I saw the way Garrid was watching her when she said that and wondered how long it would be before he gave her a gem of some kind.

We knew we were getting close to the queen's chamber when we came to the next door. It was more ornate than the first, with crudely printed letters that Garrid told us meant, "Keep out! This means you, Dunderhead!" It was obvious that the sentry had left in a hurry. Not only had he forgotten his club, but he had shut the door without making sure that it had actually closed. When Eadric set his hand on it, the door creaked open.

The room beyond was as unexpected as the gem-decorated passage had been. It was draped in fabrics of garishly bright oranges, pinks, purples, and reds that covered the stone walls so that it seemed more like a tent than a cave. Equally bright carpets had been scattered across the uneven floor, hiding holes and bumps and making walking difficult. Here and there matching pillows were mounded in piles like the leavings of some outrageously colored beast. Even with all the fabric, the room was chilly and damp and smelled strongly of mildew as well as rotten eggs.

I saw cracked urns overflowing with the feathers of exotic birds, and benches made of bone and antlers with the skulls still attached. A dainty table of tarnished silver held drinking vessels of all sorts, from rude clay mugs to finely wrought chalices made of gold. Whereas some held the dregs of a dark liquid, others held only dust.

I was walking toward the table when I nearly kicked over a basket of fruit that had been left on the floor beside one of the mounds of pillows. The grapes were withered, the apples brown and mushy, the rest so rotted that I couldn't tell what they were. When I tried to go around the basket, my foot slipped into a hole under the carpet and I stumbled, landing on my knees. I started to push myself up and found that I was looking into the glazed-over eyes of a troll. I recognized her at once. It was the troll queen, and she didn't look at all well.

I stood up and retreated a pace. The troll queen lay sprawled on her back behind the pile of pillows. All four of her heads were soaked with sweat and had tangled hair and cracked lips. Dark purple spots made random patterns on her faces. Although the head with the long brunette hair appeared to be asleep, the head next to it was delirious, turning from side to side and mumbling, "Too many birds in pie," and "Rampaging better in winter." Even though misery had distorted her face, I recognized her as the red-haired head who had threatened me over my farseeing ball.

182

I was startled when the head with reddish, light brown hair blinked and stared at me with wary eyes. "You here," she said, her hoarse voice almost too faint to hear. "Army searching river. Move on, we say. She not there anymore. We knew you come. He said so."

"Who said I'd come?" I asked, bending down to hear her better.

A head with strawberry blonde hair stared at me through eyes as big as cartwheels. "What she do, Grunella?" she asked with a catch in her voice. "She want hurt us? Wish Fatlippia awake. Ingabinga all right?"

"Quiet, Tizzy!" barked the head named Grunella. "No start crying. I not know what human do now."

"Emma, what did you find?" asked Eadric from across the room.

Li'l fluttered toward me, making funny little sounds when she saw the troll queen. "She found her! Emma found the queen!"

"For goodness' sake, get away from her!" Eadric exclaimed as he jumped over a pile of pillows and staggered across the uneven floor.

The troll queen's hand shook, and her fist started to clench. Then it went limp and Grunella groaned. "I not move stupid thing. Not since Fatlippia start raving." She nodded toward the delirious head next to her. "Wake up, Fatlippia! Company here!"

"Fish follow Fatlippia home, so I . . ."

"Fatlippia, wake up! Need control hand!"

"Name him Scales. That good name, you not think?"

"Fatlippia! Need hand to . . . Oh, you no help." The head twisted aside and spat at the wall, then turned back to look at me. "You be happy Fatlippia sick. If she awake instead of Grunella, Fatlippia find way stop you. You kill us now and steal treasures?"

"No," I said. "We never intended to hurt you. We just want Bradston back along with your promise that you'll leave him alone."

One side of her mouth quirked in a half smile. "Give you word, but not do any good. Smart troll never keep promises. Promises for weak soft-skins. But I not want him. He more trouble than worth. You tell him Grunella say so."

"Say," said Garrid. "Look at this. What do you suppose it's for?"

I had to stand to see what he was holding. When I realized what it was, I nearly broke my neck tripping over the basket of fruit as I ran to take it from him. I hadn't wanted to let Eadric know how worried I was about the magic-seeing ball, but if this was actually it . . . "Let me see that," I said, snatching the gray-green ball from his hands. I carried it back to where the troll queen lay and held it up for her to see. "This is what you used to see me when I did magic, isn't it?"

Grunella glanced at the ball, then looked away, but

the flicker of recognition I saw in her eyes was almost enough. Almost, but not quite. "We'll just see then, won't we?" I said. Raising the ball so everyone could see it, I made up a small spell on the spot. It felt wonderful to use my magic again!

> Make this chamber smell like flowers.
> Make the smell stay here for hours.

And just like that, the odor of mildew and rotten eggs was gone and the room smelled like a heady bouquet of roses and lilacs and the lilies my mother had had planted all around the moat. I was watching the ball the whole time, so I saw when it clouded over and a tiny version of me appeared standing in the troll queen's room.

"Pew!" said Grunella. "What that stench?"

"It's how your world smells right before this thing is destroyed," I said, heading toward the door. "Excuse me, everyone. I'll be back in a minute."

I hated that someone had made a magic-seeing ball that was focused on me and would know whenever I used my magic. Rather than have it fall into someone else's hands, I was going to do whatever it took to destroy it. The ball was heavy and hard to break, but I threw it against the wall until it split. I bent down to pick up the pieces and found an auburn hair same color as mine stuck to the inside of a larger fragment. "That's odd," I muttered, then remembered that whoever had made it had to have something of mine to focus it. The hair didn't just look like mine; it *was* mine. Whoever had made the magic-seeing ball must have been close to me at some point, or at least knew someone who had been. Jorge had been in our castle, although he was in our dungeon the entire time. I had never gone to see him, but it was possible that someone had given the hair to him. Thinking about his room and the furniture he'd been using, it was even possible that he'd gotten it off my old bed.

After stuffing the hair into the pouch I wear at my side, I smashed the pieces until they were small enough that I could grind them under my heel. Once I was finished, I felt much better.

When I returned to the troll queen's chamber, Tizzy was pouting. "Why you do that? Tizzy thought ball pretty."

Grunella sighed. "You happy now?" she asked me.

"Not yet," I said. "Tell me—how many of those were there?"

"Grunella not tell you!" said the head.

"Why you ask?" said Tizzy. "You want break other one, too?"

"Tizzy!" wailed Grunella. "Now she know is other one!"

"Thank you," I said. "I don't suppose you'd care to tell us where we can find Bradston?"

"Not in million years," Grunella said, chortling.

"She not staying that long, right, Grunella?" asked Tizzy.

"Prince Eadric, over here!" said Garrid. "Li'l found a door behind the cloth. If someone can hold the cloth aside . . ."

"Uh-oh," said Tizzy. "They find it!"

Grunella glared at the other head. "Tizzy! You not talk anymore!"

"Let me help," said Eadric. Grabbing a fistful of the fabric, he tore it from the wall, exposing a door that was as short and wide as a troll. It groaned like one, too, when Eadric forced it open. The room beyond was dark, the torches lighting it having fizzled out. I peered around Garrid and Eadric as they bent down to enter the room, taking our torch with them. It was the same room that Eadric and I had seen in the banshee's mirror.

Only a few paces inside the door Bradston lay on the floor, his head pillowed on his arms. The two trolls we'd seen in the mirror lay side by side in the corner, their faces spotted, their breathing loud and nasal. "Bradston!" Eadric said, his brother's name catching in his throat. "Poor little guy! What have they done to you?" The boy's face was dotted with scabs, but otherwise he looked fine to me.

"Uh, Eadric," I began.

"They must have infected him with their horrible

187

disease," said Eadric, shaking his head. "Look at his face! Who knows what this is going to do to him."

"Not much, once the scabs heal," I said. "Eadric, your brother was sick first. Your mother didn't tell us what he had, but it looks like it was chicken pox. I had it when I was five. Aside from a scar on my arm where I picked off a scab, I was fine. He will be, too, but I'm not so sure about those trolls. I don't think they gave it to him. I think he gave it to them."

"That can't be. Look at how still he is. Bradston, wake up. It's me, Eadric. We're here to rescue you. Did you see that?" he said, turning to me. "He doesn't respond. I'm sure there's something seriously wrong with him." I sighed and shook my head, but Eadric was adamant. "You wouldn't understand. You've never had a little brother."

Kneeling on the floor beside his brother's inert body, Eadric bent down to scoop the boy into his arms, and got clonked soundly on his nose when Bradston sat up with a start.

"Ow!" howled Eadric, holding his hand to his nose. Blood was already seeping between his fingers when Bradston looked up and laughed. "That was a good one! I got three trolls that way, and now you!"

"You little monster!" said Eadric.

"Why'd you bring her with you?" Bradston asked, looking at me. "Mother calls her the nasty little witch who cast a love spell on you. Is it true?"

"Of course not," I said indignantly. "I never cast a love spell on Eadric."

"I meant the nasty little witch part," said Bradston. "She said a lot of other things, too. Want to hear what they were?"

"No!" Eadric and I said in unison.

Bradston stood up and stretched. "So, you came to get me out or what? You sure took your time. Do you know how awful it's been? There's nothing to do here. Trolls have to be the stupidest people in the world. Say, you didn't bring something to eat, did you? I'm starved."

"He talk too much," called Grunella from the other room.

I saw a satisfied smile flicker on Bradston's lips and shuddered, feeling a rush of sympathy for the trolls.

We were back in the troll queen's chamber when Bradston noticed Li'l. "Am I the only one who saw that there's a bat in here? Give me a rock and I'll kill it."

"You'll do no such thing!" I said. "You stay away from her! That bat happens to be one of my best friends."

"That figures," said Bradston. "A witch and her bat. I bet you're really an old woman who drinks bat juice or something to stay young. I bet you're a whole lot older than you look."

"Bradston, that's enough," growled Eadric. "And to think that my mother dotes on him."

"Does she know he acts like this?" I asked.

Eadric shook his head. "She hasn't the least idea. He acts like an angel when she's watching."

"I can silence him for you if you'd like me to, Emma," offered Garrid.

Bradston stuck out his tongue at Garrid, then turned to me and smirked.

Eadric sighed. "Please forgive him. He's ill and doesn't know what he's saying."

"He's not that ill," I said. "And he knows exactly what he's saying."

"My parents are never going to let you marry him," the boy said. "I heard them talking. They're going to send Eadric far away and see that he gets engaged to some other princess. They said that anyone would make him a better wife than you would."

"I should turn him over my knee," said Eadric.

"Don't bother," I said, having had enough of Eadric's younger brother. "I have a better idea. Why don't we just turn him over to your mother? I think they deserve each other."

Choosing one of the cleaner rugs on the troll queen's floor, I said a quick spell to enable it to fly. Bradston was eager to take his seat beside Eadric, and even let his big brother put his arm around his shoulders to keep him safe. With Garrid seated beside me and Li'l cradled in his hands, I made the carpet rise before saying,

Take us to the young lad's mother.
She awaits his quick return.
Keep him there until he grows up.
He still has so much to learn.

Never more than five or six feet
Should this wayward youngster stray.
By his mother's side he'll linger
Till his twenty-first birthday.

"Does that mean what I think it does?" Eadric asked as a breeze sprang up around us.

"Yes," I said. "Bradston is going to be a real mama's boy."

Thirteen

"That was the best thing I've ever done!" exclaimed Bradston as the carpet settled to the floor of Queen Frazzela's solarium. "It was even better than stealing eagles' eggs or dumping trash over the parapets onto people! Give me the rug. I can think of all sorts of places I'd like to go."

"Really?" I said. "That's funny, because I can think of a lot of places that I'd like to send you. I'm not going to give you a magic carpet, though." Although the carpet was resting on the floor, a ripple ran through it every few seconds as if it wanted to fly away. Certain that the boy would try to take it when I wasn't around to stop him, I said a quick spell to turn the carpet back into an ordinary rug. It went limp with a soft, breathy sigh.

"Why'd you do that?" squeaked the boy. "You're mean! If you don't make it fly again, I'll tell my mother that you did and then . . ."

"Oh, look, there's your mother now!" I said, gesturing

behind him. "I'm sure she'd be very interested in whatever you have to say."

Queen Frazzela sat open-mouthed, making funny little gurgling sounds. We'd flown through her solarium window, landing between her and a group of ladies. One of the ladies fainted when she saw us, and most of the rest just looked dumbfounded. At a word from Queen Frazzela, the other ladies-in-waiting helped their friend from the room, leaving three other women behind. My grandmother Olivene and my aunt Grassina looked delighted to see me. My mother looked perturbed.

"Bradston, is that really you?" said his mother.

The boy didn't look happy, but I didn't know if it was because I'd denied him something he wanted or because he'd said some things in front of his mother that he'd rather she hadn't heard. He covered it well, however, forcing tears to come to his eyes and throwing himself into his mother's arms. "Oh, Mama," he said. "It was awful!"

Queen Frazzela drew him into her arms and kissed the top of his head. "My poor little darling," she said, rocking him back and forth as if he were a baby. She was cooing and patting his back when he peeked over her shoulder and gave me a sly look of triumph.

Just wait, I thought, remembering my spell.

"My poor boy! Thank goodness you're all right. Those horrible trolls. You must have been terrified. And I bet you didn't sleep a wink." She turned to my relatives, saying, "Bradston needs his rest. He's been through a terrible ordeal. You'll have to excuse me. . . ."

"Of course, my dear," said Olivene, giving mother and son a sympathetic smile. Bradston was walking dutifully beside his mother when he looked back and stuck out his tongue. Grassina looked surprised, but Olivene just smiled all the more widely and winked at me.

As soon as Frazzela and Bradston were gone, Garrid cleared his throat and said, "Eadric, Li'l and I need to take naps. If you could suggest somewhere quiet and dark . . ."

"You'd probably like the top room in the old tower. No one goes there anymore."

"Perfect," said Garrid.

When Garrid left the room with Li'l on his shoulder, he still looked like a man. Then a whiff of something cold and dank drifted in from the hall, and I knew that he hadn't waited long before turning into a bat.

"It's good to see you both safe and sound," said my mother. "Queen Frazzela told me that the trolls had killed you, but Olivene and Grassina assured me that you were unhurt. I've never known them to be wrong."

I glanced at where they sat side by side on a bench in the sunlight. Grassina smiled and tapped the farseeing ball she wore on a chain around her neck.

"Why didn't your mother thank you after you rescued Bradston?" my mother asked Eadric.

"She doesn't like magic," he replied.

"Neither do I, but I appreciate what it can do for us and know enough to respect it. Apparently your mother does not."

"I'm afraid her attitude is common in this kingdom, Mother," I said.

"Then I fear for your mother and your people, Eadric," she said. "And my respect for both has been woefully diminished."

"We knew there was something wrong with Frazzela when she came to the tournament," said my grandmother. "Your mother was so rude to our Emma."

"I remember," said Eadric. "I've already spoken to her about it."

"Tell us what happened after the army ran back here with their tails between their legs," said Grassina. "I saw them coming in my farseeing ball. I think I've spent more time looking into it these past few days than all the other times I've used it put together."

"We were preparing to follow you when I asked Grassina to see how you were doing," said my mother. "She saw that something had gone amiss, although she couldn't tell what. Her reports were so confusing: you were safe, you were in danger, you were fine . . . We stopped only three times on our way here. I've never felt so rushed in my life. When she saw you enter that mountain, your father almost set out after you, but Grassina still insisted that everything was all right."

"And it was, wasn't it?" said Grassina. "Tell me about the cockatrices. I want to hear how you got out of that one."

"And the banshee," said Grandmother. "Don't forget about her."

My mother stood and straightened her skirts around her. "If you're going to talk about such things, I might as well leave. Although I must say I was delighted when Grassina reported that you were able to accomplish so much without using magic for a change, Emma. I'm . . . proud of you," she said, sounding as if she'd surprised even herself. Gathering her embroidery, she started for the door, pausing on her way out to say, "That young man with the bat looked familiar. Have I met him before?"

"At Father's tournament," I said. "Did Father accompany you here?"

"Yes, and so did Haywood," said my grandmother. "We arrived yesterday."

"About that young man who came with you," said Mother. "Why would he want to sleep in a tower? Wouldn't he prefer to have a room?"

"He doesn't need one," said Eadric.

"Oh," my mother said, the muscles around her eyes and mouth tightening. "Don't tell me any more. I'm sure it's something that I'd rather not know anything about. Mother, Grassina, I'll see you at supper. I believe that I'll go for a walk in the garden. I trust that no one will be discussing magic there."

"Now," said Grassina after my mother had gone. "We want to hear everything. Start with how the trolls attacked in the middle of the night."

So Eadric and I told them about the trolls and the devices they'd used to sense my magic. Although I'd smashed the queen's magic-seeing ball, her army must still have theirs. I put finding it on my mental list of things I had to do.

We told them about the sea monsters and the cockatrices. Grassina said that she might like to turn into a weasel and hunt cockatrices someday. We told them about the banshee and the vampires. Olivene wondered if the banshee knew an old acquaintance of hers—someone she'd met when she was under the family curse.

They were particularly interested in the troll queen's mountain and its tunnels and caverns. Olivene and Grassina told us that the monsters sounded familiar. When we told them about the sick trolls, they said that it sounded as if they had troll pox, a nasty yet rarely fatal disease. We were still discussing the pox when Queen Frazzela returned with Bradston in tow.

"I thought the boy was going to rest," said my grandmother.

Bradston's expression was sour, and I could tell he wasn't happy to be back with us.

"He refuses to leave my side," said Queen Frazzela. "I tucked him into bed, but he jumped out and followed me when I left. The experience with the trolls must have been too much for the poor child." She patted his head, then leaned down to kiss him on the cheek, not noticing his pained expression.

I was trying not to smile when my eyes met my grandmother's. She winked at me and I had to look away.

"It occurred to me that I've been remiss," Queen Frazzela told Eadric. "I should have thanked you for what you've done. You brought my baby back to me when I thought he was gone forever. I've never heard of anyone getting a child back whom the trolls had taken. Thank you, Eadric."

"And Emma," Eadric said, giving my hand a squeeze.

Queen Frazzela sighed. "And Emma. I must admit, I never thought I'd say this, but after what Bradston told me, I, well . . ."

"Can see how magic might be useful at times?" said Eadric.

"Yes, exactly!" The queen looked relieved that she hadn't had to say it herself.

"And it might be handy to have a witch in the family?" Eadric continued.

"I never said . . . but I suppose . . . well, yes, that, too."

"I'm curious," said my grandmother. "What did Bradston tell you, exactly?"

"He told me about the trolls, of course. They were horrible to him. And he told me about the dangerous passages and the cave where he was held prisoner and the horrid monsters he saw." The queen dabbed at her eyes with a cloth she pulled from her sleeve. "When I think about what my poor boy had to endure . . . Thank you for getting him out of there!" she said, and this time she looked straight at me.

Bradston looked disgruntled. I was convinced that he'd probably described his plight to his mother to gain more sympathy, not so she could picture what we had gone through to get him out. He kicked at an uneven spot on the floor, looking as if he'd rather be anywhere else but there, yet he stayed by his mother's side when she collected her embroidery and sat down.

Eadric yawned, exaggerating it until his mother couldn't help but notice. "I need a nap," he said.

"So do I," I said, following his lead.

"There will be a feast tonight," said Queen Frazzela. "In honor of Bradston's safe return."

"Good," said Eadric, yawning again for real. "We'll be there."

Supper was hours away, however, and we were too hungry to wait. Eadric was showing me the way to the kitchen when we ran into his father in the Great Hall. "Eadric, my boy! I knew you could do it! Congratulations! Into the trolls' mountain and out again safe and sound. It's an extraordinary accomplishment. You'll have to tell me how you managed it. A little magical help from your Emma, I presume. I must say, after everything that has happened over the past few days, my opinion of magic has changed. I've never really understood it, but then maybe it has its place whether you understand it or not. It certainly saved the day this time. I heard all about the trolls attacking and how you kept the bulk of their army off my men with that thing you did to the stream, Emma. I wish I had someone like you attached to my army!" King Bodamin winked at me, and I could see that Eadric was as surprised as I was.

"We're grateful, the queen and I, although she might not know how to say it. She dotes on that young scamp. I'll have to give him a talking-to when he's feeling fit again. Shouldn't have gone off like that. Not with trolls and who knows what else outside the castle walls. We'll have to see that he doesn't stray again. Assign him his own guard perhaps."

"That won't be necessary," I told him. "I don't think he'll go far from his mother now."

"Good, good," the king said, beaming. "We can't have this sort of thing happening again. It caused quite an uproar, didn't it? Why, I was telling King Limelyn . . . You do know that your parents are here, don't you, m'dear? They arrived yesterday along with so many carts and carriages that . . . Well, I'm sure you understand."

Eadric had waited until his father paused to take a

breath. "If you'll excuse us, Father, we were on our way to get something to eat."

"Quite right, Eadric. Quite right. You must be starved. Come see me after you've eaten."

"I will, Father. We have a lot to talk about," Eadric said, giving me a meaningful glance.

His father nodded, saying, "Indeed we do, my boy. Indeed we do! Now, don't eat too much. I understand that there's to be a special supper tonight. Make sure you save room for the stewed eels. They're my favorite."

It didn't take us long to get a bite to eat. The kitchen staff fawned over Eadric, congratulating him and offering him the best cuts of leftover roasts and the freshest fruit. They smiled at me, a big difference from the disapproving looks I'd gotten from the residents of the castle a few days earlier.

When we'd finished eating, we left the kitchen and were crossing the Great Hall when my father hailed me. "My darling Emma, how are you?"

"Better," I replied without explaining that it was because I could use my magic again.

He nodded as if he understood. "Please join me for a moment," he said, and he led us to a bench away from the bustle of the Hall.

Eadric put his arm around me as we sat, pulling me close to his side. My father cleared his throat and said, "King Bodamin and I have agreed that there's no reason to put off your marriage any longer. You two make a perfect match and will unite our kingdoms in a way that would benefit both. As I have no other heirs, Emma will be queen of Greater Greensward one day. Bodamin assures me that Eadric will rule Upper Montevista. Eadric, you have shown great strength of character and bravery, two qualities that your father had hoped to see in his heir. There's no reason you can't rule both countries side by side. I must admit, I'd thought Bodamin was against the marriage, but I was surprised by how quickly he agreed to it. He mentioned something about family members helping his army. I didn't quite follow that, but he might have been alluding to the way you took care of the trolls."

"So he gave his permission?" I said, not quite believing what I thought I'd heard.

My father nodded. "The wedding will be tomorrow. Everyone we would have wanted here for the wedding is already at the castle, although I daresay that Chartreuse and Frazzela will have others they want to invite. Bodamin and I will see that the appropriate documents are drawn up. He sent word to the local priest right after we spoke. Ah, there's your mother now. She's handling the rest of the arrangements."

I was stunned. I'd been afraid that we'd never get the approval of Eadric's parents, and now we were having the wedding the next day. I didn't know if I should be happy and excited, or frightened and tell them to wait because I wasn't ready. I would have liked to discuss it with Eadric, but he took off when we saw my mother bearing down on us with a determined look in her eyes.

"Did your father tell you about the wedding?" she asked me as Eadric hurried away.

I turned to my father, but he had already retreated across the Hall. "Yes, he did," I said. "Don't you think tomorrow is a little soon?"

"Of course I do, but the men have made up their minds. I'm determined to make the best of things, however, and you should, too. Although I may not have long to make the arrangements, I'm going to see that this wedding is done right, not like your aunt Grassina's. Now come with me. I have Maude waiting to start on your gown, and Frazzela has sent both of her seamstresses to assist. This shouldn't take long with three pairs of hands working on it."

I shouldn't have been surprised that Mother had brought her favorite seamstress with her from home. She usually traveled with a full entourage, just in case she needed someone's special talents. I followed her up the stairs reluctantly, unable to think of any plausible reason to get out of it.

Maude was very businesslike when we stepped into Queen Frazzela's solarium, as were the two older women helping her. They were finishing the last of my measurements when Queen Frazzela came to the door. I could hear her arguing with my mother from where I stood in the middle of the room, so I was curious when my mother came back alone.

"What was that all about?" I asked.

"Nothing really," said my mother. "Frazzela wanted to see what fabric you've chosen, but I told her she couldn't come in. She had Bradston with her and he refused to stay outside. That boy has become so insecure since you brought him home. He hasn't left his mother's side yet."

"That's odd," I said, pretending to watch the seamstress.

"She did tell me that she has the wedding feast well under control. She also said that the guests have begun to arrive. Those friends of yours, Oculura and Dyspepsia, are here. Your grandmother insisted that she be in charge of the invitations."

"What is Grassina doing?" I asked.

"She's taking care of the flowers. I just hope they aren't like the ones she had at her own wedding."

When the initial fittings were done, the seamstresses said I could go but had to return when they sent for me. They seemed smug in their ability to tell me what to do, even if it was for a short time, but I was happy just to have gotten my freedom back long enough to go see what was going on.

I was on my way to the Great Hall when I saw Eadric

very briefly. He was going to his own fittings, but was so nervous that he couldn't stand still and paced the whole time I was talking to him. "So the wedding is tomorrow," he said.

"Can you believe it? I didn't know what to say when Father told us."

"Are you all right with it being so soon? I don't want you to feel rushed."

I smiled, warmed by his concern. "I think it's wonderful," I said, realizing that I really did.

"It looks as if we have enough people to help out," he said, gesturing toward my aunt, who was bustling through the hall with an armload of ferns.

"Mmm hmm," I replied. "I just wonder whom my grandmother is inviting."

"I saw her waiting by the drawbridge. She seemed to be expecting someone."

"Dyspepsia and Oculura are already here. I think I'll go talk to Grandmother," I said, "and find out exactly who's on her list."

I didn't have to go far to find her. Some of her friends from the Old Witches' Retirement Community had arrived, and she was escorting them across the courtyard. After they'd offered me their congratulations, Grandmother sent them inside while we talked.

"Who else did you invite?" I asked.

"Grassina helped me with the list. We invited Pearl

and Coral, but Coral is still visiting her friends and Pearl has gone to see her sisters. I thought about inviting that little dragon friend of yours along with his parents until Grassina pointed out that Bodamin and Frazzela might not appreciate having three dragons in their castle."

"So who is coming?" I asked.

"We've invited all the fairies from Greater Greensward and Upper Montevista. I made sure that we didn't leave anyone out. You know how irate fairies can be if they think they've been slighted."

"Oh dear. I didn't think of them. We needed to invite the fairies, of course, but we'll have to make sure that everyone is extra nice to them, even the more peculiar ones. The last thing we need is another curse cast on the family. I'll explain it to Queen Frazzela and King Bodamin so they can tell everyone else."

"Good," said Grandmother. "It will be for only one day. Fairies don't like spending the night away from their own homes."

My search for the king and queen took me to the courtyard and all the public rooms, but it wasn't until I started asking if anyone had seen them that a maid said they were in the family corridor. I found them talking to Bradston outside the room where Eadric was getting fitted for his clothes.

". . . just for a little while," said the queen. "You're

perfectly safe here. No trolls will ever get into the castle. There's nothing to fear from . . ."

"I'm not afraid," Bradston said, looking more irritated than frightened.

The king threw up his hands. "Then why can't you stay in your room without your mother? You're too old to be following her everywhere. You haven't left her side since you came home. The poor woman can't even use the garderobe without you waiting for her on the other side of the door."

"Don't you think I'd like to stop following her?" said Bradston. "I just can't, that's all, and don't ask me why because I don't know the answer."

I'd been standing in the hall, wondering if I should leave and come back later, when Queen Frazzela glanced up and saw me. "Bodamin," she said, tilting her head in my direction.

The king turned to me, smiling. "Ah, there you are, my dear. All set for the big day tomorrow?"

"I'm sorry to interrupt, but that's what I wanted to talk about. I guess it's a good thing that I found all three of you together. We have some guests coming tomorrow who are a little unusual. Some are from Greater Greensward and some are from Upper Montevista. They're very sensitive, you see, and . . ."

"They're witches, I suppose," said Queen Frazzela.

"I should have known you'd open my home to the worst sort of people."

I took a deep breath, trying to keep myself calm. "They aren't witches, although we did invite a few, and I expect them to be treated with as much courtesy as any other guests," I said, looking straight at the queen. "The people I'm talking about are fairies. We invited them because they would have been insulted if we hadn't, which wouldn't bode well for either kingdom."

Bradston snickered. "You're going to have little fairies at your wedding? That's the stupidest thing I've ever heard!"

"Then listen to me, Bradston," I said, barely controlling my temper. "The stupidest thing would be if someone were to insult one of these fairies. They're very powerful and could make you miserable for the rest of your life if you so much as look at one of them in a funny way."

"I'm not surprised that you consort with fairies in your kingdom, but it's unheard of in Upper Montevista," the queen said in a voice I'm sure she thought sounded superior.

"I wouldn't say that exactly, my dear," said the king, rubbing his chin with his thumb and forefinger. "My father's older brother had some fairy friends. One day he told my father that he had fallen in love with a fairy lass and was going to attend one of their dances. He disappeared that night and no one ever heard from him again."

"Your mother told me that he died very young and that that's why your father inherited the throne," said the queen.

"My mother didn't want people to know what had really happened. I'm sure that most of the stories she told you were altered to fit her version of the truth. She refused to let anyone tell me fairy tales when I was growing up. She'd say that they were all lies, then check the doors and windows as if she feared that someone might have heard her."

"She was right to be afraid," I said. "If any fairies had, they might have taken offense. It's a mistake to ignore fairies, but it's an even bigger mistake to be rude or unkind toward them."

Bradston snorted as if he thought I was making it up, but King Bodamin looked thoughtful when he said, "You say the fairies who live in my kingdom are coming here tomorrow? How many should we expect?"

I shrugged. "I'm not sure. My grandmother might know."

The king nodded and looked at his son. "Bradston, I order you to be respectful toward all our guests. None of your tricks, understand?"

The boy hesitated as if he wanted to make a snide remark, then seemed to think better of it and said, "Yes, sir. If *you* say so." His parents were both looking my way when Bradston stuck out his tongue at me.

"I'll see that this gets relayed to the rest of the castle. Frazzela," the king said, turning to his wife, "regardless of your feelings, you're to treat them as honored guests."

The queen glared at me. "We would never have had to worry about any of this if Eadric had chosen a normal princess."

"Oh really?" I said. "And would that be a princess who had slept for a hundred years or one who cleaned house until her fairy godmother helped her go to a ball? I don't know about you, but I'm not sure I've ever met a normal princess."

King Bodamin chuckled. "She's got you there," he said to his wife. "It doesn't matter whether they should have been invited or not. They have been, so we'll do as Emma has asked. This should be interesting. I've always wanted to meet a fairy."

Wonderful, I thought, heading back to the Great Hall. *With Frazzela and Bradston around, something is bound to happen.* I began to wonder if my family was doomed to end one curse just to fall prey to another.

Fourteen

hen I couldn't find Eadric, I decided to take a nap before I had to face everyone again at supper. The chamber I'd used before was just as I'd left it, which meant that the person who usually slept there had not come back. Because I didn't want to be disturbed, I said a spell to lock the door, and another to keep any outside noise from getting in, then lay on the bed and closed my eyes. I was almost asleep when I remembered what the troll queen had said. Although I'd asked her whom she meant when she told me, "He said you would come," we'd been interrupted before she answered, and I'd forgotten to ask her again. *Whom did she mean?* I wondered as I drifted off. *Why were they talking about me?*

I was exhausted and slept through supper and on into the night. It was midmorning when I woke again, feeling more refreshed than I had since leaving Greater Greensward. My grandmother was sitting at a table across from the stairwell waiting for me when I went downstairs.

"Come sit down," she said, waving me over. "I'll fill you in before your mother gets her hands on you and you don't get a chance to breathe."

"Is she upset that I slept so long?" I asked, taking a seat across from Grandmother.

"I wouldn't say she's upset. Livid, yes, upset, no. I understand she almost beat your door down trying to wake you. That must have been some spell you used to keep her out. Be prepared for a royal scolding," she said, smiling at her own joke. "She wanted you for more fittings for your gown, but I'm sure she's made do just fine."

A page ran past carrying a basket of flowers. Three others stood on ladders while hanging garlands over doorways. Grassina and Haywood presided over them all from the center of the Hall.

"I thought I should tell you before you heard it from someone else," said Grandmother. "We already had our first fairy-related near-disaster. But don't worry, I took care of it."

"What happened?" I asked with a sick feeling in my stomach.

We waited while a serving maid approached the table and set a mug of cider in front of Grandmother. She smiled at both of us and left to get one for me.

Grandmother looked around as if to make sure that we weren't about to be interrupted again, then said, "Sir Geoffrey, a very sweet and well-intentioned knight, was

212

returning from patrol when he dismounted to pick a wildflower for Lady Eleanor, one of Frazzela's ladies-in-waiting. Unfortunately, a flower fairy on her way to the wedding had stopped for a sip of nectar and was inside the partially closed flower when he snapped the stem. Sir Geoffrey had almost reached the gate when the furious fairy turned him into a chipmunk. A guard who saw the knight disappear into his clothes came looking for me. I was the logical choice since I'd already let everyone know that I'm a witch."

"You didn't!" I said.

"Of course I did. I'm not ashamed of who I am. All this tiptoeing around the subject gives me a headache. If these people have a problem with magic, it's their problem, not mine. As I was saying," she said, giving me a pointed look, "I calmed the fairy and got her to reverse her magic. She was very understanding once I explained it all to her. Fairies believe in true love just like you and me. There was one condition, however."

"And what was that?" I asked, fearing the worst.

Grandmother smiled. "They have to get married and invite her to their wedding, that's all. Neither of them minded in the least."

"Was that the fairy's condition or yours?"

Grandmother's smile got bigger. "Does it matter? Either way, they're getting married next month and I'm invited, too."

I smiled at the serving maid who gave me my cider, then said to Grandmother as the girl walked away, "What happened when you told everyone that you're a witch? How did they take the news?"

"They were a little standoffish until I said a spell to fix the broken pots in the kitchen and another to rebuild a crumbling section of that causeway they're all so worried about. They became quite friendly after that."

"I didn't know they were having any problems," I said.

Grandmother peered at me over her mug of cider. "Everyone has problems. You just have to keep your ears open and help where you can."

"How is Queen Frazzela today? Is she still upset because we invited the fairies?"

"Not at all. She was quite taken with them after she saw one this morning. Listen, I think I hear more arriving now."

She was right. When I tuned out the voices of the people in the Hall, I could hear a faint sound like wind chimes. The sound grew louder as I ran to the courtyard, wanting to make sure that someone was ready to greet them. Queen Frazzela was there already, so caught up in the fairies' arrival that she didn't notice me.

Unlike the flower fairy, these fairies were as big as humans, although finer boned and with more delicate features. The queen seemed captivated by their sweet voices and the graceful way they moved. She smiled and was gracious to them, just the opposite of the way she'd treated me. I even heard her claim that she had insisted that we invite them and that she was so glad they had come.

Bradston was there, too, of course, and was as curious about them as any ten-year-old would have been. I saw him surreptitiously touch the wing of one of the fairies, and held my breath when the fairy turned around, startled. Seeing the boy, her face relaxed in a gentle smile and I knew that what I'd heard was true: fairies were more tolerant of children than they were of adults.

I was going back into the castle when my mother finally found me. "There you are!" she said. "I hate it when you lock your door that way. I can never get in to see you when I have something important to discuss. You knew you had more fittings to do. Why did you sleep so late? Frazzela got Eadric up at dawn and he's been busy ever since."

"We can go see about those fittings now if you'd like," I said, not wanting to argue with her.

"It's too late for that," she said. "Maude had to work with what she had. That gown had better fit, that's all I have to say. It will be your own fault if you look gawky. Three seamstresses working together might have been able to disguise some of your flaws, but even they can't work miracles without fittings."

"I can always use magic to make it fit," I said, then bit my lip when I remembered who I was talking to.

My mother glared at me. "If I'd wanted my daughter

215

to wear a dress made with magic, I wouldn't have had Maude and the others stay up all night to work on it. You will wear it as it is and be thankful that I went to so much trouble."

"Yes, of course, Mother," I said, feeling sorry for Maude.

"Go to your room and wait for us," Mother ordered. "I'll send a serving girl to tell Maude to meet us there with your gown. And for goodness' sake, don't lock your door!"

Although I would have loved to go to the Great Hall to watch the guests arrive, I knew better than to cross my mother again, so I hurried up to my room. I was just shutting the door behind me when Li'l appeared at my window. Flying to the tapestry on the wall, she latched on with her claws and hung upside down to talk to me. "You'll never guess who I saw in the courtyard! The witches from the Old Witches' Retirement Community!"

"I know," I said. "They arrived yesterday."

"No, not them," said the little bat. "I meant the rest of the witches. Your grandmother didn't invite a few of her friends. She invited all of them!"

I sighed and started to take my hair out of its customary braid. "Poor Frazzela. She won't like that one bit."

There was a knock on my door, and before I could answer, my mother rushed into the room. "Good, you're here. Maude will be along in a moment. She has your gown and Lucy is going to do your hair. You've never

216

been any good at doing it yourself. I don't think you even know how to brush it," she said, poking at a lock of my hair as if it were some loathsome creature she didn't want to touch. "Thank goodness I'm here to see that you look decent for your wedding."

I glanced out the window at the tinkling sound of wind chimes and saw a brightly colored flock fly by. At first glance I thought they were birds or butterflies; then I realized that a large contingent of fairies had arrived. I saw them again as they circled the castle to appreciative applause from the courtyard below. A few minutes after they landed, Grassina came to the door.

"Did you see them?" she asked, out of breath from running. "The fairies from Greater Greensward are here. They all came together, which is amazing in itself. I think this is the first time in years they've done anything as a group. You know they consider this a special event when you see the swamp fairy wearing a new dress of green leaves."

There was another knock on the door, and Maude and Hortense came in carrying my gown and slippers. Maude couldn't stop yawning as she laid the gown on my bed. Lucy squeezed in past them, looking horrified when she saw the size of my room. "I'd better go," said Grassina. "You need the space. Call me if I can help in any way."

My grandmother was the next to arrive. When she saw how many people were already there, she pushed past them and took a seat on the bed. Hortense was helping me into my gown when Queen Frazzela came to the door. Once again, my mother wouldn't let her in because Bradston was with her. "But I have to talk to Emma," said Queen Frazzela. "The guards have cornered a dragon in the courtyard. Eadric saw them and interceded before they could dispatch the beast. He says the dragon should have received an invitation, but the beast didn't know about the wedding until the fairies told him. Can you imagine? Eadric actually insists that the creature attend the ceremony! I can't understand what's gotten into that boy. Before he met Emma he would have killed it himself. I nearly fainted when I saw it, and he wants to put it in the buttery until the ceremony begins."

"Is it a very big dragon?" I called through the door.

"No, it's quite small as dragons go," Queen Frazzela called back. "But what possible difference could that make?"

"Quite a bit, actually. A large dragon would never fit in the buttery."

"You don't understand," said the queen. "We can't have dragons in the castle! I've come to ask you to talk some sense into him."

"Who, Eadric or Ralf?" I asked. "I agree that Ralf shouldn't have come by himself. He's too young to travel this far without his parents. I think Eadric was right, though. Ralf will be fine in the buttery."

"You'll have to excuse us now," my mother told Queen Frazzela. "The ceremony will begin soon and Emma isn't nearly ready." I smiled when she shut the door firmly in the spluttering queen's face.

My gown was everything a bride could want. It was made of a finely woven cream-colored fabric that hugged my hips and fell to my feet in soft folds. The three seamstresses had embroidered the hem and cuffs with gold and green threads, using designs of vines and flowers. My mother had given me a heavy gold chain to wear low on my hips and a more delicate one to wear around my neck. Lucy took great pride in dressing my hair, brushing it until it glowed and looping a third and even finer gold chain through it. My mother then produced a gold circlet that she set on my head. It was the closest thing I'd ever had to a crown, but far lighter than what my parents wore for formal events. When they had finished, I felt beautiful and everyone assured me that I was.

We waited until Grassina brought me a lush bouquet of roses, lilacs, and lilies, then my mother led the way down the stairs to the Great Hall. The fairies caught my eye right away. Wearing their best and brightest clothes, they would have been dazzling if the sun hadn't already started to set and the Hall hadn't been lit with torches. I saw flower fairies lined up on the window ledges tickling each other and giggling. The ones sitting on the garlands were harder to see because their flower-petal skirts blended in with the brightly colored blossoms. Most of the larger fairies were gathered together at the sides of the Hall as if so many humans made them uncomfortable, although I did see a few scattered fairies seated among the other guests. One fairy was dressed all in moonbeams that made her seem less real than the fairies around her. Another wore a trailing gown of willow leaves that shivered when she moved. The gown of a third was made of violets, the blossoms having been sewn together so carefully that they remained unblemished.

I was ready when my father took my arm to walk me the length of the room. I could hear people murmuring and the priest clearing his throat, but the loudest sound was that of my own heart. Glancing from side to side, I looked to see who was there, my smile frozen in place. I saw Haywood and Grassina gazing at each other with love in their eyes. Hortense was already crying, as was Oculura, who dabbed at her eyes, then took them out and replaced them with fresh ones. Dyspepsia was muttering to her sister about the lateness of the wedding, how she didn't like going home in the dark and how itchy her new gown felt. King Bodamin smiled warmly at me, oblivious to his wife, who stood beside him trying to take a straw away from Bradston. The boy was using the straw to poke the bubbles that covered the gown of the fairy next to him. My grandmother looked wistful and my mother looked distracted, as if she were thinking of a hundred things about my wedding that she wished she had done differently.

And then I looked straight ahead and saw Eadric, and suddenly I didn't have eyes for anything else. He was standing beside the much shorter priest and looked so handsome that I felt my heart skip a beat. His cream-colored tunic and hose had been embroidered in gold and green to match my gown, and a gold circlet identical to mine held his brown curls back from his forehead. But even if he hadn't been dressed in such finery, he would have been the handsomest man there.

When I finally stood beside Eadric, I began to feel shaky and a little light-headed. Eadric must have seen something in the way I looked, because he took my hand and squeezed it. His hand felt warm in mine, and was as reassuring as always.

The priest was young and nervous. He started with a speech that sounded memorized, saying that although love wasn't essential, it was an important building block in the foundation of a good marriage. Eadric squeezed my hand when the priest paused. We turned to see what he was looking at and saw Li'l and Garrid nestled in the shadow of a banner.

The priest started over, then got as far as the next building block, loyalty, before losing his place again. A minor scuffle had broken out when one of the guards had stepped on Ralf's tail. It seemed to take forever before the priest reached the third element, friendship.

Eadric squeezed my hand once more and I returned

the pressure, knowing that all three building blocks were already ours. The priest hadn't said anything that we didn't already know. Eadric must have thought so, too, because he winked at me and grinned. After that I missed half of what the priest said because I was looking into Eadric's eyes and remembering how they had looked on the day we met. He had been a frog and I'd thought he was obnoxious. Back then I never would have imagined that I would marry him, or that I could love anyone so much.

The priest droned on, interjecting the appropriate questions here and there. I suppose I must have said what I needed to, because before I knew it he was saying, "I now pronounce you man and wife. You may kiss the bride," and Eadric was. It was a long kiss, a warm and sweet kiss full of shared memories and the promise of things to come. It would have lasted even longer if a soldier hadn't clattered into the hall and barged past the assembled guests to King Bodamin's side.

Although the soldier spoke in a lowered tone, I heard everything he said. "We have a situation, Your Majesty. A patrol has sighted trolls carrying clubs coming this way in great numbers. Should we raise the drawbridge?"

"By all means!" exclaimed King Bodamin. "Hurry, man, go give the order."

Apparently I wasn't the only one to hear him, because the fairies and some of the witches began repeating what

222

the soldier had said. He had already gone, but as word spread, knights began to hurry from the Hall as well.

Of the people who remained, the fairies seemed the most agitated. Eadric and I were still standing in front of the priest when one of the fairies from Upper Montevista fluttered her wings and flew over the heads of the other guests to join us. "We apologize, Your Highnesses, but we must go," she said. "We are grateful that you invited us to help celebrate your wedding. However, we believe that the trolls are about to attack this castle. As we must preserve our neutrality in such matters, we think it best that we leave before any fighting begins."

"You're leaving?" Eadric said, sounding incredulous.

The fairy nodded. "Unfortunately. We'll return when the battle is over, provided that the castle is still here. Congratulations on your wedding. It was a lovely ceremony." The fairy raised her hand as a signal to the rest. Within a minute, there wasn't a fairy left in the castle.

"I can't believe it," said Queen Frazzela. "That was the rudest behavior I've ever seen! They accept our gracious invitation, enjoy our hospitality, then can't be bothered to help us when we most need it. I knew all along that we shouldn't have invited them!"

Bradston tugged on her sleeve. "But you said . . ."

"Never mind," the queen snapped, looking doubly annoyed. "Some things do not bear repeating."

Fifteen

The approach of the trolls made it impossible for anyone to leave by conventional means, which meant that everyone not charged with defending the castle had to gather in the Great Hall or other rooms of the keep, the most defensible area. As it was dark out, Eadric and I collected torches to carry up to the battlements to learn what we could. Ralf wanted to accompany us, but we convinced him that he could help more by staying behind to protect the women and children. He decided that this meant watching over Bradston and his mother, so he plopped down in front of them and growled when anyone came near. Queen Frazzela nearly fainted the first time he did this, although Bradston seemed delighted with the little dragon.

When they saw us going, Grassina, Haywood, and my grandmother followed us to the courtyard and up the steps to the battlements, where my father and King Bodamin were already watching the trolls. Neither of them seemed too worried at first. "They can't do anything from there," said Bodamin as the trolls jumped up and down and shouted at us from the far side of the gap separating the ridge from Castle Peak.

While the trolls milled around, lighting torches and bumping into each other, a few of the old witches from the retirement community joined us. The witches were trying to guess what the trolls would do next when the troll queen strode down the middle of the ridge, pushing aside anyone who got in her way. Although she was shorter than most of them, she had more heads than any of the rest. Even the bigger trolls seemed to be afraid of her. When she reached the point on the ridge where the drawbridge would have landed had we set it down, she stopped and shouted with all four heads at once, "King Bodamin!" The volume was impressive, even from so far away.

"That's the troll queen," I told him. "I think the second head from the right is in charge. Its name is Fatlippia."

"What kind of a name is that?" said the king. Cupping his hands around his mouth, he shouted back, "What do you want? Why are you here?"

"We want prince!" shouted Fatlippia.

King Bodamin's eyes went hard and his hands squeezed into fists. "Never!" he shouted. Turning his back on the queen, he told us, "She's not getting Bradston back, even if she lays siege to this castle for a hundred years!"

"Then we come get him!" screamed the head called Ingabinga. "That prince ours! He promise marry queen!" The troll queen turned and was storming away when the strawberry-blonde head called Tizzy looked over her shoulder and stuck out her tongue.

"Marry!" said King Bodamin. "I can't believe Bradston would promise to marry her."

"I don't think he did," said Eadric.

A new troll had arrived and was barking orders, arranging the troll army in a raggedy line. He had two heads like the one who had seemed to be in charge during their attack near the stream—the one who had held the magic-seeing ball. We were wondering what he had planned when he shouted something at the first troll in the line, gesturing from him to us. The troll balked at what must have been an order. When he didn't move, the commanding troll shouted at the second troll. The two trolls squabbled, then the second shoved the first over the edge of the causeway.

The commanding troll barked his order again. Now that the second troll was at the head of the line, he didn't seem to like the order any better than the first had. Instead of waiting for the troll behind to push him, however, he shouted at his commander, then jumped as far as he could with his arms flailing as if they could carry him all the way to where we stood. They didn't, of course, and we watched as he passed out of sight, wailing the whole way down.

"What are they thinking?" my father said as the trolls continued to line up and jump. None of the trolls was getting anywhere near us, yet that didn't seem to deter their commanding troll. One by one they leaped and fell wailing onto the rocks below.

"Trolls don't think," said King Bodamin. "Their brains are smaller than ours."

Eadric had been leaning over the edge of the battlement with a torch in his hand, trying to see farther down Castle Peak. "Emma, could you make me some witches' lights?" he asked when the torch wasn't enough. Whatever moon was out that night was hidden behind the mountain looming above us. Aside from a few twinkling stars, the only light was what we provided. After I'd made him a score of lights, he had me send some of the glowing balls down into the ravine separating Castle Peak from the ridge. Peering over the edge again, he grunted and stepped back. "Look down there," he said, pointing. "Their brains may be smaller, but some of them can think just fine."

From where we stood on the battlement, if we craned our necks just right and leaned out just so, we could see where some of the trolls had landed. Instead of splatting on the rocks, they had grabbed hold and were climbing hand over hand.

"Does anyone know how they're doing that?" asked my father.

When no one could answer him, Grassina took out

her farseeing ball and asked to see one of the climbing trolls. The image in the ball was small, but it was enough to see that the troll was digging his long fingernails into the rock itself, not even bothering to look for crevices.

"Wow," said Eadric. "If their nails are that strong, it's no wonder they're so long. They probably can't even be cut! Look at those trolls go!"

Nearly a dozen trolls had climbed into view, and more appeared as we watched. I glanced at their commander and saw that he was still ordering the trolls over the edge one at a time. Some wailed, but the more resigned ones fell silently.

"I know what to do," said King Bodamin, and he turned to an officer awaiting his orders. They spoke for just a moment, then the officer strode off and the king returned to where we stood. "Now watch," he said. "This should take care of them."

While some soldiers ran down a ramp, others began shooting arrows at the trolls, moving so quickly that the projectiles looked like a swarm of oversized wasps. The arrows bounced off the trolls' backs, although one went straight into the open mouth of a troll who was looking up. He bit down, then smiled, grabbed the next arrow that came near him, and devoured it, too.

Within a few minutes, the first group of soldiers returned, lugging a pot of boiling oil up the ramp. Hauling it to the edge of the parapet, they poured it over the edge onto the trolls below. We could hear the oil splashing on the rocks, but none of the trolls fell, and not one made a sound when the boiling oil drenched them.

"That won't do anything except clean them off and make them smell better," said my grandmother. "Their skin is much thicker than ours, more hide than skin really. It can't be cut, pierced, or burned, unless of course you have a magical ax made specifically to use on trolls." She glanced at King Bodamin. "I don't suppose anyone here has . . ." When he shook his head, Grandmother sighed. "No, I didn't think so. Perhaps we could hold them off until dawn, when daylight will turn them to stone."

King Bodamin snorted.

"I admit that you don't see stone trolls very often," said Grandmother. "Trolls are very conscious of what their fate would be if they didn't get under cover before the sun came up. That's why they attack only at night."

"This has to work," said King Bodamin. His brow was creased and his eyes were hooded when he came back from speaking with his officer a second time. Instead of talking to us, he went to the parapet and leaned over to watch.

The soldiers tried boiling oil again, sending the contents of a dozen enormous pots onto the heads of the trolls. When that didn't work, they tried pot after pot of boiling water. When they ran out of water, they poured dirty water from scrubbing the kitchen floor and the remnants of a cream-based soup that had gone bad the day before but hadn't been thrown out yet. None of this fazed the trolls, who just kept climbing higher.

The king had his men try stones next. The smaller gravel sounded like rushing water when it fell, tumbling over the trolls and clearing off debris. The larger ones bounced against Castle Peak, breaking off chunks. The largest stones knocked a few trolls off the wall, but they just started climbing all over again.

"There must be something you can do," King Bodamin said to Grandmother, Grassina, Haywood, and me. "Some magic that would get rid of them. We know you can turn people into frogs. Can't you turn trolls into something equally harmless?"

"We could try," said Grandmother, "but it wouldn't make any real difference. Our magic doesn't work on trolls the same way it does humans."

King Bodamin's face flushed red. "I know how it is! This isn't your castle, so you don't care what happens to it. You can just fly away on your broomsticks and leave us here to face them when they . . ."

"Oh, all right," said Grandmother, sounding exasperated. "I'll show you what I mean. Do you see that horrid-looking fellow with the big ears? Watch what happens to him."

The troll she was talking about had almost reached the base of the castle itself. He was reaching for his next fingernail-hold when Grandmother cast a spell to turn him into a mouse. The troll paused for a moment, swatting at the air around his head as if a swarm of flies was bothering him, then continued to climb. We all peered down at him, wondering if anything had happened. As he came closer, we saw that he had changed, but not the way the king had wanted. His ears, usually big and pointed, were now small and rounded. His face had become pointier with a row of tiny teeth, and a long, thin tail sprouted from a hole in the seat of his pants. Unfortunately, he was as big and mean and troll-like as ever.

"All right," said King Bodamin. "You can't change the trolls themselves, but surely you can do something else."

"We could call up a storm," I said. "Although I doubt it would do much."

"A storm . . . Yes, that might work," said the king. "A big, fierce storm that will blow them from here to tomorrow."

"All right," I said, "but everyone who isn't a witch has to go inside. A storm strong enough to blow trolls off the side of a mountain will most certainly be strong enough to blow you away as well."

King Bodamin protested, as did Eadric and my father. I relented and let them stay as long as they tied themselves down, but insisted that the soldiers leave, saying that I wouldn't begin until they did. When everyone was ready, I started the storm by myself; then the other witches joined in, adding their strength to mine. It was impressive, with winds that sent boulders flying like specks of dust and ripped the words from our mouths before we could speak.

The other witches and I used magic to keep us in place, so I was able to look over the edge to see how the storm had affected the trolls. Most of them had stopped climbing. Although the trolls' fingernails were still embedded in the rock, the rest of their bodies were flapping like clean laundry in the wind. Only the trolls who had thought quickly enough to use their toenails as well were making any headway, but slowly because they had to move one foot or hand at a time.

We kept the winds blowing until it was obvious to everyone that it wasn't going to work either. Even King Bodamin admitted that we had to give up, if only so we could try something else. We couldn't think of anything else to try, however. The trolls had almost reached the top of the castle walls when my father ordered us inside. King Bodamin protested, still hoping that we could do something that would rid him of the trolls.

Grassina dragged me to the steps leading down to the courtyard. I was partway down, pushed along by the press of old witches behind us, when I realized that Eadric wasn't there. "Where's Eadric?" I called out. "Has anyone seen him?"

"He's back there," shouted a witch at the end of the

line. "I heard him talking about someone named Birdy."

"You mean Ferdy?" I turned and squeezed past my aunt and the other witches, heading back up the stairs. If Eadric was out there, he must think that his magic sword could work against trolls. "Ferdy doesn't have the right kind of magic!" I shouted, running up the last few steps.

"Shh!" said Eadric's father from where he stood just outside the door. "Let him see what he can do."

"But . . . ," I began.

My father grabbed my arm and pulled me out of the way. "If the man wants to try, why not let him?"

Eadric was facing the meanest-looking, ugliest troll I'd ever seen. He was hunchbacked, knock-kneed, and had a nose like a potato. He also had tiny, rounded ears and sharp little teeth that . . . It was the troll that Grandmother had tried to change into a mouse.

The troll hopped off the parapet, landing with a *thunk!* He didn't seem to notice that he had grown a long, thin tail until it snagged in a crack in the parapet. Eadric was already pulling Ferdy from his scabbard when the troll grunted and stopped to look behind him. Seeing his tail, he grabbed it and yanked, howling when it hurt. He forgot his tail, however, when Ferdy began to sing.

> A troll, a troll, I've never fought a troll
> Though there's been many times that I've
>   wanted to.

> To fight a troll—that has become my goal.
> I'll take a couple whacks, then I'll run him
>   through.

The troll roared, opening his mouth so wide that we could see his tiny teeth and his huge gullet. Ferdy didn't wait for him to finish. He whacked the troll, just as he said he would—one, two, three! Neat slits appeared in the troll's ragged clothes, but his hairy hide was unharmed underneath. However, Ferdy wasn't about to give up.

> This troll is tough, his skin so thick—
> Defeating him won't be so quick.
> Give me just a minute more
> And he'll be laid out on the floor!

The troll lumbered as far as his still-caught tail would let him while Ferdy whacked away until the raggedy clothes hung in ribbons. When the troll reached for Ferdy, the sword jumped aside, then whacked the creature's hands like a teacher slapping a wayward student.

The troll growled, unhurt but obviously angry. "Hold still!" he bellowed. "Me get you!"

Instead of going for Ferdy again as I thought he would, the troll buffeted the sword aside and reached for Eadric, wrapping his beefy hands around his neck. I shrieked, then bit my lip and thought furiously, knowing that with a twitch of his fingers the troll could snap Eadric's neck in an instant. Because trolls seemed to be constantly hungry, I thought a little distraction might help. The troll's mousy tendencies gave me an idea for the spell.

Stop that troll, if you please.
Hit him with a wheel of cheese!

A huge wheel of yellow cheese shot out of nowhere, thumping the troll soundly in the chest. He looked surprised, then delighted when he saw the cheese spinning on the floor where it had landed. "Yummy!" he bellowed. Letting go of Eadric, the troll lunged after the cheese, jerking to a stop when he reached the length of his tail.

While the troll struggled to free himself, I ran to Eadric and grabbed him by the back of his tunic. "Come on," I said, trying to pull him toward the steps.

Coughing and rubbing his throat, Eadric turned and followed me. Our fathers were already halfway down when we reached the stairs. Hearing another troll land on the floor lent us speed, and we dashed down to the courtyard, nearly stepping on the kings' heels.

One after the other the trolls crawled over the parapet. As we crossed the courtyard, heading for the keep, the first trolls started down the steps behind us. Haywood was waiting for us, and the moment we crossed the threshold, he said a spell that made the door as immovable as the stone walls around it. Now nothing could open that door until he undid the spell. We were discussing what we should do next when we heard something heavy crash against the door, but it was stronger now than its original wood, and the trolls couldn't even make it rattle.

"What about the other doors?" asked my father.

"The witches from the retirement community are taking care of those," said Haywood.

"The trolls are climbing the walls of the keep!" Grassina shouted from the entrance to the Great Hall.

"They must be going for the windows," said Haywood. "We'll have to take care of those next."

The arrow slits were too narrow for a troll to fit through, but the windows facing the valley were wide enough. When Grandmother's friends had finished with the doors, they went from window to window, shrinking them so that even a troll's hand wouldn't have fit. Although the rest of the castle might be overrun with trolls, the keep would be impenetrable once every door and window was blocked.

As soon as the witches were finished, we met in the Great Hall to try to come up with some way of evicting the trolls. "We're safe enough here," said King Bodamin. "I have soldiers stationed around the keep, watching the trolls through the arrow slits. They'll keep us posted if the trolls try anything new."

"We're trapped, aren't we?" said my mother.

King Bodamin's expression was fierce. "Only magic could get us out now."

"Has anyone seen the troll queen?" I asked. When no one could answer me, I took out my farseeing ball and asked to see her. At first I couldn't figure out where she was. She was using her nails to climb up a small, narrow space. Her four heads made hideous faces as they squeezed through the opening and she climbed out into . . .

"That's the garderobe down the hall from my room!" Bradston shouted into my ear. I hadn't known that he was peering over my shoulder, so I jumped when he shouted, and the image in the ball disappeared. I knew the garderobe he was talking about, however. It was a tiny room that jutted out from the side of the castle like a wart on a troll's nose. The hole of the garderobe emptied into the valley, making an easy entrance for anyone who climbed the wall on that side, provided they weren't too squeamish.

"She's in the castle?" said Queen Frazzela, her voice high and shrill.

Bradston pointed overhead. "She's . . ."

Then we all heard her, whooping and yelling as she thundered through the corridor *above* the Great Hall, growing louder as she drew closer. Queen Frazzela became so pale that I was sure she was about to faint. "Can't someone do something?" she whispered.

The troll queen tore down the steps, her four heads

screaming. Each was wild-eyed and covered with filth. A row of soldiers stood ready to defend us, forcing us to peer around them to see the queen. The closer she came, the better we could see her faces, lumpy with dried scabs left by the troll pox, and colored with garish paint that highlighted her eyes and mouths.

The troll queen fought the soldiers, their swords and pikes bouncing off her as she beat them back with the cudgels she held in her hands. She was almost through the line when Eadric tried to pull me behind him, but I stood my ground and said a spell that would have stopped most people. I didn't know if it would hurt her, but then I didn't know if anything could.

> Let the ground beneath her open
> To a deep and noisome pit.
> Put inside it snakes with venom
> Of the kind that bite or spit.

One moment the troll queen was coming after me, the next the ground had opened under her and she'd disappeared. I cringed, wondering if I'd gone too far. I'd never intentionally hurt anyone before, and the thought that I had made me feel cold inside. Everyone froze, listening for some sound from the pit, afraid that they might actually hear it. After a dreadful silence the witches began arguing about who should retrieve her body. My father suggested that I seal her in, but King Bodamin didn't want me to, saying that if the troll queen was still alive down there, she might find some way to undermine the castle foundations and kill everyone.

While the two kings debated what to do, the witches prepared to draw straws to see who would go into the hole. I was watching them when Queen Frazzela shrieked and pointed at the hole. The troll queen's heads had risen over the edge and she was crawling out, dragging herself by her nails.

However frightening she'd looked before, it was nothing compared with how she looked now. Her filthy clothes had been torn when she'd fallen into the snake pit, and what was left of them writhed as if they'd taken on a life of their own. Bulges rippled and slid across her stomach, then over her chest and down her arm. A snake slipped out of a hole in her sleeve, its tongue flicking the air. She grabbed it just behind the head and bit it while the tail thrashed and twitched. After she'd eaten the entire snake, savoring each bite, she used her nails to dig the scales from her teeth.

More soldiers had positioned themselves between the troll queen and the royal family. I'd have to do something before she hurt anyone else, but first I needed some questions answered. "Why do you want the prince?" I said. "Do you honestly want to marry him?"

"Prince promised to me. He mine!" Fatlippia said as the troll queen stopped short.

Queen Frazzela gasped and began to cry.

"Did you promise the troll queen that you'd marry her?" King Bodamin asked his youngest son as he shook him by the shoulder.

Bradston gulped and shook his head. "I didn't promise her anything."

"Then what is she talking about?" asked the king.

"Who promised that you could marry the prince?" I called to the troll queen.

"Two humans," said Tizzy. "Young one and old one. Came through magic mirror. Said if queen took young prince, queen have husband and human kingdom. Humans warn queen about you. Old one say you come if queen took prince. Gave queen two balls show magic. Young one tell where prince hunt eggs."

"What did the humans look like?" Eadric asked, pushing me to the side.

Grunella leaned toward Fatlippia, whispering, "That prince I tell about."

After studying Eadric a moment, Fatlippia nodded and whispered back, "I see what Grunella mean." Raising her voice, she told him, "Young one hair color of straw and eyes like summer sky. Old one no hair on top and big belly."

Eadric glanced at me. "Sounds like Jorge and Olebald."

"They had no right to promise you the prince," I told her. "Bradston can't go with you."

Curling her lip, Fatlippia shook her head. "Queen not want that one. He talk too much. Queen want that one," she said, pointing at Eadric. "Grunella say he prince, too."

Eadric grunted as if he'd been hit in the stomach. "You can't have him either," I said. "I just married him. He's mine now."

I could have sworn I heard Fatlippia growl. The other heads looked at her as if they were expecting something to happen. "No human tell queen what can and can't do," she said, narrowing her eyes. Raising her clubs to shoulder height, she began to twirl them like a child might twirl a length of rope. The clubs went faster and faster, making an awful whining shriek that hurt my ears. When the troll queen reached the soldiers, her clubs were an unstoppable force that cut them down like grain before a scythe. After finishing with the soldiers, the troll queen turned her eyes on me.

"Kill her, Fatlippia! If she dead, prince not belong to anyone," called the head named Grunella.

Everyone except Eadric and I had fled to the back of the Hall. Unlike my family's castle, however, there were no doors there to allow them to escape. The only thing behind the Great Hall in Upper Montevista was the valley and a thousand-foot drop. "Get back!" Eadric shouted at me, pulling Ferdy from his scabbard.

"A troll, a troll . . . ," the singing sword began.

"No," I told him. "You heard the queen. This fight is

241

mine!" And then I did something I'd never intended to do in front of my new husband's family again. The first time I'd done it, it had made them hate me and could have ended any chance I had of marrying my one true love. Now I didn't see that I had any choice if I was to save him from the troll. Closing my eyes, I said the same spell that I'd used at the tournament and many times since.

The shriek was torn from my throat as my body began to burn. I felt as though the spell was peeling off my skin and replacing my bones with lava. It was excruciating, but when it ended abruptly, I stood before the troll queen a peridot green dragon, more than twice as long as she was tall, ready to defend all the humans in the room.

"Look!" said Ingabinga.

"Maybe we go home now," said Grunella.

"I not quitter!" growled Fatlippia. "That prince mine!" Roaring her rage, she launched herself at me, her clubs moving so fast that they were hard to see.

I reared up, glad that I'd eaten gunga beans and hot flami-peppers only the week before. As the troll queen twirled her clubs, I took a deep breath and exhaled, igniting her clothes, her hair, and the banners hanging on the walls behind her. The witches in the Hall doused the flames and wafted the smoke out the window while the troll queen began to pound me with her cudgels. I beat my wings once and rose above her now-hairless heads.

Although the troll queen was strong, I knew that I was

stronger. With the witches waiting to undo any damage I might accidentally inflict on the castle, I whipped around and hit her with my tail, knocking her through the tables and benches so that she hit the far wall with a crash.

The queen staggered to her feet and shook her heads, then came after me with a roar. Hitting me with both clubs at the same time, she sent me spinning upward so that I slammed into the ceiling. The beams cracked; the ceiling disintegrated. The witches caught the debris before it could hit anyone while I snagged the troll queen with my claws. I tried to bite her, but she rammed her hand into my mouth and tried to pull out my tongue. I shook her like a dog does a rat, so she hit me over the head with her clubs. When I opened my jaws and dropped her onto the floor, she sat up, cursing.

I landed beside her, my sides heaving as I gasped for air. "You can't have him," I said when I had the breath to speak.

The troll queen's breathing was ragged when she wiped the ashes of her singed-off hair from her unscathed scalp. "I not take him now, but I not give up. I come back later when you not look."

"Are you sure you want him?" I asked.

Trying to turn Eadric into a dragon would surely kill him, but there was something that I could do that might work just as well. While the queen pushed herself off the floor, I thought of the magic that Olebald Wizard had used in the battle against my father's army. His dragons had been illusions, complete except for their lack of a dragony smell. I could use something like it, but only if the troll queen wasn't as observant as I had been.

"*Psst,* Eadric," I whispered. "Just play along."

"What are you planning?" he asked.

"You'll understand in a minute," I said, and I whispered the spell that seemed to transform Eadric.

The dragon appeared so suddenly that all four of the troll queen's heads gasped. He was an orange dragon, just as Olebald's had been. And just like Olebald's pretend dragons, he was huge. When he reared back, his head nearly touched the ceiling. Even though I had made the magic and knew that he wasn't real, I was impressed.

"Go home," said Eadric, although it sounded as if the dragon were speaking. "I'll never marry you. If you try to take me back to your cave, I'll become my true self and eat you alive."

Fatlippia and Grunella leaned toward each other until their foreheads touched. They began to whisper, but I could still hear what they said.

"This worse than first prince," said Grunella.

"First prince may be dragon, too," Fatlippia said. "Maybe whole family is."

Grunella shuddered. "I not want dragon husband. Cannot tell what to do."

"Then why marry human?" said Fatlippia. When she sighed, she actually sounded sad. "Maybe marriage not for us. Being spinster not so bad. Still have one another."

The last sound I heard as the troll queen stomped from the Great Hall was the mournful wailing of the other three heads.

Sixteen

*J*f the troll queen hadn't been so awful, I might have felt sorry enough for her to help her find someone else, but she was mean and nasty, and I wouldn't want to inflict her on anyone I knew, unless . . . The most wonderful idea popped into my head, and the more I thought about it, the more I liked it. The queen wanted a prince for a husband, and I knew the perfect man for her. He would be just what she wanted, and she would be just what he deserved.

The troll queen was about to try bashing down the door with her clubs when I found her. Rather than have another door to fix, I asked Haywood to remove his spell. Everyone else stayed behind while I followed the troll queen outside.

"What you want?" she snapped at me as her trolls assembled behind her. I was still a dragon, so they were careful to keep their distance.

I made myself comfortable on the paving stones and

wrapped my tail around me. "Just because you can't marry Eadric or Bradston doesn't mean that you can't marry anyone," I said. "I happen to know an available prince who would be just right for you. You've already met him. It's that young man, Jorge, who came to see you through a magic mirror. Do you think he would do?"

Grunella's eyes lit up while Ingabinga and Tizzy began talking at once. "He do fine!" said Tizzy. "How we find him?" asked Ingabinga. "We not know where he live."

"But I do," I replied.

"I not sure this idea good," said Fatlippia.

Tizzy stuck out her lower lip. "It not fair. We always do what Fatlippia want."

Grunella nodded. "We going even if Fatlippia not like!"

Fatlippia seemed surprised by their vehemence. "If that what three heads really want . . . ," she said.

The other heads cheered. Following their lead, the troll army shouted and stomped their feet even though they had no idea what was going on. When the ruckus died down, Fatlippia turned to me and said, "Where you say prince live?"

"I'll tell you, but first I want the other ball like the one I broke," I said.

"I not tell . . . ," began Fatlippia, but I wasn't looking at her. Tizzy's eyes had darted to the commanding troll standing in front of the troll queen. He shoved one of his hands behind his back, but not before I saw the reflection of something shiny.

"Let me see that," I said, uncurling my tail and getting to my feet. When the troll looked like he was about to turn and bolt, I stretched my neck and grabbed him by his leather tunic, then shook him until he dropped the ball. The troll queen dove for it, but I was there first, stepping on it with a loud *crack!*

"Look for the prince in East Aridia," I said, using my claws to scrape the shattered ball into a pile. "Go over the mountains and cross the River Sludge. His castle is in the city of Raveen."

Fatlippia scowled at me, but it was Grunella who said, "We go now. It time troll queen have husband!"

I remained a dragon until the last of the trolls had crossed the drawbridge and were well on their way to East Aridia. Repairs to the castle had already begun when Eadric found me in the courtyard, a human once again. Hand in hand, we retreated to the sheltered base of an undamaged tower to steal a few moments alone.

"When was the last time I told you that I love you?" I asked after I'd kissed him quite thoroughly.

"At least a few hours ago. I must warn you that my parents can't wait to thank you for getting rid of the trolls, but I'm going to keep you to myself a while longer."

"That sounds good to me," I said, leaning into another kiss.

"You know," Eadric said eventually. "I think my father likes you. He can't stop saying nice things about 'that wonderful Emma.'"

"And what about your mother?"

"I think she's getting tired of Bradston and his tricks. I actually heard her say, 'I've had just about enough of you, young man.'"

"Is that so?" I said. "Tell me, when is your mother's birthday?"

"In a few months. Why?"

"Because if she can manage to be nice to us from now until then, I just might have the perfect gift for her. What do you think she'd say if I ended the spell and gave her some time to herself?"

"I'd say that she'd be mad if she found out that you cast it in the first place."

"And if I told her that if she wasn't nice, I'd do it all over again?"

"Then I think you'd have the nicest mother-in-law in the world."

"Mmm," I murmured as he kissed me again. "That would be perfect. I already have the very best husband in the world."

"And you, my love, are the most unpredictable wife!"

The tinkle of wind chimes announcing the return of

our fairy guests made us both look up. Our chance to be alone was going to be shorter than either of us had hoped.

I sighed and brushed an errant dragon scale from Eadric's tunic. "Someday when we have lots of time, remind me to tell you what you mean to me."

Eadric tilted my head back so he could gaze into my eyes. "I can tell you what you mean to me with just one word."

"Let me guess," I said, smiling up at him. "Maybe I make you happy because you no longer have to enter kissing contests to find the best kisser? Do I bring excitement into your life because I can whisk you away to exotic lands on my magic carpet? Or do you find me delightful because I can conjure food whenever you're hungry?"

"No, that's not . . . Wait, what was that last one?"

I laughed and shook my head. "Never mind. So tell me in one word, what *do* I mean to you?"

"That's easy," said Eadric. "Everything!"

The
Salamander
Spell

One

ike everyone else, Grassina knew exactly how important the Green Witch was to Greater Greensward.
Not only did the Green Witch have to defend the kingdom from invaders, whether magical or mundane, she
also had to ensure that everything was in good working
order, like the roads, the moat, and the castle itself. It was
a full-time job, made doubly hard when she had royal duties as well.

Grassina's mother, Queen Olivene, had been the Green
Witch since before her daughters were born. Although
the queen wasn't very old, everyone knew that someday,
someone would have to replace her. Since the title usually
passed from mother to daughter, the whole kingdom had
been watching Grassina's older sister, Chartreuse, for some
sign that she had inherited her mother's talent for magic.
Unfortunately, that sign had yet to show itself, and everyone was getting tired of waiting, especially thirteen-year-
old Grassina.

Grassina set her hand on one of the thistles that grew at the edge of the moat and jerked it back, scowling. It wasn't fair. Chartreuse always got whatever she wanted— a horde of suitors, lessons in magic, a new kitten... Grassina, on the other hand, had to make do with her left-overs, just because she was the younger sister. Even her instructor in deportment, Lady Sophronia, had taught Chartreuse first, something the old woman mentioned daily. Whereas Chartreuse had been a prize pupil, Grassina was sadly lacking. Her curtsies were either too deep or not deep enough. Chartreuse's had been exactly right. Grassina's small talk wasn't witty. Chartreuse knew how to captivate everyone in the room. Grassina had yet to master the air of command that Lady Sophronia insisted all princesses must have. Everyone from scullery maids to the greatest noblemen paid attention to Chartreuse. Grassina's ineptness with her lessons didn't bother her at all; although she loved to learn, she didn't think anything Sophronia had to say was important enough to worry about. Chartreuse, of course, had considered her own deportment lessons vital.

Grassina was sure that even if Chartreuse hadn't mastered the art of courtly behavior, she would have been the court favorite. While Grassina hated her carrot red hair and too many freckles, Chartreuse was always tossing her honey gold curls and admiring her creamy complexion in the mirror. No matter what Chartreuse did, she was always pretty. She even looked good when she cried, because it made her blue eyes dewy so that she seemed sweet and vulnerable. All crying did to Grassina was turn her face red and splotchy.

Wiping a drop of blood from her pricked finger, she sat back on her heels, waiting impatiently for her sister to finish her lesson. Grassina had been kneeling beside the moat for so long that her legs were getting numb. That morning she'd overheard her mother telling Chartreuse where they would meet for their daily magic lesson, giving Grassina just enough time to look for a hiding place. The pile of stone blocks left over from repairing the tower was only a few yards from the edge of the moat, close enough to listen in on the conversation. It hid her if she stayed put, but wasn't big enough to conceal her if she moved more than a foot in either direction. Grassina shifted her weight ever so carefully, trying not to make a sound. Leaving before the lesson ended was out of the question since she wasn't supposed to be there in the first place and her mother was bound to see her if she stood up.

A medium-sized fish chased a school of minnows just below the smooth surface of the moat. Queen Olivene sighed and shook her head, turning to her older daughter. "You need to sound more confident when you recite a spell, Chartreuse. Listen closely. I'll do it again so you can hear what I mean. It's very simple, really. Just trace the letters in the water with your finger and say,

> Bubbles small and bubbles large,
> Put yourselves within my charge.
> On the water, write my name.
> 'Round it set a lovely frame.

Bubbles formed, gathering on the surface of the water until the name *Olivene* became legible and a circle of bubbles surrounded the word. The queen's name floated in place until a curious gray green fish rose to the surface and tried to bite one of the larger bubbles. The bubble burst with a loud *pop*, scaring the fish away. Grassina giggled, then clapped her hand over her mouth to stifle the sound. Chartreuse turned around and glanced in her direction, wearing a haughty look of disdain, which might have been more intimidating if Grassina hadn't caught her practicing that very same expression in a mirror that morning.

Knowing that there was no use hiding any longer, Grassina sighed and stood up. Queen Olivene frowned at her younger daughter. "Did you skip your lesson in deportment again? I'm sure Lady Sophronia is looking everywhere for you."

"I finished my lesson," said Grassina, her legs prickling as she shifted from one foot to the other.

"You're always poking your nose into things that don't

4

concern you," said Chartreuse. "It isn't as if you're going to get any magic. For two hundred years the firstborn daughter in our family has been the Green Witch. As the eldest . . ."

"I can't help it if I'm curious," said Grassina. "I love watching you do magic, Mother."

"It's your sister's turn now," said Olivene, and she turned back to Chartreuse. "I want you to try it again, but this time you have to show me that you believe in what you're doing."

"That's just it," said Chartreuse. "How can I believe it will work when it never has before?"

"It will in due time," said Olivene. "My grandmother didn't come into her magic until she was seventeen."

"So you've told me," muttered Chartreuse, her lips pursing into a pout. Dipping her finger in the water, Chartreuse wrote her name while repeating the spell in a more commanding tone. When nothing happened, she sighed and turned to her mother. "Tell me again what Father said about your magic when you first met."

A slow smile lit Olivene's face. "He told me that even without my magic, I was the most fascinating woman he'd ever met, but with my magic I was irresistible. I don't know how many times he said that he was honored that my parents had chosen him."

Chartreuse sighed. "That's so sweet. When I get married, it will be to a man who feels that way about me. He's going to love me to distraction and put me above every-thing else. He'll bring me gifts and take me to tourna-ments and write poems about my beauty just like Father did for you."

"That was a long time ago and we were both young," said Olivene. "Most husbands aren't so attentive."

"Mine will be," said Chartreuse. "I'm going to marry for love. Maybe Torrance or Limelyn. They're both very handsome."

For the last few months, one prince after another had come to visit from various kingdoms, hoping to win Chartreuse's hand in marriage. She had enjoyed all the at-tention and had been delighted when some of her more serious suitors decided to remain at the castle until she made up her mind.

"A handsome face isn't all you should be looking for," said Olivene.

"I know that. They have other good qualities, too. Torrance writes songs about me. He has the most won-derful singing voice, and his eyes . . . Have you noticed what a lovely shade of blue they are? Some of my friends fancy themselves in love with him. I think I might be, too. He says he'll have another song for me tonight."

"Prince Torrance comes from a good kingdom," said Queen Olivene. "But he wouldn't be your best choice. He's a second son, and his elder brother is reputed to be exceedingly healthy."

"There's also Limelyn," said Chartreuse. "He's terribly brave and has the nicest smile. I feel tingly when he kisses my hand."

Grassina stood up and stretched. "Have you noticed that she doesn't care if either of them has a brain or is honest or true? The man I marry must have a good heart and love me for myself. He must be smart and caring and—"

"No one asked for your opinion, pipsqueak," said Chartreuse.

Queen Olivene didn't look happy. "Limelyn is also a second son. His kingdom is small and poor. He wouldn't bring enough to the marriage to make it worth your while."

Chartreuse extended her hand over the water. "I'm going to try that spell again. Maybe if I concentrate harder . . ."

"Careful," said Grassina. "You'll give yourself a headache."

Chartreuse smiled sweetly at her sister. "Be nice, Grassina, and maybe I'll let you marry one of the other princes. Not Stephen or Clarence; they're both too serious, and I've never seen either one smile. Miguel, perhaps. You like animals and such, so you won't mind that he doesn't talk about anything except horses and dogs. I think he's a tremendous bore. I'm sure you'd find him fascinating."

"You're too kind," Grassina said.

"Or perhaps you'd prefer Rinaldo. He acts more like a merchant than a prince, but some people might think that's endearing. Princesses should never lie, Grassina, so be honest. Don't you think one of them would be ideal for you?"

Olivene looked annoyed. "Don't be so quick to dismiss them, Chartreuse. Miguel and Rinaldo may not share your interests, but they are both the sole heirs to sizeable kingdoms. Either one would be a good choice."

"Not for me, Mother," said Chartreuse. "All either one cares about is his own kingdom. I want a husband who will care about Greater Greensward. Now be quiet, Grassina, so I can try this spell again."

Grassina held her breath as her sister recited the simple poem. Chartreuse had tried one spell after another over the last few years, but so far not one of them had worked. Part of Grassina wanted her sister to succeed. After all, the kingdom needed a Green Witch in every generation, taking over when her predecessor was no longer strong enough to protect the people of Greater Greensward. Another part of her, however, was so jealous that she got a sour taste in her mouth every time she thought about Chartreuse being able to work magic. It would mean that one of her greatest fears was about to be realized: she, Grassina, would be the untalented nobody in a family of special people.

After reciting the spell, Chartreuse waited expectantly as a few errant bubbles drifted across the water. She'd worn her hair loose that morning, so when she leaned close for a better look, a curl fell forward to trail across the water's surface. Chartreuse wasn't aware of it until a large fish, mistaking her hair for a floating insect, snapped at the curl and yanked. "Ow!" she squeaked as she lost her balance. She fell in the water far enough to drench her face and hair, and might have tumbled in all the way if her mother hadn't grabbed the back of her tunic. When she sat up spluttering, Chartreuse had bits of water weed plastered to her face.

Grassina laughed. "Now, that took talent! I'm sure your suitors will be impressed when they hear what you can do!"

"Don't you dare tell them!" cried Chartreuse, lunging at her sister.

Their mother stepped between the girls. "That's quite enough," Olivene said. "Chartreuse, princesses do not strike their sisters, so stop trying."

"But she's so aggravating, Mother!" complained Chartreuse.

"And as for you, Grassina," Olivene continued. "I expect that you will show discretion and refrain from telling anyone about your sister's lessons."

Grassina started backing away. "I won't say a word as long as no one asks me how Chartreuse's magic is going. But you know that princesses must always tell the truth." Hiking up her skirts, Grassina turned and ran.

9

"You'd better watch out!" shouted Chartreuse. "When I'm the Green Witch, I'll teach you not to be such a brat!"

"You'll have to get your magic first!" puffed Grassina as she disappeared around the side of the castle. "And I'm not holding my breath until you do!"

Two

$\mathcal{K}$ ing Aldrid and his men were tilting, taking turns riding at the quintain—the figure of a knight that spun around each time they hit it with a lance. Grassina knew that the quintain had been rebuilt that spring, but it already looked battered and ancient. Since the king was an avid jouster, he and his knights practiced nearly every day.

Grassina was passing by when her father rode to the front of the line. Staying well out of the way, she found a good vantage point and stopped to watch. King Aldrid's horse snorted, jerked its head, and danced a few feet to the side. Grassina held her breath as her father shifted his weight in the saddle and leaned forward. Then, moving as if they were one, horse and rider thundered across the hoof-chewed dirt, sending clods flying and stirring up enough dust to create a cloud behind them. The king's lance slammed into the quintain, spinning it as he galloped past while avoiding the flying weight attached to the other side. Bouncing on her toes, Grassina clapped until

11

the palms of her hands stung, although her father was too far away to hear her over the thud of his horse's hooves and the shouted congratulations of his knights.

While the knights debated who would go next, Grassina slipped past the quintain, heading for her tree house. In a copse of trees out of sight of the practice field, it had been her favorite place to play when she was young. Her mother had made it for her to share with Chartreuse, and it was special in ways only an accomplished witch could manage. Although the miniature cottage was nestled in the branches of an oak well above the ground, it was roomier inside than its outside dimensions suggested and had a working fireplace that kept the cottage warm and cozy. Made with magic, the tree house still looked as new as the day it had been built with its sharply pitched roof and arched windows.

Even before Grassina set foot on the ladder, she could smell the wildflower and honey scent that always lingered around the tree house. Her copper finches began to chirp as she started up the rungs, growing louder as she climbed and bursting into song when she reached the platform. Grassina had purchased the birds on a trip to the magic marketplace with her mother. She had wanted to keep them in her chamber, but they had kept her awake the first night with their chattering. The next morning she had moved them to the tree house.

"Good morning, pretty ones," she said. When the

birds chirped back, she copied their song, smiling when they fluttered their wings and chirped louder. Because part of her mother's magic ensured that nothing could enter or leave the tree house without the girls letting it, the birds were uncaged and allowed to fly free.

There were other birds in the room as well. Shortly after Grassina had purchased her two copper birds, Chartreuse had insisted on going to the marketplace. Visiting a different vendor, she'd bought a dozen birds of pale blue glass. She'd also bought a glass branch that she set on the tree-house floor, providing a perch for her precious birds. That had been years ago, and now only five birds remained intact, the rest broken when they flew into the walls or each other.

While the birds fluttered above her, Grassina knelt beside the wooden chest at the foot of one of the tree house's two benches. "You may come out," she said, lifting the lid, "but only for a few minutes. I won't be staying long today."

A small wooden horse whinnied and tossed its head when Grassina reached for it. A rag doll yawned and sat up, wiping its black-dot eyes. Both toys had come from the magic marketplace, gifts from her mother years before. There had also been a tiny chicken made of straw, but it had gotten too close to the fireplace one winter's day and burned itself to ashes. Since that day Grassina had kept the toys shut in the chest when she wasn't there, hoping to keep them out of trouble.

When Grassina had set both toys on the floor, the doll struggled to climb up her leg while the horse trotted around the room, cantering when it reached the long, open space between the two benches, slowing to a walk as it rounded the leg of the table. It was trotting again when its hoof became wedged between two of the floorboards. The horse grew frantic when it stumbled and couldn't get loose. Thrashing and screaming, it might have damaged itself if Grassina hadn't intervened. At first the horse was too frightened for her to touch it, but she calmed it with her voice and gentle hands until it stood still, trembling, and she could pull the hoof free.

"Poor Hector," said the doll, running to throw her arms around the horse's neck. "Are you all right?" she asked.

"He's fine, Marniekins," said Grassina. "Just a little chipped paint."

Hector whuffled his lips, then left to investigate the floor under the bench. Grassina was watching him when she heard someone on the ladder. The copper finches twittered as a head appeared over the top rung. It was Chartreuse, visiting the tree house for the first time in years.

"Princess Chartreuse, is that really you?" squeaked Marniekins. The little doll ran to the princess as fast as her wobbly cloth legs could carry her, falling in a heap when they bent the wrong way. Hector nickered hello and galloped to where Chartreuse stood by the door. On her feet again, Marniekins clambered across the floor to grab hold of the edge of Chartreuse's gown. "Pick me up!" said the doll.

Shoving the doll aside with her foot, Chartreuse crossed to the window and peered out, waving at someone below. "I'm surprised to find you here, Grassina. Torrance and I were going for a walk and heard your voice. Aren't you too old to play with dolls? I'm sure your time would be much better spent learning how to manage a castle or play a musical instrument."

Marniekins had tumbled head over heels, landing in a dusty heap under the bench. She sobbed, curling up in a ball, and wrapped her arms around herself. Unable to make tears, her faded cheeks remained dry. Hector tossed his head and snorted at Chartreuse before trotting after Marniekins. He poked the doll with a consoling nose until she rubbed her eyes.

Grassina glared at Chartreuse. "Now see what you've done!" Peering under the bench, Grassina reached for Marniekins. She cradled the doll in her lap, soothing her as best she could. Marniekins whimpered, hiding her face behind Grassina's hand.

Upset by the turmoil, the copper finches twittered in agitation while Chartreuse's birds fluttered madly overhead. When one of the glass birds collided with a copper finch, a glass wing broke off and the bird fell, shattering on the floor. At the sound, Marniekins howled and buried her face in the cloth of Grassina's gown.

Chartreuse gave the doll a disgusted look. "Don't you dare make me out to be a villain," she said, turning back to Grassina. "They're just dolls. I climbed that ladder to ask you to stay away from my magic lessons. You ruined my lesson today. I was getting close to making the spell work. The magic was building up inside me; I could feel it! If it hadn't been for you, today would have been the day we've all been waiting for."

Grassina glanced up from Marniekins and snorted at the anger on her sister's face. "I've never heard Mother say anything about feeling the magic inside of her. If you felt something, it was probably your breakfast disagreeing with you. And if you're so sure that your magic is about to show itself, I'm sure one day won't make any difference. You'll be able to do the spell tomorrow."

"Not if you're there to distract me! My magic lessons are very important and . . ."

Grassina laughed. "Magic lessons! They aren't lessons unless you can do magic, too. Otherwise they're just demonstrations."

Chartreuse's eyes darkened and her nostrils flared. "It's all a game to you, isn't it? Well, it isn't to me. I take those lessons seriously. Greater Greensward needs a Green Witch; I *have* to learn how to work those spells! You don't need to know about magic, so go play somewhere else, little girl, and leave the important work to the adults!" Turning on her heel, Chartreuse flounced out of the tree house and stomped down the ladder so hard that Grassina could feel the floor of the little house shake.

Long after Chartreuse was gone, Grassina sat on the floor, calming the doll and the horse. Some of what her sister had said stung, perhaps because she was close to being right. Grassina had heard all her life that as long as anyone could remember, there had been only one witch in the family for each generation and that witch had always been the firstborn girl. Since she and everyone else in the family were convinced that she wouldn't have the magic, it seemed only natural for her to make a joke out of it.

Grassina was still stroking Marniekin's flax hair when she realized that the doll was asleep. Hector, too, stood with his eyes closed. Moving carefully so she wouldn't wake them, Grassina carried the toys to the wooden chest and laid them inside. "Sleep tight," she whispered, closing the lid.

Half the afternoon was gone, and she had yet to visit the swamp.

Chartreuse was only two years older than Grassina, and they had once been the best of friends. But after Chartreuse decided that she had to prepare herself to be the Green Witch, she no longer had the time to waste on a younger sister. Grassina began to spend increasing amounts of time on her own, exploring the castle and the area around it. Although she had always known about the swamp, which lay just beyond the practice fields and the woods where the tree house stood, it wasn't until she was on her own that Grassina actually visited it. On the very first visit, Grassina fell in love. After that, no one could keep her away.

Despite her parents' fear that she would become lost or injured, Grassina always managed to slip away when no one was watching. Her parents fought to keep her out of the swamp until the day her father had one of his men follow her to see what she did there. When he reported that she seemed to have an instinct about where to place her feet and that she was more careful than most adults, her father gave her permission to visit the swamp provided she had an escort. Her appointed escorts tried to stay by her side, yet she invariably lost them in the swamp and returned home on her own. More than one adult had to be rescued, although Grassina never did. It wasn't long before no one would go with her. Grassina was ten years old when her parents gave up.

The shy wildlife that Grassina loved to watch, the mysterious pools that could conceal just about anything in their muddy depths, and the graceful willows that hid her in their sheltering boughs called to her in a way that no one else in her family could understand. What Grassina considered mysterious, Chartreuse found frightening. What Grassina found fascinating made her sister turn up her nose in disgust. Unlike her sister, who reveled in the company of others, Grassina appreciated having somewhere she could go alone, away from the eyes, ears, and wagging tongues of the crowded castle, somewhere she could be free to do whatever she pleased. When she wanted to be alone with her thoughts, there was no better place to go than the swamp.

Grassina's first stop was a pond with cattails at one end and a pebbled bank at the other. She watched a turtle sunning itself on a log and an otter chasing fish in the shallower water. When the otter disappeared upstream, Grassina started down a path that wound across the marshy ground and was so faint that only the most experienced tracker could have found it. The path led to the northern side, where the swamp bordered the enchanted forest. She had seen creatures of all kinds drinking from a tree-shaded lake there. Although it wasn't the safest place in the swamp, it was the only spot where the more unusual plant life grew.

As she grew older, Grassina had developed an interest in the flora of the swamp. She had studied with an old woman from a nearby village, an herbalist who was delighted to have a princess as a pupil since it meant that she ate well on lesson days and was paid in real coin. During her years of study with the old woman, Grassina's interest in plants had become a passion, but the old woman had died the year before, leaving Grassina to study on her own. In her mind, that meant spending even more time in the swamp looking for specimens.

Although Grassina loved the swamp, she wasn't blind

to its dangers and was particularly careful when visiting the lake that bordered the enchanted forest. Once, while picking leaves from a variety of marsh mallow that grew at the edge of the lake, she had heard a shrill cry coming from the tall reeds between her and the forest. Looking up, she had seen a flock of crows descending on the reeds and whatever creature they hid. Armed only with a few stones she'd found on the ground, Grassina had gone to investigate. A doe, mauled by something in the forest, had wandered into the swamp to die. Although she was hidden from most eyes, the crows had found her and were impatient to begin feeding. The doe was close to death when Grassina saw her, but alive enough to turn her head. Their eyes met; one look was enough. As the doe lay her head on the ground again, Grassina threw her first stone into the flock of crows, being careful not to hit the deer. The birds squawked and flew off as one stone after another hurtled into their midst, missing most, but hitting enough to frighten them. Grassina had stayed to chase away birds even after the doe was no longer moving. She would have stayed all day if a bear attracted by the scent of blood hadn't shuffled out of the forest.

Knowing that her poorly aimed stones would do little more than irritate a bear, Grassina retreated farther into the swamp. The very next day she collected stones again. Instead of skipping them across a pond, she threw them at the gnarled knot in a tree trunk, hitting the tree but only rarely the knot. The next day she was back again, staying until her arm was sore and her aim was better. Within a month she could hit whatever target she chose. Within two months she could do it while running. Although she rarely needed to use the stones, it made her feel better to know that she could.

Fortunately, on this particular day she saw no sign of anything larger than a deer in the vicinity, so she continued on, searching for certain plants. Finding a specimen with blue-flowered spikes that had opened its blooms since her last visit, she picked one stem, leaving the rest to grow and spread. She was tucking her new find into the leather sack she'd brought when she caught the faintest whiff of smoke.

"There must be a dragon nearby," Grassina murmured. It was time to head for home.

Tilting practice was ending when she passed the field, so she sought out her father and joined him as he passed his horse's reins to his squire.

"Hello, sweetling," he said when Grassina appeared at his side. "I thought I saw you coming. What have you been up to today?"

As they started toward the castle, Grassina told him about her morning, including her conversation with Chartreuse. "It isn't fair," she said, kicking a pebble with the toe of her shoe. "Chartreuse is going to be the queen and the Green Witch just because she's older than me. All I'm going to do is marry some old, boring suitor that Chartreuse doesn't want."

King Aldrid tugged on his daughter's braid. "Chartreuse may think that fortune favors her now, but give her a few years and she'll think that you're the lucky one. With either of those titles comes a great deal of responsibility. Bearing both titles can be overwhelming. Just ask your mother. She never wanted to be the Green Witch. Given a choice, she would have preferred to do only small magic the way many of the village witches do."

"Really? If I were a witch, I'd specialize in big spells that would make a big difference and really help people. I wouldn't waste my time with the little ones like spelling my name with bubbles. But I don't understand why Mother never told us how she felt about magic."

Her father shrugged. "She knew that your sister would be the next Green Witch someday, so she wanted to let Chartreuse form her own opinion about magic. Seeing how the responsibility of being the Green Witch had affected her mother was what turned your mother against the job."

"What did it do to Grandmother?"

"We all thought your grandmother was crazy; your mother thought it was because of the things she had to do to protect the kingdom as the Green Witch. The monsters she had to face . . . The horrible things they did if she wasn't there in time . . . It was enough to give anyone nightmares."

22

"But the Green Witch is the most powerful witch in the kingdom. She can handle anything!" said Grassina.

"Yes, but at a tremendous cost. The horrors she has to deal with . . . Not to mention that her responsibilities as the Green Witch take precedence over her private life. Your mother never got to spend time with you the way she would have liked. Even now, she has no time for all the little things that she used to enjoy so much."

"I didn't realize . . ."

"As for whom you'll marry . . . You'll have a say in choosing your future husband. I'll see to that. Chartreuse, however, will marry whomever your mother and I decide would make the most suitable husband for someone in her position. The man who marries the queen of Greater Greensward must meet the kingdom's needs before his wife's. Whoever marries the Green Witch must not be someone who would try to misuse her magic. Chartreuse's choices are far more limited than yours will be."

"You're not saying that just to make me feel better?" asked Grassina, studying her father's face.

Her father laughed and shook his head. "I wouldn't dare try to convince you of anything. I know you too well. Just don't let Chartreuse upset you when she talks about her brilliant future. Nothing is ever exactly what we expect it to be."

Three

*Y*ou've changed and I don't like it," said the queen on the other side of the closed door. Her voice was ill-tempered and angry, which was unusual for her. Grassina had been about to knock, but she dropped her hand and hesitated, torn between wanting to hear what her mother said next and knowing how upset the queen would be if she knew that someone was eavesdropping.

"I don't know what you mean," said King Aldrid, sounding puzzled.

"You were so attentive when we first met. Don't you remember singing love songs outside my window at night until my father threatened to have you dragged off to the dungeon? You gave me so many gifts that I didn't know what to do with them all. You even begged me for a lock of my hair to keep by your heart. After we were married, you took me to tournaments and on that grand tour. We were so happy together, and you promised that it would never end."

"I remember," he said. "We were young then and didn't have the responsibilities that we have now."

"Don't talk to me about responsibilities! I know exactly what's expected of me by you and everyone else in this kingdom. All I'm asking for is a little romance ... some sign that you still love and cherish me and that I'm still important to you and not just because of what I do for our kingdom. I want you to be the man you used to be. I want to feel the way I used to feel."

"I didn't know you weren't happy," said King Aldrid. "You've never said anything before. What brought this on?"

"Nothing, really. I was talking to Chartreuse and I remembered how it once was, that's all. She's so bright-eyed and certain of her future, like I was at her age. I suppose I just need to know ... Are you still the Aldrid I married? Do you still love me the way you once did?"

"Of course I do!" the king said, beginning to sound irritated.

"You certainly never show it!" The queen's voice was louder, as if she were coming closer. Grassina stepped back a pace, not wanting to be caught listening.

"You have to tell me what you want. I can't read your mind!" said the king.

"That much is obvious!" The queen had almost reached the door. "You never even *tell* me that you love me anymore."

"I shouldn't have to say it."

"Perhaps not, but it would be nice if you did it without having to."

Grassina's heart was pounding when she darted down the corridor and slipped behind a wall hanging that covered a small, drafty alcove. Peeking out from behind the hanging, she searched her mother's face as the queen passed by and was dismayed to see tears streaking her cheeks. As a child, hearing her parents argue had frightened Grassina, perhaps because they did it so rarely. It upset her even now, although she couldn't have explained why. Talking to someone about it might help, but it had to be someone who felt the same way she did. Only one name came to mind.

Grassina often forgot just how big the castle was until she had to find someone. She looked for Chartreuse in her chamber, but it was empty. Even her sister's new kitten was gone. Chartreuse wasn't in the Great Hall either, nor their mother's chamber, nor any other room where she might usually be found. To her surprise, she finally found her in the kitchen.

A few years before, Grassina had developed a love for cooking and had persuaded the cooks to give her lessons. She still visited the kitchen often to try her hand at new dishes, but as far as she knew, her older sister had never set foot in the kitchen. Grassina could tell from the sour expressions on the cooks' faces that they weren't pleased about Chartreuse's current visit.

Chartreuse was standing at the long table where she'd shoved aside a mound of vegetables, leaving a cleared space for her to work. A book, a bowl of flour, a saltcellar, a lump of butter, and a dozen apples lay on the table in front of her. An orange-striped kitten sat on the table at Chartreuse's elbow, lapping a bowl of milk. Supper was hours away, but roasts were already turning on the spit, making Grassina's mouth water from the aroma of the sizzling juices. She was wondering if the cook might give her something to tide her over when Chartreuse began to read aloud from the book.

> Pour the flour and the salt.
> Drop in a bit of lard.
> Mix it till it's nice and smooth.
> Add water—it's not hard.

Although Grassina was watching carefully, nothing seemed to be happening. "A cooking spell," she murmured. "I wonder where she found that."

> Roll it flat and roll it wide.
> Cut squares with a blade.
> Lay the apple slices there.
> Don't stop—it's nearly made.

The ingredients hadn't budged from the table. "It's not working," said Grassina. "Why are you going on with the spell if it's not doing what it's supposed to? And why are you wasting your time on a cooking spell in the first place? You can cook without magic. Now if *I* were trying to do magic, I'd do something big that could make a real difference that I couldn't make any other way."

Chartreuse looked up from the table to glare at her sister. "If I wanted your opinion, I'd ask for it. Go away. I'm busy."

"But I need to talk to you," Grassina said, glancing at the cooks and their score of assistants. Although none were looking in the sisters' direction, they were all working so quietly that she was sure they were listening. "It's about our parents," she told Chartreuse in a fierce whisper.

"Didn't this afternoon's conversation sink in at all?" asked Chartreuse. "I don't want you anywhere near me when I'm doing my magic!" Picking up the book, she pointedly turned her back on her sister.

Chartreuse's kitten licked its paw, then used it to wipe its face. Cat hairs floated in a sunbeam coming through one of the windows set high in the wall. Grassina crinkled her nose when some of the hairs drifted into the bowl of flour. She picked up the kitten to set it on the floor, and it mewed, earning her a nasty look from Chartreuse.

"I have to talk to you," said Grassina. "This is important. They've been fighting."

28

Chartreuse slammed the book on the table and spun around. "So you think that what I'm doing isn't important? Get out of here and leave me alone! And that goes for my kitten, too. I never said you could touch it." Giving her sister a nasty look, she snatched the kitten off the floor and set it on the table. The kitten backed away, bumping into the bowl of flour. The bowl overturned and the flour splashed out, coating the kitten from head to toe. Howling, the kitten jumped to the floor and dashed around the kitchen, leaving a white, powdery trail.

A scullery maid was carrying a bucket of water when the kitten ran under her feet, tripping her. The bucket went flying, the water gushing over the spitted roasts, drenching them and extinguishing the fire. The head cook roared and, grabbing a broom, flailed at the kitten. Terrified, the kitten tore out of the kitchen and down the corridor toward the Great Hall. Chartreuse snatched up her book and ran after her pet. Grassina grabbed some apples and was only a few paces behind.

Although most of King Aldrid's hounds had gone outside to pester the stable boys, one hound had stayed behind to take a nap by the fireplace. Woken by the still-yowling kitten, the hound scrambled to its feet and took off after the dusty white ball of fluff. Bigger and faster than the kitten, the hound would have caught it if, just as its jaws were about to close, the flour puffing off the warm, furry body hadn't tickled the hound's nose. The hound sneezed, giving the kitten enough time to launch itself onto one of Queen Olivene's prized tapestries decorating the closest wall. Its needlelike claws dug into the woven fabric as the kitten climbed until it was too high for the hound or anyone else to reach. This didn't discourage the hound, who leaped at the tapestry, barking hysterically. Dragged down by the weight of the hound, the tapestry tore at the top where it was fastened to the wall and began to sag.

Chartreuse glanced at Grassina. "Now see what you've done!"

"You're blaming me?" said Grassina. "It's your kitten!"

"We were fine until you came in!"

The hound jumped again, scrabbling at the tapestry with its paws.

"I'll get the hound," said Grassina. "You get your kitten."

Grassina reached for the hound's collar, but the animal snapped at her when she came close. She looked to see if her sister was having any better luck. Chartreuse was thumbing through her book, licking her finger before she turned each page.

Grassina was still trying to decide how to approach the hound when Chartreuse began to read a spell for getting things down from high places using a loud, decisive voice. Grassina shook her head. "I can't believe she's trying magic now!" she muttered.

While Chartreuse concentrated on the spell, Grassina looked around for something she could use to scare off the hound. She was about to go back to the kitchen when she remembered the apples. "This should do it," she said, hefting one in her hand.

The apple hit the hound in the ribs, surprising it so that it took off yelping with its tail between its legs. When the kitten still didn't come down, Grassina threw another so that it hit the tapestry directly above the kitten's head. Startled, the kitten pulled its claws free and fell. Chartreuse took her eyes from her book just as the kitten landed in Grassina's arms.

"Did you see that?" Chartreuse asked, her voice a high squeak. "Did you see what I just did? My magic finally worked! I told you today was my day!"

Grassina tried to keep a straight face, but the twitching of her lips almost betrayed her. "Yes, indeed. The way that cat came down was pure magic. Congratulations, Chartreuse. I didn't know you had it in you!"

"But I did!" said Chartreuse. Clapping her hands, she twirled on her toes and did a little jig. "I did it! I did it! I have to go tell Mother right away."

The pages sitting at a nearby table were trying hard not to laugh, but when one snorted with the effort, they all broke up, guffawing and slapping the table. Princes Torrance and Pietro had just come into the room when Chartreuse noticed them. She waved and smiled again before

31

turning back to the pages. Her smile evaporated as she said, "Why are you laughing? Did I say something funny?" Her eyes narrowed when they grinned back at her. "I didn't do it, did I? It was something you did, wasn't it?" She turned to glare at Grassina accusingly.

Grassina nodded, then giggled in spite of herself. "Maybe today wasn't really your day after all."

"You are so immature," Chartreuse said, looking from Grassina to the still-laughing pages.

"At least I know my limitations," Grassina murmured as her sister stalked off.

Four

The next morning, Queen Olivene sent for her daughters, telling them to meet her by the moat. Chartreuse arrived first and looked disappointed when her sister appeared on the drawbridge. "What are you doing here?" she asked.

"The same thing you are," said Grassina. "Don't bother telling me to go away. Mother told me to come."

Chartreuse was about to reply when Queen Olivene stepped off the end of the drawbridge. "Come along, girls. We have much to do today. I've invited you to join us, Grassina, because Sophronia has gone home. She told me there's no use trying to teach someone deportment and the courtly graces if that person can't be found. Finished with your lesson, indeed!"

"Well, I was," said Grassina. "Lady Sophronia just didn't know it."

"And so I'm stuck with you," muttered Chartreuse.

"It could be worse," said Grassina. "It could be Prince Rinaldo."

"I hope we can get through this fast," Chartreuse said as the girls turned to follow their mother. "The princes are waiting for our morning walk."

"All of them?" asked Grassina.

"Of course," said Chartreuse. "You wouldn't want me to play favorites, would you?"

"Not yet," Grassina said under her breath. "You're having too much fun the way it is."

The queen took the girls down the road leading away from the castle. When they reached a farmer's hayfield, they picked their way through the stubble left over from a recent cutting until they reached the overgrown thicket that divided the field from the one beyond it. Using an impromptu spell, Olivene cleared away a strip of ground facing the thicket and had the girls sit on either side of her.

"Now listen carefully, Chartreuse," said the queen. "I'm going to teach you a spell to call animals. This spell is longer than the one I showed you yesterday. Pay particular attention to the tone of voice I use. That's critical in a number of spells."

Resting her hands in her lap, the queen opened her mouth to begin, but a voice called out, "Pardon me, my dear. I must speak with you." The king was walking toward them with one hand behind his back, looking pensive the

34

way he did when considering a serious problem. "Girls, please leave us. Your mother and I need to be alone."

Gathering their skirts around them, the girls took their leave, although they didn't go far. When Chartreuse would have returned to the castle, Grassina stopped her, saying, "We can't go home. They're going to fight, I know it."

"It's none of our business," hissed Chartreuse.

"Of course it is," said Grassina. "They're our parents. Everything they do is our business. Did you see the expression on Father's face? He looked odd."

"Fine, we'll listen in, but only because we care."

"Precisely," said Grassina.

Moving as quietly as they could, the girls crept through an opening in the thicket and down its length until they could see their parents while remaining hidden.

". . . a lesson," said the queen. "Chartreuse is doing so well at memorizing the spells."

"Very nice," King Aldrid said, sounding as if he wasn't really paying attention. He cleared his throat with a loud *harumph* before saying, "I thought about what you said yesterday. I wrote a poem for you. I know it isn't very good, but I never was much at writing, although you always seemed to like whatever I wrote. Here it is."

> *Though I forget from day to day*
> *To find the words I ought to say,*

You're half my heart and half my soul.
Without your love I can't be whole.
So please forgive me if I fail
To say how much I love you.

"That was so sappy!" whispered Grassina. "I can't believe he said that!"

Chartreuse sighed. "I think it was terribly romantic."

Tears glittered in the queen's eyes. "It was perfect," she said, smiling up at him.

"I got you these myself," he said, pulling a bouquet of wildflowers from behind his back. "I didn't have time to get you anything else. I hope you like them."

The queen gasped, her eyes growing wide when he laid the bouquet in her lap. The petal of a daisy brushed the back of her hand, and a breeze sprang up, carrying the heavy scent of roses and lilies, although there were none in the bouquet.

Grassina suddenly felt uneasy. She turned to look around her, thinking that the weather might be changing or someone might be coming, but nothing had happened as far as she could tell. The sun was still shining in a cloudless sky, the birds were still twittering in the thicket, the fields were still empty, and her parents . . .

It was then that she noticed that her mother had begun to change. Her softly curling strawberry blond hair was becoming lank and dull, turning the color of

36

wet mud. Her well-shaped nose was growing long and hooked, nearly meeting her increasingly pointy chin. The once-flawless skin of her cheeks was becoming bumpy and coarse, and her gentle eyes were now beady and piercing.

Unfortunately, her appearance wasn't the only thing that had changed. "What are you staring at?" she rasped. The voice that had been declared the sweetest in the kingdom now sounded like a rusty saw sharpening on a dull whetstone.

Grassina and Chartreuse gasped behind the concealing thicket and reached for each other's hands. King Aldrid's sun-bronzed cheeks went pale. "Then it was true," he said, his voice hoarse. "Your mother told me of the curse, but you said she was crazy. I thought she was, too. She was afraid of so many things—men wearing pointy hats, shadows in the snow, red shoes on little girls. We never thought any of it was real."

"What are you yammering on about, you addle-pated fool?" demanded Queen Olivene. "And men say women talk too much."

"If only I'd realized that the old woman was right about the curse. She said that if you touched a flower after your sixteenth birthday you'd turn into a horrible hag. To think that it's my fault that you've—"

"Enough of this blathering!" the queen snapped. Pointing her finger at her husband, she chanted,

Go hide inside your hidey hole,
You mumbling, bumbling rat.
Stay in the dungeon till I say
You've had enough of that.

There was a squeak like a rat might make, and King Aldrid disappeared.

Chartreuse cried out and hid her face in her hands, while Grassina jumped to her feet, shouting, "No!"

Queen Olivene's head whipped around. "So you were spying on me? I hope you got a good eyeful."

Ignoring the thorns that tore at her clothes, Grassina forced her way through the thicket. "Where's Father?" she asked. "What have you done with him?"

"I sent him to the dungeon, where he can talk all he wants and I won't have to listen to him." Olivene chuckled, making her long nose quiver. "Serves him right. He didn't say anything that I wanted to hear."

"What happened to you?" asked Grassina, unwanted tears thickening her voice. "Are you going to be like this for good?"

"For good or ill, who's to say? Why, do you have a problem with it?"

Grassina held out her hand to the queen. "I want you back the way you were!"

Queen Olivene hopped to her feet and stuck out a long, crooked finger. Prodding Grassina's collarbone, she said, "Well, we" *poke*, "don't always" *poke*, "get what we want." With one last poke, she pushed so hard that Grassina fell backward into the thicket, crying out as the thorns scratched her.

Hot tears stung the cuts on Grassina's cheeks. She sobbed, turning her head aside so she wouldn't have to look at Olivene's awful, leering face.

Olivene's lips curved down in disgust. "Look at that! Frightened of your own shadow! Why, you're as scared as a rabbit!" An idea occurred to her, changing her expression to one of glee. "In that case," she said, "if you're going to act like one, maybe you should be one and see what it's really like." Pointing her finger at Grassina, Olivene chanted,

> Turn this silly, wretched girl
> Into a frightened rabbit.
> Let her see how she would feel
> Were fear a lifelong habit.

"No!" cried Grassina, struggling to get out of the way of the crooked finger, but the thorns held her in place like a skewered roast in the kitchen. She cried out when her skin began to prickle and her skull began to itch. When the world seemed to tilt, she shut her eyes and tried to hold back a sudden swell of nausea.

Although Grassina had never known her mother to turn herself into an animal or talk about it if she had, she had seen her turn someone into a dog once. A soldier had beaten a homeless hound, so the queen had changed the man into a small, ugly cur until he'd agreed to mend his ways. The soldier was a changed man after that, but it wasn't what had made the biggest impression on Grassina. It was the way he had looked while he transformed, shrinking in some ways, growing in others, his clothes melting into him as his fur sprouted and his hands and feet became paws. It had frightened her at the time, watching the man change while his expression vacillated from horrified to pained and back again. The experience had given her nightmares for weeks, but she'd never thought she'd have to live through it herself.

Thankfully, the pain wasn't nearly what Grassina had expected. In fact, it didn't hurt exactly, although it did feel extremely odd. As her hands and feet curled into paws and her ears lengthened and moved to the top of her head, she kept waiting for the pain to begin. It hurt a bit when her body shrank, but it was more of an ache than a pain and didn't last very long.

Her ears had nearly stopped growing when she heard a chicken squawking and a nasty, rasping laugh. Frantic, Grassina wiggled free of the last few thorns that held her in place and looked around her. There was no sign of her mother or Chartreuse, but that didn't mean they weren't close by. A snapped twig made her go deeper into the thicket where the leaves concealed her from anyone outside.

Learning how to hop the way rabbits do wasn't easy in the confines of a thicket. Grassina managed, however, tripping only a few times and hitting her head only once. She found it hard to avoid catching her ears on thorns, and her fluffy tail was almost yanked off after it got snagged, making her move even more cautiously.

When she heard a whisper of sound nearby, Grassina had already worked her way so far into the thicket that all she could see was a wall of green. She crouched down to make herself as small as possible and froze, listening to the muted rustling, scraping, and scratching common to a thicket. It occurred to her that she wasn't alone and that some of the other animals might be bigger and meaner than a rabbit. Any predator that came along would be unlikely to know or care that she was really a thirteen-year-old girl.

Unfortunately, Grassina had always had a vivid imagination. With each new sound, she pictured all sorts of creatures that could live in a thicket, any one of which might enjoy a nice rabbit meal. When nothing appeared, she began to worry about other things like whether her mother's transformation was temporary or permanent and whether the queen would come looking for her. She thought about her father and how he must feel, then began to worry about what would become of her family if her mother didn't change back. When nothing new happened, she worried that she was going to have to spend the rest of her life as a rabbit.

"Oh dear," said a voice from somewhere close by. Grassina pricked up her ears, swiveling them in the direction of the sound. She froze again when she heard the whisper of something brushing against the leaves. "And I thought thingss couldn't get any worsse," moaned the voice. "What should I do now?"

Although it wasn't Chartreuse's voice, it had to be her. Who else could be in this thicket, talking in a way Grassina could understand? Their mother must have changed both of her daughters at the same time. And if it was Chartreuse, it sounded as if she'd been hurt, perhaps by the magic that had changed her.

Moving as quietly as she could, Grassina crept through the hedge, listening for her sister. There was a sound—over there. It was close, too. If it was Chartreuse, whatever she had been turned into should be visible by now. Grassina couldn't see her, but she did smell an unfamiliar, musky scent. She was watching the play of dappled light on the shadowy green foliage when a long narrow head moved, two glistening black eyes looked her way, and the shape that had blended into the thicket so well suddenly became apparent.

"Chartreuse?" Grassina whispered to the snake. "Is that you?"

"Go away!" whispered the snake. "Don't come near me. Ssomething bad will happen if you do!"

Grassina hopped closer. "Don't be silly, Chartreuse. It's me, Grassina. What's wrong with your tail?"

The snake had twisted around itself until the last few inches of its tail rested on the top coil. Part of it looked flatter than the rest, and whole rows of bright green scales were missing. "You don't want to know. It'ss a very long sstory."

"I don't have anywhere to go," Grassina said, stretching out on the cool soil to listen.

The little snake sighed. "If you inssisst, but I warned you! It'ss my bad luck, you ssee. I've been plagued with it ssince before I wass hatched. My mother abandoned me, sso I wass all alone in the world when I broke out of my shell. I wass crawling to another branch when I fell out of my tree. It took me an entire morning to climb back up. The next day a witch named Mudine ssnatched me from my jungle where I was nice and warm, dropped me in a bassket, and whisked me away to her cottage in thesse cold, cold woodss. She locked me in a cage and fed me inssectss that made my sstomach hurt.

"Then bad thingss began happening to her. A sstorm made her roof leak and ruined her magic bookss. A rat wandered in and ate her mosst important herbss. Her potion sscorched when she took a nap. That'ss when she told me it wass all my fault; she ssaid that her bad luck began the day

43

she brought me home. She called me a jinx, and I knew she was right. Bad luck followss me wherever I go."

"I'm sorry to hear that," said Grassina as she took a step backward. Apparently, this wasn't Chartreuse after all.

"Yessterday a hairy monsster broke into the cottage and ssmashed everything. The witch wass out, you ssee, or she would have turned him into a mousse and fed him to me. When the monsster broke my cage, I thought I'd finally be free. I wass almosst out the door when he sstepped on my tail. I thought he wass going to kill me, but he changed hiss mind and I got away after all. I sstill have bad luck, though. I can't go far with a tail like thiss. Ah, I ssee you undersstand. That'ss it, move away from me. Maybe my bad luck won't hurt you if you leave now."

Grassina kept backing away until she bumped into the thicket behind her. Despite what the creature said, it wasn't its bad luck that she found frightening. "You're a real snake!" she said, her eyes widening as she realized something else. "Then why can I understand everything you're saying?"

"Why wouldn't you be able to undersstand me, unlesss . . . Is there ssomething wrong with the way I talk?" the snake asked, becoming agitated. "Are my wordss getting sslurred? Iss my voice getting faint? I'm going to die now, aren't I? The end iss near. I can feel it! It'ss my bad luck, I tell you. That monsster musst have hurt me more than I thought when it sstepped on my tail!"

44

"I doubt it. You sound fine. It's just that I'm really a human girl, not a rabbit, and I shouldn't be able to understand you . . . unless . . . Is it because I *am* a rabbit now?"

"You're crazy," said the snake. "That explainss a lot. Only a crazy rabbit would want to hear my sstory. Monkeyss are crazy, and if you're like them . . ."

"I'm not crazy. I'm a human girl who . . ."

"You're no human; you're a rabbit. Jusst look at that little twitchy nosse and fluffy puff of a tail! I think that . . . Shh! What wass that?"

A leaf rustled. Fur brushed a twig. A padded paw scraped an exposed root. Grassina raised her head to sniff the air. There was a new scent, like her own rabbity smell, yet completely different. This scent set her whiskers quivering and made the fur along her spine bristle. Whatever the creature was, she already didn't like it.

Turning her head ever so slowly, Grassina glimpsed a flash of russet fur and the tip of a pointed ear. It was a fox, and it was only a few feet away inside the tangled thicket.

"Thiss iss the end," whispered the snake. "Now ssomeone iss going to die becausse of my bad luck. I can't sslither fasst with my tail like thiss, and you're crazier than a butterfly that thinkss it can sswim. We don't sstand a chance!"

Caught between the instinct to run and her desire to help a creature in need, Grassina paused for only a second before saying, "I'm not crazy, and I'm not leaving you

45

here to die. There must be something we can do." Her eyes fell on a broken twig. When she tried to pick it up, she had to use both paws to hold it, being careful not to prick herself on the wicked-looking thorns.

The twig wobbled as Grassina raised it between her paws and turned to face the fox. Smiling, the fox skirted a prickly branch while its eyes flicked from her to the snake. "What have we here?" it said, licking its lips.

"You don't want to fool with me," Grassina said.

The fox smirked. "And why is that?"

"Because I have this!" she said. Raising the twig over her head, she hopped once and brought it down on the fox's skull as hard as she could. The fox jerked its head away, but Grassina followed, raining blows on it with the thorny twig.

"What are you doing?" the fox barked. "You're a rabbit. You're supposed to be afraid! Stop that! Ow! Ow!"

The fox dodged, trying to evade her blows. Grassina was still walloping the animal when her skin began to tingle, her paws to prickle, and her ears to ache. She paused and took a deep breath, but her vision blurred, making it hard to see when the fox turned to face her, its lips curled back in a snarl. Shaking her head to clear it made her feel woozy, so she almost didn't notice the fox tensing its muscles to pounce. When she did, she swung at the fox one last time even though she was feeling so light-headed that she was afraid she might faint. She was halfway through her swing when her paws lost their grip on the twig; the tingling had grown until she could feel nothing else.

Grassina's entire body shimmered, but she had her eyes closed, so she didn't see it. Nor did she see the horrified look on the fox's face when she began to change.

The fox turned tail and ran when Grassina's body began to push the thorns aside, breaking some and bending others as she grew. The thorns scratched and bit into her flesh as she returned to her normal size and shape, leaving trickles of blood on her face, hands, and clothes. When the tingling stopped, she felt the thorn-inflicted pain in a rush of sensation that made her cry out. Her eyes fluttered open and she flinched; the thorns were so thick around her that she was afraid to move. Biting her lip at the pain of each new prick and scrape, she pushed the twigs aside as she forced her way through the thicket.

"Well, I'll be . . . ," whispered the little green snake at her feet.

Grassina looked down. "I can still understand you!" she said. "Now do you believe me? I told you I was a human." Something rustled in the thicket only a few yards away. After glancing in that direction, Grassina turned back to the snake. "I don't want to leave you here to get eaten. Come with me and I'll . . ."

The snake drew back, rearranging its coils deeper under the protective thorns. "Pleasse don't try to hurt me! Issn't it bad enough that my tail iss ssquashed?"

Grassina was aghast. "I don't want to hurt you! I have to go home now and see my family, but I don't want to leave you here. If you go with me, I can keep you safe while your tail heals. You won't bite me or anything if I pick you up?"

"Well, you did protect me from that fox," said the snake. "I ssupposse I can trusst you. But I have to warn you that if you take me with you, my bad luck will come, too."

"You don't need to worry about that," said Grassina. "I don't believe in bad luck." Gritting her teeth, she touched the snake, expecting it to feel cold and slimy. Instead it felt nice, not cool, but not exactly warm either. Its scales were smooth, and it tickled when it slid across her palm and wrapped itself around her wrist.

"Ssay," said the snake. "You're not a witch, are you? You're not going to sstick me in a kettle with toe of bat and ear of rat or ssome other dissgussting combination?"

Grassina laughed and shook her head. "You don't need to worry about me. I don't have a lick of magic. I told you, I just want to keep you safe." Pushing aside the last branch, she stepped out of the thicket and stopped to tug her gown free of the thorns. She looked around, afraid of what she might see. The farmer's field was empty except for a flock of scavenging crows; there was no sign of either her sister or her mother. She would have to go home to find out what had happened to her family.

Over the years, she had learned enough about magic to realize that because her mother had cast the spell that changed her, Olivene had to be the one to change her back. She had reverted to her human form, so perhaps her mother's own transformation had been only temporary and she was her normal self again. But if she wasn't . . . Grassina began to hurry, taking long ground-eating strides as she thought about her father's disappearance. And then there was Chartreuse. Who knew what their mother might have done to her?

Grassina would have to tend to the snake first, of course. "Hold on tight. I don't want to drop you."

"I wouldn't blame you if you did. It would jusst be my bad luck again. But I should be fine. I *wass* hatched in a tree, after all. You know, you're the firsst human I've ever talked to. Mudine talked *at* me, but she never tried to talk *to* me."

"And you're the first snake I've ever wanted to talk to," Grassina said, still amazed that she could converse with an animal.

Five

hat are you doing?" demanded Grassina, ducking out of her sister's way.

Chartreuse waved the broom handle, swatting at a web and ripping it down the center. A spider dangled from one of the broken threads. "Vandals! Thieves!" it shouted in a voice no louder than a whisper.

"That should be obvious," said Chartreuse. "Mother told us to collect spiders' webs. Do you know of a better way?"

Grassina put her hand on the broom so that her sister couldn't swing it again. "You don't have to be so rough. We could try asking for them."

"Ask who?" Chartreuse glanced at the stable boy mucking out a nearby stall. "I'm not asking him, if that's what you mean."

Grassina shook her head. "Ask the spiders, of course. The webs belong to them."

"You want to talk to spiders?" Chartreuse sounded incredulous.

"You could do it if you'd like. I think talking to animals is fun."

"You would," said Chartreuse. "But I don't. It's beneath a royal princess to talk to animals. We have a responsibility to our subjects to maintain some decorum. If you'd paid attention to Lady Sophronia, you'd know that we are supposed to set examples for our less fortunate subjects."

"Something awful happened to you when Mother turned you into a chicken, didn't it? You never did tell me what it was like."

Chartreuse gave her such a venomous look that it could have wilted plants. "I told you never to mention it again! It was a nightmare, and I don't want to talk about it!"

Soon after returning home, Grassina had discovered that she hadn't been the only one to have a transformation spell cast on her. Holding up her hands in surrender, she said, "All right, I'm sorry! But if you won't talk to spiders, at least let me try."

"Even you can't think that—"

"We shouldn't use a stick anyway. Did you see how it tore the web? We have to be gentle with them. Mother wants us to keep the webs intact."

Chartreuse sighed. "Then go ahead and do it your

way. I want to get this over with so I can go to bed. I have plans for the morning and need to get up early."

"I just bet you do," muttered Grassina. Spotting another web near the ceiling, she waved her hand at it, calling, "Yoo hoo! Over here."

The spider crouching in the center of the web glared down at them. When it spoke, its voice was scarcely louder than the breathing of the horses in the closest stalls. Grassina wouldn't have heard it if she hadn't been trying her hardest. "Stay away from me, you monsters," said the spider. "I saw what you did to Inez's web."

"I'm sorry," said Grassina. "That was a mistake. It won't happen again."

"You bet it was a mistake," the spider said, waving a leg in the air for emphasis. "That was a beautiful web! Inez is known throughout the stable for her craftsmanship."

"I'm sure she is. I've never seen such lovely webs as the ones I've found here. That's why my mother sent us to get them. She said they were the best in all the land, and she needs them for a very special project."

"I thought we came to the stable because we didn't know where else to look," murmured Chartreuse.

"Shh!" said Grassina, darting an angry glance at her sister. Turning back to the spider, she smiled and said as graciously as she could, "We've come to ask if we might have a selection of your finest webs."

52

"What sort of special project?" asked the spider, sounding interested in spite of itself.

"Don't you dare listen to her, Corinne," whispered the spider named Inez. "You can't trust a web beater."

"She didn't beat your web," said Corinne. "The other one did."

Inez turned from Grassina to Chartreuse. "They all look alike to me."

"Tell me about the project," Corinne said again.

"Oh, right, the project." Grassina thought fast, trying to come up with something convincing. "My mother is the queen. She's made a wager with another queen that our spiders are finer weavers than any human in her kingdom. Of course Mother wants the best webs she can find to show the other queen—"

"Then it's no wonder you came here," said Corinne. "But you were going about it all wrong. Here, I'll show you." The spider darted to the edge of the web and worked one of the anchoring threads free. "You can have this one. It's one of my best efforts, if I do say so myself."

"Don't do it, Corinne!" shouted Inez. "They don't deserve it."

"Stop being an old stick in the web," said Corinne, loosening a second thread. "I've heard about contests like this. The spiders always win if their webs are half decent. I'm giving the queen the best webs we have." Working on one thread after another, she freed the web until it began to sag.

Olivene had made the girls boil vinegar to wash the webs, then gave them a gray powder to mix with the vinegar, saying, "That should do the trick!" The resulting concoction had smelled so strong that Chartreuse had made Grassina lug the pail to the stable, saying that the odor gave her a headache. Grassina crinkled her nose at the smell as she held up the pail to catch Corinne's falling web.

"Is this going to take much longer?" Chartreuse asked, stifling a yawn. "It's getting late, and I would like to get to bed sometime tonight."

"How many more do you need?" the spider asked Grassina. "Morris! Francine! Your webs should do very well. The queen will need one of Astoria's special weaves, too. Tori, if you undo that end, I'll get started on this one."

By the time the spiders had finished donating their webs for the queens' wager, Grassina had collected more than two dozen. Chartreuse waited impatiently at the stable door while Grassina thanked the spiders.

"That was some story you made up," Chartreuse said as her sister joined her.

"I know, I know, I shouldn't have lied, but what did you expect me to tell them—give us your webs so our mother can use them in a potion? I'm sure that would have gone over well."

Chartreuse patted her sister on the back. "Don't be so prickly. I thought your story was good."

"Maybe," said Grassina, "but I didn't like deceiving them that way."

"Don't let it worry you. They're just bugs."

"So it's all right for a princess to lie to certain people?"

"Certainly not, but spiders aren't people, are they? Now, let's finish these horrid webs. I'm sick of them already."

"Where should we wash them?" asked Grassina.

"Your chamber will do. The smell will keep me awake if we do it in mine. Your room already reeks of all those plants you have drying."

"I'd rather have it smell like herbs than the way that kitten makes your room stink," Grassina muttered as she shifted the weight of the heavy bucket from one hand to the other.

Whatever the powder was that their mother had given them, it kept the webs from clumping or dissolving and made them sparkle as they sloshed around in the pail. Grassina's burden seemed to grow heavier as she climbed the stairs, and she had to stop now and then to rest. Chartreuse finally offered to take a turn, but she did it grudgingly and complained the entire time.

The stars were shining outside Grassina's window when the girls reached her room. Rather than find someone to light her candles for her, Grassina borrowed a flame from a torch in the hall and lit them one by one. A draft from the window made the drying plants hanging from her ceiling rustle and carried their pungent odor down to the girls. Chartreuse wrinkled her nose, but Grassina liked the smell and turned her face up with a sigh.

"What are you waiting for?" said Chartreuse. "I don't have time for this. Don't you realize how late it is?"

"Oh, I realize . . . ," Grassina grumbled, reaching for the bucket, "since you keep reminding me." Although she washed the first web by herself, she was afraid it would tear when she took it out. "Help me with this," she said, glancing at Chartreuse.

"Say *please*," her sister told her. "Princesses must never forget their manners."

"Please," Grassina said through gritted teeth.

"I don't see why you can't do it yourself," Chartreuse said as she helped carry the dripping web to the windowsill. After they'd draped it over the ledge, she shook her hands to dry them, splattering her sister with droplets. "I'm sure you can handle it from here. It shouldn't take you much longer, so I'll be off to bed now."

"We're supposed to do this together," said Grassina.

"We did. I have to go. I'm too tired to stay awake a minute longer."

"We've barely started . . . ," Grassina began.

"Good night, Grassina," Chartreuse said pointedly as she closed the door behind her.

Grassina reached into the pail for another web. The vinegar was cold and stung the little cuts she hadn't known

56

she had, but she handled the webs as carefully as she could. It was very late when she realized that only a few remained in the pail. Even so, the castle wasn't completely silent. The sound of the guards making their rounds on the battlements carried through the still night air. The yowling of cats in the courtyard seemed extra loud and made Grassina feel edgy. She was relieved when a hound broke up the catfight.

When she'd laid out the last web to dry, Grassina tumbled into bed and fell asleep instantly. It seemed only a few minutes had passed before she woke to a voice screeching in her ear, "Get out of bed, you lazy lump!" Startled out of a deep sleep, Grassina lurched bolt upright with her heart trying to thud its way out of her chest.

Olivene stabbed her collarbone with one long, crooked finger. "It's almost dawn. Why are you lying around when you have work to do? I need you to find me a toad with seven warts."

"Can't I sleep a little longer?" Grassina asked, rubbing her eyes. "I was up most of the night washing the spiders' webs."

"No, you can't sleep! I need that toad now if I'm going to get my potion to work. Your sister is already on her way to her next chore. Why can't you be more like her? Get up and get busy!" Olivene waved her hand, using magic to tilt Grassina's bed so that it stood on end, dumping the girl and all her bedding onto the floor.

"Ow!" Grassina exclaimed. Untangling herself from her blankets, she glared at her mother. "You didn't have to do that! I was going to get up."

Olivene cackled and rubbed her knobby hands together. "I know! That's why it was so much fun." Turning to leave, she stomped out the open door, stopping only long enough to say, "Make your bed before you go anywhere. This room is a pigsty! Say, that gives me an idea—" Olivene pointed her finger at her daughter, but before she could do anything, Grassina had scrambled off the floor and slammed the door in her mother's face. The sound of hysterical laughter faded as Olivene walked away.

Grassina looked at her upended bed and bit her lip. It had been five days since her mother had become this awful creature, and every one of them had been terrible. Fortunately, Grassina had learned a lot since then, such as what she could and couldn't do around the queen. She knew better than to show fear in her mother's presence or to let her see that she was upset. It had surprised her to learn that standing up for herself was her best defense because it seemed to amuse her mother instead of making her angry. Chartreuse had yet to learn any of this, however, even though she'd spent the first day as a chicken.

It didn't help that Olivene had decided to make the girls assist with her magic, sending them on errands and giving them chores around the castle. Claiming that she didn't trust anyone but her own daughters to do the work, she'd had them collect milkweed pods in barrels, then made them take off their shoes and stockings, climb into the barrels, and stomp on the pods until the milky liquid squelched between their toes. Olivene had siphoned off the milk herself while sending the sisters to collect old snake skins from the woodpile and press them with hot irons, being careful not to damage the scales. Although they hated that job, it was less taxing than collecting the rainwater that puddled in the right footprint of left-handed people. That chore had taken most of one drizzly afternoon and had given both girls the sniffles. Not only had Olivene been unsympathetic, but she'd seen them returning to the castle and had immediately sent them to gather the dust under the benches on the western side of the Great Hall.

Grassina sighed. Finding the toad wouldn't be easy, but at least she could do it in the swamp, away from her mother's ever-watchful gaze. As she righted her bed and straightened the bedding, she wondered what chore her mother had devised for Chartreuse. A least they wouldn't be working together.

"Iss she gone?" whispered the little snake, whom Grassina had named Pippa. Complaining that she was cold, the snake had taken to sleeping under the blankets at the foot of Grassina's bed at night. Having a snake sleeping beside her feet had made Grassina nervous at first, but she and Pippa had soon grown used to each other. Each day after Grassina got out of bed, Pippa explored inside the castle walls, where she ate the mice that threatened to overrun the castle now that Queen Olivene was no longer maintaining her housekeeping spells.

Grassina had wrapped the snake's injured tail in a bandage, immobilizing it so it could heal. Because the tail was mending nicely, Grassina was already thinking about where she'd release Pippa when she was completely healed. Unfortunately, if the queen was going to make unannounced visits to Grassina's room, the chance that she might see the snake was something they couldn't risk.

"She's gone," Grassina said, feeling guilty that she hadn't done more to hide the snake. This was the first time her mother had visited the room since she'd changed, but Grassina was mad at herself for thinking that meant Olivene never would. Bending down, she picked up Pippa, saying, "You can't stay here any longer or Mother will see you. Who knows what she'd do to you then."

The little snake sighed. "It'ss my fault your mother actss the way she does. My bad luck changed her, and it keepss making her do awful things. You never should have brought me here. Don't missunderstand; I'm grateful for all you've done. You've given me a ssafe place to ssleep and all the fresh mice I can eat, but I jusst know you'd be better off without me."

"That isn't true!" said Grassina. "I told you before, I don't believe in your so-called bad luck. I'm sure that

60

witch blamed you for all her problems because it was easier than blaming herself. If she'd patched her roof, or shut her door, or stayed awake, none of the bad things you mentioned would have happened. And as for my mother—my father would have brought her the flowers whether you were there or not. You had nothing to do with the curse. Now come with me and I'll take you somewhere safe where no one will bother you until your tail finishes healing."

"Will I be alone there? I don't want my bad luck to hurt any of your friendss."

"But I just told you . . ." Grassina shook her head and sighed. "Yes, you'll be alone, although I will come to see you as often as I can." With Pippa wrapped around her wrist, Grassina stroked the top of the little snake's head and wondered if there really was anywhere she could take her that would be truly safe.

Six

The guards had grown used to lowering the drawbridge early in the morning so the princesses could do their mother's bidding, which made it easy for Grassina to smuggle Pippa out of the castle. What wasn't so easy was getting the little snake to stay hidden when she wanted to see everything that was going on around her.

Grassina had almost reached the drawbridge when Chartreuse called from the center of the courtyard. "Grassina! Wait for me!"

Although she considered pretending not to hear, Grassina knew Chartreuse wouldn't believe her. Sighing, Grassina stopped and turned, hoping she wouldn't have to wait long. Instead of hurrying, however, Chartreuse dawdled as if looking for someone, glancing back at the castle as she walked. Finally, a young man came through one of the doors. Chartreuse's face lit up, and she waved gaily when he looked her way. It was Prince Miguel, dressed for a morning ride.

While Grassina watched her sister smile coyly and laugh at something the young man said, Pippa poked her head out of the leather sack the princess was carrying. Grassina didn't look away from the flirting couple until she felt the little snake wiggle, making the sack thump against her hip. "What *are* you doing?" Grassina asked. "I told you to stay hidden."

Pippa peered up at her. "I wanted to know why we sstopped. It'ss imposssible to ssee anything from insside thiss sstuffy old bag, and the rockss in the bottom pinch my tail. I ssupposse it could be worsse though. With my luck it could have been filled with prickerss."

Grassina glanced at the closest guard. "Shh! Keep your head down," she whispered to the snake. "We stopped so we could wait for my sister."

"Really?" said Pippa. "I've never met your ssisster."

"And you're not going to, either. She'd probably scream and make a fuss, which is something I'd rather avoid."

"I bet she'ss like mosst humanss and doessn't like ssnakess."

"Lately, the only creatures she likes are handsome princes, so unless you're really an enchanted prince . . ."

Pippa sighed. "I'm not an enchanted anything, although I wish I were. Then maybe my luck would be better."

"Come along, Grassina," said Chartreuse, hurrying across the paving stones. "I don't have time to waste. Mother thinks I already left to start my chore, but I'd promised to have breakfast with the princes. If I finish the chore early enough, I'll be able to meet Prince Miguel in the garden when he comes back from his ride. Oh, look! There's Prince Clarence! Wait right here. I'll be just a moment."

"Not another one," said Grassina as her sister hurried toward a prince riding his destrier from the stable. Both the horse and the prince were dressed in armor, and neither one looked happy to be delayed.

"Where are you headed so early in the day, Clarence?" Chartreuse asked in her sweetest voice. "You didn't mention at breakfast that you were going anywhere."

"My squire told me that there's talk of a dragon in the woods only a few miles from the castle, dear princess," said Clarence. His highly polished armor reflected the morning sunlight directly into Grassina's eyes. She squinted, but didn't stop listening.

"Your squire must be mistaken," said Chartreuse. "No dragons would dare come so close."

"Perhaps, perhaps not," said Clarence. "But I feel it is my duty as your suitor to investigate the allegations and protect you if need be. Rest assured, sweet princess, if there is a dragon in those woods, I, Clarence, prince of the Mucking Peninsula and Outer Saltfort, will dispatch the monster so that it cannot possibly harm a single hair on your glorious head."

Chartreuse's eyes grew misty as she gazed up at him.

"Then ride, my champion, and take my token with you, knowing that I will await your return with bated breath."

"Could she be any more sappy?" Grassina muttered.

After searching her clothing for something that she could present to him, Chartreuse gave the prince a dazzling smile and said, "Just a moment." The prince waited while Chartreuse turned and ran to Grassina. "Quick!" she whispered. "You have a ribbon lacing the front of your tunic. Give it to me!"

"What?" squeaked Grassina. "Don't you have something you can give him?"

"No, and he doesn't have time to wait while I go to my room. Don't worry, I'll give you one of my ribbons later."

"This is so unfair," Grassina grumbled as she turned her back and unthreaded the pale green ribbon.

Chartreuse snatched the silky strip of fabric from her sister's hand and hurried to the prince's side. After pressing the ribbon to her lips, she tied it on his horse's bridle, saying, "Take this personal token of my high regard for you, my prince."

Clarence's armor clanked as he reached to touch the ribbon. "I shall carry it with pride, my princess."

"If it's my ribbon, is he my champion?" Grassina murmured.

"Why did she give your ribbon to that horsse?" asked Pippa, the tip of her nose peeking out of the leather sack.

"Shh!" whispered Grassina. "Here she comes."

65

"There you are, sister dear," said Chartreuse over the clopping of the destrier's hooves. Taking Grassina by the arm, she hustled her to the drawbridge, nodding when the guards greeted them. "I never realized that the boy cared so much for me," Chartreuse whispered when they'd passed by the men. "To think he'd be willing to give his life for my well-being. He must really love me!"

"Or love hunting dragons," Grassina said under her breath. Then she added in a louder voice, "Do you really think there aren't any dragons in the woods?"

"I'm sure I would have heard about it if there were. Since Mother lost interest in anything but her magic, I've been trying to stay informed about what's going on in the kingdom. When I'm the Green Witch, I'll be the one to deal with any problems. Unless Clarence goes deep into the enchanted forest, he's not likely to encounter anything more frightening than a bad-tempered squirrel. Now tell me, what does Mother want you to do? I have to collect blue butterflies, and I know just where to look. It shouldn't take me long, unless you keep dragging your feet."

"She wants me to get her a toad with seven warts."

Chartreuse looked shocked. "Is that all? That's not fair! She gave you the easy job."

"I thought you said you knew where to find blue butterflies," Grassina said, pulling her arm out of her sister's grasp. "Finding a specific toad will probably take a lot longer."

66

Chartreuse's expression brightened. "That's true. In that case, I'm glad I don't have that one!" After patting her sister on the back, she left her at the drawbridge to go her own way.

Pippa peeked out of the leather sack to watch Chartreuse. "How many princess want to marry her?"

"More than she can count," said Grassina. "A lot of princes want to marry a princess who'll be queen in her own right as well as a witch who could help their kingdom."

"There might be another reasson," said Pippa. "She might have shed her old sskin recently. Then she'd be nice and ssmooth. That might make her more attractive to maless."

Grassina laughed. "Maybe that's it. I'll have to ask her sometime."

Knowing that she didn't have long to take Pippa somewhere safe, Grassina decided to go to her tree house. It was on the way to the swamp—a perfect place to look for toads—and was unlikely to attract any other visitors.

When they approached the trunk of the tree that supported the miniature cottage, a squirrel chattered, "Go away!" Jerking its tail in anger, it skittered around to the other side of the tree when Grassina began to climb the ladder. Once inside the tiny house, the princess opened the sack and let the snake loose to explore. She'd brought a waterskin with her from the castle and used it now to fill a bowl for the snake. "It's just for a few days," she said, setting the bowl on the floor. "Your tail should be healed soon."

"It's nice and warm in here," said Pippa, raising her head to look around the room. She stopped when she saw the fireplace where the embers were still warm in the grate.

"That fireplace lights itself whenever the tree house gets cold," said Grassina.

"A ssnake could get ussed to this," Pippa said, slithering toward the hearth.

The copper finches twittered overhead while one of the few remaining glass birds rustled its transparent feathers, making them click softly. Pippa tested the air with her tongue, looking disappointed when the birds didn't smell real.

"You'll be safe here," said Grassina. "I have to go to the swamp to find a toad for my mother."

"Why? Doess she eat them?" the snake asked, her eyes glistening.

Grassina laughed and shook her head. "I have no idea what she plans to do with them, but at this point, nothing she does would surprise me."

"Doess anyone live here? Asside from the birdss, I mean."

"It used to be a playhouse for my sister and me," said Grassina. "No one comes here much anymore."

"Good," said Pippa. "Then my bad luck won't hurt anyone elsse."

Although Grassina had considered introducing Pippa to Marniekins, she decided that it might not be such a good idea. Pippa would probably fret about her bad luck more if she thought someone else might be hurt, and there was no way to tell how the doll would react to a snake.

Confident that her mother's old spell would keep Pippa safe inside the tree house, Grassina climbed down the ladder while clutching her toad-collecting sack. Starting at the base of the tree, she began lifting leaves and moving stems until she found a fat toad under a skunk-cabbage leaf near a mostly collapsed stone wall.

"Pardon me," Grassina said, picking up the toad to count the lumps on its back.

"What are you doing?" croaked the toad. "Put me down! This is so undignified! Why, I never . . ."

"I'm sorry," said Grassina. "I need to count your warts. These bumps are warts, aren't they? Mother told me to find a toad with seven warts, but I'm not sure these are what she meant."

The toad squirmed in her grasp and leaked something clear onto her fingers. "Ick!" she said. "What is that?"

"It's your own fault. You startled me. I can't help it if I have an incontinence problem when I'm startled. Now, if you wouldn't mind putting me down, we'll forget this whole thing ever happened and—"

"I can't put you down. Hold still so I can count your warts!"

"They're not warts! They're ... uh ... signs of age and wisdom. Yes, that's what they are. I'm not as young as I once was."

"Are you sure?" said Grassina. "They look like they could be called warts."

"Of course, I'm sure," said the toad. "It's my back, isn't it?"

Grassina sighed and crouched down, setting the toad back where she had found it. "There you go," said the toad. "That's right ... put me on the nice soft moss and I'll ... hop off as fast as I can!" The toad hopped wildly away from the skunk cabbage and into a crevice in the jumbled stones of the wall. "You won't catch me again. No, sirree! I'm safe in here, warts and all!"

"You little liar!" said Grassina. "I never should have believed you."

Resolving not to listen to any other toads no matter what they said, Grassina straightened her back and strode into the swamp, the empty sack swinging from her hand. It took some time before she found another toad, but it didn't have the right number of warts. Knowing that her mother would make her life miserable unless she returned with the desired toad, Grassina kept searching.

She found another toad in the short grass beside the edge of a pond, but it didn't have enough warts. A toad under the old willow had too many. All three toads that she found on the way to the northern edge of the swamp had too few. The sun was at its highest point when Grassina found the toad she needed. It was partially hidden under a rotting log, and she would have missed it if it hadn't made the dry leaves rustle when it moved.

Grassina bent down to peer under the log. The toad looked up at her and blinked. Before it could get away, she reached down and picked it up, counting the bumps on its back out loud. ". . . five, six, seven. You have seven warts. Finally! I was beginning to think I'd never find one like you."

"Now, isn't this just perfect!" said the toad. "As if my day isn't bad enough, a human has to come along and . . . Hey, what are you doing?"

Grassina carefully lowered the toad into the sack. "Taking you home with me," she replied, forgetting her resolution not to talk to the toads.

"Really? But we just met. Aren't you being a little presumptuous?"

"My mother needs someone like you," she said, peering into the bag.

"What for?" asked the toad.

"I'm not sure. She didn't say and I didn't ask."

"Is she a nice person or should I be worried?"

"She used to be very nice, but lately . . . Let's just say that she's not quite the same person anymore."

"In that case . . . ," said the toad, and with a giant leap, it flew out of the bag, hit Grassina squarely on the chin, and landed sprawling in the mud.

"Ow!" said Grassina. "Hey, come back here! I need you! My mother will turn me into something awful if I don't bring her a toad with seven warts!" As the toad hopped away, Grassina chased it, half bent over and nearly stumbling over the hem of her gown. She was still chasing the toad when she noticed the first paw print in the mud. It looked like it might belong to one of her father's hounds, only it was bigger and slightly longer. "That's odd," she said to herself.

Seeing another paw print a short distance from the first, she forgot about the still-hopping toad and knelt down to examine the prints. Grassina was familiar with nearly every kind of creature that had ever set paw in the swamp, yet this print was new to her. She went on, hoping to see which way the animal had gone, and stopped short. Another print was placed right where the creature's next step would have landed, yet it was different enough from the first that it could have been made by some other, perhaps larger, beast. The pads were longer and set farther apart. The print beyond that was also different, and the one beyond that was . . .

Grassina looked up at the sound of leaves rustling in the underbrush. It was a very little sound, yet it was loud in the still afternoon air. There was a smell as well—a musky kind of odor that was as unusual as the paw prints. Grassina shivered with the feeling that someone or something was watching her. Slipping her hand into the leather sack, she wrapped her fingers around one of her smooth, round throwing stones. She glanced at the prints again as she backed away. Whatever had made them was heading toward the enchanted forest. From the way the prints seemed to change with every step, Grassina was almost sure that it had come from there as well.

The rustling stopped as she backed away, but the sudden silence made her uneasy. Pulling the stone from her sack, Grassina took two more steps backward, then turned and started back the way she'd come, her ears straining to hear anything unusual behind her. The same sixth sense that had kept her safe so many other times had told her it was time to go home.

Grassina left the swamp and was passing the practice field when Chartreuse called out, "Grassina, is that you? Come over here and give me a hand!" Chartreuse tapped her toe with impatience until Grassina reached her side. Handing her younger sister the small wooden bucket she'd been carrying, Chartreuse said, "Mother is ruining my life! It didn't take me long to find those butterflies, but when I took them to her, she sent me out to pluck dande-lion fluff. And I so wanted to talk to Prince Pietro. I told him how much I like poetry, and he was going to write me some. But look at what that fluff did to my fingers! No one will want to write poetry to my beauty after this." Still talking, she shoved pink fingertips under Grassina's nose. "It felt soft at first, but I've pulled so much of it that my fingers are worked nearly to the bone. It was bad enough that they were practically pickled in that vinegar last night. My hands are probably scarred for life. A princess shouldn't have to do things like this. It's a disgrace! I'm so tired, I could lie down right here and fall asleep—if the ground was cleaner. What have you been doing?"

"Looking for the toad I told you about," Grassina said, her face flushing as she remembered that she'd let the toad get away.

"And it took you all day? Just be glad you didn't have to pick dandelion fluff. My back is so sore from bending over that I feel like an old crone. Take that in to Mother for me," Chartreuse said, pointing at the bucket. "I need to wash before supper. I just hope I don't run into any of my princes before I change out of these dirty clothes."

Without the toad in her possession, the last thing Grassina wanted to do was go see her mother. "If that's what you want, but won't Mother think that I picked it all?" Swinging the bucket for emphasis, she raised it in such a big arc that the soft fibers threatened to fall out.

"Never mind!" Chartreuse said, snatching the bucket away. "I'll do it myself."

When they reached the castle, the two girls parted; Chartreuse went in search of their mother while Grassina headed for the dungeon. She knew she'd have to face her mother sometime, but she hoped to find another toad first. In the meantime, she wanted to talk to her father, the one person who could truly commiserate with her.

"I can't really talk to Chartreuse about it," she said from her seat on an old chest that her father had had carried down to the dungeon. Grassina was sitting in the room he'd taken over when Olivene decided that he'd been a rat long enough and changed him back into a human. It was a lot more comfortable than it had looked the first time she'd seen it; he'd had it cleaned out and a few pieces of furniture brought in, making it almost homelike. "When I try to talk to Chartreuse," Grassina continued, "everything is either about her or the kingdom. I don't think she cares about anything else. She can't see any of this from my point of view, or yours, and certainly not from Mother's. Although I suppose I can't blame her for that last part. Mother is terrible now. I know she hasn't been like this for long, but it's getting harder to remember her any other way."

"Not for me," said King Aldrid. "I can still close my eyes and picture her exactly the way she was the day we met. I started loving her that very first moment and never stopped, despite what she might have thought. It was my fault she became a victim of her family curse, and I'll never forgive myself. If only I'd listened to her mother."

"But you said that everyone thought Grandmother was crazy. I don't remember her very well, but I do remember that she did the strangest things. Once she had me stand with my feet in two buckets of water for most of an afternoon. She said she was trying to protect me from the fairies."

King Aldrid sighed. "That sounds like her. Maybe she knew something that we didn't. And now your mother . . ."

"Mother isn't crazy, she's cursed. There's a difference. A curse can be undone, and when I'm older, I intend to find out how. I want Mother back the way she was."

"We all do, sweetling," said the king. "Everyone that is, except your mother. She seems content with her new condition, although that might be part of the curse, too."

"She should be happy, since we're doing so much work for her," grumbled Grassina. "Even so, if we don't do exactly what she wants, she turns us into all sorts of things. I told you about being a rabbit. I was a mole yesterday morning. Chartreuse was a chicken for a few hours, but she won't admit to anything else."

"At least your lives are interesting," said the king.

Grassina laughed, but not because she thought it was funny. "Too interesting, if you ask me." Seeing a wistful expression on her father's face, she asked, "Is it that bad down here, Father?"

"I don't mind it," said her father. "I even like it in a way. My men come to see me, so I'm current with everything I need to do. And when I'm not working on the affairs of the kingdom, I've found time to write. I started creating a history of Greater Greensward years ago, but never had the time to finish it. I've been able to make some real headway the last few days because it's so quiet. I can't even hear the squabbling going on upstairs."

Grassina turned her head, unable to meet his eyes. She knew that at least part of the problem was the way she and Chartreuse couldn't get along. Even though she'd known that their arguing had disturbed their father, she'd never really tried to stop. And now that there seemed to be more than ever to argue about, she didn't see that it would ever end.

Grassina slid off the trunk. "It's getting late. I'd better go. But first," she said, remembering why she'd returned from the swamp, "I meant to tell you about something I saw today. There were paw prints . . . like a dog's or a wolf's, but very odd. They changed from one step to the next. I've never seen anything like it."

King Aldrid's gaze was sharp and direct. "How did they change?"

"The paw seemed to grow longer, the pads wider. . . . Why? Is it important?"

"I'm afraid so," said her father. "I was wondering when something like this would happen. I just wasn't expecting it so soon."

"Expecting what?" she asked.

"Paw prints like that belong to werewolves, my dear. It's a sign that things are about to go very wrong in Greater Greensward."

Seven

$\mathcal{G}$rassina got up early the next morning, borrowed a basket with a lid from a scullery maid, and made her way down to the swamp. This time she was going to be prepared; no toad would get away from her again. She had just set her wicker basket down and lifted the lid when something hurtled over the lip, making the wicker creak. "What was that?" she said, peering inside.

A surly-looking toad blinked up at her and said, "I'm a *who*, not a *what*. The least you can do is be nice to me, considering I put myself in here."

Grassina picked up the basket. "Why did you?" she asked, already counting the toad's seven warts.

"I don't rightly know," said the toad, sounding genuinely puzzled. "There I was, slurping up a worm, when all of a sudden my legs just carried me in. I'd jump out if I could, but my legs are locked up tighter than a snake's jaws on a muskrat. I don't suppose you'd want to take me out and set me back on the ground so I could finish my breakfast?"

"Not a chance," Grassina replied, closing the basket's lid. "You have seven warts, so you're just what I need. I'm not one to look a gift toad in the mouth."

"I never said I'd open my mouth so you could look in," said the toad, his voice muffled by the wicker. "You're awfully arrogant, thinking I would do that for you."

Grassina slid the little piece of wood to latch the lid. "I would like to know what compelled you to do it. Toads don't just jump into baskets for no reason. Something or someone," she said, looking around her, "*made* you do this. I wonder why."

"Because they're mean and ornery and hate me for no good reason that I can think of?" said the toad.

"Maybe . . . or maybe someone is trying to help me. Whoever you are," she said, raising her voice, "thank you!"

"Yeah," grumped the toad. "Thanks a lot!"

Pleased that she finally had the toad she'd been ordered to find, Grassina hurried to take it to her mother. She found the queen alone in the Great Hall, crouched on a bench while she pulled leeches off her dripping legs.

"That moat's full of leeches," said Olivene, glancing up at her daughter. "Good thing, too. Means I have a steady supply. A little boiled leech paste and . . . What is that you have there?" The queen's long nose quivered as she eyed Grassina's basket.

"It's that toad you asked for. I brought it as soon as—"

Olivene's lips pursed, and her eyes grew as cold as

iron. "I told you to get that toad yesterday! A day late is almost as bad as not at all. I think you need a little lesson about being slow, my girl."

The color drained from Grassina's face when her mother raised her arm. Setting the basket on the floor, she backed away, saying, "I'm truly sorry, Mother. It won't happen again! I've already learned my lesson."

"I'll be the judge of that," sneered Olivene. "Next time I'm sure you'll do whatever it takes to be prompt!"

The turtle skirted a moldy clump of tansy, shaking its head in disgust. The herbs that covered the floor of the Great Hall should have been replaced weeks ago, but ever since the queen had fallen prey to the family curse, a lot of things had been neglected in the castle. Two pages were just returning from watching the knights practice with swords and lances when one of them discovered the turtle. The freckle-faced boy, the son of a minor noble and the youngest page in the castle, stopped to poke the plodding turtle with his shoe. "Look at this! How do you suppose it got in here? Do you think it belongs to somebody?" The boy picked it up and flipped it over to examine its underside. Startled, the turtle pulled its head and limbs into its shell and squeezed its eyes shut.

A page with curly black hair rapped on the shell with his knuckles. With the authoritative air of someone a full year older, he said, "Nobody brings a turtle into the castle unless it's meant for supper. I love a good turtle soup."

"Maybe it escaped from the kitchen," said the first page. "Do you think Cook will give us a reward if we take it back?"

"Let's see if she has any tarts left from last night," the older boy said, reaching for the turtle. "Give it to me! I'll take it to her."

"And claim all the tarts for yourself? I don't think so!" Snatching his prize back, the younger boy took off running with his friend right behind.

Acting in a very unturtlelike manner, the captive stuck its head out of its shell, looking for a way to escape. Its head bounced painfully on its scrawny neck as the boy ran, but the turtle knew what would happen if it reached the kitchen: a little discomfort was the least of its worries.

"Cook!" shouted the page. "We found your turtle!"

"My what?" The head cook blinked sleepily at them from her seat by the fireplace, where she'd been dozing with a cat on her lap. She peered at the turtle as the pages held it up for her to inspect. "Ah," she murmured, "it's a nice turtle, too. Thank you, boys. I like a bowl of turtle soup now and then. Give it to Lettie there. She'll know what to do with it."

Thrusting its legs out of its shell, the turtle struggled to get down, but the boy held it away from his chest so that his captive had nothing to push against.

"Drop that right in this pot," said a chubby young woman with cheeks bright red from the cooking fire. "Oh, that's a good-sized one, that is! This water's cold, but it'll soon heat up over this nice hot fire, so . . . I say, what's this? Turtles aren't supposed to glow like that, are they?" The scullery maid was staring down into the pot with eyes as big as trenchers.

"What are you going on about, Lettie?" Cook said, dislodging the cat as she leaned forward in her seat.

"Agh!" shrieked the scullery maid. She dropped the pot, which had suddenly become too heavy to hold. It hit the floor with a clang, splashing water everywhere. While the maid backed away from the fire, the pages fought to see around her. They gasped when a person shot up out of the pot and went sprawling on the floor.

"Well, I never!" said Cook.

Grassina groaned and rubbed her head where she'd hit it on the edge of a table. Shaking her foot until it came unhooked from the pot handle, she sat up and looked around. "Sorry about the mess," she said, seeing the scullery maid's horrified expression.

Lettie gulped. "That's quite all right, Your Highness. Think nothing of it."

"Does this mean we won't get a tart?" the freckle-faced page whispered to his friend.

Grassina's cheeks were crimson as she hurried from the kitchen, leaving a trail of wet footprints behind her.

Avoiding the eyes of everyone she passed, she fled to her room, shivering in her damp clothes. It was the first time she'd had an audience when she changed back, and she felt oddly embarrassed. "I shouldn't worry about what other people think," she muttered, wriggling out of her clammy gown and into a clean one.

Grassina glanced out the window when she heard the rumble of thunder. The sky had darkened, and rain was already pattering on the sill. A breeze blew the dried plants that hung from her ceiling, making them rustle the way they had while alive. When the door flew open behind her, Grassina turned to see Chartreuse stalk into the room. "I heard what happened," said Chartreuse. "The whole castle is talking about it. What were you thinking of, turning back in front of so many people?"

Grassina flipped her braid over her shoulder. "I didn't have any choice. It wasn't as if I wanted to be a turtle or could choose when I turned back."

Sighing like someone carrying a great weight on her shoulders, Chartreuse flung herself on her sister's bed so that she was lying on her back with her arm covering her eyes. "It's bad enough that she likes turning us into things, but does she have to make it so obvious? My princes are bound to find out now, and I've tried so hard to keep it quiet. I've sent them on every errand I could think of just to keep them away from Mother. Clarence isn't back yet or I would have sent him, too. What's the point, though, if

84

Mother insists on making these spells so public? Someone is bound to tell my princes sooner or later. I'll never be able to live this down! Greater Greensward is going to be the laughingstock of all the kingdoms! On my way here, everyone stared at me as if I was about to turn into some awful creature. How could she do this to me?"

Chartreuse rolled over onto her stomach and stared accusingly at her sister. "Come to think of it, the entire thing must have been your fault. She turns us into horrid beasts when she wants to teach us a lesson, which means you did something to make her angry. What did you do this time?"

Grassina looked away and shrugged. "I was a little late bringing her the toad, that's all."

Chartreuse sat up abruptly. "I've nearly killed myself doing whatever she's asked me to do, but you couldn't bring her one stinking toad! Would it be too much for you to make a little effort to please the woman?"

The rain began to fall in grass-flattening sheets. A cackle of laughter as loud as thunder drew Grassina back to the window. She jumped when a jagged bolt of white light struck the ground at the edge of the moat, the boom so loud it made her ears ring. Wrinkling her nose at an acrid smell, she stepped closer to the window. The flash of lightning had shown her something so unbelievable that she had to look again to see if it was true. A figure dressed all in black was capering in the field below with her skirt hitched up and her skinny legs dancing across the lightning-singed ground. Her hair was flying as she twirled and spun, making snatching motions with her hands all the while.

". . . if you would just think of others. Oh, for . . ." Chartreuse hopped off the bed, grabbed Grassina's shoulder, and spun her around. "Have you heard a word I've been saying? I told you not to make a spectacle of yourself like that again! We're going to be the talk of the entire kingdom. No one will want to marry either of us!"

"I don't think they'll be thinking about us at all," said Grassina. "Not after they see what's going on outside."

"What are you talking about?" Chartreuse said, peering out the window. "There's nothing out there except . . . Is that Mother? What is she doing in the rain?"

A bolt of lightning hit the ground, narrowly missing the prancing woman. Leaping into the air, she kicked her legs high and flailed her arms, then hunched over and slapped the ground. Although the girls had to clap their hands over their ears to still the ringing and make the thunder bearable each time another bolt struck, they were unable to look away from the cavorting queen.

"This is horrible!" Chartreuse shouted during a lull. The thunder had been so loud that everything else sounded muffled and distant. "We can't let anyone see her like that!"

"And what do you propose we do about it?" Grassina shouted back.

86

"We can . . . You should . . ." Chartreuse's voice trailed away as she tried to think. Then, nodding to herself, she declared, "We'll go see Father. He can talk to her."

"What can he do?"

"I don't know. He's her husband. She'll listen to him before she'll listen to us."

"Are you crazy?" Grassina asked, following her sister into the corridor. "You know what she's like now. She doesn't listen to anyone."

Chartreuse stopped long enough to glare at Grassina. "If you have a better idea, I'd be happy to hear it!"

Grassina swallowed and shook her head. For the first time in ages, Chartreuse actually wanted her suggestions. It was too bad that she didn't have any to give.

Flickering torches lit the girls' path through the dungeon, making shadows jerk and waver around them. Because every surface was made of stone, every sound had its echo, with a hollow note that made even the most innocent noise seem sinister. Water seeping between cracks made the floor glisten and slippery to walk on and the air already sour with mold and decay smell even more pungent. One section of the corridor was so cold that Grassina could see her breath, yet there were no crosscurrents of air and there was no reason why it should be colder. Chartreuse shivered and hurried on, calling to Grassina when she lingered to look around. They were passing a cell with rusty bars in the tiny window when Grassina thought she heard voices; she peeked inside, but no one was there.

The only sign of life they encountered was a spider weaving its web across a doorway. "Listen!" said Grassina when she thought she heard something faint and far away and . . . Someone coughed and the sound echoed in the nearly silent hall. Following their ears to the door of their father's cell, they peeked inside and found him sitting hunched over a small table. "And to what do I owe this honor?" he said, having looked up from his quill and parchment when he heard the girls' hesitant knock.

"We've come to ask for your help," said Chartreuse. "Mother is dancing in the thunderstorm and making a spectacle of herself."

King Aldrid looked puzzled. "I'd like to help you girls, but I don't know what I can do about it. The queen has been avoiding me. We haven't spoken in days."

"I knew we shouldn't have asked him," Grassina blurted out. "He can't even leave the dungeon."

Chartreuse gave her father a pitying look. "Don't worry, Father. As soon as I come into my magic, I'll get you out of here."

King Aldrid cleared his throat. "That won't really be necessary. Your mother's spell kept me here for only three days. I could have left any time after that."

"Then why didn't you?" asked Grassina.

"To be honest, I've been avoiding your mother. As long as she doesn't see me, she leaves me alone. I've been able to handle the kingdom's business from down here, probably better than I could if I were upstairs running into Olivene. One flick of her finger and I'd be a rat again. Believe me when I say that no one wants a rat ruling the kingdom. If word got out that the king of Greater Greensward had been turned into an animal . . ."

"So what are we supposed to do about Mother? She has to be insane to do what she's doing!" said Chartreuse.

"She could get herself killed!" said Grassina.

"Your mother isn't insane. Just because she doesn't behave the way she used to doesn't mean that she doesn't know what she's doing," said the king. "I'm sure that whatever her reason is, it has something to do with her magic."

"But does she have to do it where everyone can see her?" wailed Chartreuse.

"She probably thinks it's more fun that way," said Grassina.

The king coughed behind his hand. "She probably does," he said, chuckling to himself.

Eight

Mwowr! screamed Chartreuse's kitten, slashing at the nose of the other cat. The larger honey-colored animal hissed and backed away, its ears flattened against its skull, its tail puffed out to twice its usual size.

Barking joyfully, a wandering hound took off after the cats, chasing them around the moat to the lowered drawbridge. A tinker stepped out of their way as the cats tore past. The kitten streaked over the gap in the boards, but the older cat missed its footing and slipped, falling through the gap and into the moat with a splash. As the kitten disappeared under the portcullis, the cat floundered in the water, its eyes frantic as it turned in circles, trying to find a way out. It might have made it had one of the larger fish that lived in the moat not come by and dragged it under the water. The cat yowled as it sank below the surface; then all that was left to show that it had been there were a few drifting bubbles.

Grassina stepped to the edge of the moat, clutching

her bucket of toadstools as she peered into the silt-laden depths. Then out of the water shot Chartreuse, spluttering and splashing, her streaming hair half covering her face. Blood mixed with water trickled from a scratch on her nose as she made her way to dry ground, paddling at first, then wading when her feet reached a rocky ledge.

"Need a hand?" Grassina asked, bending down to reach for her sister.

Chartreuse looked startled when she saw her and not at all pleased. "No," she said, her lips stiff as she climbed out of the water. "I don't need anyone's help, especially not yours. I hope you're happy. Rinaldo left at dawn this morning, and it was your fault. I just know he heard about your turtle incident."

Ignoring the gaping mouths of the farmers and merchants who had witnessed her misfortune, Chartreuse pushed her way through the usual morning crowd that had come to do business in the castle and limped across the drawbridge. Grassina saw her stiffen when Pietro passed under the portcullis, giving him only the briefest of nods. The prince turned as if to follow Chartreuse, but seemed to think better of it and continued across the drawbridge. Grassina shook her head when he stopped to talk to a group of farm girls carrying heavily laden baskets. She was watching the girls vie for his attention when her gaze fell upon a middle-aged man in homespun on the back of an old plow horse, its sides lathered from running too long and too fast. The man's face was pale despite his exertion, and his eyes had a hunted look.

The man was still astride his horse, arguing with the guards stationed at the end of the drawbridge, when Grassina approached them. "I'm telling you," one of the guards said to the man, "you can't see the queen. She's indisposed and won't see anyone."

"But it's important! A terrible thing has happened, and Queen Olivene needs to know. I have to talk to her."

"Perhaps I can help," said Grassina, stepping up to the guards.

Seeing the princess, the guards dipped their heads in deference, then swatted the man when he didn't do the same. "'Tis Her Royal Highness Princess Grassina," said one of the guards. "Show some respect."

"Pardon, Your Highness," said the man, slipping off his horse and turning to Grassina. "My name is Hal of Darby-in-the-Woods. Dare I ask if you can help me? I must see the queen, yet these men tell me it isn't possible."

"What would you see her about?" asked Grassina. "I need to know if I'm to help."

The man shuddered as if what he had to say was too horrible for words. Glancing furtively at the guards, he inclined his head toward Grassina and whispered, "A pack of werewolves attacked my village last night. I came at first daylight. We need the help of the Green Witch. Three men are dead and two others were bitten, yet still live. We locked them in farmer Gib's shed, but who knows if it will hold when the change comes on them."

A sick feeling soured Grassina's stomach. "The guards were right, you can't see my mother now, but maybe I can talk to her for you."

"Would you?" Hal asked, hope displacing some of the fear in his eyes. "We're in sore need of her help. Frankly, we're surprised she hasn't come already, seeing that the Green Witch knows everything that goes on in Greater Greensward."

"Not everything," said Grassina. "And it's come as a surprise to us as well. I'll go see the queen, but I don't know if she'll help."

"Thank you, Your Highness," said the man. He looked so grateful that Grassina found it almost embarrassing.

The day before, Olivene had moved her magical paraphernalia down into one of the cells, turning it into a workroom where she could concoct her potions and practice her spells. Grassina had yet to visit her there and had been putting off taking her mother the toadstools she'd demanded. Now, after promising the villager that she would talk to her mother, Grassina could no longer delay.

She thought at first that it might be hard to find her mother in the warren of rooms that made up the dungeon, but a thump, her mother's screech, and an even louder crash told her where to look. Grassina bit her lip, wondering what her mother had done this time. Following a loud tapping sound, she turned a corner where a damp fog smelling of rotting meat and skunk cabbage enveloped her. The fog was oozing out of the wall just outside her mother's door, growing thicker the longer she stood there. It was enough to make her eyes water, so she wiped them on her sleeve and tried to take shallow breaths as she took one step, then another. When the wall in front of her bulged and receded, she had to rub her eyes. Everything looked different from inside the fog. The ceiling seemed to shift above her, the floor rippled at her feet, and a window opened in a wall, then closed with a snap. Taking two quick steps, Grassina left the fog behind, and suddenly everything looked normal again.

Light flashed in staccato bursts from a doorway up ahead. "Oh, no, you don't!" shouted Queen Olivene. There was a thump and the light flashed brighter, then died down to a wavery, uneven glow. Steeling herself against whatever her mother might do, Grassina reached the door and peeked inside. Olivene was standing in front of a large cauldron, stirring its contents with a spoon as long as her arm. Each time the spoon made one full circuit of the pot, it hit the rim with a loud tap.

A book lay open on a table near the door. Grassina craned her neck to read the spell titled "Releasing Trapped Magic." She'd read only a few words when she smelled the fog again, so she stepped into the room to get out of its way and bumped into the table.

Olivene spun around and glared at her daughter. "What are you doing here? Don't just stand there staring like a gargoyle—come in and give me those toadstools." Before Grassina could move, Olivene had crossed the room and snatched the bucket from her hand. "Here," she said, thrusting the spoon at her. "Make yourself useful."

While her mother examined each toadstool individually, Grassina stirred the viscous liquid, wrinkling her nose at the frothy, hairy scum that floated on its surface. "There's something I need to tell you," she said.

"When I'm finished," her mother grumbled. Then she sniffed another toadstool.

Light flashing in the corner of the room made Grassina turn her head. A lidded wicker basket sat on the floor, isolated from the rest of Olivene's belongings. Tiny lights sparked through the gaps in the weave, like coals flaring in a dying fire. Suddenly, the basket fell on its side with a thump and began to roll. As it passed Olivene, she kicked it without looking up from what she was doing, sending it thudding into the wall. The basket buzzed angrily, then rolled back into the corner and flung itself upright.

"Let this be a lesson to you, girl," Olivene told Grassina. "Never collect insects in a thunderstorm expecting to get more effective lightning bugs. The darn things spark, but they don't have any real light. The crickets are the worst—it made them bad-tempered and smarter than they should be. Can't do a thing with them!"

"Why did you choose crickets?"

"Bugs are bugs, aren't they?" Glancing at the cauldron, Olivene said, "Watch what you're doing!" and pointed a crooked finger at the bubbling liquid. Grassina looked down to see it burble and ooze over the rim. "Hit it!" shouted Olivene. "Use the spoon and whap it hard!" Grassina whapped the concoction with the spoon, sending droplets flying. The liquid stilled, then slurped back into the cauldron.

"What's in this pot, anyway?" Grassina asked.

"None of your business!" Olivene snapped. Elbowing her daughter aside, the witch dropped in three carefully selected toadstools one at a time. When the third one was sucked in with a *glorp,* the liquid frothed as high as the rim of the pot before settling back down to a steady seethe.

Olivene's long nose quivered when she leaned over the pot and sniffed.

"I really need to tell you something," Grassina began.

Her mother held up her hand imperiously, saying, "Not now! Can't you see that I'm busy?" After another deep sniff, she dumped the rest of the toadstools into the pot, crowing with delight when it turned a sickly shade of blue. While Grassina retreated to the doorway, Olivene took a grisly-looking hook off the wall and dipped it into the pot, pulling out a dripping stocking.

"If you want something done right, you have to do it yourself," said Olivene, draping the stocking on a ring embedded in the wall. "That makes two pairs. Get a little potion on your clothes and suddenly no one wants to wash them for you. I was going to make you do it, but I decided that the wash water would work just fine as the base for my next potion. Hand me those leech lips and stand back. I should get a good reaction when I add them!"

Grassina studied the bottle labeled "Leech Lips." Some of the little, brown, squiggly things inside smacked themselves while others smiled or pouted. She told herself that it was the water's sloshing that made them move, but she wasn't so sure.

"I came to tell you that werewolves attacked a village last night," she said, handing the bottle to her mother.

Olivene's eyes brightened. "Really? Where?"

"Darby-in-the-Woods. A man came to see you about it."

"Did they kill any of the werewolves? Darby-in-the-Woods isn't far from here. I could be there and back in two shakes of a snake's tail."

"I don't think they did."

"Then why are you telling me about it? Unless someone has collected a werewolf's whiskers or the last hair on the tip of its tail, I'm not interested." Uncorking the bottle, Grassina held it over the cauldron and shook out a few blubbering lips. The liquid seethed for just a moment, then became as placid as a lake in winter. "Drat!" muttered Olivene.

"You're the Green Witch," said Grassina. "It's your duty to protect the kingdom."

"Duty schmooty! Do you see a ring on this finger?" Olivene shoved her hand under her daughter's nose. "I'm no more the Green Witch than you are. If you don't mind, and even if you do, I have to get back to work. Now scat! I don't have time for all this tongue flapping."

"If you're not the Green Witch, then who's going to protect the kingdom? And what should I tell the man? I'm sure he's going to want . . ."

The basket filled with lightning bugs fell over with a *whump*—bursting open and letting all the bugs escape in a crawling, skittering, leaping, flying rush. "Now see what you've done?" shouted Olivene. "You've distracted me. It's going to take hours to catch those pesky pests, and I still haven't finished my laundry!"

"Maybe I could . . . ," Grassina began.

"Get out!" her mother shrieked, taking off her shoe and hurling it at her daughter.

Grassina darted from the room, ducking when the

second shoe sailed past her head. Olivene was still shouting at the insects as Grassina turned the corner, grateful that her mother had cast a shoe and not a spell.

"What's the ruckus about?" King Aldrid asked from an open doorway.

Grassina stopped and turned. She hadn't realized that her mother had claimed a room so close to her father's. "Did you know that Mother is no longer the Green Witch? It makes sense, of course. I mean, the Green Witch is the most powerful and the nicest witch in the kingdom, and no one can claim that Mother is nice anymore. But if she isn't, then who is? Do you think we should . . . Wait a minute. What's wrong with you?" She took a step closer, noting his sunken cheeks and the dark circles under his eyes. "You look awful!"

"It's good to see you, too," he said, giving her a weak smile.

"I didn't mean . . . I just . . . Are you all right?"

Her father had begun to cough so hard that he shook with the effort and had to look away until it was over. "I've seen better days," he wheezed when he could talk again. "Why did you come to see your mother? Is something wrong?"

Grassina nodded. "A man came to tell us that werewolves attacked people in his village!"

"And your mother doesn't intend to do anything about it, does she? Then I'd best see to it."

99

"You can't hunt werewolves. You're ill!"

King Aldrid shook his head. "There won't be any hunting involved. Werewolves turn back into their human form during the day, so my men and I will set traps and check them tomorrow. I was very adept at catching werewolves before I met your mother, but I haven't had to trap one since I moved to Greater Greensward. There was no need with the Green Witch watching over the kingdom. We were spoiled when your mother protected us, but now that she isn't doing that, we'll have to handle it ourselves the way rulers of other kingdoms do."

"But you should be resting."

"It's just a cold. I'll be fine. A little fresh air will do me good."

Grassina was worried. She followed her father out of the dungeon, returning to her own chamber while he sent for the men he intended to take with him. She already had the necessary plants dried and hanging from her ceiling, so it didn't take long for her to mix a tonic for his cough. To her dismay, he and his men had already departed by the time she returned downstairs. With the tonic tucked safely in her purse, Grassina hurried to the stable and had her palfrey, Buttercup, saddled. Since she didn't know the way to Darby-in-the-Woods, she was glad that the head groom insisted on accompanying her. Normally, she would have chatted with the groom as they rode, discussing the weather, the crops in the fields they passed, and any unusual plants they happened to see, but she was so worried about her father that she couldn't think about anything else.

The sun was still climbing when they reached the point where the road to the village entered the forest. At first Buttercup seemed to enjoy the cooler air of the forest shade, pricking her ears and looking around with great curiosity, but after a time, she began to act nervous, startling at the smallest sound and snorting when the shade grew deeper. The groom's normally placid horse also seemed uneasy, prancing sideways when a squirrel ran in front of him. Buttercup shied at a dark spot on the road, fighting the reins until Grassina brought her under control.

They reached Darby-in-the-Woods without further incident just as her father and his men were riding out of the village in the opposite direction. Of all of Chartreuse's suitors, only Prince Limelyn had elected to accompany the king. The two royals rode side by side through the strangely quiet village, the single road dividing the cluster of cottages devoid of children, dogs, or geese to challenge a stranger's approach.

Here and there anxious faces peered from doorways, but no one came out to speak to Grassina as she passed by. A silent group of men stood in the shadow of the last cottage watching the king and his knights, turning their attention to Grassina only after Buttercup whinnied to the other horses. One of the villagers, a tall man with long dark hair, stared at Grassina openly without any of the deference commoners usually paid to a princess. He made her feel so uneasy that she urged her horse to a gallop, joining her father in a shower of dust and pebbles.

"Grassina!" he said, turning his horse to face her. "What are you doing here?"

"Looking for you," she replied. "I brought you this." Reaching into her leather sack, she drew out the bottle of tonic and held it up for him to see. "It's for your cough."

"I appreciate your thoughtfulness, but that was neither necessary nor wise. These woods aren't safe if there are werewolves around."

"But you said that werewolves were active only at night."

"That isn't the point. Men from the village are already trying to track them down. Any hunters still out here will be using whatever means they can. It's during times like these that I particularly want you to stay close to the castle. Fear can make people do terrible things.

The king looked around, letting his eyes fall on two of his men. "Stay behind and see that we're not followed. There were no dogs in that village, which probably means that the werewolves have already disposed of them. Werewolves hate dogs because dogs hate werewolves and can find them when no one else can. I would have brought my own if I'd been thinking straight. No matter now. Just keep your eyes and ears open. Some of the villagers may have been turned into werewolves already and would be happy to see where we place our traps. And as for you," he said, looking at his daughter, "you'll have to stay with me now. We'll be returning to the castle as soon as we've dug some . . ." King Aldrid broke off when a deep, wracking cough made him close his eyes and grip his saddle to keep his balance.

Grassina watched with concern until her father's cough subsided. "Please try the tonic," she said, uncorking the bottle and handing it to him.

"Did you make this or did your mother?" he asked, sniffing it suspiciously.

"I did. It should help calm your cough."

"You're a very thoughtful girl," he said before taking a sip from the bottle. "Just like your mother used to be," he added, wiping his mouth with the back of his hand.

No one spoke as they rode into the forest, leaving the village and the two knights behind. They hadn't gone far when a horse whinnied deeper in the woods. The party stopped to wait while Prince Limelyn and three knights rode off to investigate, returning with an armored destrier, its head hanging as it limped across the forest floor. "I think that's Clarence's horse," said Grassina. Even in the shade of the tall trees she could see that the armor of

103

the riderless horse was no longer bright and shiny, but was smudged with something dark.

Slipping off her mare, Grassina ran to the destrier and reached for his bridle where a singed scrap of pale green ribbon still dangled. A smear of black came off on her finger. It was soot. As her father rode up, she raised her hand to show him. Rubbing her thumb and forefinger together, she said in a subdued voice, "I guess there really was a dragon after all."

With the destrier slowing them down, the knights didn't go far before stopping to lay the first trap—just far enough that no one from the village could hear them. While some of the men dug a deep hole, others cut down branches and saplings, whittling the ends to make sharpened stakes. Once King Aldrid declared the hole deep enough, one man was lowered in to line the bottom with the stakes, angling them upward so they'd impale anything that fell in. When he was finished, they rode on to the next likely spot, leaving two more men behind to cover the hole and erase any sign of the trap.

"How do you know where to put them?" Grassina asked her father when they'd stopped once again.

"We dig the traps near the road where a werewolf might lie in wait for an unsuspecting traveler. Werewolves are stronger and faster than either men or wolves. They have the wolves' fangs and a man's intelligence, yet they avoid fair fights whenever possible. For all their nasty, brutish ways, werewolves are basically cowards. They hide from their prey where the wind will carry their scent away, sneaking up when they are sure to take them by surprise. Only stout locks and tall trees will keep them at bay, because they can neither manipulate locks with their paws nor climb higher than they can jump."

Grassina shuddered as she peered into the deeper gloom of the forest. "What should I do if I see a werewolf?"

"Just stay in the castle," said her father. "It's the only place you'll be truly safe, especially if there are dragons around as well."

Nine

$\mathcal{G}$ rassina was still in bed the next morning when a buzzard smelling of its recent meal of rotting muskrat flew in through her window and dropped a note on her. "She was right," said the bird as it landed on the sill. "Although why anyone would be in bed this late in the day is beyond me."

Rolling over, Grassina blinked, then sat up with a start when she saw the filthy bird. The buzzard snickered at the frightened look in her eyes, clacking its beak in irritation when the note fluttered off Grassina and onto the floor.

"Don't just sit there," said the buzzard. "Pick it up and read it! Why do you think I'm here? She said you were slow as well as lazy and that I should lend you a wing if you needed it." Extending a wing covered with dried blood and reeking bits of offal, the bird snickered again when Grassina retreated to the far side of the bed. "She said you'd be prissy. You might as well get the note though. I'm not leaving until you do."

Keeping her distance from the bird, Grassina slipped out from under her covers and knelt on the floor, reaching under the bed for the wayward note. "Good," said the buzzard. "It's officially delivered, so I'm off. I'd read it right away if I were you. You don't have much time since you've already slept away most of the morning."

Grassina glanced out the window as one of the castle's roosters crowed. The sun was just rising over the tops of the trees in the distance, and the first rays had yet to reach the cold stone walls. The buzzard flapped its wings and flew away, shedding a loose feather that drifted onto Grassina's bed. She didn't notice, however, because she was already trying to decipher her mother's handwriting.

Grassina,

Get your lazy rump out of bed and go to your precious swamp. Find enough eggshells from just-hatched blackbirds to fill a washtub and bring them back to me before midnight tonight. If you fail to do this, go straight to the moat and make yourself comfortable, because I'll be turning you into a slimy, loathsome snail.

Signed,
Queen Olivene (your mother)

P.S. Have Cook bring me some rotten grapes, stale bread, and a flagon of brackish water. Yesterday's breakfast was so good I can't wait to taste it again.

"How am I supposed to do that?" Grassina muttered, thinking about the size of the washtubs she'd seen in the kitchen. The task was so daunting that she was tempted to give up before she'd even begun, but she couldn't—not if she didn't want to become a snail for who knew how long.

This time when Grassina sought out a scullery maid, she asked for the smallest washtub. Unfortunately, even the smallest tub was unwieldy when the princess tried to carry it herself. Grassina staggered under its weight as she lifted it with both arms and lugged it out of the castle and across the drawbridge. She had to set it down twice so she could rest before reaching the tree house, groaning each time she picked it up.

Grassina was setting the washtub down once again when she thought about Pippa. It had been days since she had last visited the little snake, but she'd been so busy, she hadn't had a chance. Grassina bit her lip. She hadn't taken Pippa any food in all that time either, and with the queen's magic keeping the snake inside . . .

Something crunched under her feet as Grassina approached the ladder. Broken glass sparkled on the ground, some of it still in the shape of feathers. Worried, Grassina hurried to the ladder and began to climb, almost falling when a rung snapped beneath her foot. She gripped the ladder with white-knuckled hands, her heart racing. After that she tested each rung before putting her weight on it and was relieved when she reached the platform. Her relief gave way to dismay when she saw the cottage. Wasps buzzed through the open window. Branches from the supporting tree had broken, smashing through the roof and some of the platform boards.

"It's like the castle," murmured Grassina. "When Mother changed, she stopped caring about a lot of things. She must have let the maintenance spells lapse." Stepping over the larger debris, she set her hand on the door, which was sagging so badly that she had to give it a hard shove to move it out of her way.

More shards of glass littered the floor inside, and the copper birds were gone. The fire was out in the fireplace, where even the ashes were cold.

"Pippa!" called Grassina. "Are you here?"

At first there was no reply, but then over the creaking of the tree's branches and the angry complaint of the wasps, Grassina heard a faint, almost tentative tapping coming from the wooden trunk in the corner. Skirting a branch that protruded through the ceiling, she reached the trunk and lifted the lid. Hector's eyes were wild when he whinnied to her, but Marniekins looked even worse. Her dress was disheveled, her wool hair a stiff corona around her head. The poor doll was so upset that she couldn't stop wringing her hands.

"Oh, Princess, I'm glad you came!" exclaimed the doll. "There was a big storm and the wind shook our tree and there was crashing and banging and it was just awful!"

"Are you all right?" asked Grassina.

Marniekins nodded until Grassina feared that her head would come off. "We're fine. We stayed in the trunk while your friend told us what was happening. Pippa was so nice! She talked to me after you left and told me about monkeys and bright-colored birds and scary lizards and all sorts of things. But then the storm came and everything changed and she left to get something to eat and never came back."

Grassina frowned, wishing she had come sooner. "I hope she wasn't hurt. She already had an injured tail."

"She told us about that," said Marniekins. "She told us about how she met you, too. Were you really a rabbit?"

"Yes," said Grassina, scooping up the doll and tucking her in her sack. "And I'll be something else if I don't find the eggshells my mother wants. I'm taking you and Hector with me. You can't stay here any longer."

"Where are we going?"

"After I do something for my mother, I'll have to hide you in the castle. Rag dolls and wooden horses don't last long outside in bad weather."

"But didn't you take Pippa out of the castle because it wasn't safe?"

Grassina nodded. "That's true. But this time I don't have any choice."

As the swamp wasn't far from the tree house, Grassina forced herself to carry the washtub without stopping once. She sighed when she finally set it down by a pond.

"This is a beautiful place," Marniekins said, peeking out of Grassina's leather sack. "But what kind of errand would your mother send you on that would bring you here?"

"I have to collect enough blackbird eggshells to fill this tub. If I don't, she'll turn me into a snail and I'll have to live in the moat."

"That's so mean! I saw your mother only a few times, but she didn't seem mean to me."

"Mother wasn't horrid until recently. A curse turned her nasty. Now she orders us around and makes us get her all sorts of strange things."

"And if you don't get them, she turns you into a snail?"

"Not always. She turned me into a turtle yesterday. And when I met Pippa, I was a rabbit, remember?" Grassina sighed. "I don't know how I'll ever find the eggshells, let alone enough to fill this tub, so I'll probably be a snail before the day is out."

A sound like muffled thunder made Grassina look up. An angry-looking cloud was forming over the trees to the north. As it grew, it seemed to writhe and churn, becoming darker and more ominous each moment. With a muffled shriek, Marniekins pulled her head into the sack and tugged it closed behind her.

When Grassina finally realized that the cloud was

111

coming her way, there wasn't time to reach shelter. She was looking up into the heart of the cloud when it started to break apart, raining bits of itself down on her. Crouching low to the ground, she covered her head with her arms, squeezed her eyes shut, and waited for whatever it was to strike. A roaring wind nearly knocked her over, carrying with it a pungent odor. The sound grew so loud, it was deafening, yet Grassina remained untouched. Warily opening her eyes, she was surprised to see blackbirds hurtling past, one after another, slowing long enough to drop something from their beaks into the washtub. Having decided that the birds weren't coming after her, Grassina sat back on her heels to watch the cloud lessen and finally disperse. When the sky was clear once again, she peered into the washtub and was surprised to see that it was filled with bits of broken eggshells.

"The blackbirds brought me the eggshells I needed!" Grassina exclaimed. "I wonder who did this." Turning her head from side to side, she tried to spot her mysterious benefactor. "Those birds wouldn't have done it on their own. It's just like when the toad jumped in the basket. Someone with magic must be doing this. A fairy perhaps . . . Maybe even the swamp fairy. Hello! Whoever you are—thank you for your help!"

When no one appeared, Grassina picked up the tub, staggering under its even greater weight. The way back seemed longer than the trip out had been, and she had to set the tub down five or six times before she had the castle in sight. Whatever magic had made the birds bring her their shells hadn't made the tub or its contents any lighter.

Grassina had passed the practice field and could smell the fetid water of the moat when she heard a woman screaming. An anguished, wavering cry of loss and despair, the sound would have made her turn and run if it hadn't been coming from the castle. Dropping the washtub with a loud thump, she ran toward the drawbridge. Her first thought was that the werewolves had somehow gotten past the defenses, but she couldn't understand how it could have happened. The moat completely encircled the castle, and the drawbridge was always well guarded. Only something with wings could have gotten over the castle walls, and even then . . .

A piercing shriek made Grassina stumble and nearly fall. The sound dissolved into a wordless wail that clutched at her heart and brought involuntary tears to her eyes. She looked up when a woman wearing a long, white gown drifted through a tower window, wailing and tearing at her streaming white hair. The woman swooped low enough that Grassina could see her bloodred eyes and gaunt features. "Woe is me!" the woman wailed. "Death and destruction shall visit this castle before the day is out!"

As the woman flew off, heading north toward the

enchanted forest, a feeling of absolute desolation swept over Grassina, leaving her feeling lonely and bereft. The guards on the battlements, the farmers delivering chickens, and the pages chucking stones into the moat were frozen in place as if the wail had the same power to render them as immobile as the frigid north wind.

When the cries of the woman had faded away, Grassina was once again able to move, although with a dragging step and a heart that ached with unnamed sorrow. The faces of the guards stationed by the drawbridge were pale, their expressions stricken. Grassina tried not to look at them too long, knowing that their faces mirrored her own and only made her sorrow harder to bear.

Her feet seemed to move of their own volition, carrying her across the open courtyard into the castle, where the sound of crying seemed natural after the heartrending wail. She found Chartreuse huddled on a bench in the Great Hall, sobbing. Prince Limelyn was sitting beside her holding her hand while Torrance sat on the other side with his arm around her shoulder. The other princes stood at the far end of the table, looking uncomfortable.

Prince Limelyn jumped to his feet when he saw Grassina, relinquishing his seat for her. "What happened?" she asked, putting her arms around her sister.

"The banshee...," Chartreuse cried. "She flew through the castle, screaming and tearing out her hair and

114

frightening everyone and saying that ... that ... Oh, Grassina, it's too awful! Father is going to die today!"

"I don't believe it, unless ..." Grassina narrowed her eyes in suspicion. "Did the banshee do something to Father?"

Chartreuse shook her head, making her honey gold curls fly. "I don't think she went near him, but then, she wouldn't have to. She's a banshee! They always know when someone is going to die."

"Have you gone to see Father? I hope he didn't hear this nonsense. Nobody in this castle is going to die today!"

"I told you ... banshees know these things."

"Well, this time she's wrong," said Grassina, helping her sister to her feet. "Now stop crying. We'll go visit Father and you'll see that he's all right."

Nearly a dozen people stopped them in the hall as they headed to the door at the top of the dungeon stairs, and they all wanted to offer their condolences. "We're so sorry to hear about your father," some said.

"He was the best king we've ever had," said others.

"Our father is fine," Grassina said each time while Chartreuse cried harder.

Chartreuse was sobbing loudly again when they closed the dungeon door behind them and started down the stairs, but even she noticed that the shadows seemed to draw closer the louder she cried. It frightened her enough that she straightened her shoulders, gave a few last shuddering sobs, and wiped her eyes with the tips of her fingers.

The sisters had almost reached their father's room when Olivene popped through the doorway and glared at them. "Where do you think you're going?" snapped the queen.

"To see Father," said Grassina. "We wanted to make sure he was all right."

"Well, he's not," Olivene said, so angry that her voice shook. "Fine daughters you are, coming to see him only after he's dead."

Grassina shook her head. "No, you're wrong. Father can't be dead. I saw him yesterday. He said he had a cold."

"He's deader than a doornail and there's nothing you can do about it, so go away and leave us alone."

"Father is dead!" wailed Chartreuse. "The banshee was right! I told you, Grassina, but you wouldn't listen!"

Grassina was too stunned to reply. She felt as if the floor of the dungeon had dropped out from under her and she was falling into an abyss. Her father was gone. The only person who understood her, the only person who she knew really loved her, was gone. "Can we see him?" she whispered, her throat feeling tight and prickly.

"No, you can't see him. I was saying my good-byes, so go away! I wasn't finished."

While the girls watched, stunned, Olivene scuttled back into the room and slammed the door. Tears trickled

116

down Grassina's cheeks as she took her older sister's hand in hers. "We'll come back later, after she's finished saying good-bye."

Something made of glass hit the door on the other side, shattering. "You're a no-good, rotten liar!" screamed the queen.

Chartreuse nodded. "Maybe she'll go upstairs soon."

There was a thud, and the door shook. "How dare you leave me?" screamed Olivene. "I was supposed to go first! It wasn't supposed to be like this."

Chartreuse glanced back at the door as her sister led her away. "Mother doesn't grieve like everyone else," said Grassina.

"I know," said Chartreuse. "But then, Mother doesn't do anything like anyone else."

Once upstairs, Chartreuse left Grassina, saying that she wanted to be alone. Grassina felt numb and empty as she slipped away to her chamber. The loss of her mother to the family curse had been a blow, but nothing like this. At least then the girls had still had one normal parent who cared about them. Now all they had was their mother, a horrible person who cared only for herself.

Grassina stayed in her room until late afternoon, when she heard a commotion outside. Wiping the tears from her eyes, she took a shuddering breath and went to

117

her window. Chartreuse and Prince Pietro were walking toward a crowd gathered around a man who was waving his arms and gesturing. When he turned his head to look at the castle, Grassina saw that it was her father's game-keeper, Milo Blum, a normally quiet and sedate man.

After splashing cold water on her face, Grassina hurried down the stairs. Chartreuse was already there talking to Milo when she arrived. Prince Pietro was lingering only a short distance away, looking irritated.

"I went to see for myself," said Milo. "The stream is poisoned. A Vila probably did it, just like the one in Upper Montevista three years ago."

"Isn't there anything you can do about it?" asked Chartreuse.

Milo Blum shook his head. "I don't know. We've never had a Vila in Greater Greensward before. I don't even know what to look for or how to track her."

"What is a Vila?" asked Grassina, stepping through the crowd.

"I've heard she looks like an incredibly beautiful young woman dressed in white. She lives in the woods and protects the animals. They say that Vili don't like hunters and poison the streams they drink from to keep them from coming back. What with the werewolves . . . and now the Vila . . . no one wants to go into the forest anymore. I told Cook that's why I won't be bringing her fresh meat for tonight's supper."

Chartreuse silenced him with another wave of her hand. "Thank you for telling us. Please keep us informed of anything else you hear. That will be all for now."

"Yes, Your Majesty," Milo said, bowing to her as if she were the queen. It struck Grassina that Chartreuse was more of a queen than their mother, at least the way their mother was now.

"So what should we do?" Grassina asked her sister as they crossed the courtyard together. "Do you think we should assemble the knights and ask for volunteers to find the Vila?"

"No," said Chartreuse. "The Green Witch has protected this kingdom for hundreds of years, but Mother doesn't care what happens to Greater Greensward now. I'm sure Father could have handled it, if he were still . . ." When her eyes started to well with tears, Chartreuse took a deep breath and blinked furiously for a moment. After clearing her throat, she added, "I may not be the Green Witch yet, but I will be someday, so I guess this is going to be up to me."

"What can you do?" asked Grassina. "You're only fifteen and don't have a speck of magic."

Chartreuse lifted her chin. "I'm going to have magic," she said, sounding defiant. "It just hasn't shown itself yet. Maybe this is what it will take to get it started. I'll go down to Mother's workroom and look through her books. I'm sure she'll have some kind of spell I can use."

"Do you really think she'll let you look at them?"

"I wasn't going to ask her! I'll just slip in when she comes up from the dungeon. Leave it to me," said Chartreuse. "I know what I'm doing."

"Then I'm going with you," said Grassina. "Two pairs of eyes are better than one."

❦

Hiding in the shelter of a nearby alcove, the girls watched the door to the dungeon stairs until their mother came into view. When she disappeared down the corridor, they slipped through the door and headed to her workroom.

"I want to see Father first," said Grassina, continuing down the hall past their mother's room.

Chartreuse stopped. "We may not have much time."

"We have time for this," Grassina said, placing her hand on their father's door. Although it felt like rough-hewn wood, the door was as unyielding as the stone around it. "It won't open," she said, pushing against it with both hands.

"Mother probably put a spell on it," said Chartreuse. "I hope she hasn't locked her workroom, too."

When their mother's workroom door opened easily, Chartreuse and Grassina slipped inside. A pallid pair of witches' lights glowed in the corner, bobbing against the ceiling like corks on a fishing line. They gave off a bluish light that made everything stand out in sharp relief, showing every line and freckle on the girls' faces.

While Chartreuse looked for the books, Grassina circled the room, examining everything that she hadn't dared approach when her mother was present. Dust-choked spiderwebs hung like lacework from the ceiling, swaying in a faint current of air. The skull of a griffin was mounted on the wall, its eyes still intact. When Grassina walked past it, she could have sworn the skull's gaze moved with her.

She had just found the basket containing the lightning bugs when something brushed against her ankles. Startled, Grassina looked down. Chartreuse's kitten was rubbing against her leg, purring so hard that its little body vibrated. "What's he doing here?" Grassina asked. "Did he follow us down the stairs?"

Chartreuse glanced at the kitten, then turned away. "I gave him to Mother. He wasn't nearly as sweet when I got to know him. I thought he and Mother would suit each other very well. They're both mean and self-centered. She's already named him Herald. Oh, good. Here they are!" said Chartreuse, standing in front of the only table in the room. A small stack of books was lying on it beside a tankard filled with a thick green liquid smelling strongly of week-old fish. "There aren't very many. I always thought she had more than this. That's good, I guess.

It won't take long to look through them. Listen, this spell is for . . ." Chartreuse had flipped to the front page and was reading the very first words when the book flew up into the air, closed itself, slapped her hands, and landed on the table. "Did you see that?" she asked with a squeak in her voice.

"Maybe you did something wrong," said Grassina. "Try another book."

Chartreuse gingerly opened the next book. "This one seems all right. It says . . ." This time when she began reading, the book flew up, fanned its pages in her face, pinched her nose, and fell back to the table, closed once again.

"I don't think they want you to read them," said Grassina.

"I don't believe this!" said Chartreuse, rubbing her nose. "No stupid book is going to do that to me!" This time the book struggled when she picked it up, but she held on tight with both hands and forced the book open. With an angry shriek, the book shouted, "Robber! Scoundrel! Set me down, you no-good book thief!" and wiggled out of her grasp. Once free, the book began to hit her until she backed away, waving her hands to fend it off.

"What's going on in here?" demanded a voice by the door. Both girls turned to face their mother, their eyes wide in dismay. Chartreuse flinched when the book gave her another solid whack.

"Were you fiddling around with my books?" demanded Queen Olivene.

"Me? No, of course not!" protested Chartreuse. "I wouldn't touch anything of yours."

"Liar!" shouted the book.

"Liar! Liar!" echoed the rest of the books on the table.

"You lied! You know what I do to liars, don't you?" Olivene asked with a malicious gleam in her eyes.

Chartreuse backed away from the table. "I wouldn't touch your crummy books! They probably wouldn't have what I need anyway."

"Hypocrite!" screamed all the books at once as they rose up and began to flap their pages at her.

Olivene chortled gleefully, rubbing her hands as her older daughter tried to dodge the books. Horrified, Grassina looked around for something she could use to stop their assault. Her eyes settled on the basket of lightning bugs, agitated now by all the noise. Although the sound coming from the basket had been little more than a soft hum when the girls first entered the room, it had risen in volume until it was almost as loud as the books, and sparks were shooting out of the holes in the weave.

"Mother, make them stop!" screamed Chartreuse as the books continued to assail her.

"It's your own fault," Olivene shouted over the din. "You're getting exactly what you deserve!"

"Then I'll stop it," Grassina said under her breath as

she kicked the lightning-bug basket as hard as she could. The basket careened into the wall, splintering the brittle wicker and freeing all the bugs. Suddenly, they were everywhere—crawling, flying, skittering, hopping, and inching their way across the room. Although Grassina ducked away from the flying insects, they flew past her in a swarm that twinkled like stars, knocking over bottles, books, and anything else that stood between them and the queen.

Olivene screamed when the first wave hit, shocking her with their wings, their legs, their bodies. She started hopping around on one foot, then the other as the crawling bugs reached her. Grabbing her sister's hand, Grassina pulled her out of the room and into the corridor where the girls threw their arms around each other, laughing.

"I'm not going back down there!" Chartreuse cried later that night. "It's a horrible place. I don't ever want to set foot in there again."

Grassina patted her sister's arm. "It's all right. I'll go by myself. I want to see if the door to Father's room is still locked. We'll have to arrange for his funeral tomorrow, but I wanted to see him first."

Chartreuse glared at her sister. "If you're trying to make me feel guilty, it's not going to work. I loved him, too, you know."

"I'm not *trying* to do anything. Mother went out, so I came to see if you wanted to go with me. Since you don't . . ." Grassina shrugged. She didn't really want to go by herself, but she would if it was the only way.

Chartreuse sputtered. "You're going down there? By yourself? At *night*? That's the stupidest thing I've ever heard!"

Grassina slipped off the edge of her sister's bed and

started for the door. "I'm sorry I woke you. I didn't want to wait any longer to see him, and I thought you'd want to go, too. Go back to sleep and I'll see you in the—"

Throwing back the covers, Chartreuse shot Grassina a nasty look. "Oh, stop being the martyr. You know I can't let you go by yourself. I'd never forgive myself if something happened to you, too. Just give me a few minutes to get dressed and we'll go to the lousy dungeon. I must be crazy to do this," she muttered, reaching for her tunic. "That is the absolute last place I want to go at night."

"I don't understand why," said Grassina. "There's nothing down there that can hurt us."

"Oh yes, there is," said Chartreuse. "Mother!"

Although it was always dark in the dungeon, it seemed even darker at night. There were only a few small windows to let in a breath of air, and none where the girls were going, yet the dungeon *felt* different than it did during the day. A sense of silent waiting pervaded the air as if the dungeon knew that something was about to happen. As neither of the girls wanted to see what that something might be, they hurried down the corridor, slowing to a quiet tiptoe only when they passed the door to their mother's workroom.

This time when they tried their father's door, it wasn't locked. The girls slowly pushed the door open, and

Grassina held up the torch she'd carried with her. Except for broken furniture and torn bits of parchment littering the floor, the room was empty.

"Where's Father?" said Grassina, peering into the corners.

"You think I keep dead bodies around here, cluttering up the place, just so people can come and gawk?" said their mother from the doorway.

Grassina turned slowly to face her. "I thought you'd gone out."

Olivene chortled. "Obviously—or else you wouldn't be here. Well, I'm here and he's not. I had him buried hours ago."

"Without letting us say good-bye?" cried Chartreuse.

"I said good-bye for you. And now I'm saying good-bye *to* you. Good-bye. Go away. I want my peace and quiet."

The girls slunk out of the room under their mother's gaze. They hadn't gone far when they stepped into the fog. It had grown since Grassina had seen it last, and it smelled even worse than before.

"What is that stench?" asked Chartreuse, wrinkling her nose.

"I think it's magic Mother released from the walls. At least I saw it coming out of the wall earlier, and I saw a spell for releasing magic in Mother's workroom."

"You saw a spell for releasing magic and didn't tell me?

Don't you see, that might work on me!" In her excitement, Chartreuse turned around and was about to go back when Grassina stopped her.

"What are you going to do, ask Mother for the book?" said Grassina.

Chartreuse shuddered. "You're right. Never mind. It probably wouldn't work on a person anyway. And if it did, it probably wouldn't do me any good, not if it was one of Mother's spells." She stopped talking to peer into the darkness that seemed to move just beyond the light of the torch. "What is that? Is someone there?"

Grassina looked in the direction her sister was pointing. "It's probably this fog. It makes things look different."

"Maybe so, but it looks so real, almost as if—"

"I may not know a lot about courtly manners, but it seems to me that pointing is rude," said a wavering voice. "Who do you think you are, chit, pointing at me that way?"

"Now Hubert," said a younger and steadier voice, "I'm sure the girl didn't mean any harm by it."

"Who are *you*?" demanded Chartreuse, looking at the two approaching figures. "Are you blind that you can't see to whom you're speaking? I'm Princess Chartreuse and this is my sister, Princess Grassina. I expect, no, I demand an apology this . . ."

Chartreuse's voice faded away as Hubert and his companion drew closer. It wasn't so much the way the old, stooped figure in the tattered tunic and his younger, well-dressed companion walked that drew her eye as the way they weren't walking at all. Both men appeared to be floating a few feet above the ground, which was convenient since neither one seemed to have any legs below their knees. The rest of their bodies began to materialize as she watched, open-mouthed, although they remained slightly transparent.

"Are you . . . Can you be . . . Is it possible . . . ," stammered Chartreuse.

"They must be ghosts," Grassina whispered in her sister's ear.

"Ghosts?" Chartreuse said, the word ending in a squeak.

"Pardon me, Your Highness," said the younger figure. "I'm Sir Jarvis, and this is my friend Hubert. At your service." With a polished gesture, the ghost whipped off his pointed cap and bowed deeply. Chartreuse gasped when his head fell off and rolled across the floor.

The head came to a stop faceup, but its lips had collected dirt as it rolled. "Pleh! Pleh!" Sir Jarvis spit, then rubbed his lips together and said, "I'm so sorry, Your Highness. There are still times I forget that I'm not all one piece."

Chartreuse's voice reached a higher octave when the headless body began patting the ground with its right hand. She swayed when its right arm dropped off.

"Don't lose your head, Jarvis," said Hubert. The hand

on Sir Jarvis's unattached arm was still patting the ground when Hubert picked up the head and set it back on his friend's neck.

"Ah, there we are," Sir Jarvis said, reaching with his remaining arm for the one on the floor. "It's been more than two hundred years since I was drawn and quartered, but one tends to forget such things."

Chartreuse swayed once and collapsed, lying sprawled on the cold stone floor.

Sir Jarvis was still talking when he shoved his arm bone into the socket. "I apologize for . . . Oh dear, I believe the young lady has fainted."

Grassina dropped to her knees. "Chartreuse! Are you all right?"

"I think we should go," Sir Jarvis told Hubert. "There's nothing we can do, and no one wants to be in such an embarrassing position around strangers."

"She must be weak in the head," said Hubert, "fainting that way and all."

"Quite possibly," said Sir Jarvis as the ghosts faded away. "Too much inbreeding in the royal lines, you know."

"Chartreuse!" said Grassina, shaking her. "Wake up! You can't stay here." When her sister didn't respond, she slapped her once on each cheek.

Chartreuse opened her eyes. "What are you doing? What happened?"

"You fainted. If you stand up, we'll . . ."

"Don't make up stories, Grassina." Chartreuse pushed herself up with her elbows. "I've never fainted in my life. I'm not one of those weak-kneed Nellies who can't . . . What is *that*?"

The fog had moved on, but something else was coming their way. A shape even darker than the deepest shadows was drifting toward them out of the gloom. About the size of a calf, it had glittering red eyes that glared malevolently at them. Chartreuse scrambled to her feet, clutching Grassina's hand for support. "Let's go, Grassina. Let's get out of here."

"I'd love to, except we have to go that way to get to the stairs," Grassina replied, gesturing toward the corridor past the shadow beast.

Grassina could feel her sister's hand tremble as they backed away. She suddenly had the urge to protect her, a feeling so unfamiliar that she surprised herself, but Chartreuse was her last living relative, or at least the last one who felt like family. As Chartreuse took another step back, the red eyes swung in her direction.

"Don't move, Chartreuse," said Grassina, but it was too late. The shadow beast was charging straight at her older sister.

"Oh no, you don't," shouted Grassina. Pulling back her fist, she stepped in front of Chartreuse and punched the shadow squarely between its glowing red eyes. With an anguished howl, the shadow beast stopped in its tracks, turned tail, and ran the other way.

"Thank goodness," said Chartreuse, her voice sounding as unsteady as she looked. Tidying her hair with one hand, she took the torch from Grassina and started for the stairs, going faster when she heard the tap of her own footsteps. Grassina was right behind her when she reached the top. As the dungeon door closed behind them, Grassina started to say good night, but Chartreuse didn't give her the chance.

"Don't you dare say a word. For once I want you to listen to what I have to say. I told you I didn't want to go down there, but you insisted. We had to go see Father, who wasn't even there. And you said that Mother was gone, except she wasn't! And then you stood there like a stick when . . . when something tried to frighten me to death, and then there was that *monster*! Were you trying to get me killed? That was it, wasn't it? You've always been jealous of me. You spoiled my lessons so my magic wouldn't start and laughed at me when I tried to learn in spite of you. You hate me so much that you want to see me dead. I think you want to see all of us dead. I bet you were happy that Father died. I bet those tears were all a pretense. You're just as bad as Mother. You don't even need a curse to turn you into a horrible person. You were born that way. Do us both a favor and stay away from me. I don't ever want to hear you or any of your ideas again. I wish you weren't my sister. I wish you'd never been born!"

Grassina was stunned. She knew that encountering the ghosts and the shadow beast had rattled Chartreuse, but even that wouldn't account for all the horrible things she'd said. Grassina watched, gasping for air as Chartreuse whirled around and strode down the hall.

Eleven

*G*rassina didn't sleep at all that night, although she tried for the first few hours. After that, she wrapped herself in her blanket and curled up on the window ledge to gaze at the night sky. She didn't know what to do. The life she'd always known was over; nothing would ever be the same again now that her father was gone. Chartreuse would probably become queen soon since she wanted it so much and their mother obviously didn't care. Because Chartreuse seemed to blame Grassina for everything bad that had ever happened, Grassina was sure that one of Chartreuse's first acts as queen of Greater Greensward would be to banish her younger sister. And if she didn't banish Grassina, she'd probably see her married off to one of the least desirable suitors. Perhaps it would be the one who hadn't bathed since the day he was born. Then again, if Chartreuse didn't marry her off, she might keep her at the castle as some sort of slave to appease Olivene, making Grassina do all the nasty chores for their mother. As far as Grassina could see, her future at the castle would be awful no matter what Chartreuse decided.

As the first rays of sunlight turned the night sky from black to gray, Grassina collected a change of clothes and all of her throwing stones, wrapping them in a blanket. Loaded down with this bundle, she was the first person to cross the drawbridge that morning.

Grassina went as far as the edge of the practice field before glancing back at the castle one last time. The sight of the mist-shrouded moat, the pennants floating from the tops of the turrets, and the silvery stone of the castle fortifications almost made her want to cry. "No more of that," Grassina muttered to herself, rubbing her eyes with her free hand. She'd cried enough over the last few days to last her a lifetime and was afraid that if she got started again, she might not be able to stop.

Hurrying past the practice field, she tried not to think about the last time she'd seen her father there, talking and laughing with his men. She ducked her head, refusing to look at the tree house. After bringing Marniekins and Hector back to the castle, she'd left them in a special hiding place in the buttery. She knew it was foolish, but she regretted that she hadn't taken the time to say good-bye. It almost felt as if she'd deserted old friends. And then there was Pippa, a new friend who must think she'd been abandoned, too.

"Pippa!" Grassina called as she passed under the ruined tree house. "Pippa, where are you?"

After pausing for a reply and hearing nothing but silence, Grassina shifted her bundle in her arms and continued walking. Pippa may not have stayed around the tree house, but she still might not have gone far. Calling the little snake's name, Grassina followed her usual route to the swamp, looking for Pippa the entire time.

She was still calling to the snake when she reached the last of the trees that grew at the edge of the swamp. Suddenly, something fell off a branch and landed on her shoulder. Grassina shrieked and dropped her bundle, then began slapping at herself with both hands.

"Hey!" Pippa said, squirming under the neckline of Grassina's tunic to avoid being slapped. "What'ss wrong with you?"

"Help! I . . . Oh, it's you. Why did you do that? You nearly frightened me to death!"

"Ssorry," said Pippa, "except it wass your fault. You kept calling me! I wanted to sstay away from you. After all the bad thingss my luck hass done, I thought you'd be better off without me. But you're my only friend, and when you kept shouting my name, I decided that you musst really need me for ssomething. Iss everything all right?"

Grassina took a deep, shuddering breath, ready to tell the little snake about her father's death and her sister's cruel words, but she found she didn't want to talk about it,

136

at least not yet. Instead she let her eyes wander from the blue sky that seemed to go on forever, to the light reflecting off the water half hidden by cattails, to the bees humming around a patch of wildflowers, and she realized that she felt better than she had in days. Her stomach had been in knots from the last time she spoke with her sister, but now that she had reached the swamp, she was finally able to relax.

"It's been awful, but I think it's about to get a lot better," Grassina told the little snake. After all, she had a friend, a place to go, and the beginning of a plan. She didn't expect the Swamp Fairy to be easy to find. If she hadn't shown herself yet, she wasn't likely to just because it was what Grassina wanted. Even so, Grassina knew exactly what to do. She'd make herself a shelter deep in the swamp at the end of one of the more difficult-to-find paths, somewhere safe where nasty relatives would never find her should they ever think to come looking. She would go out during the day and look for the Swamp Fairy, who was bound to want to meet her face-to-face eventually. Grassina wasn't sure what she would do then, but at least she could thank the only person who'd helped her. In the meantime, there would be plenty to eat, at least for the rest of the summer, and she was sure she'd meet the fairy before the weather grew cold.

Although she doubted that anyone would care enough to try to find her, Grassina planned to hide her trail by stepping on rocks and avoiding the softer mud. Taking the less obvious routes, she could go places that only she knew existed.

"I'm going to live in the swamp for a while. Things have gotten worse at the castle and I have to get away," said Grassina.

"It got worsse when I wassn't even there? Maybe my bad luck rubbed off on you!"

Grassina sighed. "I don't think you have bad luck. If anything, I think your luck is good, at least for you. When that monster broke into the witch's cottage and wrecked everything, he set you free, didn't he?"

"Yess, and sstepped on my tail!"

"Which wasn't bad enough to kill you. Think about what would have happened if he'd stepped on your head!"

"That'ss true," said Pippa. "But what about your little housse in the tree?"

"It was ruined, which was lucky for you when you think about it. I hadn't brought you any food; if the tree hadn't broken the cottage roof, you couldn't have gotten out and found something to eat."

"I never thought of it that way!"

"That's what I mean. It's all a matter of how you look at it. So I don't want to hear any more about your bad luck," Grassina said as she set her feet just so, to avoid the sucking mud.

"All right," Pippa said. "But I have sso many other

thingss I want to tell you. Even though I've been frightfully cold, I've learned a lot during the lasst few dayss. Did you know that dollss can live in trunkss and don't need to breathe?"

"Most of them don't talk either," muttered Grassina.

"What did you ssay?"

"Nothing. What else have you learned?"

"That thosse metal birdss couldn't ssay anything but nonssensse. I don't think they have any real thoughtss in their headss. Mice aren't too bright either. They go the ssame placess time after time, which makess them eassy to catch."

"I'm sure it does," said Grassina.

"And the hairy humanss who run on all fourss are much fasster than the oness who aren't hairy and run on two feet."

Grassina stopped walking. "Hairy humans? Do you mean werewolves? Have you seen any around here?"

"A few. They were on their way to your casstle. They came back talking about the guardss and the fori . . . forfif . . . the moat and wallss and sstuff."

Grassina nodded. "You mean the fortifications. They're the things that keep the castle safe. Have you seen any hairy humans today?" she asked, glancing behind her.

"I never ssee them when the ssun iss out. Do you think they could be related to owlss? Owlss come out at night, too."

"I'm sure there's no connection," said Grassina. "Please do me a favor. Tell me if you see any sign of those hairy humans. I'd like to know where they are and what they're doing."

"Ssure," said Pippa, "although I don't know why anyone would want to talk to them."

While the little snake kept watch for the hairy humans, Grassina followed the secret pathways that only she knew, zigzagging where the hidden path required it, jumping across patches of quickmud to another path when the first arrived at a dead end. She thought she smelled smoke, but the wind changed direction, carrying the odor away before she could locate its source. The possibility of dragons in the area made her walk faster, yet it still took her most of the morning to reach the heart of the swamp.

Grassina knew exactly where she would build her cozy little home. An island about a quarter the size of the Great Hall supported a spring and a scattering of wild plum trees. With its own moat of quicksand and open water surrounding it and a thick screen of trees and brush concealing it, the island was almost impossible to find let alone reach unless one knew exactly where to look. Grassina had visited it many times and was familiar with every tree and rock.

To her surprise, when she arrived at the island the little grove of plum trees was occupied. A makeshift lean-to stood between two of the larger trees. Only a short distance away, a pile of kindling and a still-smoldering log marked a fire pit ringed with stones. Draped over the branch of one of the plum trees, a ragged tunic and a pair of breeches dripped water onto the trampled grass, evidence that someone had been washing laundry. Even so, one quick glance around the tiny island showed her that no one was home.

"Now what will I do?" Grassina murmured.

"Iss *that* where you're going to live?" asked Pippa. "It doessn't look very warm."

"That lean-to isn't mine," said Grassina. "I don't know who made it. It wasn't here the last time I came this way."

She considered turning around and going in search of another likely spot, but her feet refused to obey. Her whole plan had been centered on this island, and to find that living there was no longer an option was almost more than she could bear. Shouldering her bundle, Grassina crossed onto the island and began to look around, wondering who had taken over her secret hiding spot.

The campsite held little of a personal nature. An old wooden trencher and a small iron pot rested on the ground beside the fire pit. Inside the lean-to she found a simple pair of leather shoes in good condition and a neatly folded blanket, clean, sweet smelling, and serviceable despite the patches that seemed to hold it together. She didn't think there was anything else to find until she picked up the blanket and saw that it had been concealing a slim wooden chest. With water marks discoloring the wood and deep grooves and scratches in its top and sides, the chest looked like it might have come from a trash heap, but there was something about it that intrigued her.

Pippa flicked her tongue at the chest. "What'ss that? Iss there a doll like Marniekinss inside? Hello there!" she called, sliding down Grassina's arm so that she was closer to the wooden chest. "Can you hear me?"

"Pippa, not so loud! I don't think a doll would fit in there. Just a minute and I'll see if I can open it." Grassina knelt beside the chest and tried to lift the lid. It stayed shut as stubbornly as if it had been made of one piece.

"That'ss not going to work," said Pippa. "Maybe if you bit it, or hit it with a sstick . . ."

"I think I know a better way," said Grassina.

Determined to know what the interloper on her island might be hiding, Grassina inserted a slim, pointed stick in the tiny gap between the lid and the base, and attempted to pry it open. Aside from jamming her thumbnail, nothing happened, however, so she took the chest in both hands and was shaking it when an angry voice behind her said, "What do you think you're doing?"

Startled, Grassina stood, bumping her head on one of the posts that supported the lean-to. The lean-to tottered and swayed. A strong arm reached out and pulled her to safety just before the shelter fell with a crash. While

Grassina staggered and tried not to fall, Pippa slipped under the neckline of her tunic.

"Ow! What are you doing? Oh . . . my . . . ," said Grassina, glancing from the scowling boy who had saved her to the jumbled branches that had formed the lean-to moments before. "I'm sorry. I didn't mean to . . ."

The boy let go of her arm and stepped back. "To what? Destroy the only shelter I have or snoop around in my personal possessions?"

"Both. Neither. I mean . . ." Grassina bit her lip. "Wait a minute. I'm not the one in the wrong. You shouldn't even be here. Who are you, anyway?"

"That's not the point," said the boy. "Hey, give me that!" Snatching the dilapidated chest from her hand, he inspected it as carefully as if it were his most precious treasure. Grassina decided that, from the way he was dressed, it probably was. The oversized tunic he wore came down past his knees. His feet were bare like an urchin's and his sandy brown hair was long and uneven, as if he'd trimmed it himself. He was taller than Grassina, although not by much, and she might have been afraid if he hadn't had such an open, honest face and warm brown eyes that would have looked friendly if he weren't so angry.

"Why are you here?" asked the boy, looking up from the chest to glare at her. "You weren't supposed to come anywhere near . . ." His voice trailed off as if he'd said something wrong, leaving Grassina wondering what it might have been. "I mean, no one was supposed to come here. This is my home, and I want to be alone."

"You can't make me leave! I have more right to be here than you do. I'm . . ." It occurred to Grassina that it might not be a good idea to tell this stranger exactly who she was. Although some people might respect her royal status, others might try to use it to their advantage. He didn't look like a bad person, but looks could be deceiving, as her old nurse used to say. Grassina didn't know anything about this boy—who he was, where he came from, and certainly not what his intentions might be should he hear the truth about her.

"You're what?" asked the boy.

"Not leaving, that's all. I spend more time in this swamp than anybody else. What makes you think you can show up all of a sudden and lay claim to it?"

"I'm not claiming the whole swamp, just this island. And I didn't just show up. I've been here for a while."

"Then how come I haven't seen you before?"

The boy shrugged. "I guess you haven't gone to the right places. It doesn't matter though. I built my home here, so this island is mine. You can just—"

"If that's all it takes to claim it, I'm going to build my cottage here, too. It will be a lot better than that thing you had. Your *home* was all crooked and wobbly . . ."

"It was a perfectly good lean-to!" said the boy, sounding indignant.

144

"It was more of a lean-from, if you ask me!" said Grassina. "I hardly bumped the thing and it fell over."

"Ha!" said the boy. "I doubt you could build anything, let alone a cottage."

"We'll see about that!" said Grassina.

"Fine!" said the boy. "Tell me when you're finished. I could use a good laugh!"

Grassina turned her back on the boy so fast that the end of her braid whipped around and stung her cheek. She was careful not to look his way as she studied the ground, trying to decide where to build her cottage. Finding a level spot, she cleared away the debris and left the island in search of long, straight branches.

Although she'd envisioned the cottage as roomy and large enough to walk around in, she began to think that might not be practical if she was going to build it all by herself. Without an ax or saw, she'd have to take whatever windfall she could find, which wouldn't leave her much to work with. She found a few branches that might suffice, although they weren't nearly as long as she'd hoped.

Grassina was about to start back to the island when Pippa said, "I'll sstay here for a while. I don't want that boy to ssee me."

"I wouldn't let him hurt you, if that's what you're worried about," said Grassina.

"It'ss not that. I don't like meeting new people. You're nicer than mosst sstrangerss. The old witch wouldn't

145

come near me without a forked sstick in her hand. She alwayss looked like she wass afraid I might bite her."

"Would you?"

"Only if I had to, but that'ss besside the point. I think it'ss better if I keep to mysself while you're around him."

Grassina shrugged. "If that's what you want."

"What I want is a nice fat mousse," said Pippa. "But that'ss ssomething elsse I'll have to do on my own."

Thinking about building a shelter was a lot easier than actually building one. It took Grassina a number of botched attempts before she finally found a method that would work. After carefully placing the branches where she wanted them, she lashed them together with willow wands, propping them up again each time they fell down. It was frustrating work, made all the worse because she knew the boy would be watching. When she had the branches angled well enough that they could stand on their own, she covered them with twigs and stuffed the spaces with mud and grass.

Pippa returned shortly before the shelter was finished. "It lookss like an upside-down bird'ss nesst."

Grassina shrugged. "Maybe, but I'm too tired to care."

"What'ss that noisse?" asked Pippa.

Rubbing her growling stomach, Grassina said, "I'm hungry, that's all. I haven't eaten all day." She glanced at the boy, wondering if he was watching her, but he was still reinforcing the lean-to he'd rebuilt and didn't seem to notice her.

"Sso, are you going to call that boy over to ssee what you did?" asked Pippa. "I'll wait in the grasss if you are. You sure showed him, making thiss housse and all. It'ss sso much better than that thing he built."

"Not really," said Grassina. "It isn't at all what I wanted to make. It's not a cottage. It isn't even big enough to call a hovel."

"That'ss all right. You don't have to show him anything. We don't want to look like we're bragging."

The sun was setting, and with the advent of nightfall came a cool breeze and the scent of rain. Grassina shivered and slipped into her cottage on her hands and knees, avoiding the still-wet mud in the walls. She was cold, her skin felt grimy, and her stomach ached with hunger. It was hard not to think about all that she'd given up—hot food, a roof over her head, clean, dry clothes, and the safety of solid stone walls. While Grassina pried a small rock out of the ground so it wouldn't dig into her side when she lay down, Pippa investigated the little bit of floor space, then slithered up the wall and disappeared among the branches.

Grassina's tiny cottage creaked as the wind picked up, finding its way through the holes she'd missed. Wrapping herself in her blanket, she huddled in the center of her shelter, yawning so hard she could hear her jaw creak. A larger gust shook her shelter, and Pippa dropped out of the ceiling. Gathering the little snake to her, Grassina curled around her friend, trying to warm her. When the wind died down for a minute, she thought she heard the boy talking, but then the rain began and the gentle tapping lulled Grassina into an exhausted sleep. Even after the rain became a steady downpour, she did little more than pull her blanket over her head and continue sleeping. As the rain grew heavier, globs of mud washed through the chinks in the walls and ceiling. *Plip! Plip!* Cold mud dripped on her blanket, trickling down her hunched figure and turning the blanket into a sodden weight.

"You might want to get out of there before this thing collapses," the boy said from the doorway, but Grassina was sleeping too deeply to hear him.

She didn't wake when Pippa slipped away, or when the boy sighed and crept into her shelter on his hands and knees, then carried her out, still wrapped in the saturated blanket. As the rain lashed them both, the boy held Grassina closer, smiling to himself when she snuggled into the warmth of his arms.

It wasn't until Grassina smelled meat roasting over an open fire that she finally opened her eyes. The sun had risen, making the drops quivering on the leaves of the closest plum tree shimmer like diamonds in a world washed clean by the night's rain. A small flock of sparrows flitted among the branches, greeting the day and each other with a chirping chorus. Confused when she didn't see the stone walls of her chamber, Grassina threw off the dry blanket that covered her and sat up. Even as the events of the previous day came back to her, she couldn't remember leaving the shelter she had built.

The smell of roasting meat was too hard to resist. Grassina climbed out from under the boy's lean-to, rubbing her back to ease the stiffness. The boy must have helped her; it was his blanket that had been covering her when she awoke, and she couldn't imagine how else she could have ended up in the lean-to. Before approaching the fire pit and the source of the tempting smells, she glanced around the clearing, expecting to see the boy. She saw her shoes, clean and drying in the sun, as well as her own soggy blanket draped over a branch, but the boy was nowhere to be found. Pippa was gone as well.

Peeking inside the shelter she had built, Grassina was dismayed at how poorly it had survived the rain. She thought the sagging roof was bad enough until she saw the mud puddle where she had sat the night before. Shuddering, she backed away and hurried to the fire pit.

Some sort of small animal had been skinned, skewered, and left with the stick resting across two forked twigs. The scent of fat sizzling on the coals of the fire was almost more than she could bear, but she rotated the stick to cook it on the other side, still expecting the boy at any moment. When he wasn't back by the time the meat began to char, she took it off the fire and blew on its golden brown surface to hasten its cooling. With no sign of the boy, Grassina could wait no longer. She tore into the crisped morsels, savoring the flavor while watching the pathway for the boy's return. Although she intended to eat only half, she was licking her fingers before she knew it, having already cleaned the bones.

After one last disgusted glance at the sorry shelter she'd made, Grassina decided that it was time to begin searching for the Swamp Fairy. While she was at it, she'd see if she could find the boy. She would thank him, but she'd also let him know that she didn't really need assistance and could take care of herself.

Grassina spent the rest of the day visiting many of the places she'd frequented before her mother had changed. She went deep into the swamp where only muskrats, otters, and wildfowl left their prints. She circled the quagmire, collecting useful herbs that grew at its edge and nibbling berries as she picked them. At the pond that bordered the enchanted forest, Grassina kept an eye open for werewolf prints like the ones she'd seen before and was relieved when she failed to find any. She did smell smoke, however, and followed it to a patch of weeds that had been crisped in a fire. Because the burn mark was so small that only a very young dragon could have made it, she decided that it wasn't worth worrying about.

The shadows were lengthening when Grassina returned

to the island with a sack full of edible roots and found that the boy was there ahead of her. He offered her some plums and a seat beside the fire where two leaf-wrapped fish baked amid the coals.

"Where did you go?" Grassina asked, watching the boy poke the steaming fish with a stick.

"Someone had to catch our dinner," the boy replied without looking up.

Grassina opened her sack to offer him some of the edible roots. "You didn't have to get one for me. I can fend for myself when I have to."

"I'm sure you can," he replied, looking pointedly at her sagging shelter.

"Who are you anyway?" Grassina asked. "How did you end up here?"

"My name is Haywood. I ran away from home. I couldn't live there anymore, not the way things were with my father. So I came here looking for someplace where I could be by myself."

"Then I guess you couldn't have found a better place than the swamp," said Grassina. "No one comes here except me . . . and the Swamp Fairy, of course."

Haywood chuckled. "The Swamp Fairy! That's a good one."

"Shh! Don't laugh. She might hear you. You don't want to make her angry."

Haywood gave her an incredulous look. "You don't

really believe . . . I guess you do," he said, seeing how serious Grassina looked.

"Of course I believe in the Swamp Fairy. She's helped me more than once. Why, if it weren't for her, I'd be a snail or something even worse."

"Really?" said Haywood. "And what exactly did this Swamp Fairy do?"

"She sent a toad when I needed one and later a flock of blackbirds with eggshells."

"How thoughtful of her. But if she's so busy helping people, I wonder why I've never seen her."

"I think she must be shy," said Grassina. "To tell the truth, I haven't seen her either."

"Here," said Haywood. "I think these are ready." Using one of the longer sticks, he deftly flipped the leaf-wrapped fish out of the fire and onto a flat rock to cool.

"You're a good cook," Grassina told him between bites a few minutes later.

"Thanks," he said. "You'd be surprised at all the things I can do."

Twelve

Although Grassina hoped to get up before Haywood left the next morning, he was already gone when the touch of the sun's rays on her eyelids woke her. Grassina had meant to repair her shelter and sleep there, but nightfall had taken her by surprise, and she hadn't done more than clean out some of the mud before it was too dark to see. The boy had let her sleep under his lean-to again while he slept at the opposite end. Grassina appreciated that, after that one meaningful glance, he never again referred to the deplorable condition of the shelter she'd built. Even so, she was well aware of how few things she'd actually accomplished since she'd arrived in the swamp and how bleak her future looked. It was almost enough to make her want to pull the blanket over her head and never come out from under it.

"Are you going to eat thiss egg or what?" asked Pippa. The little snake was curled beside an egg that had been carefully placed just beyond the lean-to. "That boy boiled it in hiss pot and left it for you. I prefer them raw, but I'm willing to give it a try if you don't want it. We could call it my good luck and—"

"I'll eat it," Grassina said, reaching for the egg. "Who knows when I'll get something else? Finding food has been harder than I thought it would be. And don't you dare tell me it's because I have bad luck. Sometimes luck has nothing to do with what happens."

"Hmm," said Pippa. "Sso tell me, why do you ssupposse the boy takess that box with him when he leavess? Maybe it'ss a deep, dark ssecret. Maybe he keepss the finger boness of a murderer in it. Or maybe there are love notess from a jilted mermaid, or a horde of deadly sspiderss trained to jump up and bite you on the nosse when you leasst expect it."

"That's a horrible thought," said Grassina. "Where do you get such ideas?"

Pippa coiled herself on Grassina's knee and rested her head on her tail. "I didn't make them up. They were part of a sspell Mudine ussed once."

"So why do you suppose Haywood takes the box with him?" asked Grassina.

"Either he takess it becausse he needss ssomething that'ss in it, or sso ssomeone, maybe you, can't ssee what'ss insside."

"I wonder which it was."

"My guesss iss," said Pippa, "it'ss probably both. Ssay,

154

are you going to eat the resst of that egg? Becausse if you're not . . ."

"I'm eating it! See!" Grassina took her second bite.

Pippa eyed a bird's nest at the top of a plum tree. "Then I ssupposse I have to go get my own food. I feel a ssudden yearning for fresh eggss, sso if you'll excusse me . . ."

Grassina finished the egg while following the path off the island. It had occurred to her that the fairy might have left the swamp on some sort of errand, but she wasn't ready to give up yet. However, she was beginning to wonder just what she would say if she found the fairy. Should she ask for a place to live? A new family, perhaps? But even that wouldn't work. The only family she really wanted was the one she'd had. Then a thought occurred to her that was so stupendous that she gasped and almost forgot to start breathing again. Maybe she could ask the fairy to use her magic to remove the curse from the queen and put everything back the way it had been. Then her father would be alive and Chartreuse wouldn't hate her and . . . How strong was fairy magic anyway?

Having started the day feeling dispirited, Grassina now had a spring in her step and a new purpose to her search. Finding the fairy could change not only her life, but that of her entire family. All she knew about the family curse was what her father had told her, so maybe it wouldn't be too hard to end.

"Swamp Fairy!" called Grassina as she waded through the tall grass beside the bottomless pit. "Oh, Swamp Fairy," she shouted across the river where the otters made their home. "Are you there, Swamp Fairy?" she wailed.

Although she searched high and low for the Swamp Fairy, Grassina never saw any evidence that the fairy was around. She was on her way back when she passed another patch of weeds burned to a crunchy black, a patch that had been lush and green the day before. Grassina shrugged and continued on, once again certain that she had nothing to fear. It was probably just a baby dragon, although she had yet to see or hear one.

It was late in the day when Grassina returned to the island and found Haywood there with dinner waiting. This time he'd found enough meat and edible roots to make a stew. Grassina had found a handful of scraggly wild onions.

"How did you find all this food?" she asked as she accepted a hollowed-out gourd filled with stew.

"Magic!" Haywood said with a wink.

Grassina shrugged. "So don't tell me." She wasn't about to pester him into telling her, not when she already planned to find out for herself. "But I have another question for you. I've been finding burned spots like a baby dragon might make. And I found werewolf prints near the enchanted forest, but that was before I came here to live. Have you seen any sign of either one?"

Haywood bent over the pot on the fire, stirring the little bit of stew that remained. "Can't say that I have," he said without looking up.

"Good," said Grassina. "Just let me know if you do."

Once again, Grassina was too tired to work on her shelter, but this time, she had another reason to go to bed early. While Haywood was banking the fire for the night, she found Pippa soaking up the last bit of heat from a sun-warmed rock on the other side of the island. "Would you wake me before Haywood leaves tomorrow morning?" she asked the snake. "You could get me up when you get up."

"If you really want me to," said Pippa.

"I do," Grassina said. "But we have to be quiet about it. I want to follow him without him knowing it."

"I get it. You want to sspy on him. And you should, too. I bet there'ss something he issn't telling you that you really should know." The little snake reared her head. "Maybe your mother ssent him to sspy on *you*!"

"He was here before I was, remember? He couldn't have been sent to spy on me before I even decided to come here."

"Well, there iss that . . . ," said the snake.

"Did you say something?" Haywood asked, coming up behind her.

Pippa slithered off into the tall grass as Grassina turned to face him. "No, I was just talking to myself."

"You do that a lot."

"I do not!"

"Yes, you do. I've seen you when you didn't know I was looking. You do it all the time."

"You do spy on me!"

Haywood blushed and looked away. "I wouldn't call it spying. I just like to look at you. I think you're beautiful."

Grassina felt heat creep up her neck and across her cheeks. "People usually call my sister beautiful, not me. Please don't say things you don't mean."

"I don't," Haywood said, shaking his head vehemently. "I think you're the most beautiful girl I've ever seen."

"Then I thank you for the compliment," Grassina said, feeling her cheeks flame. Although her father had often told her that she was pretty, no one else ever had. She had always assumed that her father had said it *because* he was her father.

A bat darted between them, catching an insect, then zigzagging away. "It's getting dark," Haywood said into the uncomfortable silence.

Grassina nodded and turned toward the lean-to. She was suddenly aware of him in a way she hadn't been before. The feeling stayed with her as she wrapped herself in her own now-dry blanket under the lean-to and closed her eyes. Hayward was good-looking in a sweet and wholesome way. His tousled brown hair was getting lighter from the sun and was now the color of drying hay.

His eyes, so angry at first, were friendly, and the crinkles in the corners made him seem that much nicer. She had believed him when he'd said he was telling the truth simply because she didn't think he was capable of lying. Tired as she was, it took her a long time to fall asleep that night.

It was still dark out when Grassina felt something brush her cheek. The feather-light touch came again, and she opened her eyes. In the radiance of the nearly full moon she could just make out Pippa's slight form only inches away, flicking her tongue at her. Startled, Grassina jerked her head back, thumping it on one of the support posts.

"You ssaid you wanted me to wake you," said the snake.

Grassina cleared her throat, careful to be quiet so she wouldn't wake Haywood. "Thanks," she said. "What time is it anyway?"

"I'm a ssnake. Do you really think I can tell time? That lasst mole I ate didn't agree with me. I've had indigesstion ever ssince I sswallowed it. I think it musst have gone bad. Well-behaved moless never give me problemss like thiss."

Grassina glanced up at the moon to check its position in the sky. "Will you look at that! It can't be later than five o'clock. I wonder why Haywood gets up so early."

"He doessn't. I did becausse my sstomach hurtss. Can I help it if I couldn't ssleep any longer? You ssaid you wanted me to wake you when I got up. That boy will probably ssleep for a while yet."

"What am I supposed to do in the meantime?"

"Go back to ssleep?"

"Will you wake me again?"

"Why, wassn't once enough for you?"

"But I . . . But you . . ."

"Now that I'm awake, I have thingss to do. Nestss to raid. Mice to catch. Maybe a nice tender mousseling will make my sstomach feel better."

"If I go back to sleep, I'll probably miss him again."

"You probably will, the way your luck iss going now. I guesss you should sstay awake," said the snake, and she disappeared into the underbrush.

Squirming around so that she was almost sitting, Grassina propped herself on her elbows. She couldn't sit up all the way because it wouldn't do for Haywood to wake and see that she was awake as well, not if she wanted to keep it a secret.

Something plopped into the water just beyond the last plum tree. A tiny creature squeaked in the grasp of a night predator. Grassina pulled the blanket up to her chin and watched the stars through the shifting branches overhead. She thought about the tapestry that had hung on the wall of her mother's chamber for as long as she could remember. The tapestry had shown her mother as a young woman standing on one of the castle's towers. It was night, and the stars were actually twinkling, just like the ones in the sky were now. Her mother had called it the Green Witch Tapestry and said that she had received it when she became the Green Witch. She never would tell Grassina any details, just that it had appeared in her room the night her own mother had died. The tapestry had disappeared when the curse changed Olivene, and no one had seen it since.

Grassina was still thinking about the tapestry when she heard Haywood begin to stir. She remained motionless while he crawled out from under the lean-to and made soft noises by the fire pit. When she finally opened her eyes, he wasn't on the path she always took; he was going in the opposite direction on a path she hadn't known existed and had the wooden chest tucked under his arm.

Watching from among the plum trees, Grassina saw him follow a convoluted set of twists and turns. She couldn't understand how he knew where to place his feet with such apparent confidence until she reached the head of the path. Two parallel rows of fireflies sat facing each other across a span of a foot or so on what she would have sworn was quicksand, lighting the way in an on-again, off-again pattern. If she hadn't seen Haywood place his feet exactly *there*, she never would have thought it safe enough to try. Grassina's steps were tentative at first, but when she found firm ground beneath the top layer of mud and water, she began to walk with more confidence.

The sun rose, banishing the fireflies and replacing them with thick-bodied black beetles, lined up like dots of ink splattered across one of her father's parchments. When the water-laden sand thickened around her like curdled milk, supporting straggly plants and not much else on its more solid-looking clumps, bright yellow butterflies fanned their wings on the only tufts that could hold her weight.

Grassina glanced up to see Haywood step onto dry land and hurry around a group of blue green leaved shrubs. She took the last few steps faster than was prudent, and her foot slipped into the water, making her half fall, half jump to solid ground. Bunching the fabric of her skirt in her fists, she ran after Haywood, convinced that she knew his secret.

It took her a few minutes to find him again as tall grass concealed where he knelt beside one of the larger ponds. A fat, silver-sided fish lay gasping at his feet, and another leaped out of the water as she watched.

"So that's it," she said, pointing an accusing finger at him. "You can do magic!"

Haywood turned to look at her, his face a study of flickering emotions. "How did you get here?" he asked. "I thought you were asleep."

"I wanted to see where you went," Grassina said. "I never guessed . . ."

"So now you know," he said, his voice sounding stiff

and wooden. "I suppose this means I'll never see you again."

"Why do you say that?"

Haywood shrugged. "If you're like any of the girls I used to know, you'll be afraid of me. If you're like my father, you'll threaten to have me locked up for the rest of my 'miserable' life."

Grassina was horrified. "Is that why you ran away? And they acted like that just because you can do magic? I can't see how anyone who knew you would ever think that you would hurt anyone, and to say that you—"

An incredulous look crept across Haywood's face. "You mean you aren't afraid of me? I thought you of all people would . . . I mean, with a mother like yours . . ."

"You know who my mother is?"

"I know she's a witch who threatened to turn you into things if you didn't do what she wanted. That's enough to make anyone afraid of magic."

"How do you know she did that? I never mentioned anything about it."

"I told you, I've heard you talking to yourself. I've been living in the swamp for a few weeks now. The first time I saw you, you were holding a toad. I heard you say that you needed a toad with seven warts for your mother. And then you came looking for blackbird eggshells. Both times you talked about what your mother would do if you didn't bring her what she wanted."

163

Grassina's hand flew to her heart. "It was you, wasn't it? You're the one who helped me, not the Swamp Fairy! I saw what you could do with insects and fish. I suppose toads and birds wouldn't be very different."

Haywood shrugged and shifted the wooden box to his other arm. "I can do only simple magic—the most basic kind that even the least gifted fey can do, like turn flax into gold and make ants separate peas from lentils. I've tried to do more involved spells, but I can get them to work only partway before they fizzle out. So far, I haven't been able to control any animal bigger than a cat."

"At least you can do some kind of magic!" said Grassina. "Even small magic is better than nothing."

"Small magic, huh? I suppose that's an appropriate name for it. I haven't given up on doing the bigger magic, though. I was trying to come up with a bigger, better spell when my sister and her friend walked in on me. I lost my concentration, and there was an accident that set the stable on fire. They couldn't wait to tell my father their version of what had happened. He never gave me a chance to explain."

"But I thought people respected magic users. The Green Witch . . ."

". . . is well respected. I know. And, because of her, so are most of the women who do magic. But men are different. How often do you hear about a good wizard? They're out there, but it's very rare to hear about the good they've

164

done. People would rather talk about the ones who misuse their magic, which makes it seem as if they all do."

"You're a good person. Surely your father could see . . ."

"My father didn't know me well enough to *see* anything. I was the fifth of seven brothers and three sisters and had never been his favorite, probably because I didn't fit into his plans. Unlike my brothers, I didn't want to be a knight or a member of the clergy. I practiced with the sword and lance when Father demanded it, but everyone knew I preferred my books. My mother had given me an illustrated bestiary shortly before she died birthing my youngest sister. The book showed every magical creature known to man. I thought they were fascinating and spent all my spare time learning everything I could about magical beasts. When my father found out, he took my books away and ordered me to practice swordplay with my brothers. I disarmed the two eldest, which seemed to anger the rest. Father didn't say a word when they all took me on at once, fresh and eager to fight while I was too tired to hold up my sword."

"That's awful!" said Grassina.

Haywood shrugged. "It wasn't that unusual in our family. My father often turned a blind eye when it suited him. Last year, I discovered that I had some small talent for magic, so I went off by myself whenever I could, hoping that I'd become good enough to make him proud of me. But it was already easy for him to think the worst of me, so he believed my sister when she accused me of purposely setting the stable on fire. You have known me only a short time, yet you've seen me more clearly than he ever did."

"Weren't you able to save any of your books? Oh!" said Grassina. "Is that what you keep inside that wooden box? You take it with you everywhere you go, but I've never seen you open it. Is it the book your mother gave you? If it is, I'd love to see it. I think that book sounds fascinating."

Haywood glanced down at the box. "It's not a book. It's something else. . . . Something too dangerous to open when anyone else is around. I keep it with me in case of an emergency and so no one will try to open it and get hurt. Now I have a question for you. I know you have a pet snake. Don't deny it," he said when Grassina opened her mouth to speak. "It's left trails all over the island. And I've seen you wearing it on your wrist like a bracelet. Why do you keep a snake like that? You're the first girl I've ever met who actually likes snakes."

"I don't like all snakes, just Pippa," said Grassina. "I met her after my mother turned me into a rabbit. Pippa's not a pet, either. She's more of a friend. I'd introduce you to her now, but she's hunting back on the island."

"Good," said Haywood. "There were too many mice there before you came. They were nibbling holes in everything, and I couldn't keep food from one day to the next."

"Thank you," said Grassina.

"For what? I should be the one thanking you. You brought the snake."

Grassina shook her head. "Thank you for helping me when no one else would. I hate to think what I'd be doing now if I'd stayed with my mother and sister."

"In that case, you're welcome," said Haywood. "Although to tell the truth, having you here has been the best thing that ever happened to me."

Thirteen

ater that night, Grassina sought out Pippa and suggested that the little snake meet Haywood. "No," said Pippa. "I heard you talking about hiss magic. If he'ss a wizard, he might put me in a cage like Mudine'ss."

"But I won't let him," said Grassina as she carried the little snake toward the campfire where Haywood waited.

"Make him promisse that he won't," said Pippa. "Tell him how horrible it iss to be locked insside a little box. It makess an animal go crazy."

"All right," said Grassina. "I'll make sure he understands."

Haywood was watching her approach with a quizzical expression on his face. "Who are you talking to?" he asked.

Grassina sighed. She wouldn't have to be a translator if only he could talk to animals, too. Hiding her hand behind her back, she stepped closer to the light of the fire. "I was talking to Pippa. She doesn't want to meet you unless you promise never to lock her in a cage."

Haywood smiled and shrugged. "Tell her I promise."

"She wants me to tell you how horrible it is."

"I'm sure she's right," he said, his smile becoming a little less bright.

"So will you promise?" she asked.

"I promise," said Haywood, although he seemed distracted.

"In that case," Grassina said, bringing her hand from behind her back, "this is Pippa!"

The little snake eyed him warily while Grassina told her about Haywood's promise. Turning her head, Pippa whispered to Grassina, who listened, then laughed out loud. "She says she's going to keep her eyes on you. She thought you were nice enough as a regular human, but she isn't so sure now that she knows you're a wizard. She says you have to be nice to me or you'll have to answer to her."

"I'll keep that in mind," Haywood said, looking as serious as he sounded.

Over the next few days, Haywood and Grassina fell into a routine of chores and practice sessions in which he tried to strengthen and expand his collection of spells. Grassina told him about some of the spells that she remembered from watching Chartreuse's lessons and was delighted when Haywood was able to work many of them.

One day, Haywood used his own kind of magic to

make a school of fish gather water grasses and weave them into a basket for Grassina. She was delighted and promptly used it to collect wild mushrooms and roots to add to their supper. When she returned from her excursion, the sky was overcast and there was a chill to the air, so she settled down to watch while Haywood tried to fashion a witches' ball. His first few attempts to make the hovering balls of light fizzled before they'd even left his hands, but eventually he was able to produce one with a faint, wavering glow that could float on its own. Grassina was admiring it when the first fat raindrops splatted on the plum trees.

Although Haywood and Grassina hurried to the shelter of the lean-to, the storm hit so quickly that they were both drenched before they could get inside. Within minutes, the wind was whipping the branches of the plum trees in a creaking frenzy and shearing the top off the water surrounding the island so that it mixed with the driving rain, soaking them until there wasn't a dry scrap of clothing between them. Grassina shivered, her teeth chattering so hard that her jaw hurt. As the wind buffeted the lean-to until it swayed and shook, Haywood drew Grassina to his side and wrapped his blanket around them both.

Lightning split the sky over the enchanted forest. A few seconds later, thunder rumbled like an angry dragon. "Tell me about yourself," Haywood said, slipping his arm around her shoulders.

"Now?" Grassina asked.

"I can't think of a better time," he said. "Why don't I start. I like to read and—"

Thunder occasionally drowned out his words, yet Haywood kept talking. He told her about his childhood, his sisters and their quests for husbands, his brothers and what they expected to inherit from their father. He didn't tell any extraordinary stories, yet Grassina found them interesting because they were about him. They also provided a distraction from the ferocity of the storm around them, which she decided was what he probably had in mind.

For a full two minutes, lightning struck so close that the air smelled acrid and their ears rang from the boom of the thunder. Haywood put both of his arms around her then, and she snuggled into his shoulder, hiding her face until the lightning moved on. She was frightened, but not too frightened to notice that he kissed the top of her head and held her closer.

Because the dark of the storm blended into the dark of night, they had no idea what time the storm ended or when they finally fell asleep. Waking early the next morning, they found that a large portion of the lean-to had collapsed and that the rest was badly in need of repair. The little hut that Grassina had built was completely destroyed, ending the pretense that she was ever going to fix it.

"Well," said Haywood as he surveyed the damage to the

lean-to. "I guess it's time to make a real shelter, something that will stand up under any weather."

Retrieving the cooking pot from a bed of mud, Grassina poured out the water that filled it. "How are you going to do that?" she asked.

"I'll use magic!" he said. "I don't know why I didn't think of it before."

Grassina was hanging things up to dry when a flood of muskrats arrived, dragging saplings and a few larger branches. When the muskrats left, the birds came, bringing so many reeds and twigs that soon there wasn't enough room to stand. After a score of robins nearly dropped their deliveries on her, Grassina picked up her basket and left the island. Rather than trying to watch from a distance, she decided that she wanted to do something nice for Haywood. It didn't take much to persuade Pippa to go with her once the little snake realized that Haywood's hammering was frightening away her usual prey.

Recalling some berry bushes that grew beside the lake fronting the enchanted forest, Grassina picked her way across the uneven ground, avoiding sinkholes and mud pits. The bushes were easy to find, the berries more plentiful than she remembered.

She was unwrapping the little snake from around her wrist when Pippa said, "I don't know why I had to come with you. It'ss not like I can help you pick berriess."

"I told you," said Grassina. "I need you to keep watch

for me. This is where I saw those paw prints. Just look around and tell me if you see anything unusual."

"I'd rather take a nap," grumbled the little snake. "My sstomach iss sso full I can hardly move. I should never have eaten a rat that wass too fat to run."

"You slept all the way here," said Grassina, setting Pippa on the ground.

"And it wassn't nearly enough," said the snake.

While Pippa slithered off to explore, Grassina began plucking the riper berries, popping a few in her mouth now and then as she moved from one bush to the next. Her basket was close to overflowing when she thought to look for the little snake again, but Pippa was nowhere to be found.

"Pippa!" Grassina said, inspecting the ground under the bushes. "Pippa!" she called, searching the bank on the swamp side of the lake.

Unable to find her, she paused for a moment as she tried to decide what to do and was surprised to hear Pippa's voice carrying across the water. "She'ss not like mosst humanss. Grasssina is actually nice," said the snake.

Although she really didn't want to go anywhere near the enchanted forest, Grassina had no choice if she wanted to collect her friend. Arming herself with two smooth stones, she rounded the pond and stepped from bright sunlight into the deep shade of the forest. She followed Pippa's voice beneath the ancient trees, certain the whole time that all sorts of creatures were watching her.

When she finally spotted the little snake at the base of a towering oak, Pippa appeared to be talking to a young woman dressed all in white. With her pale skin and mass of auburn hair, the woman almost didn't look real. Grassina took another step and nearly stumbled over a tree root. She glanced down to get her balance; when she looked up again, the little snake was alone.

"Psst! Pippa!" said Grassina. "What are you doing here? It's time to—"

Twigs snapped in the forest. Seconds later, a doe hurtled over a rotting tree stump and darted toward Grassina. Veering to avoid her, it panted, "Hurry! It's coming!"

Pippa swung her head around to face Grassina. "It'ss bad luck that you came now," said the snake. "Lissten to me and don't assk questionss. Climb that tree and don't sstop until you can't go any higher. There iss a beasst on itss way that you don't want to meet."

Grassina stared at her, too astonished to move. "Go!" Pippa said as a pulsating rumble reached Grassina's ears. Shoving the stones back into her sack, Grassina turned to the gnarled old tree behind her and strained to pull herself onto the lowest branch. Her feet scrabbled against the rough bark, and then she was up, clutching the branch until she could get her legs under her.

The sound grew louder, becoming the *whump*, *whump* of mighty wings. Three deer darted under the tree Grassina was climbing. She needed no encouragement to grab the next branch and the next after that. A buck bounded into sight when she was halfway up the tree. Then a shape as dark as night and the size of three of her father's biggest horses smashed through the forest, shattering branches as it descended on the unfortunate deer. It was a dragon, dark on dark in the gloom of the forest, its eyes and claws appearing to glitter with a light of their own. The buck leaped again, but the dragon met it in midair, snapping its neck with one bite.

Grassina wrapped both arms around a sturdy branch and squeezed her eyes shut, her breath coming in high-pitched wheezes as she tried not to scream. "That'ss a big one," whispered Pippa from beside Grassina's ear. "It musst be a male. The maless sseem to be bigger than the femaless. I came to the foresst after the tree broke your little housse. I've sseen dragonss of all ssizes here."

Grassina bit her lip and tried not to listen to the crunching of bones and tearing of flesh. She didn't dare open her mouth for fear of the sounds that might come out.

"They tear their food apart like that before they sstart eating. You know, I've been thinking. My luck iss pretty good. Here I am in the foresst with monssterss all around, but I'm too ssmall for any of them to care about, whereass you're probably jusst what they'd like. If anybody hass bad luck, I think it'ss you. Look, he'ss almosst finished. He'll be leaving ssoon."

The forest was growing darker when the beast finally

abandoned the remains of the deer carcass and flew off, the beat of its wings creating miniature tornadoes that swirled leaves and broken bits of branches in its wake. Grassina fought to stay in the tree, tightening her already fierce grip on the branch. Because her quaking muscles had been locked in one position for so long, she was in no condition to climb down even after the forest grew quiet. Instead, she struggled to reach one of the wider branches where she could sit for a moment. Her arms and legs were still shaking when she leaned back against the trunk, took deep breaths to calm herself, and willed her heart rate to return to normal.

Grassina was resting on the branch when she heard a sound at the base of the tree. Leaning forward, she glanced down, freezing as a silver body passed below her. It was a wolf, its coat shining in the darkening gloom. As she watched, the wolf raised its head and looked directly at her. For an instant, Grassina could have sworn their eyes met, but it turned away and went on, sniffing the air as it walked.

The wolf paused and raised its head. Grassina shrank back against the tree as the beast's hackles rose, its lips contracted in a fearsome sneer, and a low growl rumbled from its throat. Although she was far enough above the ground that the wolf couldn't possibly reach her, Grassina pulled herself onto a higher branch before looking down again. The wolf had turned so it was facing away from the tree, back the way it had come. Even from behind, the wolf's flattened ears showed its dislike for whatever was approaching.

Grassina looked past the wolf to the darkness beneath the trees and gasped when she saw a figure there, keeping to the thickest shadows, its belly so low it nearly brushed the ground. Another appeared behind it and another after that until half a dozen indistinct shapes surrounded the wolf. When one passed through a patch of moonlight, Grassina caught her first real glimpse of it and had to press the back of her hand against her mouth so as not to cry out. It was a wolf, yet not a wolf, its body chunkier, its head coarser, its paws broader. Grassina shuddered: it was a werewolf.

Although she wanted to look away, Grassina found herself unable to stop watching as the largest one detached itself from the shadows and walked stiff-legged toward the real wolf. "The girl is mine," the werewolf growled.

"Then come and take her," snarled the silver wolf, stepping away.

As the werewolf advanced, the silver wolf waited until they were only a few yards apart before it lunged, landing on the werewolf's back, sending them both tumbling across the ground. Snarling, they raked each other with their claws, ripping at ears and faces, throats and backs in a tangled frenzy of fangs. When they separated, blood flowed freely from gashes on the silver wolf's neck and shoulders as it stood panting, head hanging, feet splayed.

The werewolf was not even winded; the bleeding from its face and throat was not enough to slow the beast as it paced a circle around the silver wolf.

Although she didn't know the silver wolf, Grassina knew that she didn't want the werewolf to win. Opening her sack, she took out a fistful of stones, braced her body with her feet and legs, then hurled the stones one at a time at the werewolf with all the strength she could muster. The first stone hit a glancing blow, making the werewolf snap at its side as if at a biting fly. The second stone hit the werewolf behind the ear. The beast turned its head and was struck on the snout, which made it yelp with pain. Another stone hit it directly between the eyes with such force that its head snapped back and blood oozed in a line across its brow. The werewolf staggered and fell to the ground. When their leader didn't get up, the rest of the pack stepped out of the shadows, the fur along their spines bristling. As they drew closer, Grassina could hear their deep-throated growling all the way up in her tree.

Forming a circle around the silver wolf, the were-wolves had begun to move in when the lead werewolf groaned and lurched to its feet. It looked groggy and un-coordinated as it shambled unsteadily back the way it had come. The other werewolves stayed in their circle until a sharp bark from their leader made them turn and slink away into the darkness.

Once the werewolves were gone, the silver wolf

heaved a loud sigh, then collapsed in slow motion until it lay sprawled across the ground with its tongue lolling in the dirt.

"Pippa?" Grassina called softly, but the little snake didn't answer. With the silver wolf at the base of the tree and no idea how far the werewolves had gone, Grassina was reluctant to climb down. It was dark as well, and a bad time to be on foot in the enchanted forest. Wincing at every little sound, Grassina wedged her body in the tree so that even if she fell asleep, she wouldn't fall to the ground, then shut her eyes, hoping that it would be morning when she opened them again.

Fourteen

"Wake up," a voice whispered into her ear, and Grassina's eyes flew open. For the second time she woke to find Pippa staring at her from only inches away.

Grassina squirmed out of the crook in the tree where she'd spent the night. Her muscles were so stiff when she tried to stand that she had to hang on to an overhead branch to haul herself up. "Is the wolf gone?" she asked, remembering why she was in a tree at all.

"Ssee for yoursself," said Pippa.

The little snake twined around her wrist as Grassina peered down through the branches. Instead of the wolf, the beautiful young woman who had been talking to Pippa the day before lay at the foot of the tree. Even in the light of day the woman didn't look quite real. Grassina rubbed her eyes, afraid that she might be hallucinating.

She almost fell out of the tree when the woman yawned and sat up. "You shouldn't be down there!" called

Grassina. Dropping from branch to branch without actually falling, she reached the young woman's side moments later. "Do you know what lives in these woods? You'd better come with me. I'll take you somewhere you can be safe." Grassina offered her hand to the woman, who laughed and pushed it away.

The woman didn't look very old, although certainly older than Grassina. She laughed again when she saw Grassina's earnest expression and patted her shoulder as she might a friendly dog. "You really do care what happens to me!" she said, sounding delighted.

A twig cracked in the forest. For a second, Grassina wondered if the werewolves were coming back.

"I told you she wass a good persson," said Pippa.

"You were right," said the young woman.

Crows took off cawing as if an intruder had startled them. Whatever was coming, Grassina thought it seemed to be getting closer.

"Do you two know each other?" she asked Pippa, feeling oddly betrayed.

"We've met," said the young woman.

Grassina looked at her with growing suspicion. "You aren't Mudine, are you?"

"By the buds of my home tree, no, I'm not a witch!"

"She'ss a Vila," offered Pippa. "She'ss here to protect the foresst and all the creaturess in it."

The Vila nodded. "That's true, and because you

chased away that werewolf for me, I'm going to honor you by making you my blood sister."

Grassina blinked. She could have sworn she'd seen Haywood's face peeking through the leaves behind the Vila, but when she looked again, his face was gone.

"Your what?" she asked. After seeing the wolves trying to tear each other apart the night before, she didn't think she wanted to be a blood anything.

"My blood sister. That means you'll be under my protection and I'll teach you all sorts of wonderful things. I don't offer this opportunity to just anyone, but since you helped me last night—"

"I didn't help you. I've never seen you before!"

The Vila made a trilling sound that reminded Grassina of a songbird. It occurred to her that the Vila was laughing. "Why, of course you helped me! I'll admit I didn't look the way I do now. I looked more like this. . . ." The air around the Vila shimmered and suddenly the young woman was gone, replaced by the silver wolf. The wolf yipped and licked Grassina's hand, then the air shimmered again and the young woman was back, wearing a smug smile.

"Get away from her, Grassina," said Haywood, stepping from behind the tree. "Vili are nothing but trouble, even the ones who claim to be good."

The Vila whirled around to face him. "How dare you!" she shouted. "All I've done is offer to take care of that girl and teach her what she wants to know. Your snake friend told me that you want to learn all about plants," she said, turning to Grassina. "I can teach you everything, far more than some sawed-off stump of a wizard can."

Grassina blanched when she saw the thunderous look on the Vila's face. "But I don't want—"

"You know who I am?" said Haywood.

"I know everything that goes on in my forest." The Vila took a step toward him.

Grassina darted around the Vila, hoping to get between the two of them.

"I even know that you won't make it back alive to that miserable swamp," said the Vila. "Out of my way, child," she told Grassina. "I'm going to see that this young man never taints my forest with his presence again!"

"No!" said Grassina, flinging up her hands as if to push the Vila away. "You can't!"

"Oh, I see how it is. He's a man, and he's used his manly influence on you. Don't worry, I know a cure for *that!* Come over here," the Vila said, taking Grassina's arm in an iron grip and pulling her toward a tree. "I'll turn you into a tree nymph. Then you can live inside the tree and forget all about men and—"

"Let go of me!" cried Grassina. "I don't want to be a tree nymph! I want to be who I am and stay with Haywood!"

"You aren't in love with him, are you?" the Vila asked, looking appalled. "Because if you are, there's no hope for you. If you know what's good for you, you'll reconsider. I would take care of you and teach you everything you ever wanted to know!"

"We can take care of ourselves!" Grassina said, struggling against the Vila. "And I'll learn what I want to know without you. Now let go of me! I mean it. I don't want to go into any tree!"

"Just a minute," said Haywood. "You claim to be the protector of the forest creatures, don't you, Vila?"

"Why, yes, I am," the Vila said, pausing with one hand on the bark of the tree and the other still clutching Grassina's arm.

"Then you won't mind if I invite some of your forest friends to a meal." Raising his voice so that it rang out through the forest, Haywood said,

Termites fast and termites slow,
This is where you'll want to go.
Come and have a tasty treat.
Eat until your meal's complete.
Bring your friends and dig right in.
Hurry so you can begin.

The Vila's head whipped around as the smell of sawdust pervaded the forest. Fallen leaves and other debris on the forest floor rose and fell in waves as a horde of termites left whatever they were eating and scurried toward the tree. "No!" the Vila screamed at the insects. "That's my tree! You can't eat that!"

"But they're forest creatures, too," said Haywood. "And you're supposed to be the champion of all forest creatures, aren't you?"

"Not all of them," cried the Vila. "Just the ones I like. And I don't like termites!" Grassina stumbled when the woman suddenly let go of her arm. While the Vila strode into the midst of the termites, Haywood motioned for Grassina to join him. She was reaching for his hand when the Vila began waving her arms in a shooing motion. A cloud of termites were flung backward through the air, but it made little difference, for the more the Vila tried to get rid of them, the more they poured out of the surrounding forest.

The moment the woman turned her back on them, Haywood began pulling Grassina behind him. "Let's get as far from here as we can before she notices!" he said. Tightening their grip on each other's hands, they ran, their feet slipping on the carpet of skittering insects.

"How did you find me?" Grassina asked as she fought to stay upright.

"When you didn't return to the island last night, I asked if anyone had seen what happened to you. A little bird told me where to look."

Suddenly, a shadow detached itself from the gloom under an ancient tree and stepped into the half-light of the forest directly in their path. "Well, well, now isn't this cozy?" said a tall, thin man with long dark hair. Grassina thought he looked vaguely familiar. With thick eyebrows that met in the middle and long incisors that glinted when he smiled, he looked threatening enough to make her shiver. "If it isn't the little princess who stopped by the village looking for her father."

As more men emerged from the shadows, Haywood turned to Grassina. "Princess?"

She shrugged. "I meant to tell you sometime. Then after a while it no longer seemed important."

"How could your being a princess not be important?"

"I just thought—"

"Excuse me!" interrupted the man. "I was talking, remember?"

Grassina wanted to tell the stranger that he was being rude, but she thought better of it when she saw the oversized knife he was wielding.

Shoving Grassina behind him, Haywood said in a commanding voice, "What's the meaning of this?"

Grassina thought Haywood was incredibly brave for standing up to the man, but when the stranger started toward them, she noticed the scabbed-over gash on his forehead and the blood encrusting his hair. "Uh, Haywood," she said, tugging on his sleeve. "That's not an ordinary man."

"I know that," Haywood said out of the side of his

mouth. "He's a lunatic with bad teeth who is threatening us with a knife."

"That's not what I mean," said Grassina. "I saw him in the village and again last night. He's a werewolf, and I bet those other men are, too."

"A werewolf?" said Haywood. "Are you sure?"

"She's a smart little thing," said the leader, "to figure out who we are."

"That wizard sent termites after the Vila's tree!" said a red-headed man with drooping eyelids. "What do you think he'll do to us, infest our coats with fleas?"

A lean man with a sly face glanced at his companion. "Then he's too late as far as you're concerned. You already have them!" The rest of the men laughed, sounding more like barking dogs than humans.

"Haywood!" whispered Grassina. "We have to do something."

"Give me a minute," he said. "I'm trying to remember what I read about them."

"He wants a minute to think!" said the scruffy man, nudging another in the ribs.

"Then today's his lucky day. He'll have plenty of time to think—while he's taking his eternal rest! Get 'em, boys!" shouted the leader.

"Have you thought of anything yet?" Grassina asked as the men crowded closer.

"Yes, run!" Half pushing, half dragging her, Haywood

hustled Grassina to an ancient oak as big around as a small hut. After boosting her into the lower branches, he turned back, ready to defend her with nothing more than a branch he'd picked up off the ground.

Grassina was digging into her sack for her stones when the men threw themselves at Haywood. He fought valiantly, jabbing and whaling at them with the branch. Grassina was about to throw a stone when the scruffy man grabbed her ankle from behind.

"Let go of me, you . . ." Kicking and shaking her foot, she held on to a sturdy branch with both hands, but the man was stronger, and she knew she couldn't hold on for long. He yanked hard, and she half fell out of the tree, her legs dangling in empty air. Grassina shrieked and tried to kick him, but he ducked and wove, avoiding her blows. She was still struggling to hold on when Pippa's head popped out of Grassina's sleeve. Hissing softly, the little snake dropped onto the man's back.

One more yank and Grassina tumbled to the ground, landing on her side with an *oof*. The man was bending over her when Pippa slithered down the neck of his tunic. "Hey!" he shouted. Letting go of Grassina, he began patting his clothes. "There's a snake! Get this—" The next instant he collapsed in a heap and lay on the ground with saliva dribbling from his mouth. He made gasping sounds while his eyes rolled back in his head.

Grassina scrambled to her feet. "What did you do?" she asked, picking up Pippa.

The little snake curled around her wrist, tickling her skin with a flicking tongue. "The ssame thing he wass going to do to you," said Pippa. "I bit him."

"Are you venomous?" Grassina asked.

"Yess," Pippa said, sounding resigned. "But don't tell anyone. People tend to look at me differently once they know. You sstill like me, don't you?"

"Of course I do," said Grassina. "Just don't . . ."

"You know I'd never bite a friend, but if I'm going to bite more like him, we'll have to wait until I make new venom. I ussed all that I had jusst then. Ssay, maybe your luck hass changed. It wass good luck that I wass there to help you!"

The men on the other side of the tree began barking jubilantly, having overwhelmed Haywood and forced him to the ground. Grassina started toward him, but a trio of men blocked her way. With only two stones left, she threw one at the first of her attackers, hitting him squarely on the forehead. He staggered and went down, but was back on his feet a moment later. The second stone struck another man on the shoulder, which just seemed to make him angry. He snarled, his lips curling like a wolf's.

Grassina studied the forest around her; she was surrounded with no place to go and no one who could help.

Looking for a weapon of some sort, she snatched a stick off the ground and held it out in front of her. "I wish I had a real weapon," she said. "Something that would work against werewolves!"

She nearly dropped the stick when it began to shiver in her hand, but she held on, as mesmerized by the light that came from it as were the men who slowed down to watch. The stick grew until it was the length of a spear, its tip becoming thick and pointed. When it stopped quivering, the glow burst into a silvery radiance that banished the half-light of the forest.

In the full light of day, the men rushed at Grassina, brandishing knives and daggers. Holding the spear as she'd seen her father's soldiers do, she hurled it as hard as she could at the man in the lead. Although her aim was off, the spear righted itself and flew directly at him. It struck, the tip slicing deep, the shaft quivering as the man fell. Grassina was defenseless now, but only for a moment as the spear slid back out of the motionless figure, rose into the air, and returned to her hand. She glanced at the fallen man, half dreading, half hoping to see that she had killed him. To her surprise, he had been infused with a silvery glow, not unlike that of the spear.

As Grassina watched, the man shuddered, and when he lay still again, all signs that he had ever been a werewolf were gone. His long incisors had grown smaller, his bushy brow had shrunk, and even his demeanor had changed. The werewolf part of him was gone, yet when he stirred and sat up, Grassina could see that his human aspect still lived.

A twig snapped behind her, and Grassina spun around. The remaining men were circling her, made wary by the spear. Grassina hefted it and took aim, throwing the spear when a man launched himself at her. It struck as truly as if she'd been a seasoned fighter, taking him out of the fray. Then, just as before, the spear flew back to her hand while the injured werewolf became fully human.

Poised for another attack, Grassina turned and drew back her spear. Having seen what had happened to their comrades, the men who were still on their feet seemed to have lost all interest in her. Even as they slunk away, Grassina hurried to find Haywood and discovered him lying sprawled on the ground, bleeding badly and barely alive.

"No!" she said, kneeling down beside him. "You can't die! Haywood, I need you!"

"He doesn't have to die," said a voice. Grassina looked up and saw the Vila.

"Can you save him?" Grassina asked. "Surely there is something you can do. . . ."

"You don't need me," said the Vila. "You have magic of your own."

"What are you talking about?"

"How do you think you got the weapon you needed when you needed it the most?" the Vila asked.

"You mean you didn't send me the spear?" Grassina glanced down at the gleaming pole she still clutched in her hand.

The Vila shook her head. "You did that all on your own. Try a healing spell. It should work."

"But I don't know how!" wailed Grassina.

"Just as I doubt you knew how to throw a spear. Try it and see. The magic will do the hard part for you."

"I don't know any healing spells."

"You must. Haven't you ever seen an injury healed through magic?"

"I did fall out of a tree once; my mother healed my broken arm."

"Good. Then think back," said the Vila, laying her cool, dry palm on Grassina's forehead.

"I don't really remember. . . . Wait. Yes, I think that's it. I'll have to change it a little, but I think it went something like this."

> Bones may break and flesh may tear.
> Neither one's beyond repair.
> Bones and flesh and sinew, too.
> With this spell make them like new.
> Mend the one I love so well.
> Use my love to aid this spell.

192

Haywood groaned and moved his head ever so slightly, but otherwise nothing happened. "It didn't work!" cried Grassina. "Now what am I going to do?"

"It didn't work because you don't love him enough," said the Vila.

"But you said yourself that I love him!"

The Vila sighed. "I'm not saying you don't, just not enough to make that spell work. However, I can assist with that if you'd like. You helped me when I needed it, and I have yet to repay you. I don't like feeling obligated to anyone, even someone who rejected the offer of sisterhood."

"I'd appreciate anything you can do if it will help Haywood."

The Vila nodded. Waving her hands over Grassina and Haywood, she said something in a language Grassina didn't understand.

"What was that?"

"A love enhancement spell. It works only when two people are learning to love each other. Your healing spell should work now."

"Thank you," breathed Grassina. Turning back to Haywood, she was surprised to see that he didn't look exactly the same as he had before. She thought he was handsomer now and so appealing that her heart ached at how helpless he looked. Eager to see the healing spell's effect, she repeated it all in one breath, then held her next breath as she waited to see if it would work.

The forest seemed unnaturally quiet, as if every creature wanted to see what would happen. Haywood took a ragged breath and then another. As color flushed his pale cheeks and his wounds began to heal before her eyes, Grassina took his hand in hers and squeezed it.

Haywood opened his eyes in response, smiling up at her when he saw her bending close. At first delighted by his smile, Grassina drew back when his incisors began to grow and a feral light filled his eyes.

"I was afraid of that," said the Vila. "It looks as if he's turning into a werewolf now that he isn't going to die. You don't have any choice. You'll have to take your spear and stab him."

Grassina was horrified. "I can't do that!"

"Of course you can. Think about what happened to those werewolves you struck with the spear. The spell didn't kill their human side, just the werewolf in them. It will do the same for your young man if you let it."

"What are you talking about?" Haywood asked, propping himself on his elbows.

"Nothing," said the Vila. "Now hold still while she pokes you. It won't hurt . . . much. No worse than a thorn prick."

Haywood jumped to his feet. "No one's stabbing me with a spear! You have to be crazy if you think . . ."

"Will it really work?" Grassina asked the Vila.

"I'm certain it will," said the Vila.

"I'm sorry, love of my life, but I must do this," Grassina told Haywood.

Haywood began backing away. "Oh no, you don't! Whatever she's told you, my darling, whatever I've done, I'm sure we can work this out."

"We'll talk all about it," said Grassina, "as soon as you're no longer a werewolf."

"I'm not a werewolf," Haywood growled.

"Yes, you are. Feel how long your teeth have grown. Your eyebrows meet in the middle now, although they didn't before. And you're beginning to smell like a dog."

Haywood continued to back away. "I admit I haven't bathed recently, but that's no reason to . . ."

"Now!" shouted the Vila as Haywood tripped over her outstretched foot.

Grassina stabbed him in the leg as gently as she could. Haywood gasped and began to struggle upright, but the light infused him just as the spear sprang back into Grassina's hand, and he collapsed again.

"That should do it," said the Vila.

"I thought you were certain it would!"

"I am . . . fairly certain," the Vila said as Haywood continued to lie motionless at their feet.

"Haywood!" Grassina cried, falling on her knees beside him. "My sweet, sweet darling! Light of my life, what have I done?" Bending over him, Grassina kissed him full on the lips.

"That was very nice, precious love," Haywood muttered against her mouth, "but can you please get up? You're kneeling on my hand."

Grassina sat back on her heels and clasped her hands together. "Oh, Haywood, you're all right!"

"Uh, yes," he said, flexing his fingers. "Thanks to you, my darling doodlebug."

Grassina frowned and turned to the Vila. "We've never called each other silly names before. What have you done to us?"

"Nothing that wouldn't have happened anyway, given a little time. You were already in love. I just made your love stronger. No spell can create love if there is none to begin with, but because of my spell, you will love each other for the rest of your days as long as you remain in the form you have now. However, if you ever get tired of it, just come see me. I can always turn you into a tree nymph, and then you'd forget all about him."

"I'll never tire of my dearest Haywood," said Grassina.

"Then in that case there's no need to thank me!"

Fifteen

They were sitting by the fire in front of Haywood's half-built hut when Grassina told him about her family. "And so Chartreuse said that she hated me and never wanted to see me again," she continued. "I left the next morning and don't ever want to go back." The last log cracked in two, showering sparks into the night air. A sleepy bird protested from its nest in one of the plum trees. Grassina leaned against Haywood's leg. "I could stay here with you, heart's delight. Between your magic and mine, we could be safe and very comfortable. There's no need for either of us to leave."

"That would be a dream come true, my treasure," Haywood said, caressing her fingers where they lay across his palm. "But I don't think it's possible. I need you, and I want you here with me, but I think Greater Greensward needs you more right now."

"You'd send me away?" she asked.

"Not because I want to. I love you, dearest darling.

197

I have ever since you built that terrible hut and were too proud to ask for help. You're the bravest girl I've ever met and the most understanding. Nothing would make me happier than to have you here with me for the rest of my life. Ordinarily, I wouldn't be able to say these things to you—you being a princess and me the younger son of a minor noble—but I think you love me as much as I love you—"

"Oh, I do, light of my life," breathed Grassina. "I have never felt about anyone the way I feel about you. I'll stay with you and we can use our magic to build a bigger home, by the river perhaps, or—"

"As much as I want that, it wouldn't be right. The kingdom needs you, precious one. Go back to your castle and see if your sister has her magic yet and if it's enough to return things to the way they were. Whatever happens, come back to me. I'll be waiting for you here."

Grassina sighed heavily. "I suppose I have to go. I thought when I ran away that my duty to Greater Greensward was over, but I guess that's never going to happen. I'll be responsible to the kingdom forever."

"All princesses are born into responsibility. There's no getting around that."

"Then stay safe while I'm gone, light of my life. I'll leave in the morning and be back as soon as I can. If you need me for any reason . . ."

"I'll send a little bird," said Haywood. "But I'm sure I'll be fine. The werewolves aren't likely to follow us here.

It's you I'm worried about. Your mother will still be the same."

"Yes, but now she won't be the only one with magic. Somehow the thought of seeing her isn't quite so daunting. I just wish I felt the same about seeing Chartreuse."

Going home felt odd, mostly because nothing seemed to have changed since the morning she'd left. The same men were standing guard at the drawbridge, looking bored and only half awake. The same cats were scrapping with bristled backs and puffed tails in front of the stable doors. The Great Hall still smelled of the old herbs that needed to be replaced, the hounds sleeping in front of the cold hearth, and the unwashed bodies of the people who passed through. Grassina almost felt as if she'd never left, yet too many things had happened to her, changing her in ways she never would have expected.

She was trying to decide if she should go look for her mother or her sister first when she heard Olivene's unmistakable screech. "I don't know why you had to show up! I was just getting used to you being gone! My life was nice and peaceful without you. Why did you have to spoil it by coming back?"

At first Grassina thought her mother was talking to her, but the queen was nowhere in sight. Following the sound of Olivene's voice, Grassina found her by the stairs

leading into the dungeon. A pile of her father's belongings had been heaped beside the door, shrinking steadily
as Olivene snatched one object after another and chucked
it down the stairs. "Here, take this!" screamed the queen.
"No one else wants your trash!"

"Mother?" said Grassina. "What are you doing?"

Olivene's head whipped around. "Oh, it's you. So you
decided to come back from wherever you've been hiding.
I don't know why you bothered. We don't need you here."

Grassina shrugged. "In that case, I'll be going," she
said, glancing toward the door to the courtyard.

"You most certainly will not!" said Olivene. "Here,
take this. See how hard you can throw it. If you do it right,
it should bounce all the way down the stairs."

Grassina took the sword from her mother's gnarled
hands. It was her father's best sword, the one he'd worn
during every important ceremony. She glanced at the pile.
His armor was there, as were his books, his clothes, and
even the dishes he'd used in the Great Hall. "What's going
on, Mother?" asked Grassina.

"I'll tell you what," said the queen. "Your father came
back the night before last. He came to see me the last time
I went down there. As if anyone wants to see *him* again."

"My father? How can that be? You mean he didn't really die?" Grassina asked, hope lighting her eyes.

"He died all right. I never said he didn't. He's still
dead, too, so don't start thinking there's been some sort of

200

miracle. He's come back as a ghost, determined to haunt me for the rest of my days. You couldn't leave well enough alone, could you, you miserable old cuss?" Olivene shouted down the stairs.

"Has Chartreuse seen him?" Grassina asked, thinking her mother was imagining things.

"That ninny? Ha! She refuses to go down there. Says she doesn't believe in ghosts. That's a whole lot of hooey if you ask me. She's just afraid; I can see it in her eyes."

"She was very upset when he died."

"Not enough to go see him now that he's back! You should visit him though. I'm sure the old stick would like to see you. Here, take this. I don't want the darn thing getting stuck in the stairwell." Grassina had to set the sword on the floor to take the armored breastplate that her mother was handing to her. She thought she saw tears glinting in her mother's eyes, but she couldn't be certain. The queen turned away too quickly, saying, "You can take the rest of this junk down there while you're at it. I don't want it cluttering up the place anymore. I'll throw it out if he doesn't want it."

"Are you sure . . . ," Grassina began, but her mother was already stomping off.

Gathering as many of her father's possessions as she could carry, Grassina picked her way down the stairs, trying not to step on the clutter Olivene had tossed there. Beady rat eyes watched her from the open doorways of some of the cells, but the only sound was that of her own feet on the stone floor. Remembering the ghosts she'd met before, she kept her eyes open for any sign of what her father might have become, but the dungeon was unusually quiet. Grassina had begun to wonder if her mother had finally slipped over the edge into insanity when she reached the door to the room her father had used.

Grassina wasn't sure if she wanted to see him there or not. Although she missed him desperately, it was the man she missed, not some disembodied wraith who floated through walls and spoke in half whispers. But when she saw a familiar shape limned in blue, though it was little more than a shadow in the flickering light of the torch in the corridor, her heart skipped a beat and she felt an overwhelming sense of relief. Her father was back, in whatever form, and now everything would be all right.

"Father, is that you?" Grassina asked from the doorway.

The figure turned around with shadows rippling on shadows. "Grassina, my darling girl," said a whispery voice as the figure drifted closer. "Your mother told me that you were gone. 'Ran away,' she said. She was making it up, of course."

"I was gone, Father, but I'm back now."

The ghost approached until Grassina could make out her father's features. Despite his hollow eye sockets and skin of palest blue, it was most definitely her father. He was so transparent that she could see the walls and broken furniture behind him, but he was there, or at least some part of him was, and just then that was enough. Grassina shivered as the ghost came closer with arms outstretched and a gentle smile on his face. She expected to be enveloped in a chilly hug, but the ghost passed right through her. Grassina felt woozy the way she did when she stood up too fast, although this was much worse. The experience left her cold, shaky, and slightly queasy.

"That was very odd," said her father, "and most unexpected." His outline wavered as if he were shuddering.

Grassina rubbed the goose bumps that had risen on her arms. "I know what you mean."

"I must apologize, my dear," said her father. "I'm not used to being a ghost and have yet to learn what I can and cannot do. In my joy at seeing you again, I forgot that I can't actually touch physical objects."

"I understand," Grassina muttered from behind her hand. Her stomach was roiling, but she didn't want to talk about it.

"I'd like to be able to write, or read what others have written, but I can neither hold a quill nor turn the pages."

"Maybe I can help you with that," said Grassina. "I can do the writing for you and turn the pages when you're ready. But we'll have to put this room to rights first. Mother certainly made a shambles of things. Just a minute while I set these over here." Grassina placed the items she'd brought in the corner of the room while her father hovered beside her. Brushing off her hands, she glanced at him, then at the pile of armor and clothing. "If you can't touch anything, I don't know what Mother expects you to do with all this."

"I don't think she knows either. I believe it's her way of telling me that she loves me. She doesn't know how to say it anymore, but I know in my heart," he said, pointing at his chest, "how she really feels. It's why I had to come back, and it's why I can't leave."

Her father had never had much in the room, so it didn't take long for Grassina to straighten it up. The larger furniture had been broken into pieces, making them easier to cram through the doorway, and the rest was light enough that she could move it on her own. After setting the sheets of parchment in two stacks that she could organize later, she folded his clothes and replaced them in the not-too-badly damaged trunk. "I'll bring everything else down now," she said, heading toward the door. "Mother has quite a pile up there. She'll throw it out if I don't move it."

"Then by all means," said King Aldrid. "I wouldn't want to upset your mother."

Grassina loaded her arms with as much as she could carry for the next two trips, but her father's armor was heavy, and she couldn't carry more than a few pieces at a time. As she was setting his helmet on the pile, she knocked over his shield, which fell on the arch of her foot. She howled and dropped the rest on the floor, hobbling to the only chair in the room so she could inspect the injury. No skin was broken, but her foot hurt almost as much as the time a horse had stepped on it.

"Why don't you rest for a moment?" said her father, floating in the air above her. "You can tell me about what you've been up to."

"There's a lot to tell," said Grassina.

Her father chuckled—a hollow sound that would have been frightening if Grassina hadn't known who made it. "I have nothing but time," he said. "You can begin with the day you left the castle."

Relieved that she wouldn't have to talk about his death, Grassina rubbed her aching foot and told him about her fight with Chartreuse. She described her feeling of hopelessness and how she'd left the castle before first light. Her father was intrigued when she told him about Pippa, and asked countless questions when she mentioned Haywood. When she described the Vila, he grew restless, becoming even more agitated when she talked about the werewolves. "You could have been killed!"

"And I would have been if the spear hadn't appeared in my hand. I came into my magic, Father! Just when I needed it most!"

"You what?" said King Aldrid, his color flaring a brighter blue.

"I thought the Vila had sent the spear to me, but later when I had to stab Haywood, she told me she hadn't."

King Aldrid's ghost seemed to shrink as he settled to the floor. "This is too much for me to take in all at once. You have magic? Wait ... Why would you stab your friend?"

"So he wouldn't stay a werewolf," said Grassina. When her father seemed even more confused, she explained it all as best she could, although she left out the part about the Vila's love enhancement spell. Even without the spell, she was sure she would have loved Haywood, but she didn't feel like explaining that to her father.

"And so I came home to see if I'm needed here. I'm sure I won't be if Chartreuse has come into her magic. . . . You haven't heard anything about that, have you?"

Her father sighed and shook his head. "Your mother hasn't come back down since she first discovered that I was here, and I haven't seen or heard from your sister."

"Then as soon as I finish bringing everything, I'll see if I can find her. I know she won't want to see me, but this isn't about what either of us wants."

"You don't have to carry the rest down yourself. Use your magic. It would be much faster and easier for you."

"Oh," said Grassina. It hadn't occurred to her that she could use her magic for anything but an emergency. The thought of reciting a spell to perform such an ordinary task made her look at her magic differently—making it less of a weapon and more of a tool. As far as she knew, there was no reason she couldn't use it for all sorts of things the way her mother had.

"That's a good idea," said Grassina. "Only I don't know any spells for moving things. I don't think I ever heard Mother mention one to Chartreuse."

King Aldrid shrugged. "Then make one up. Your mother always did."

Grassina stood at the top of the stairs, poking the pile of clothes and weapons with the foot that wasn't sore. It had sounded good to say that she could make up a spell, but now that she was faced with the task of actually doing it, she had no idea where to begin. She debated telling her father that it wouldn't work, then decided that it wouldn't hurt to try. Clearing her throat, Grassina pointed at the pile and said,

Carry this from here to there.
Haul it down the dungeon stair.
Take it to the tiny room
Where my father met his doom.

A fly landed on the pile, tasting the old leather of the undercoat that her father had worn beneath his chain mail. Grassina was beginning to think that she'd done something wrong when the pile seemed to quiver, then collapsed, disappearing in a nearly silent whoosh and taking the fly with it.

"It worked!" she said, delighted with herself as well as the knowledge that she wouldn't have to carry everything down the stairs.

"It certainly did!" crowed her mother behind her. "You have your magic! I should have known you'd be the one!"

Grassina twirled to face Olivene, too elated about her magic to feel nervous around her mother. "Did you see that? Wasn't it wonderful?" Her smile faded when she saw that her sister was there as well, looking as angry as she'd ever seen her.

"Simply marvelous," said Chartreuse in a flat, tight voice. "It was some kind of trick, wasn't it? You don't really have magic; you just want us to believe you do so we'll forget that you ran off the way you did. First Clarence goes off to fight a dragon and gets himself killed, then Pietro disappears. They say he went to find the Vila. He never could resist a pretty face. And then you ran away, leaving me desperately afraid that something awful had happened to you, too. Don't you think I care about you? You're the only sister I have. And you know I need you here. Greater Greensward needs you here. I can't handle *everything* myself!"

"Don't be such a sourpuss, Chartreuse," said Olivene. "You'll make a competent queen, but you'll never be the

Green Witch. Just because you can't do it doesn't mean that your sister can't. I saw her do it with my own two eyes and so did you. I've been sorely disappointed in you, Chartreuse, but now I know why you never came into your magic. It wasn't in you and it never will be. Magic runs true in our family—goes to the most deserving, I'd say. Does your father know, Grassina? I'm going to go tell him."

While Olivene thumped down the stairs, Chartreuse glared at her sister, standing with her feet firmly planted and her fists on her hips. "I bet you're proud of yourself and think you're really special," said Chartreuse. "Well, you're not. Look at your hand. If your magic was as good as Mother seems to think it is, you'd have the Green Witch's ring on your finger. Don't try lording your magic over me, miss. The ability to do a few simple tricks doesn't impress me. Mother will see soon enough what you can do. And there's no saying I won't still get my magic, and then we'll see who's better at it!"

Grassina put up her hand as if to stop the flow of words. "Chartreuse, I—"

Chartreuse shook her head. "I don't want to talk to you, so do us both a favor and don't say another word. But while you practice your magic or whatever it is you're going to go do, keep in mind that I'm not the only one with a responsibility to the people of this kingdom!"

Sixteen

$\mathcal{G}$rassina sat on the edge of her bed staring at the wall across from her. She hated to admit that Chartreuse was right, but it looked like this time she was. It hadn't occurred to Grassina until her sister mentioned it that she might have earned the Green Witch's ring if her magic had been strong enough. With the ring on her finger, she would know that she was capable of protecting the kingdom however necessary. Without the ring, Grassina wasn't sure that she could protect much of anything.

After Chartreuse's tirade, Grassina had fled to her room, hoping that even if the ring wasn't on her finger, the tapestry might have appeared on her wall. It hadn't been there, of course; she hadn't really expected that it would be. Now it was even clearer that there still was no Green Witch to protect Greater Greensward.

It had been only one day since she'd returned to the castle and it already felt like an eternity. Nothing was the way it had been. Her mother was making Chartreuse do all the chores. Chartreuse hadn't spoken a word to Grassina since they'd met outside the dungeon door, which was probably just as well.

It didn't help that Grassina missed Haywood dreadfully and thought about him all the time, or that worrying about the ring had kept her from sleeping most of the night. All the next day, she'd drifted through the castle, unsettled and unsure about what she should be doing. By late afternoon, she'd once again returned to her room to stare at the empty wall.

Grassina was still sitting on her bed when she heard someone sobbing. Opening her door, she peeked out and found Lettie, the scullery maid, crying. "What's wrong?" Grassina asked.

Lettie's face was even redder than usual, and her cheeks were streaked with tears. "Oh, Your Highness," she wailed, "I didn't want to disturb you, but I don't know who else to turn to. They say you helped that man from Darby-in-the-Woods, so I was hoping you could help me, too."

"Are you having a problem with werewolves?" asked Grassina.

"Yes! Well, not me exactly. My Basil is a soldier. He was on patrol last night, and he went missing along with some of his friends. He told me he'd be safe enough— they weren't going beyond sight of the castle—but he never came back, and I think the werewolves got him!

What am I to do, Your Highness? He was just about to propose to me, I know he was!"

"I wish I could help, but I don't know what I could do. I'm not the Green Witch," said Grassina, holding up her ringless hand.

"And your mother isn't either! We've all seen that she's lost the ring, and everyone knows that Princess Chartreuse hasn't a magic bone in her body. Everyone's saying that it's you who has the magic now, so I thought . . ."

"I'm sorry, I'm not the one to do this. You'll have to find someone else," Grassina said, pulling the door closed behind her.

Turning toward her bed, Grassina paused, her hand still on the latch. She could hear Lettie sobbing as she retreated down the corridor, and Grassina couldn't blame her. There wasn't anyone else, and everyone knew it. Ever since she'd faced the werewolves in the forest, she'd been hoping she'd never see them again. She'd even harbored the unlikely thought that they could have left altogether, scared off by the power of her spear. However, deep down inside she'd known this wasn't true; it was the reason she'd been awake most of the night. Ridding the kingdom of the werewolves was going to be up to her, for even her small bit of magic was more than anyone else who cared seemed to have.

"Perhaps Father has some advice," she murmured, squaring her shoulders as she turned back to the door.

She found King Aldrid exactly where she'd seen him last, drifting silently in the darkened room. He seemed to be as lost as she had felt since her return. "I need your help," she said, plunking herself down on the only chair. It wobbled on its cracked leg, so she hopped off and sat on the trunk instead. Seeing the stack of parchments on the floor, she remembered her offer to help with his writing and to turn the pages so he could read—yet another thing only she seemed able to do.

Her father's ghost sighed. "I don't know how much help I can give you. I can't even go upstairs."

"Really?" said Grassina. "You mean you've tried?"

King Aldrid nodded. "I think it's because I have no substance. I can go through walls and doors, but I can't climb the steps. I pass right through them, too."

"There must be something you can do."

"I'm sure there's a trick to it," he said, rubbing his ghostly chin. "I'll just have to keep trying. Now, you said you needed my help?"

Grassina nodded. "It's the werewolves. They're coming as close as the castle. Some of our guards are missing."

"That's bad," said the king. "Very bad. But there isn't anything I can do."

"I know," said Grassina. "I'm going to handle it myself. All I want from you is advice on how to get rid of them. What do werewolves fear? Is there anything special I can use to chase them off?"

"Silver," he said promptly. "A silver-tipped arrow lodged firmly in the heart should do the trick."

"But there are so many of them, and I'm just one person. I can't possibly shoot them all. Isn't there anything else I can use?"

"Silver-tipped arrows are the most effective weapon that I've ever employed, although I suppose if you cut off the werewolves' heads . . ."

Grassina shuddered. She was willing to fight them if she had to, but she couldn't imagine cutting off anyone's head. "Thank you, Father," she said, getting to her feet. "I'll be sure to keep that in mind."

Something crashed in a nearby cell, and Olivene shrieked wordlessly. "Has Mother started coming to the dungeon again?" asked Grassina.

"Since yesterday," said her father's ghost. "We talked about your magic. She's very proud of you, although I think she's being a bit hard on Chartreuse."

"I'd help Chartreuse if I could," said Grassina.

"As would I," said the king. "I just need to find a way out of here."

"I think I'll go talk to Mother and see if she has any suggestions about the werewolves," said Grassina.

"She might," said the king. "Although I don't know if you should do *anything* she says."

Grassina found her mother standing on top of a pitted green leather trunk, hanging bird skeletons from the ceiling. "Oh, it's you," she said when Grassina appeared in the doorway. "Hand me that grackle. No, not that one, the one with the chipped beak. Good. Now, what do you want? I know you didn't come to watch me redecorate. Speak up. I'm busy. No time for idle chitchat."

Grassina ducked to avoid the skeleton of a raven. "I've come to ask you about werewolves. Do you have anything that I could use to get rid of them?"

Olivene guffawed, opening her mouth wide enough to show the gaps between her blackened, rotting teeth. "You make those werewolves sound like fleas in your underthings," she finally said. "Any way to get rid of them? Hah! Watch out, that buzzard is coming after you." Grassina jumped out of the way as one of the larger skeletons clipped her shoulder with its wing. She scowled at the bird, who looked as if it were scowling back. "Werewolves, huh?" Olivene continued. "I've never had much to do with them. Why are you asking?"

"I told you about the werewolves in the enchanted forest. They're still there and are moving this way. Would you like to take care of them, or should I?" Grassina asked, still hoping that she wouldn't have to be the one to face them.

"Is that a trick question? Because I don't like trick questions, unless I ask them myself. Can't you see that I'm busy? If I don't get all these hung, they'll fly into a tizzy and get their bones mixed up. Hey, don't hurt that raven! Do you know how long it took to get it up there?"

The raven skeleton had grabbed hold of Grassina's braid with its claws and was trying to fly off with it, but it could only circle around the point on the ceiling from which it hung. Grassina took hold of her braid and yanked, pulling it free and bringing three of the bird's claws with it.

"I know what you need," Olivene said, snapping her fingers. Hopping off the trunk, she threw the lid open and began rummaging inside. "Here, take these." Removing a bundle of stiff gray hairs tied with a silver thread, she pulled out two and handed them to Grassina. "They're werewolf whiskers, good for tracking anything within fifty miles. If you're going to use them to track werewolves, do it at night. They won't do you a bit of good otherwise. And this is a witch's tooth that . . . Wait, that's mine. So that's where it went," she said, jamming the blackened bit of bone into her gums. "Then there's this . . . No, I might need it. And this . . . Isn't it a ghastly color? I think I'll keep that. Ah, here you go. I suppose you could have one of these, seeing that I have an extra." Olivene handed Grassina a ridged tooth at least two inches long dangling from a golden chain.

"What is it?" Grassina asked, watching it twirl.

Instead of answering, Olivene scuttled across the floor and tossed the basket of lightning bugs to Grassina. "You might as well take these, too. They're of no use to me, and I'm sick of their infernal din. Now get out! You've taken up too much of my time as it is. So long, good riddance, and all those other things you're supposed to say when an idiot is staring at you big-eyed and jaw-dropped like you are. Shut the door on the way out. I don't want any more unwelcome visitors taking advantage of my good nature."

Although her hands were full, Grassina managed to close the door behind her. The visit hadn't been at all what she'd expected, but then, she didn't have any idea what to expect when she saw her mother. Having set the angrily buzzing basket on the floor, she tucked the werewolf hairs and the tooth in the sack she carried. At least now she had a few things that she might be able to use, even if her mother had neglected to tell her how.

Seventeen

It was almost dusk when she found Haywood squatting beside the fire, feeding the flames with kindling. A filleted fish lay on a rock beside a pot of water. "I was hoping you'd come back today, my sweet precious, at least to tell me how things were going," he said after they greeted each other with a kiss. "Would you like some fish stew? It won't take long."

"I'm too nervous to eat," Grassina replied. Then she sat down to tell him what she had done and why she had come back when she did. Haywood nodded but didn't interrupt, for which Grassina was grateful. Telling him about her family and the werewolves was already hard enough. "But I think I'll need your help," she said when she'd finished. "You know things about magic that I don't. Together we might know enough to make this work."

Haywood took her hand in his and squeezed it. "I'd go in your stead if I could, but I know my magic isn't strong enough to defeat a pack of werewolves. And your magic

218

hasn't been fully tested. I'm not sure if our magic com-bined—"

"It has to be," said Grassina. "Someone has to deal with them before the kingdom is overrun. They're getting bolder all the time. They've already been seen near the cas-tle. It won't be long before they turn one of our own men into a werewolf and get inside the castle, too. Greater Greensward needs us, my darling. There isn't time to waste. I'll be leaving as soon as it gets dark. The werewolf whis-kers Mother gave me to track them will work only at night."

"And your father . . ."

"He can't help us. He doesn't even know how to help himself yet. And my mother isn't interested, although to be frank, if she were, she might side with the werewolves instead of us. It really is up to you and me."

Haywood sighed and got to his feet. "Let me get my things. I'll be ready in just a minute."

"You mean you'll come?" asked Grassina, her eyes shining.

"Of course. I would never let you do this by yourself."

Grassina collected her spear and was leaving the hut that Haywood had finished in her absence when Pippa wrig-gled through the interwoven branches, landing on the ground in front of her. "What are you doing here?" Grassina asked, startled.

"Making ssure that you don't leave me behind again. You have a habit of doing that."

"Sorry. I didn't dare take you to the castle. It would have been too hard to hide you from my mother."

"I'll forgive you thiss time," said Pippa. "At leasst I had Haywood for company. Did you know that he'ss very good at finding mice?"

"I thought you looked a little plumper."

"Are you almost ready?" Haywood called from the head of the path. "It's nearly dark out."

"We're both coming," Grassina replied as she picked up the little snake. "We have one more weapon to take with us. Pippa wants to go, too."

❧

The stars were shining overhead as they neared the edge of the forest. Grassina reached into her sack, took out the whiskers, and held them up to the light of Haywood's witches' ball.

"These are the werewolf whiskers that Mother gave me," she said. "They don't look like much, do they?" She turned them over in her hand and bit her lip while she thought. "Do you have any idea what to do with them? Mother forgot to tell me."

Haywood shrugged. "I've never seen anyone do tracking magic. Have you?"

"It wasn't included in my deportment lessons. I don't

know if Mother ever showed Chartreuse either. I guess I'll have to make up something again. I hate doing this, but here goes."

Holding the hairs on the palm of her hand, Grassina thought for a minute, then said,

> As a bird flies to its nest
> And a fox runs to its den,
> Show us where the werewolves are—
> The wolves now, not the men.

"I hope it workss," said Pippa. "That wass really awful."

"Don't be so critical," said Grassina. "I'm new at this, remember?"

"Look," said Haywood. "They're changing color."

At first it was difficult to see in the flickering light of the torch, but it soon became obvious that the whiskers were turning red. Before long they were glowing a brilliant scarlet. Rising into the air, they rotated until they were both pointing in the same direction, and then they took off like two flaming arrows.

"Hurry!" shouted Grassina, sprinting after the whiskers. "I don't have any more. If we lose sight of those, we'll never find the werewolves!"

"Too bad you didn't usse one at a time!" Pippa said into her ear.

"Don't you think I know that now?" puffed Grassina.

"Save your breath for running," said Haywood. "Look, they're over that ravine."

While Haywood slid down the steep incline, Grassina picked her way more carefully, grabbing hold of branches and crouching when she slipped. Haywood had almost reached the top of the other side when he saw two glowing lines waiting just above his head. He was reaching for Grassina's hand to help her out of the ravine when the whiskers took off again.

"They went that way!" Grassina shouted, stumbling when Haywood jerked her toward him and started running.

Concentrating on keeping up with the racing red streaks, running without regard to being stealthy or quiet, Grassina and Haywood soon forgot why they were running. They kept going until their lungs burned and they had stabbing pains in their sides. They ran until they thought they couldn't run anymore, then they stopped thinking and just put one foot in front of the other. When the whiskers finally grew still and hovered over the remains of a fallen log, Grassina and Haywood didn't notice at first and nearly stumbled past them. In the distance, the full moon rising behind the castle showed them exactly how far they had gone.

"Do you see . . . the werewolves?" Grassina asked, gasping for air.

"Is that...them...by those rocks?" Haywood whispered back, pointing beyond the last of the trees at a jumble of boulders. A shape moved, jumping onto the tallest rock so that the body was silhouetted against the night sky. Larger than an ordinary wolf, the creature was more muscular as well, as if he were a throwback to a beast of an earlier age that had required greater size and strength to survive.

When the werewolf turned his head and looked directly at them, Grassina whispered, "He knows we're here! Look, the others are spreading out. They'll surround us if they can!"

"If we could keep them together somehow...," said Haywood.

"That gives me an idea," said Grassina, "but I'm going to need your help." Unwrapping the blanket she had wrapped around the basket of lightning bugs, she set it on the ground and stepped back.

"What is that?" asked Haywood.

"Some very angry insects," said Grassina. "You're good at controlling birds and such. Can you tell these bugs to circle around the werewolves and draw them together?"

"Now *that* I can do," said Haywood. Flexing his fingers, he pointed at the basket and murmured something under his breath. "Go!" he said in a louder voice and kicked the basket over.

As the lid fell off, the angrily buzzing swarm of lightning bugs hopped, skittered, crawled, and flew straight at the pack, shedding sparks along the way. The lone were-wolf poised atop the pile of boulders leapt to the ground and began padding toward Grassina and Haywood. The first lightning bugs hit him in the chest, shocking him so that he fell back, whining and snapping at his fur. Other werewolves tried to bypass their stricken leader until the bugs flew at their eyes and they, too, were driven back. Bugs hopped into their open mouths and crawled over their paws, shooting sparks and shocking them at each point of contact. With sparks lighting the way, the lightning bugs herded the werewolves back toward the rocks. Even after they'd rounded up the entire pack, the bugs continued to shoot off sparks so that it looked like an invisible fire was burning in the forest.

While Haywood strode purposefully toward the pack of werewolves, Grassina followed with her spear poised to throw, just in case.

"What have you done?" snarled the werewolf who had watched them from the rocks. "Get these things away from us now or I'll rip out your throat!"

"Isn't that what you plan to do anyway?" Grassina asked.

"You understood it?" asked Haywood. "What did it say?"

"I suppose you have to have been an animal to understand one," said Grassina. "Maybe you can try being one someday. The beast was threatening us, that's all." Turning back to the werewolf, she pointed her spear at him, saying, "Your threats mean little to me. I can kill you whenever I choose. However, if you promise to leave this kingdom, I'll let you go on the condition that you never come back."

"Leave the . . . Have those insects crawled through your ear holes and infested your brain? We're not making any deals with you! You're a human and nothing more. When I get past these pests . . ." The werewolf swatted at a lightning bug and yelped when it shocked him. Swiping at his paw with his tongue, the werewolf glared at Grassina. "I'll find a way to get around these bugs. When I do, I'll eat your heart while it's still beating."

"Grasssina," Pippa whispered into her ear. "Bad luck. I think that sspell iss wearing off."

"What spell? You mean . . . Oh!" Although the lightning bugs had formed a flashing, sparking wall only moments before, large gaps were beginning to appear as insects deserted one after the other, called away by the clear night sky and the temptations of the forest floor.

The head of the werewolf pack was still watching them when Grassina whispered to Haywood, telling him about the spell. "That's one thing about my kind of magic," replied Haywood as they both backed away. "You can't go against a creature's nature if you want the spell to last. They are only insects after all. We can't really expect them to act like anything else for long."

"I wish you'd told me this before!" said Grassina. "Can't you repeat your spell?"

"I could, but it wouldn't do anything. My spells never work a second time on the same batch of animals."

Grassina frowned and reached into the leather bag. "I suppose I could try this," she said, pulling out the tooth on the chain.

"What kind of animal did that come from?" asked Haywood.

"I was hoping that you could tell me."

Haywood shrugged. "I've never seen anything like it, but whatever it was it must have been big. Look at the size of that thing."

"I hope it was mean, too," said Grassina. "Mean enough to take on a pack of werewolves. But I guess we're about to find out. Here goes." Holding the tooth at arm's length, Grassina said,

> Use this tooth to let us see
> That which you were meant to be.
> When you are what you'll become,
> Chase the wicked werewolves from
> This, the kingdom we love so.
> Do not tarry, don't be slow.

While saying the last few words, Grassina tossed the tooth outside the ring of fire and waited. The tooth landed behind a patch of ferns so at first they couldn't see it. Then the plants began to shake, twitching violently as an oversized manlike head appeared. Covered with a great mane of tawny hair, the creature opened his mouth wide, showing three rows of teeth, identical to the one from which a golden chain still dangled.

As a tawny back arched above the ferns, a musky smell reached Haywood and Grassina. A trencher-sized paw crushed the plants flat, cracking a branch beside them with a sharp report. When the beast shook himself, a tail tipped with a dense ball of bone and fur twitched, thudding as it hit the ground. Turning to face the werewolves, the horse-sized beast roared, sounding more like a trumpet than a living creature.

"That's a manticore. I've seen drawings of them, but never the real thing," Haywood whispered to Grassina. "He's magnificent!"

"I don't care what he is as long as he gets rid of the werewolves," Grassina replied.

Pippa peeked out of Grassina's sleeve. "How will you get rid of the manticore once he'ss chassed away the werewolvess?"

Grassina bit her lip. "That's a good question."

"I could bite him if you need me to," offered the little snake.

"Thanks," said Grassina, "but I hope that won't be necessary."

Having heard the manticore, the werewolves turned to face this newest threat. When they growled deep in their throats, Haywood put his arm around Grassina and drew her closer to his side. Walking stiff-legged, the werewolves approached the rocks, the fur bristling along their spines. The manticore crouched down, his tail twitching behind him as he eyed the closest werewolf. Suddenly, the beast leapt from atop the rocks, snatched the werewolf in his jaws, tossed it into the air, and caught it on the way down. The werewolf struggled to free itself and actually succeeded for a moment. Then the manticore pounced on it again, batted it with a paw, and let it go just to knock it down again.

"The manticore is playing with the werewolf the way a cat does a mouse," Grassina whispered to Haywood.

He nodded. "It seems we got what we wanted. Those monsters don't stand a chance."

When the werewolf no longer responded, the manticore bit off its head with a horrifying crunch and flung the body aside like a broken toy. Another werewolf approached from behind, so the manticore swung his tail, crushing the creature's skull with one blow of the ball. The carcass hadn't even hit the ground before the rest of the pack turned tail and ran as fast as they could with the manticore close on their heels.

Grassina shuddered and looked away. "I should have

used my spear on them. At least then they'd be turned back into humans and not . . . not . . ."

"Eaten?" said Haywood. "Except you never could have turned them all back. One of them would have gotten to you first, and then you would have been missing a few vital organs."

"Maybe, but what that monster just did makes me sick to my stomach."

"What do you have in mind now?" asked Haywood.

"We'll go to the castle and tell them what happened. Will you go with me?"

"As far as the gates, but I'm not going inside," Haywood said. "I don't think this is the right time to meet your family."

Hand in hand, they started toward the castle, studying the field around them with wary eyes. "Do you see that?" Haywood said suddenly. "There, by those trees. It looks like . . . Yes, I think it is. The manticore is back!"

As the manticore bounded across the farmer's field, Grassina turned to face the beast, gripping her spear firmly. "I wish I knew what he wanted."

"Whatever it is, it can't be good," said Haywood. "Manticores aren't known for being overly friendly."

The manticore stopped only a dozen yards from them and crouched, his wicked-looking tail flicking across his back like an angry pendulum. "You got what you wanted," growled the beast. "I killed a few and scared off the rest." He took a step closer, his shaggy head weaving from side to side. "They won't be back as long as they can smell my scent, which is why you won't kill *me*." Another step and the beast seemed impossibly huge. "If you did, you'd have to face the werewolves all over again."

As the manticore continued his approach, Grassina backed away, uncertain if she should throw her spear or not. One more step and his eyes were boring into hers. "You said I should be quick. Was I too fast for you? I got back before you could run away. I'm sure that wasn't part of your plan. I'm sure this wasn't either."

In a fraction of a second, the manticore rushed at Grassina, knocked the spear from her hand, and swatted her so that she flew into the air. It happened so fast that all she had time to think about was that she was going to die. She didn't realize that she was screaming until her throat hurt. Closing her eyes, she expected to hit the ground hard, but suddenly something soft and fluttery enfolded her in its embrace. Her eyelids flew open. A cloud of moths had surrounded her, breaking her fall. "Haywood!" she breathed as the moths laid her on the ground, then scattered into the night.

Although Grassina was on her feet in an instant, the manticore was already there. This time when the beast batted at her, a flock of owls caught her clothes in their talons and lowered her gently to the farmer's field. She had no intention of playing the manticore's game of cat and mouse, so when the beast pounced on her and rolled her over with its paw, she shouted, "Now, Pippa, bite him!"

Growling deep in his throat, the manticore pinned her to the ground with his paws, letting his decay-scented breath wash over her. Up close, his shaggy head was even bigger than she'd thought; it was at least three times the size of hers, with a mouth large enough to swallow her head and shoulders in one bite. The monster's drool was running into Grassina's ear when Pippa slithered out of her sleeve. Winding herself around the manticore's leg, the snake latched on with her fangs.

A strange look came into the beast's too-human eyes. As the little snake's venom coursed through the monster's veins, the manticore swayed and shook his head. His pupils were dilated, and his breathing was shallow when he slumped toward Grassina. Certain the creature was collapsing just like the werewolf had when Pippa bit it, Grassina tried to squirm out from under him. Instead of crushing her, however, the manticore shook his head again as if he had just awakened from a deep sleep, blinked, and said, "My! I feel so relaxed!"

"Uh oh," said Pippa. "That wass *not* ssuppossed to happen!"

Grassina tried not to flinch when the manticore smiled down at her, grinning so broadly that it looked as if his face might split in two. "I did what you wanted," he said. "Now I'm going to do what *I* want. You never said that I couldn't eat you."

"I wish you—" began Grassina.

"Uh, uh, uh," said the manticore, covering her mouth with his paw. "No magic spells out of you, witch!"

"Hey, monster, over here!" shouted Haywood.

The beast's great head swung toward the young wizard, his eyes narrowed to glittering slits. "Wait your turn. I'll get to you next."

Grassina struggled to breathe, but the manticore's huge paw covered her mouth and her nose. She was writhing under the weight, desperate to break free, when Pippa sank her fangs into the manticore's leg, but without enough time to replenish her venom, her bites had little effect.

Then Haywood shouted, and a moment later the manticore screamed. When he suddenly lifted his paw from her mouth, Grassina gasped for air.

"Ow!" exclaimed the manticore. "Those things can bite! Ow! That hurts!" Plopping down on his haunches, the manticore kicked at his head with his hind foot, then began twisting and thrashing as he snapped at his sides.

"Run!" Pippa said into Grassina's ear, sliding beneath the neck of her tunic.

The beast was rolling on the ground whining when Grassina scrambled out of the way and turned to look. Fire ants were streaming across the monster's fur, biting as they went.

"Quick, over here!" said Haywood, taking her hand. Riddled with crevices, the boulders offered more shelter than anything else they could reach. As they ran, Haywood used his magic to call a bat to lead them to a hiding place. They followed the little creature, climbing over the boulders while the manticore continued to rage. The opening the bat had found was awkwardly placed halfway up the pile of boulders, and almost too narrow for Haywood's shoulders. He squirmed in first, then helped Grassina wriggle through. The manticore had followed them and was sniffing at the bottom of the pile as Grassina pulled her feet in after her.

"Do you have anything elsse in that bag that could help?" asked Pippa.

Grassina shook her head. "That was all I had. I can try to think of a spell, but I'm not very good at it."

"Ah!" said the manticore from outside their hole. "Here you are!"

Grassina lurched backward when the manticore's paw reached inside to grope the air only inches away from her. "I know you're in there! Do you honestly think a few rocks are going to stop me?"

"About that spell . . . ," said Haywood.

A grinding sound made them scoot as far from the opening as they could manage. The manticore was moving the boulders, trying to force his way inside. "I can't think when he's doing that!" said Grassina.

Haywood sat back and placed the wooden box on his lap. "Then I guess it's up to me. I was hoping I'd never have to try this, but I don't have any choice. What I'm about to do is very dangerous, so don't come any closer."

Grassina held her breath while Haywood muttered a spell and removed the lid of the wooden box. For the first time she could see what was inside. A bed of hot coals filled the box, and on the bed slept a small red lizard, glowing even brighter than the smoldering coals.

"Who is that?" asked Pippa.

"*What* is that?" asked Grassina.

"It's a red salamander," said Haywood. "I was learning how to handle it when I started the fire in my father's stable. Red salamanders know more about fire than any other creature, besides dragons, that is, but they are very hard to control."

"You've had that with you all this time and never told me? Oh!" she gasped. "Is that what made those burn marks in the swamp? And I thought it was a dragon! But that salamander is so little. What can it do against a monster like the manticore?"

"You'll see," said Haywood. "I have a spell I can try. . . . I just hope it works."

> little salamander friend,
> Take your flames and with them wend
> 'Round the manticore so dire

234

To protect us with your fire.
Make a wall to force him back
And forestall his next attack.

When Haywood held up the box, the salamander took a burning coal in its mouth and scurried out the opening of the shelter. Once out of the box, the little creature shed crackling flames wherever it went. Smoke wafted back into the hole where Grassina and Haywood had taken refuge, making them cough and rub their eyes.

The manticore bellowed close enough to the hole that the rocks around them shook, and Grassina feared that they would be buried alive. Frightened, Pippa wrapped herself around her wrist so tightly that Grassina's hand began to turn blue.

The commotion outside continued, then suddenly grew fainter, and the rocks around them stilled.

"Thank goodness!" said Grassina. "I'm glad you thought of that salamander spell. I didn't know that small magic could make such a difference. I guess it depends on how you use it."

"That's true of any magic," said Haywood. "Have you come up with your spell yet? The salamander won't get rid of the manticore, just hold him off for a while."

"I think I'm ready," said Grassina. "But I want to see him when I say the spell to make sure it actually works."

"I'll go firsst." Unwinding her body from Grassina's

wrist, Pippa slithered out the opening. "That manticore almosst got in. He moved a lot of rockss. You can come out now. He'ss too bussy to notice you."

Getting out of the shelter was easier than getting in had been; the manticore had moved most of the smaller rocks out of the way. Grassina crawled out on her hands and knees, saying, "Haywood, I'm glad you had that box with you to . . . Oh, my!" She had spotted the manti-core.

It had run about a hundred feet from the rock pile before the salamander had trapped it. A wall of flame rose up around the manticore; each time the beast tried to leap over the fire, the flames shot higher, singeing its fur and making it fall back, bellowing.

"This is close enough," Haywood said as he got to his feet behind her.

Grassina nodded. "I think so, too." Raising her arm, she pointed at the manticore and said,

> Fierce and nasty you may be,
> But you will not frighten me.
> Though you're big and though you're strong,
> You won't stay that way for long.
> Shrink in strength and shrink in size
> Till you wear a kitten's guise.
> Let your scent be all that stays
> To remind us of your ways.

The manticore was pacing within his fiery cage when he began to shrink. He was smaller than a newborn lamb when the salamander ran off into the night, letting the flames die away. Having extinguished his fire, the little creature was almost impossible to see in the dark.

"Where's he going?" asked Pippa.

Haywood shrugged. "I don't know. I doubt I'll ever see him again."

"But I will," said Pippa, raising her head to taste the air with her flicking tongue. With her head still raised, she slithered off after the salamander.

Grassina hadn't taken her eyes from the manticore. It had stopped shrinking when it reached the size of a three-week-old kitten, but looked in every other way exactly as it had before. "Why doesn't he look like a kitten?" she asked. "He was supposed to after that spell."

"A manticore's a magical beast," said Haywood. "Our magic doesn't work the same on them."

The manticore tried to bellow, but instead of the blare of a trumpet, it sounded more like the tootle of a flute. Frustrated, the beast ran at Grassina as if to attack her again. When it reached her feet, she clucked her tongue and picked him up by the scruff of his neck. The manticore mewed pitifully when she held him at arm's length. "That's much better," said Grassina.

"What have you done to me?" squealed the kitten-sized beast.

Grassina set the creature on the ground, hardly noticing when he swung his tail and tapped her on the wrist with the ball. "Nothing that you don't deserve," she said. "You were right when you said I didn't want to kill you, but then, I didn't want anyone else to be killed either. Good-bye, little one. You should be happy. You wanted to be free to do whatever you desired, and now you are."

As the manticore darted off into the grass, Haywood once again took Grassina's hand in his. "What's this?" he said.

"Hmm?" said Grassina. Turning back from watching the manticore, she let her eyes follow Haywood's. There was a ring on her finger now, a green ring made of a single stone carved to look like overlapping leaves. "Oh," she breathed and glanced up at Haywood. "Do you know what this means? That's the ring of the Green Witch!"

"Which means that you hold the title now," said Haywood, his words clipped and dry. "I'm so happy for you."

"Isn't it wonderful?" said Grassina. "I have to go tell my family. Greater Greensward has a Green Witch again!"

"It is wonderful," said Haywood, "for the kingdom."

Eighteen

rassina and Haywood had almost reached the castle when they ran into an armored party mounted on horseback. Prince Limelyn was at the head of the column, leading King Aldrid's ten bravest knights. "What are you doing here, Princess?" he said, his armor rattling as he doffed his helmet. "It isn't safe. We've come to do battle with a terrible beast that's been heard in the forest. We'll escort you back to—"

"That won't be necessary," said Grassina. "It was a manticore, but we've already taken care of it."

Prince Limelyn looked astounded. "Was it you, good sir?" he asked Haywood. "Tell us how you were able to perform such a marvelous deed!"

"I helped, that's all," said Haywood. "Princess Grassina did most of it herself. Look!" he said, holding up Grassina's hand. The green ring glittered on her finger as it caught the morning sun.

"Is that . . . ?"

"It must be!"

"Princess Grassina is the new Green Witch!"

The knights urged their horses forward, forming a circle around Grassina. Removing their helmets, they gazed at her with respect and admiration. Although she tried to keep hold of Haywood's hand, he had seen the expressions on the knights' faces, and it seemed to make him uncomfortable. "Good-bye, my darling," he said, raising Grassina's hand to his lips. "I must go now. You have to tell your family your news. I'm sure there will be work for you to do as well. You don't need me any longer. These gentlemen will see you safely home."

One of the knights struggled to dismount under the weight of his armor. When he finally had his feet on the ground, he stood between Grassina and Haywood. Draping the reins across his horse's neck, he turned to Grassina, saying, "Your Highness, please do me the honor of riding my steed back to the castle."

"Just a minute," she said, trying to look around him. "Haywood! I need to talk to you. Don't go!"

The knight stepped aside, but Haywood had already slipped past the horses. "Your Highness," said the knight. Leading her to his mount, he helped Grassina into the saddle. She could see farther once she was seated—far enough to see Haywood disappear into the morning mist.

Grassina was still thinking about Haywood when the horses clattered across the courtyard to the foot of the stairs. She didn't notice that her mother and sister were waiting in the midst of Chartreuse's suitors until Olivene called out, "Is that you, Grassina? What are you doing with those men?"

"We have excellent news," said Prince Limelyn as his squire helped him dismount. "Princess Grassina wears the ring of the Green Witch on her finger!"

"She can't!" blurted Chartreuse. When all the princes turned to look at her, she added, "I mean, she wasn't wearing it yesterday."

"Let me see!" crowed Olivene. "I know what it looks like better than any of you." Grabbing Grassina's hand, she yanked so hard that she nearly pulled her daughter off the horse. "That's it, all right. Congratulations. You now have the worst job in the kingdom. It's about time someone in this family did a little work around here, besides me, that is."

"Well, I never . . . ," sputtered Chartreuse.

"See, she admits it. She never could do a decent lick of work."

"Mother!" cried Chartreuse, blushing scarlet.

Prince Torrance pushed his way to the front. "Princess Grassina, may I be the first to congratulate you."

"No!" snapped Olivene. "I already did!"

"And I'd like to wish you well," Torrance continued. "I've always considered you remarkably intelligent and beautiful. Being the Green Witch will simply add to your long list of accomplishments."

"I'm going to be ill," muttered Olivene.

"I can't believe my ears!" exclaimed Chartreuse. "Just the other day you told me that you were glad Grassina wasn't around anymore to distract you with her silly prattling!"

Torrance looked irritated when he glanced at Chartreuse. "I'm sure you must have misunderstood me. I would never be so unkind as to say such a thing about dear, sweet Grassina."

"I say," piped up Prince Miguel, "you do sit that horse well, Grassina."

Prince Stephen scowled. "She'll make a good witch. We could use someone like her in my kingdom. Might keep the minor nobles in line."

"What's going on here?" said Chartreuse. "She's still the same person she was the other day when none of you had time for her. And now you're talking to her and ignoring me!" As if someone had opened a sluice gate, tears flowed from Chartreuse's eyes, and her bottom lip quivered. Dabbing at her eyes, she turned her back to her suitors. "I'm sorry. A princess should never cry in public."

Prince Limelyn was at her side in an instant. "Your Highness," he said. Taking her hand in his, he spoke to her in a voice so quiet that only she could hear it.

"Do you mean that?" Chartreuse asked through her

tears. "You want to marry me whether I have magic or not?"

"With all my heart," said the prince.

"What do you intend to do as your first act as the Green Witch?" Torrance asked Grassina.

"Um . . . I . . ."

"More to the point," said Prince Stephen, "have you thought about getting married? I have a lot to offer a wife."

Chartreuse's eyes flashed. "*I* would like to make an announcement. I have chosen the prince who will become my king. He is brave and true," she said, giving Torrance a nasty look, "unlike some others I could mention. I have decided to marry Prince Limelyn."

"Good for you," said Prince Miguel. "Grassina, you haven't answered Stephen's question. Have you thought about marriage?"

"You're not too young," said Torrance. "If anything, Chartreuse is a bit on the old side."

"Do you mean it, Chartreuse?" Limelyn asked, cupping her face in his hands. "Do you really want to marry me?"

"Yes," she replied. "It would make me the happiest woman in the kingdom. There is no one with whom I'd rather spend the rest of my life." Limelyn was drawing her into his arms when Chartreuse whispered to Olivene. "Don't try to talk me out of it, Mother."

Olivene snorted. "Why would I? You can marry whomever you wish. After all, *you* aren't the Green Witch."

Limelyn had already wrapped his arms around Chartreuse, and so didn't see the stricken look on her face.

"Come, Grassina, we're all waiting to hear your answer," said Stephen. "Because if you're not interested in getting married, I might as well go home. I've already wasted too much time here as it is."

"As a matter of fact," said Grassina, "I do intend to marry, and I know exactly who my husband will be."

"Good!" said Torrance. "Which one of us is it?'

All three princes crowded closer as if expecting to hear their own names.

"None of you. I met him while I was away. He's kind, thoughtful, and brave. He loves me for me, not for my title or for what I can do for him. He's the perfect man for me," she said, turning to Olivene. "Mother, I know you'll love him as much as I do. He has magic, too!"

"Really?" said Olivene, arching her eyebrows.

"Then I'm leaving!" announced Prince Stephen as he shoved past everyone else on the steps. "Stable boy, saddle my horse!"

"I might as well go, too," said Torrance. "I've heard there's a princess in North Aridia who isn't half bad."

"Care for some company?" asked Miguel. "They're said to have excellent horseflesh in North Aridia. Even the women are accomplished riders."

"Congratulations, Grassina," said Limelyn. "When will I meet this lucky fellow?"

"You already have," said Grassina. "Now I just have to let *him* know how lucky he is!"

⌘

After visiting her father to share the good news, Grassina hurried back to the swamp. She didn't see Haywood at first, but the fire was burning in the circle of rocks, so she knew he had to be close by. When she sat down to wait for him, she found Pippa stretched out on the rocks beside the fire.

"Pippa, how did you get here so quickly? I thought you were looking for the salamander."

"I found him! Princesss Grasssina, I want you to meet my friend, Igniss."

The fire flamed higher, and something shifted in its depths. Grassina glanced down and was surprised to see the salamander resting comfortably among the glowing embers. "It's nice to meet you, Princess. Pippa has told me all about you," the salamander said in a husky voice.

"It's nice to meet you, too," Grassina replied.

"The moment I saw Iggie, I knew we were meant to be friendss," said Pippa. "He'ss warm and friendly and warm and honesst and. . . . Did I mention how warm he iss? With him around, I'll never be cold again. You were right about my luck. I musst be the luckiesst ssnake in the world to have found a good friend like Iggy, and it wouldn't have happened if Haywood hadn't ssaid hiss ssalamander sspell! It'ss amazing what ssmall magic can do."

"I've been thinking about it, and I don't believe we should call any magic small; certainly nothing Haywood does. He is quite wonderful. Do you know—"

"After I found Iggie, I perssuaded him to come with me," said Pippa. "I told him that I knew of a nice ssafe place where he could live. We were on our way here when we ssaw Haywood and he gave uss a ride."

"Where is Haywood now?" asked Grassina.

"I'm right here," said Haywood, rounding the hut. His eyes brightened when he saw her, but then he shook his head and turned away, although not before Grassina saw his eyes cloud over with despair.

"I was wondering if you'd come to say good-bye," he said.

Grassina shrugged. "I had to come. We have too much left to say."

"No, we don't," said Haywood, turning back to her. "You don't have to explain anything to me. I saw how those men looked at you. You told me about your sister's suitors. I'm sure that you'll have even more now that everyone knows you're the Green Witch. You'll marry a prince, not someone as lowly as me. I'm not worthy of you. I have nothing to offer other than a hut in a swamp. Please, be kind and make this quick. Seeing you is hard enough."

"I don't know why," said Grassina. "Hearing that someone loves you to distraction and wants to marry you shouldn't be all that difficult. Why, when I told the princes back at the castle that I'd already chosen the man I wanted to marry—"

"You want to what?" Haywood asked, blinking at her in confusion.

"Marry you, of course. I've never met anyone who suited me better. Since I couldn't possibly live without you, there's no need to talk of anyone being unworthy. Those princes couldn't hold a candle to you. And I'm the Green Witch now, which means that I can live anywhere in the kingdom and no one can tell me what I can or can't do. Greater Greensward needs me too much. Chartreuse won't dare try to order me around. She's getting married, too, you know. To Prince Limelyn, the only one of the lot whom I could stand."

Haywood pulled her into his arms and kissed her. Wrapping her arms around his waist, Grassina kissed him back and sighed when it was over. She was thinking about how happy she was when Haywood pressed his cheek against the top of her head and said, "But what will your family say? Your mother—"

"My mother will love you. I'm sure of it. And if she doesn't, what can she do? The Green Witch is always the most powerful as well as the nicest witch in the kingdom. No one will dare get between you and me. Just wait and see. Everything will be wonderful. You and I are about to find out what it really means to live happily ever after!"

The Dragon Princess

PROLOGUE

Though she was just a few minutes old, everyone agreed that the baby was beautiful. She had eyes like those of her mother, Princess Emma, and a shock of blond hair much like that of her grandmother, Queen Chartreuse. Emma swore that her daughter had Eadric's smile, but her mother, her aunt, and her grandmother all claimed that the baby was too young and wouldn't really smile for some time yet.

When she was only three months pregnant, Emma had dreamed that the baby was going to be a girl. After that, she and her husband, Prince Eadric, had never worried about a boy's name. The baby would be named Millie, after the second Green Witch, Emma's long-ago ancestor.

Although Emma wanted to show Millie to Eadric right away, the midwife and all the other women in the room insisted that they wash the baby first. Unfortunately, an over-eager lady-in-waiting hadn't bothered to warm the water before bringing it to the midwife. The midwife, rattled in the

1

presence of so much royalty, most of whom were witches, splashed the cold water on the baby. With a startled cry, the baby turned red as a strawberry, and her thin wail broke the calm of her parents' bedchamber. Emma sat up to see what was wrong. At that instant, the air seemed to sizzle and the baby turned from a beautiful human newborn with honey-blond hair into a baby dragon with scales of the palest green. Queen Chartreuse screamed. Two ladies-in-waiting fled the room. The midwife fainted.

Emma sighed and reached for her baby. "I was afraid of this," she murmured, gazing down at the squalling infant. Turning to her aunt Grassina, she added, "This is what comes of spending half my life as a dragon."

One

Not quite fifteen years later

$\mathcal{P}$rincess Emma, the Green Witch of Greater Greensward, was sitting at her worktable copying spells onto fresh parchment when a slender green dragon darted through her window and landed on the floor behind her.

"Millie's home!" squawked the green-and-yellow parrot perched on the edge of a precariously balanced stack of books. The bird flapped its wings, making the whole stack sway. Emma gestured at the books as they started to fall, and they shivered back into place.

"I know, You-too," said Emma. "You don't need to tell me when she's standing right here. And as for you, Millie," she said, turning to the dragon, "what upset you this time?"

The dragon sat down and wrapped her long, spiked tail around her. "The scullery maid dropped a pail of muddy water at the top of the stairs just as I was coming up. I'd already put on my new gown for Prince Atworth's visit and the water ruined it. I changed into a dragon

3

before I could help it. Yes, I know you can fix the gown, but I didn't think of that until later. Anyway, the girl started screaming, so I flew out the window. She was terrified— as if she thought I was about to bite off her head. I don't understand. After all these years, why are some people still so afraid of me? I've never hurt anyone while I was a dragon, at least, not since I was a little girl and didn't know any better. You'd think everyone here at the castle would remember that."

"I'm sorry, darling. It's human nature to be afraid of dragons. I'm sure you handled it very well."

Light shimmered around the dragon and a lovely young girl appeared. Her honey-gold hair framed her face in soft curls and cascaded down her back. Except for her dainty nose, her face was much like her mother's and her eyes were the same shade of deep green.

"What a mess!" screeched the parrot.

Millie glanced down at her gown and sighed. The pale green skirt was splattered with mud and the real blossoms sewn onto the bodice were broken and wilted. She touched one of the stems, wishing she could fix it herself. Although Millie had a magic of her own, she was unable to perform the simplest kind of spells that most witches found easy. "Would you mind fixing it for me, Mother?"

"Not at all. I'll just—"

"Zoë's here!" shrieked You-too, and both mother and daughter turned to the window where a little bat had landed

4

on the ledge. "I don't know why we have a door if everyone comes through the window," the parrot grumbled.

"I don't mean to intrude," said the bat. "I was on my way over when I saw Millie come through the window, so I thought I'd look for her here."

"We were just talking," said Emma. "Come right in."

Zoë fluttered into the room and settled on the floor beside Millie. A shadow passed over the bat and a puff of cool, dank air made Millie sneeze. When she looked at her friend again, Zoë was no longer a bat, but a slender girl whose head came up just past Millie's shoulder. Her hair was such a pale blond that it looked almost white; her eyes were blue-gray and shining.

The parrot flapped its wings and squawked, "Watch your necks! Vampire in the room!"

"You have to be the rudest bird I've ever met," said Millie. "I don't know why you keep him, Mother."

"He was a wedding gift from Olefat Wizard to your father and me. I've heard that Me-too, You-too's father, still lives with Olefat and gets more obnoxious every year. Sometimes I wonder if that wizard didn't give us the bird for revenge. The old wizard hasn't gotten his hands on any new spells since the day I helped your great-aunt Grassina make him stop stealing witches' memories."

"If You-too gets too obnoxious, just let me know," said Zoë. "I've never bitten a parrot before. What do you suppose their blood tastes like?"

You-too opened his beak to say something but apparently thought better of it and closed it with a snap. When Millie and Zoë began to laugh, he turned around so his back was to them and hunched his head down into his feathers.

"Would you really want to bite a parrot?" Emma asked.

The girl laughed again, her smile lighting up her pale face. "Don't worry, Your Highness. I've never bitten a bird or any creature larger than a grasshopper, much to my father's dismay. He's disappointed that I'm not embracing his family's lifestyle."

Emma frowned. "How can you do that? Don't vampires *have* to drink blood?"

"Full vampires do, but I'm lucky enough to have a choice. I just turn into an ordinary bat whenever the urge to drink blood comes over me, and then I eat insects. It's the same for the boys and little Suzette."

"How are your mother and the new baby?" asked Emma. "I haven't seen Li'l since right after the baby was born."

"They're doing well, thank you," said Zoë. "Mother sends her love." Turning to Millie, she glanced at her friend and frowned. "What happened to your gown?"

"A minor disaster," said Millie. "I was just asking my mother to fix it. Prince Atworth is on his way here. I saw him when I was flying over the forest. He has a small party

6

with him—only a squire and a page. They should arrive fairly soon. I wanted to talk to you about that, too, Mother. Don't you have something else you can try that might help me? Not a potion, but a spell, perhaps? It would be a catastrophe if I turned into a dragon while he's here. He's the fifth prince to come courting, and I can't afford to frighten away another!"

"I can't believe you want me to try magic on you again," said Emma. "You know my magic never works the way it should on you. I think your dragon side changes it somehow. You remember that potion I gave you the last time a prince came to visit . . ."

"Those green swellings were horrible!" said Zoë. "They were the size of my fist and they jiggled when you moved."

Millie grimaced. "I never told you, but they glowed in the dark, too. Even after I drank the second potion to reverse the effects of the first, the swellings didn't go away for days."

"I still don't understand how Prince Leopold made you angry. He seemed nice enough to me," said Zoë.

"I thought so, too, at first, but then he started telling me all the things he would do to 'improve' our castle if we got married, which meant tearing down half of it. He would have made it squat and ugly. And he criticized everything, from the moat to the shape of the castle keep, and acted like he knew more about castles than anyone else. I tried to tell him that I loved the castle just the way it was, but he told me I didn't know what I was talking about. I kept expecting to feel the change come on, so I was thrilled when it didn't. Then those boils or whatever they were started to pop out all over me, and I knew he was going to leave as soon as I saw the look on his face. I don't want another potion, Mother, but maybe a spell . . ."

"I really don't think it's a good idea, sweetheart. Who knows what the side effects might be. And to do it right before a prince is coming to visit—"

"But that's the whole reason I need your help. I'm never going to find the man I'm supposed to spend the rest of my life with if I keep scaring them away!"

"You still have plenty of time, Millie," said Emma. "You're not that old."

"I'm turning fifteen the day after tomorrow!" Millie wailed. "By the time you were fifteen you had already fallen in love with Father. And just last night Grandmother read a letter to me that she'd received from her old friend Queen Isabelle. Her son is marrying a girl that he just met. She was locked in a tower for most of her life and he was the first prince she'd ever seen. The girl is a year younger than me! Grandmother says that there aren't very many good princes around and if I don't hurry, they'll all be taken."

"Chartreuse always was helpful that way," Emma muttered. "I wouldn't worry about it," she said in a louder voice. "When I was young, she told me that no prince would marry me, and tried to make me marry the first one who asked. And then I met your father, who was exactly right for me. I'm sure you'll meet the right man, too, someday."

"But what if Atworth is the right one and I scare him off by turning into a dragon the first time we argue?"

You-too fluttered into the air and landed on Emma's worktable, his long green tail dragging behind him. "Then you'll be an old maid!" he squawked, nearly knocking over a pot of ink.

Emma frowned and snatched the pot out from under the parrot's wing. "Watch yourself, You-too, or I'll send you to the chicken coop."

"What would a parrot do in a chicken coop?" he asked.

"Who says you'd still be a parrot?" Emma replied.

"*Thppt!*" the parrot said, sticking out his tongue in a rude sort of way.

"Shoo!" said Emma, waving her hand at him. "I can't work while you're sitting on my table."

The parrot snapped at her fingers before darting to the window ledge. As he flew above the table, his tail knocked over the pot of ink, dousing Emma's parchment. Scowling, she gestured at the ink while muttering under her breath. The ink reversed its flow and ran back into the pot, which righted itself with a *thunk*, leaving the parchment as clean as before.

9

"Please, Mother," said Millie. "I need you to say a spell. I don't want to be an old maid."

"Oh, all right," Emma said, looking resigned. "But don't say that I didn't warn you." Tapping her finger on her chin, she studied her daughter for a moment. "I think we'll try a different approach. The potion I gave you last time was meant to prevent you from turning into a dragon if you got angry. Why don't we see if we can curb your temper instead?"

"If you think it will work," said Millie.

"I can't guarantee anything, but we'll try this."

> Quench this girl's temper
> And make her mood light.
> Don't let her get mad—
> At least till tonight.

"What do you mean 'at least till tonight'? What's so important about tonight?" asked Millie.

"You said that those swellings didn't disappear right away when I gave you the second potion. I didn't want to make this spell last too long in case it has side effects you don't like. If it works the way you want it to, I can always try to make it more permanent."

"That sounds reasonable," said Zoë. "I wonder what the side effects will be."

10

Millie darted an indignant glance in her direction. "I hope there won't be any."

"I think it's so romantic that Prince Atworth is coming for your birthday," said Zoë.

"It would have been more romantic if I'd met him before this. I'd never even heard his name until his messenger brought his letter."

"Someone's coming!" screeched You-too. "Three boys on horseback. Maybe one of them is that prince."

"Let me see," said Millie as she and Zoë raced to the window. The dragon part of her gave Millie excellent eyesight, but she had to wait until the horses trotted from behind some trees before she could see them. "He's very handsome. And he has dragons on his crest. If he likes dragons, maybe he's the one for me."

"Let's go meet him," said Zoë.

Millie turned away from the window. "Are you coming, Mother?" she asked, her cheeks flushed with excitement.

Emma smiled and reached for her daughter's hand. "I wouldn't miss this for anything, but don't you want me to do something about your gown?"

They were on their way down the curving tower stairs when Millie glanced behind her and said to Zoë, "I can't believe all you have to do to change is think about it. I wish it was that easy for me. I can never change when I want to. Do you know how frustrating it is to have so little control over your life?"

"I can imagine," said Zoë. "It must be awful."

As the prince's party approached the steps, Zoë stood on tiptoe to whisper into Millie's ear, "You were right when you said he was handsome. He's even better looking than Leopold."

"Isn't he, though?" Millie said, admiring his long dark hair and chiseled features. She also liked the flag his squire carried, with the golden dragon emblazoned on its center.

"Greetings," said the prince as he dismounted. He handed his reins to his squire while eyeing Millie and Zoë. "Go fetch the princess, and tell her that Prince Atworth has arrived."

Millie giggled and said, "I'm Princess Millie."

Zoë poked her in the side and whispered, "Did you just giggle? You never giggle."

"I know," Millie whispered back, giving her friend a confused look. "I didn't mean to." She glanced at Atworth and saw that he had swept off his cap in a courtly bow and was waiting for her to notice.

"You may rise, fair prince," Millie said as she held out her hand. Atworth took three steps and enfolded her hand in his. She giggled again when he turned it over and kissed her palm.

While the prince began to tell her how excited he was to meet her and how much he had been looking forward to his visit, Millie fought down a rising sense of panic. She thought the maids who flirted with squires looked brainless when they batted their eyelashes and giggled. The last thing she wanted to do was act the same way.

Emma had stopped to send word to Eadric and her parents that the prince had arrived, but she appeared now and nudged her daughter so that Millie's eyes lost their glazed expression. While the prince spoke to her mother, Millie fought the urge to giggle every time he looked her way. When he mentioned that he was hungry, Emma invited him to join them in a midday meal, even though it was still early.

"That sounds delightful," said Atworth, squeezing Millie's hand, which he still held in his.

A giggle erupted from Millie, making everyone, including the prince, look at her in surprise.

Millie wanted to tell her mother about how she couldn't keep from giggling, but when Emma's glance met hers, she realized that her mother already knew. It had to be a side effect of the spell and, in a way, she thought it was worse than the last one. The swellings just made her look awful. Uncontrollable giggling made her look and feel like a fool.

Millie was trying so hard not to giggle that she paid little attention to what Atworth was saying as they walked side by side to the Great Hall. Her grandparents and her father were already there when they arrived, and they greeted Atworth, gesturing for him to sit beside the old king. Limelyn had always doted on his granddaughter, so he studied the prince with great interest.

It was a simple meal of cheese, cold meat from the night before, fresh bread baked that morning, and berries from the castle's garden. "This is delicious," said the prince as he helped himself to another slice of roast pork.

"Cook is saving the best food for the day after tomorrow," said Millie. "Everyone in the kitchen has been cooking all week for the party."

"You're having a party in my honor?" said Atworth. "I'm surprised you have enough food."

Zoë frowned and leaned forward to see past Millie. "Actually, the party is in Millie's honor. Her *birthday* is the day after tomorrow."

"I see," said the prince, but he looked confused. "How can you use the food for a party when you're in such dire straits? I understand that you have a large dragon population in Greater Greensward. Don't they carry off your sheep and cattle and burn your crops to the ground with their foul breath?"

Millie giggled, although she didn't think he was the least bit amusing. "Why no," she said. "Not at—"

"When I heard about your dragon problem, I knew that Greater Greensward was the place for me. I'm quite an accomplished dragon slayer. I have nearly fifty trophies mounted on the walls of the Great Hall at home. I see that you don't have any," the prince said, looking around.

"We don't—," Millie began.

"You must have different dragons in your kingdom than we do back home. I saw a green one on my way here today. I was thinking how well its head would look on my wall, but since your birthday is coming up, I can kill it tomorrow so I can give you the head as a birthday gift."

Millie knew she should be angry at the awful butcher who had unknowingly offered to present her with her own head for her birthday, but all she could do was giggle. The more she thought about it, the more she giggled. When she tried to stop, her face turned red from the effort.

King Limelyn gave his granddaughter a sharp glance and said to the prince, "Did I hear you say that you kill dragons?"

"Yes," said the prince. "It's a real shame that no one in your kingdom is brave enough to slay them. The beasts must have been breeding here for some time for the dragon population to grow as large as it has. I've heard from travelers that there are dragon sightings in Greater Greensward every day. You may breathe easy now that I've come to help you with your infestation. I'm sure we'll be able to work out some sort of arrangement for my services. Say, half the kingdom and Princess Millie's hand in

16

marriage? I'll rid you of all the dragons and, of course, I get to keep the heads, except for the one I'd give to you for your birthday, my dear," he said, turning to Millie. "You are quite lovely, you know, and not too overburdened with brains. I think we'll get on very well."

Millie tried to stifle a giggle and ended up gasping. "I really . . . don't think—"

"It would help if you could tell me where the dragons' lairs are located. I could find them myself, but the whole thing would go much faster if I knew where to look."

This time the urge to giggle was more than Millie could stand. She giggled so hard that she was afraid she might faint for lack of air. "I have . . . to go," she wheezed. Although she welcomed Zoë's offer to help her from the room, Millie was unable to make it farther than the corridor outside the Great Hall, where she let go of Zoë's arm and sank to the floor. "How long . . . until nightfall?" she asked.

Zoë shrugged. "Eight hours or so. It's summer, Millie, so the days are longer. If you're wondering about the spell, there's no saying when it might end. Your mother was right when she said that the spells she casts on you never work the way she intends."

"I wish I . . . could get angry," Millie said, fighting for control. "I'd like to . . . turn into a dragon . . . and fry him to a crisp!"

"And he'd like to chop your head off," Zoë reminded her. "I hope neither of you gets your wish."

Millie giggled and clapped her hand over her mouth. When the urge had passed, she said in a strangled voice, "I swear, I'll never ask my mother to put another spell on me, no matter what. I was foolish to ask her to do it this time."

"You weren't foolish," said Zoë. "Just desperate. But I think we know one thing for sure now. Prince Atworth is not the right one for you."

"You can say that again," said Millie.

When Millie was finally calm enough to return to the Great Hall, the mood in the room was very different than it had been at the start of the meal. Her mother's mouth was set in a grim line and she was looking at the prince as if *she* wanted to take off *his* head. Her grandmother was biting her lip and watching King Limelyn. Both Millie's father and grandfather were glaring at Atworth.

"Ah, there you are, Millie," said the prince. "Your grandfather and I were just about to seal our deal."

"I beg to differ, young man," said the king. "I was just about to tell you to leave my kingdom and never come back. We don't need you to kill any dragons, and even if we did, my granddaughter would not be part of any *deal*. I suggest you go back to whatever minor kingdom it is that you came from and stay there."

Prince Atworth blinked. For once, he didn't seem to know what to say.

Eadric stood and strode the length of the table. "Let me help you out," he said, taking the prince by the arm.

He had dragged the boy from his seat when Atworth planted his feet and said, "You don't have to give me Millie's hand, or even half the kingdom, but would you mind if I stayed to slay a few dragons? You wouldn't have to pay me at all."

Millie was proud of her father when he said, "You don't have our permission to hunt so much as a butterfly in Greater Greensward. If you even look as if you are trying to slay a dragon, I will come after you myself!"

"As will I!" shouted King Limelyn.

Both Chartreuse and Emma clapped as Eadric hustled the prince to the door. He was scarcely out of sight when Emma pushed back her chair. "I'm going to the top of the tower to keep an eye on Atworth. When he's out of sight I'll watch him with my farseeing ball. If he doesn't move quickly enough to suit me, I'll cast a spell to rid us of him for good. You need not worry about him, Millie," she said, stopping by her daughter's seat. "Are you all right? You look awfully pale."

"I'm fine," Millie said, and giggled. "But I'll feel even better when this spell wears off."

"I'm glad I put a limit on it," said Emma. "Let's just hope it ends when it's supposed to."

Three

The spell hadn't ended when Millie went to bed that night, so she was too worried to fall asleep for the longest time. When she finally did, it seemed as if it was only minutes later that daylight was streaming through her window and her parents were standing beside her bed.

She was still groggy when her mother said, "A messenger arrived from Queen Frazzela this morning, and, well . . . I know you had other plans, but we need to go to Upper Montevista today."

"What day is it?" Millie asked, rubbing the sleep from her eyes. "Isn't my birthday party tomorrow?"

Her parents exchanged a wary look she'd seen all too often. "You'll still have your party," her mother told her.

Millie sat up, suddenly wide awake. "Not if we go to Upper Montevista. It will take days since we always have to travel by carriage when we go there. How can we celebrate my birthday while we're traveling? You promised we could have my party here."

"We promised we would be with you for your birthday," said her mother. "We never said we had to have the party in Greater Greensward. Your grandmother has written asking us to celebrate your birthday in Upper Montevista. Frazzela said that she hasn't seen enough of you lately and has a very special present for you. I'm working on a spell that will get us there today."

"But I don't want to go now. My friends can't come to my party if we have it there!"

Her father put his arm around her mother's waist, as if to give Emma support. "We've already sent our reply, Millie," he said. "We're going to Upper Montevista. As your grandmother reminded us, she and your grandfather are getting old. Who knows how long they'll be with us? People on my side of the family don't stick around as ghosts like your mother's family do."

"Why can't your parents come here if they want to see me?" Millie asked her father. "They've never come to visit us."

"My parents don't like to travel," said Eadric. "Besides, your mother and I would have gone there right after your party, anyway. They're having a problem with sea monsters in Chancewold and—"

"I knew it was something like that. I've been looking forward to my birthday party for months and now you have to spoil it just so you can take care of somebody else's problem!"

21

"The sea monsters aren't someone else's problem, they're ours," said Emma. "If there's an emergency in Upper Montevista or Greater Greensward, it's up to us to take care of it, but we won't attend to the sea monsters until after your party."

"Why can't you ever think about what I want?" said Millie, her face turning red. "Why do your two stupid kingdoms always have to come first?"

"Here we go again," her father said under his breath.

"It's always Greater Greensward this or Upper Montevista that!" Millie knew she was being selfish and unreasonable, but she was so upset that she didn't care. She was angry, too, and getting angrier the more she thought about how unfair they were being. They were her parents. Shouldn't she come first? Suddenly the air seemed thick, the walls too close. She was glad when she felt the change begin. At least now she could get away. Millie paused to take a breath, and in that instant the bone at the base of her spine lengthened into a long tail, her eyes moved farther apart as her skull changed shape, and her skin prickled as scales emerged. A heaviness between her shoulder blades told her that her wings had come out.

"You're never here when I need you and now you're dragging me off with you so you can take care of *another* crisis!" When she finished changing, Millie was about seven feet long, with scales ranging from pale green to deep emerald. She wasn't a very big dragon, but then,

22

nearly fifteen-year-old dragons never were. "I don't think you care about me at all!" she said, her eyes flashing. Throwing back her head, she spread her wings and flew out of her bedchamber, drawing her wings to her sides only long enough to fit through the window.

As she beat her wings, flying high above her family's castle, Millie was so angry that smoke leaked from her nostrils. She didn't notice the flock of starlings that veered away when they saw her, nor the cows that bellowed and ran as her shadow passed overhead. She was thinking about how much she wished her parents would stay home just this once when she noticed a cottage surrounded by a lush garden nestled on the bank of a river.

Even though it was still early in the morning, a knight in armor stood in a clearing just beyond the garden, swinging his sword and lunging at a dummy made of wood and leather. Millie flew lower, and the knight looked up at the sound of her beating wings. She was in the mood to fight, so, instead of flying away, she landed on the ground not ten feet from the knight and puffed a ball of fire in his direction. The knight stepped to the side, trampling a patch of daisies.

"Good," declared the knight, as he waved his sword at Millie. "A worthy opponent! It's been many days since I slew my last dragon."

"You shan't slay me, fair knight," growled Millie, "for I am no ordinary dragon."

"And I am no ordinary knight!" he shouted just before he lunged.

Millie danced away and the knight's sword whistled past her shoulder. "You'll have to do better than that!" she cried. Whirling around, she lashed her tail at the knight, who leaped nimbly over the tip despite his armor.

The knight grabbed a shield that had been leaning against a fence post and raised his sword again. "Then how is this?" he shouted, as he ran straight at the dragon with his sword aimed at her heart.

Taking a deep breath, Millie exhaled a ten-foot-long flame that hit the shield and flared out to the sides. The knight slowed, but didn't stop advancing, so she kept her flame going until she was gasping for air. She was trying to get another flame started when he swung his sword and hit her hard enough to chip one of her scales.

Startled, Millie gasped and narrowed her eyes, but instead of striking her again, the knight began to dance around the clearing, waving his sword in the air and yelling, "I hit her! I finally hit her!"

"We're not finished yet!" shouted Millie, flaming at the knight just as he raised his shield. Once again, the knight came after her with his sword raised, but this time Millie backed away until her tail was in the river and she had to dig her claws into the bank to keep from slipping in.

"I've got you now!" the knight cried. Just as he lunged at her with his sword, Millie stepped to the side and spun around, hitting him with her tail so that he fell, flailing, into the water.

Knowing that the river was shallow there, she waited at the edge, expecting the knight to pop up at any second. As time passed, however, and he didn't emerge, she stepped closer and dipped her head into the murky water to see what had happened to him. She had just started to look around when the knight jumped up with a *whoosh*, wrapped his arms around her neck, and pulled her in after him. Millie gasped, and her mouth filled with water, half of which trickled down her throat. She could feel the fire in her belly go out as the water reached it. A moment later, she and the knight were sitting side by side in the waist-deep water, each laughing at how ridiculous the other looked as steam seeped from her mouth and water dribbled down his face inside his helmet.

"You almost had me," she said when she finally stopped laughing. "You should have pressed your advantage when you chipped my scale. By the way, you owe me for that," she said, glancing down at the marred surface of her dripping shoulder.

"What about me? My armor could rust after getting wet like this," said the knight, reaching up to pull off his helmet. Millie leaned away from him as the young man with straw-colored hair and laughing green eyes shook his head so that water splattered everywhere.

"Not if I know you, Francis," she said, getting to her

feet. "The spell you put on your armor to make it light probably made it rustproof, too. I bet you never even have to polish it."

"Hey," said the young man as he tried to stand on the slippery river bottom. "I use my magic only to help me be a better knight. I can't help it if . . ." With a startled cry, Francis's feet went out from under him and he landed in the water with a splash.

Millie sighed and reached into the water. Clamping her jaws gently around his arm, she pulled her cousin from the river and helped him climb up the slick mud to drier ground. Nudging him up the last few feet with her nose, she said, "If you give me a few minutes till I get a flame going again, I'll dry you off."

"And risk getting cooked like a sausage in a skillet? I don't think so!" Francis said, scrambling to his feet.

"May I suggest you put a spell on your shoes to make them grip slippery surfaces better? What if you really were fighting an unfriendly dragon?"

"Good idea," said Francis. "I'll see what I can do. So, tell me, what made you mad enough to want to bite some-body's head off this time?"

Millie didn't bother asking him how he knew that she'd been angry. Everyone close to her knew that she turned into a dragon when she got really mad. Francis was the only one who had taken advantage of this and had talked her into fighting with him when she was a dragon, just so he could have the practice. Ever since he was a little boy, Francis had wanted to be a knight more than anything. He had practiced day and night for years, much to his parents' dismay; although he had inherited their talent for magic, he hadn't inherited their interest in it. He was already adept with the sword and the lance, but no matter how hard he'd tried, he'd never been even close to beating Millie before.

Millie sighed and settled on the ground beside the bench where Francis always sat. He was taking off his armor when she replied, "My parents have to go to Upper Montevista to take care of another *crisis*. They say we're going today."

"What about your party?" asked her cousin.

"That's what I asked them. Apparently, my grandparents want me to have my party there. They got me a special present and everything."

"I wonder what it is," said Francis. "Maybe it's another gown like last year, although I don't know why anyone would call that special."

Millie shrugged. "Who knows? Anyway, I got mad because it's so unfair that my parents have to drag me to Upper Montevista when everybody was already coming to my party here, but they don't care what I want."

"Parents are like that," said Francis. "Mine want me to practice my magic when they know how much I want to be a knight. I don't have time for silly things like turning coachmen into rabbits."

"Do they actually do that?" asked Millie.

Francis snorted. "Them? I've never seen them turn a person into anything. I think it's because my father spent all that time as an otter."

"I bet you're right," said Millie.

"So, what are you going to do about your party?"

"I'll have to go, of course, but that doesn't mean I'm going to like it."

Four

By the time she had finished talking to Francis, Millie was calm enough to become a human again, but she waited to do it until she had returned home. She was going to fly through her chamber window and change there, but when she saw that a maid was in the room packing gowns into a small trunk, Millie swerved away and went looking for somewhere private. No one was in the sheltered niche behind the stables, so she changed back into her human form in the dust under old cobwebs and was on her way into the castle when she heard the clatter of wheels crossing the drawbridge. Curious, Millie turned back to the courtyard and was surprised to see the elegant carriage belonging to Zoë's family slow to a stop. A moment later, Zoë stepped out of the carriage holding the hands of her two younger brothers.

"Millie, isn't it exciting?" Zoë said as she hurried over to join her friend. The two little boys with pale blond hair ran to keep up. "We're going to Upper Montevista with you. Papa needs to start his annual visit to all the relatives, so when your mother's invitation came, he decided that we should all go. I can't wait to see your grandparents' castle."

"I'm so glad you're coming!" said Millie, giving her friend a hug. "I hated the idea of having my party without you."

Three carriages belonging to her own family rumbled across the stones of the courtyard, which was suddenly bustling with activity as trunks were loaded and the other travelers arrived. Millie was happy that her grandparents King Limelyn and Queen Chartreuse were going, but she was thrilled when Francis and his parents appeared.

"We got your mother's invitation right after you left," Francis told her. "I packed all my stuff in an acorn I bought at the Magic Marketplace. You'd never believe what you can fit in one of those things. Say," he said, squinting into the shadows beneath the wall of the keep, "is that Great-grandfather?"

Millie yelped and ran to greet the ghosts of her great-grandparents, who had come to say good-bye along with some of the other castle ghosts who were her friends. Although they were hard to see in the shadows, they would have been nearly invisible in the bright daylight, which was one of the reasons they rarely ventured out of the dungeon during the day.

"We heard that you were going to Upper Montevista," said her great-grandmother. "We hope you have a wonderful time."

"I'm so sorry you won't be able to come to my party," said Millie. "I really wanted to have it here."

"We can't understand why Frazzela would make you have it at her castle," said a ghost named Sir Jarvis.

"Just be careful on the road," said King Aldrid. "There were bandits on the way to Upper Montevista when I was alive."

"Don't worry, Great-grandfather," Millie said. "My parents chased the bandits away years ago. I'm sure we'll be fine."

A shadow passed overhead. Terrified, the horses harnessed to the carriages began to rear and scream. Men were rushing to control them when a familiar voice called hello. "It's Ralf!" Millie said as a twelve-foot-long blue dragon landed on the cobblestones.

Emma was reciting a spell to calm the horses when two more dragons landed in the courtyard behind the first. Although the red dragon was huge at nearly twenty feet, the blue-black dragon was the biggest of all. Over thirty-five feet long, it had deep-set eyes that could make even the bravest knights quake. Millie wasn't afraid of any of them. Ralf's parents had often looked after her when she was a baby; they were like a second family to her. "Ralf! Flame

31

Snorter! Grumble Belly!" she cried, flinging her arms around Ralf's neck before running to hug the others. "Are you coming to Upper Montevista, too?"

"Upper Montevista? Why would we go there?" asked Ralf. "We stopped by to see if you wanted to go swimming in the ocean with us before your party."

"Oh, Ralf, I'd love to," Millie exclaimed. "But I can't today. We're going to Upper Montevista for my birthday. We're having my party there this year."

"Really?" said Ralf. "Can we go, too?" he asked, turning to his parents.

His mother shook her head. "Sorry, Ralf, but you know how Millie's other grandmother feels about dragons. She told her archers to shoot us the next time we drop in."

"I'm sorry, Ralf," said Millie. "I was supposed to have my party here, but there's been a change in plans."

"That's okay," he said, but his ears drooped and his ridge went limp. "Maybe I should give you your present now. Here." Reaching under his wing, Ralf pulled out a small leather sack tied shut with a silver cord.

"Thank you, Ralf," she said. "This is so sweet of you." Millie pulled open the drawstring and removed a handful of bright-colored crystals, holding them up so everyone could see. "What are they?"

"We found them in a cave. You eat a couple before you flame and they make your fire come out a different color.

They're really crunchy and kind of sweet," Ralf said, licking his lips.

"Thanks," said Millie. "I'll have to try them next time."

Her parents gave each other worried looks.

"We should go now, Ralf," Flame Snorter said. "Millie's family is going on a trip and we're keeping them from getting started."

"Good-bye, everyone," said Grumble Belly. "Ralf . . ."

"I'm coming," said Ralf, spreading his wings wide.

"Happy birthday, Millie!" the dragons shouted as they took to the air.

"Thank you!" Millie replied, waving with one hand while holding on to the side of a carriage with the other.

As the dragon family took off, the wind their wings created blew the green pennants off the lower towers, knocked over a half-filled water barrel, swept a young page off his feet, and destroyed the carefully arranged hairdos of all the ladies present.

"They *would* have to come now!" said Queen Chartreuse as she straightened her clothes.

"Is everyone ready?" Prince Eadric asked. "Millie, I need to talk to you." He waited while she walked around the toppled water barrel before saying, "Your mother has come up with a marvelous spell that will take all our carriages to Upper Montevista in just a few hours. You'll be traveling with your mother and me. We have something we want to discuss with you."

33

"But Zoë and Francis—," Millie began.

"—are traveling with their own parents," interrupted her father. "Go get in. We're about to leave."

She had started for the carriage when her mother cried, "Millie, watch out for the horses!"

A groom was walking a fresh pair of horses to her grandparents' carriage. They were only a few yards from Millie when they smelled her. With flaring nostrils and frantic eyes, the horses tossed their heads and backed away from Millie. She hurried to her parents' carriage and climbed in, shutting the door behind her. Horses had never liked Millie. Her mother said it was because she had so much dragon in her. Horses could smell her dragon side even when she hadn't been one for a long time; they refused to go anywhere near her. Unlike most princesses her age, Millie had never learned how to ride.

When everyone else was ready, Emma and Eadric climbed into the carriage with their daughter. Millie loved hearing her mother's spells, so she listened eagerly while Emma recited the one she had made up just for the trip.

> Horse and carriage, you'll now speed
> Through the countryside.
> Take us to Frazzela's home
> With the smoothest ride.

34

Slow to a more normal pace
When people are around.
Then hurry up until we fly
Over rock and ground.

Get us there before the sun
Sets on this lovely day.
Take the shortest route you can—
Neither stop nor stray.

The carriage lurched as the horses started out, then settled into a pace so fluid that Millie had to look out of the window to see if they were really moving. They were already outside the castle walls by then and when she looked down the ground was hurtling past. Sliding off her seat, Millie leaned out of the window to see the horses. They were running just as they normally would, but the ground itself seemed to be rushing under their hooves.

"I wish we could fly there," Millie told her parents as she returned to her seat. "It would be so much simpler."

Her mother was idly gazing into the farseeing ball that she always wore on a chain around her neck. Glancing at Millie, she let go of the chain and said, "Maybe we'll be able to in a few years, but the people of Upper Montevista still expect to see us travel like royalty. They accept my magic much more than they used to; it's just that they still aren't ready to see us arriving on a flying carpet. Besides, your father and I wanted to talk to you and the wind can be so loud when we fly."

Eadric cleared his throat and said, "You know we love you very much and we think you're wonderful just the way you are . . ."

"What have I done wrong now?" Millie asked.

"Nothing. It's just that we want you to be careful while we're visiting your grandparents. Please try very hard not to lose your temper. We've done our best to keep your grandmother from hearing about . . . you know."

"You mean that I turn into a dragon? I know that's why we've visited them only a few times. I figured that out years ago. But how have you kept them from hearing about it from other people?"

Emma couldn't quite meet her daughter's eyes as she said, "I cast a spell when you were just a baby. If anyone who wasn't a friend or part of the family came near you, he was struck dumb if he tried to tell someone new about the way you change. Unfortunately, there isn't a thing we can do about it if your grandmother actually sees you, which you must try very hard not to let happen. There are certain things we still can't do around Frazzela."

"She likes fairy magic," Eadric reminded Millie. "For some reason, my mother finds fairies fascinating. It's gotten so she can't seem to get enough of them."

"That's true," said Emma, "but she doesn't like it when

I turn into anything. I had to become a dragon the day of our wedding—"

"Because the trolls attacked the castle," said Millie. "I know. I've heard the story."

Emma nodded. "And ever since then, I don't dare turn into anything when your grandmother is around. She became hysterical during one of our visits a few months later, when she saw me turn into a hawk. She threatened to outlaw witches in Upper Montevista."

"Which she could never do," said Eadric. "Not with all the witches my father has helping his soldiers now."

"But she could make it uncomfortable for them again," said Emma.

"And that's why you don't want her to know that I become a dragon, too? It's not like I do it on purpose!" said Millie.

"Which might frighten her even more. Uncontrolled magic would probably terrify her. All we're asking you to do is try hard not to lose your temper, which I know is very difficult at times."

"I'll do the best I can," said Millie.

Five

They made good time going north, having slowed only twice—once when they went through a small village, and again when they passed a group of hunters who would surely have noticed the speeding carriages. Millie was watching the trees in the forest flash past when water splattered the carriage and they stopped with a lurch so sudden that she slid off the seat and landed on the floor at her parents' feet. A loud moan shook the carriage and another deluge struck with a terrific *splat*.

"What happened?" Millie asked as she untangled herself from their legs.

Her father reached for the door, saying, "I'm going to go see."

There was a series of loud booms and the forest floor shook. If Eadric hadn't been holding on to the door, he would have fallen out headfirst.

"I'm going, too," said her mother, pausing to give Millie a stern look. "You stay here until we get back."

"But I want to—," Millie began.

"Not this time, Millie," her mother said as she peered out the window. "I don't need to worry about you and whatever is going on out there, too."

While her mother shut the carriage door behind her, Millie scooted toward the window. "I'm not a little girl anymore," she muttered. "I don't know why I have to stay inside." Millie reached for the latch when she saw Li'l, the bat, fly out of her carriage, and her daughter Zoë climb down as a human. When she saw her grandparents get out of their carriage, and Francis and his parents get out of theirs, Millie couldn't wait any longer. A deep rumbling sound was making the trees vibrate when she opened the door and slipped out. The sound rose and fell as Millie crept around the back, hoping to see what was happening without being seen herself. The ground was wet and muddy, so she had to pick her way carefully and didn't see Francis until she bumped into him.

"What are you doing?" he asked.

"Sh!" hissed Millie. "My mother told me to stay in the carriage."

"It's giants," whispered Zoë as she joined them. "There's a whole crowd. They're standing around talking to your parents, Millie. Come here and I'll show you." Zoë led the way to the edge of a ditch tall enough for a man to stand in without his head showing over the top. It was nearly twenty feet wide, and on the other side rested a stack of logs well over sixty feet long.

Millie leaned over the ditch, trying to see past the closer trees to where two giants had crouched down to talk to her parents. There were four giants all told, not the crowd that Zoë had mentioned, but even four giants was a lot. Millie thought it must be a family, with a mother, a father, and two boys who were almost as big as their parents. The adults were talking to Emma while the boys stood behind them, each with a hand on his mother's shoulder. Huge tears trickled down her cheeks, which, Millie decided, explained the water that had hit the carriage.

Although the rumble of a giant's voice could make the ground shake, the giants who were talking to her parents were courteous enough to whisper, yet even from a distance, Millie could hear most of what they were saying.

"We were felling trees so we could make a boat," whispered the father. "We want to explore the Eastern Sea. Our friends have already gone to start a new life on one of the islands."

"My Penelope . . . ," the mother cried, wiping her eyes.

The father shook his head. "She's just a little girl. She could be anywhere."

"She's only three," the mother whispered. "I was watching her and I turned away for a minute to catch a tree

40

that was about to hit my boys. And then when I looked for my little Penelope, she was gone." The giantess sobbed and dabbed at her eyes with a cloth that could have covered Millie's bed.

Millie couldn't hear what Emma said, but she saw her pick up her farseeing ball and move her lips. An image must have appeared in the ball, because the giants bent closer to peer into it and were smiling and laughing when they stood up.

"I know where that meadow is!" boomed the father, forgetting to whisper. The trees around them whipped back and forth as if caught in a terrible storm. Twigs and leaves rained down on Emma and Eadric, who clutched each other so they wouldn't blow away. Millie could feel the wind from where she stood, and she had to step away from the ditch so she wouldn't fall in. It was even worse when the giants turned and started to run through the forest. "At least they're going the other way," Millie shouted to Francis as the ground bucked and lurched beneath them.

Trees crashed as the giants pushed them aside, and then there was silence, but it lasted for just a moment before the entire forest shook from the giants' laughter.

"Your parents are coming back," Francis said, and Millie hurried to the carriage.

She glanced toward the trench in time to see her mother move the logs with her magic while Li'l watched from a nearby tree stump. Then Li'l was on her way back, stopping long enough to talk to Zoë. They were already in their carriage when Millie's parents returned.

"What happened?" Millie asked as her parents took their seats across from her.

"A family of giants was felling trees," said Emma. "Their little girl wandered off while they were working and they didn't know where she'd gone. I used my far-seeing ball to find the child."

"She was asleep in a meadow," said Eadric. "You should have seen their faces when your mother told them where she was."

"I'm glad you stayed inside where I told you to," said Emma, leaning across the space between the seats to give Millie a hug. "I don't ever want to lose you the way that mother lost her baby."

"Mama, I'm not a baby anymore."

Emma kissed her on the forehead and said, "You'll always be my baby, Millie, even when you're a hundred years old."

The sun had almost set when the carriages slowed for the last time. Millie stuck her head out of the window as they approached the narrow causeway that led to the royal castle of Upper Montevista. She had been there only a few times in her life and then only for very short visits; all she remembered about the castle was that it was cold, dark,

42

and uninviting. When she finally spied it through the carriage window, she remembered another reason she hadn't liked the castle—it was ugly. Unlike the light and airy castle in Greater Greensward, with its slender towers and many windows, this castle's thick, nearly windowless outer walls and four massive towers made it look squat and heavy, like a fat toad sleeping on a rock.

Zoë's brothers were the first ones out of their carriage. Unlike their father, who couldn't come out of the curtained carriage in the daylight, sunlight didn't bother the children. Millie wondered if the three boys had traveled as bats or as vampires, but either way they shot out of the carriage as humans and with so much pent-up energy that it carried them whooping and yelling around the courtyard. Zoë chased them, calling to her brothers to come back, but they ignored her and didn't stop running until a young man with curly brown hair like Eadric's stepped forward and scooped up the two smaller boys in his arms.

"Who is that?" Millie asked her father as he helped her down their carriage steps.

"That's your uncle Bradston," Eadric said, reaching for Emma's hand. "It looks as if everyone has come to welcome us."

Millie knew who Bradston was, of course, although she had been a small child the last time she visited Upper Montevista and he had been a teenager who hadn't paid her much attention. What she remembered most about him came from her favorite bedtime story: the retelling of how her parents had rescued him from his troll kidnappers. Her mother always finished the story with the spell she'd cast to make Bradston stay close to his mother until he nearly drove Queen Frazzela crazy.

Servants were lighting torches in the darkening court-yard when Millie and her parents joined the people waiting by the door. As the sun went down behind a distant mountain, Garrid emerged from his carriage, although there was no sign of either Li'l or baby Suzette. Eadric had already begun the introductions when Francis ran up to join Millie, leaving his parents to follow.

"That was great!" Francis whispered into Millie's ear. "I wish every carriage ride was like that. I'm going to have to learn that spell so I can use it, too."

Millie turned her head to whisper back, "But I thought you wouldn't use your magic unless it helped you as a knight."

Francis opened his mouth to reply, but Millie didn't hear what he had to say because just then someone squeezed her cheeks between two fingers and turned her head to face forward. An older woman with frizzy brown hair streaked with gray was smiling down at her, saying, "This must be our Millie. My, but you've grown since I saw you last. Of course, if your parents brought you around more often, you wouldn't be such a stranger. Look at her, Bodamin. Doesn't she look like Eadric when he was her

44

age?" King Bodamin didn't answer his wife because he was talking about hunting with Millie's other grandfather, King Limelyn. Queen Chartreuse was there beside Frazzela, however, listening to every word.

"Actually, I think I look more like my other grandmother, Queen Chartreuse," Millie replied between lips puckered like a fish's.

"She does have my hair color," murmured Chartreuse.

"Perhaps," said Queen Frazzela, releasing Millie's face.

Millie rubbed her cheeks as her two grandmothers led the way into the castle. Francis had disappeared and she was about to go looking for him when her father said, "Millie, I'm sure you remember your uncle Bradston." Her father had his arm around the shoulders of the young man she'd already seen. A pretty young woman stood on Bradston's other side, and beside her was a boy not much older than Millie.

"It's nice to see you again, Millie," said Bradston. "This is my fiancée, Lady Maybelle, and her brother, Lord Eduardo."

"Hello, Millie," said Maybelle in a surprisingly high-pitched voice. Millie thought her pale blond hair and light blue eyes made her look almost ghostly in the torchlight. "You never told me that she was pretty," Maybelle said to Bradston. Turning to the boy on her other side, she added, "She might be just what you're looking for, Eduardo."

Taking a step forward, Eduardo bowed to Millie and

45

took her hand in his. "I've heard wonderful things about your kingdom and your mother, the Green Witch," he said. "Do you have magic as well?"

Millie nodded and swallowed hard. Unlike his sister, Eduardo had dark hair and piercing brown eyes, but he was as handsome as Maybelle was pretty. The look he was giving Millie was so intense that she could feel her face grow hot.

"Maybe we should go in now," said Francis, bumping into her arm.

"Uh-huh," said Millie, but her eyes didn't leave those of Eduardo, who still held her hand in his.

"Did you see where my parents went?" asked Zoë. She was holding her youngest brother, Ivan, who had fallen asleep with his head on her shoulder.

Francis tugged on Millie's arm. "Come on. We have to go help Zoë."

"Why do you let your servants talk to you like that?" Eduardo asked Millie.

"What?" said Millie, confused until she saw where he was looking. "They aren't my servants. This is my friend *Princess* Zoë and my cousin *Lord* Francis."

"My mistake," Eduardo said. "Their clothes . . ."

Zoë glanced down at the simple shift she was wearing, then looked up at Eduardo, her eyes flashing. "We've been traveling."

"If you'll excuse us," Francis said through stiff lips, "we have to go."

Eduardo squeezed Millie's hand before releasing it, murmuring, "Until later."

"Uh . . . right, later," Millie told Eduardo over her shoulder as Francis dragged her away.

As they entered the castle, Zoë said, "I don't like that boy."

Francis frowned. "Neither do I."

"I think he's all right," said Millie, glancing over her shoulder one last time.

Six

illie was exhausted. Once she reached the chamber she was to use, she lay down on the bed to rest her eyes. It was a cozy room, having been made that way by her mother many years before. The tapestry on the wall and the comfortable bed made it seem like home, and before she knew it, Millie was asleep. She missed supper and would have slept until morning, but halfway through the night her door flew open and a flock of bats fluttered in. Millie sat up, rubbing her eyes as one of the bats settled on her bed and turned into Zoë.

"Guess what?" said her friend. "My parents have to go, but they said I can stay here with you!"

Another bat landed on the floor and a moment later Garrid was shutting the door. He had the same blond hair as Zoë, and the same sharply defined features, but unlike his daughter, the prince was tall and extraordinarily handsome, while Zoë could only be considered pretty. "Li'l said that she can manage without Zoë as long as the boys remain bats," said Garrid, "so I spoke to your mother and father and they said it's fine with them. I'm sorry we're going to miss your party, but at least you two will be together."

"Zoë," said Li'l, a small brown bat, "you can fly us to the castle wall, then I want you to go to bed. You and Millie are going to have a busy day tomorrow, so you should get some sleep now."

"But Mama, I slept all the way here!" wailed Zoë.

"I'm sorry, Zoë, but you'll have to live like a human, at least for a little while. Queen Frazzela and King Bodamin don't know anything about you, so just let them think you're human while you're staying with them." Li'l fluttered around Millie, brushing the girl's cheek with her wing. "Happy birthday, Millie!" Li'l said. "Behave yourselves, and don't get into any trouble."

"See you in the morning!" Zoë told her friend before turning back into a bat and flying out the window with her family.

It seemed as though Millie had just fallen asleep again when she woke to the sound of people running in the halls and the tinkling laughter that could only belong to a fairy. She sat up and was about to get out of bed when suddenly her door burst open and a flood of full-sized fairies poured in as a flock of tiny fairies flew in through the window. Laughing and shouting, "Happy birthday!" the fairies crowded around Millie's bed, showering her with kisses so delicate that she could scarcely feel them.

Tiny fairies began to jump on her bed, shedding fairy dust in their excitement. They didn't seem to mind when a larger fairy swept a dozen or so of them aside so she could sit by Millie's feet. "Happy birthday!" she said, giving Millie's toes a pat. It was the Swamp Fairy. She had become a particular friend of Millie's parents around the time Millie was born, claiming that she had a special tie to them because she had known them for so long.

Millie felt a tug on her hair. The tiny fairies were swarming around her head, vying with each other to arrange her locks in a special birthday style. Not to be outdone, the big fairies began rooting through Millie's trunks, pulling out one gown after another, then discarding them, declaring that they were too plain or too ugly. Her shoes were also dismissed as being unsightly, and tossed under the bed.

When the tiny fairies finally let go of her hair and hovered around her to admire their handiwork, Millie reached up to feel what they had done. Somehow, they had turned her hair into a giant knot that she couldn't get her fingers through. Millie winced when her fingers snagged the knot. "Um, thanks for trying, but . . ."

"Now it's my turn," said the Swamp Fairy. With a wave of her hand, the knots came out of Millie's hair with a *whoosh* and flew in a whirl around her head, settling in an intricate arrangement of curls. A mirror flew out of the trunk on the floor, stopping inches away from Millie's face. She had to lean back to see her hair, which wobbled and bounced each time she moved her head. "Uh, very nice, but—"

"Let me!" cried another fairy.

"No, me!" cried another.

Millie gritted her teeth and tried to look like she was enjoying it as the bigger fairies used their magic to rearrange her hair. Curls, loops, ringlets, braids, poufs, and buns all gave way as her hair changed from one style to the next. From what she could see in the mirror, none of the styles were anything she would actually have worn, although a few gave her some ideas.

"Hello!" called an overly cheerful voice, and Queen Frazzela stuck her head into the room. "What's going on in here?" she asked, smiling broadly.

The Swamp Fairy frowned. "We were just leaving," she said. "Happy birthday again, sweet bud," she said to Millie, and gave her another kiss on the cheek. Then, in a sparkle of fairy dust and a tinkling sound like wind chimes, fairies big and small fled the room.

Queen Frazzela scowled at Millie. "They didn't have to leave," she said, and turned to study the mess on the floor. "I hope you brought a maid to clean this up." Still scowling, she stomped from the room and closed the door with a loud *thunk*.

Millie sighed and slid out from under her covers. Although she could do some simple magic of the ordinary kind, most of her magic was related to being a dragon. This meant that while her relatives could clean a room with a quick and easy spell, Millie had to ask a maid to do it or do it herself. It didn't take long to pick up all her gowns, but her shoes were under the bed and she had to crawl on her stomach to reach them. She was still trying to grab the last slipper when the door opened again and Zoë and Francis came in.

"Looks like your party already started," said Francis.

"The fairies came to see me," Millie said, crawling out from under the bed.

"Is that what happened to your hair?" asked Zoë, stifling a giggle.

Millie reached up to touch her hair. "Is it that bad? I haven't found the mirror yet."

"It's not *that* bad," said Zoë, grinning. "It's worse. Here, let me help you." The last fairy to arrange Millie's hair had left it in stiff coils that sprung from her head like tiny snakes. Taking a boar-bristle brush from the trunk, Zoë brushed out her friend's hair and braided it in one long plait. "There, now you can go out in public without frightening everyone."

"Am I the only one who's hungry around here?" Francis asked.

"I'm famished," said Millie, heading toward the door.

"You would be," said Zoë, as she followed her friends. "You slept through dinner last night. Your mother told us not to wake you."

Millie laughed. "Which your whole family did, anyway."

"That was different," said Zoë. "They came to say good-bye."

"Your parents left?" asked Francis.

"Let's go get some breakfast," said Millie. "We'll tell you about it on the way."

Millie and Zoë took turns telling him what had happened. They were still talking when they reached the entrance to the Great Hall and ran into the witches Ratinki and Klorine, two of the more frequent visitors to Emma and Eadric's castle.

Although they always wore ordinary clothes when they visited Greater Greensward, today Ratinki and Klorine were dressed alike in dark green gowns and short, sleeveless, gold-colored tabards embroidered with King Bodamin's double-mountain crest. Their clothes were the same, but Klorine was smiling as if she was happy to see them while Ratinki's wrinkled face looked sour and grumpy.

"Look, it's Millie!" Klorine shouted in her loud and distinctive voice.

"I suppose this means I should say 'happy birthday' or some such drivel," grumbled Ratinki. "No one wishes me well on my birthday, so I don't know why I should say it to anyone else."

"I gave you a new pair of shoes for your birthday not six months ago," Klorine bellowed, looking puzzled.

"Goody. Shoes," grumbled Ratinki.

"But you asked for them. I thought you liked the shoes! You have them on your feet right now."

"You didn't give me what I really wanted. I asked for you to stop shouting, but that hasn't happened yet."

"Why . . . that's . . . ," sputtered Klorine.

"It's good to see you both," said Millie.

"What are those for?" Francis asked, pointing at their golden tabards.

"King Bodamin gave us jobs. We're his Magic Brigade," Klorine said proudly in a quieter voice that was still louder than everyone else's. "We work with the army to make stronger armor and weapons that don't break so easily. The king gave us space in the dungeon to do our work and another room to sleep in. It's small, but not nearly as drafty as my cave."

"And no one's come to burn it down the way they did my hut," said Ratinki. "I wonder if it's still repairing itself. I should go and see one of these days. Maybe I should let the cat out, too."

"How long have you been here?" asked Francis.

"Two years," said Klorine. "I didn't know you had a cat, Ratinki."

"That's because it's none of your business," said the old witch. "The cat's probably run out of food by now," she mumbled to herself.

"Maybe one of the villagers let it out," said Millie.

Ratinki curled her lip in a half snarl. "Maybe one of the villagers stole it. They always were stealing my food."

"Speaking of food," said Francis, "we're on our way to get breakfast. Would you like to join us?"

"No, thanks," said Klorine. "Three bowls of porridge is enough to start my day."

"I have work to do," Ratinki grumbled. "I want to see if I can find a way to make the opposing armies' spears shatter before they reach our men. Maybe when the spears are in the air . . ."

Klorine nodded. "We could do that. Or maybe before the soldiers throw them."

"Sometimes you come up with good ideas, for a ninny-head," Ratinki told her, as the two turned and started for the dungeon.

When Millie and her friends finally entered the Great Hall, housemaids and grooms were sweeping the floor and hanging garlands from the windowsills. The tables had already been rearranged for the party, with room for musicians on the raised dais where the king and queen usually sat. The only people sitting down were Maybelle and her brother, Eduardo, who smiled and stood up when Millie entered the room.

"Won't you join us?" Eduardo said, indicating the bench beside him.

Millie was happy to share a bench with such a handsome young man. She'd decided that all she had to do was steer the conversation away from anything that might make her mad and see how well they got along when she didn't have to worry about side effects or her fear that she could change into a dragon.

"Where are all the fairies?" asked Zoë as she took a seat across from Millie.

"They went off with some woman named Grassina," said Maybelle. "She said they could help her with the flowers for the party."

"Grassina is my mother," said Francis.

"That's nice," Maybelle said, looking bored.

Eduardo turned so that he was facing Millie, even though she was sitting right next to him. Francis scowled but didn't say anything until after the cook's helper had set a bowl of porridge in front of each of them and returned to the kitchen.

"How long are you staying in Upper Montevista, Eduardo?" asked Francis.

Eduardo looked annoyed as he said, "Are you talking to me? . . . What was your name, again? You have a better memory than I do, Maybelle. What is the boy called?"

"Francis," Maybelle said, giggling.

"It's Lord Francis to you, *Ed*," said Francis.

"That's right! Grassina is the younger sister of Greater Greensward's queen, which makes you Millie's first cousin once removed, doesn't it? As the son of the younger daughter, there isn't much chance you'll ever sit on the throne."

Maybelle clapped her hands and squealed. "Five gold pieces says my brother is right!"

Zoë gasped. "You're both very rude!"

Eduardo turned to face her, his lip curled in a sneer. "You're supposed to be a princess, aren't you?"

"My father is Prince Garrid," said Zoë.

"I notice that no one has mentioned your kingdom. Is it because you don't really have one?"

"Why, I . . . you . . . I can't believe . . ." It was obvious that Zoë was flustered. Although her father was a prince, his subjects were scattered across countless geographic kingdoms. Zoë didn't dare mention that he was the prince of vampires.

"I bet we can uncover the truth before the day is over," said Maybelle.

"My sister likes to wager," said Eduardo.

Maybelle sniffed. "No more than you."

"Perhaps," said her brother. "But I gamble only about things that really matter. And you," he continued, turning to Zoë, "should work on your lies. You aren't very convincing."

Millie no longer found the young man charming. "I can't believe you're calling my friend a liar," she said, sliding away from him on the bench. "Because if you are, you're calling me one, too. I told you who she was last night."

"Ah, but that was a joke, wasn't it?" said Eduardo.

"No more than you are a gentleman," Millie replied.

Francis had two spots of red on his cheeks as he said, "You've insulted my cousin and our friend. You, sir, have no honor. Would you care to meet me on the jousting field so I can teach you a lesson?"

Eduardo laughed. "I don't joust with children!"

"You can't be more than a year or two older than I," said Francis. "I could best you at any weapon you choose."

"Don't flatter yourself, boy," said Eduardo. "You may be related to royalty, but you'll never be my equal."

"Why I ought to—," Francis began, just as a witch seated on the handle of a pitchfork zipped into the Hall, shouting, "There's the birthday girl!" Suddenly there were witches everywhere, pushing and shoving as they streamed through the windows and doors.

Millie stood to watch the witches arrive. Although some of them rode brooms, others rode farm implements, chairs, and magic carpets. One witch even rode a cobbler's bench, which trotted to the corner to wait until its rider was ready to leave.

"Oh, my!" said Maybelle as the witches crowded around, laughing and jostling each other as they tried to get close to Millie.

Smiling until she felt as if her face might crack, Millie returned their hugs and greeted each one by name. Francis and Zoë joined Millie in greeting the witches they knew, while Maybelle and Eduardo shrank away from the witches as if afraid of touching one.

It was some time before the friends had said hello to everyone crowding around them, but once they had, three witches who'd been waiting in the back stepped forward. Dyspepsia and her sister, Oculura, lived in the Enchanted Forest near Zoë's family. Millie had never seen the third witch before. "My sister and I have someone here we'd like you to meet," said Dyspepsia. "This is Mudine. Our cottage used to belong to her."

Zoë gasped and clutched Francis's arm, while Millie's smile vanished. Mudine was the name of the witch who had caught Li'l and kept her tied with string to a rafter in an old, run-down cottage. Li'l had been unable to leave the cottage even after Mudine had gone; it had been Emma who had freed the little bat.

The old witch stepped forward and looked at them with eyes as piercing as a blue jay's. "Where can I find the little witch called Emeralda? She took something of mine."

"I'm her daughter," Millie said, squaring her shoulders and raising her chin. "Maybe I can help you."

"Not unless you can tell me where I can find my bat. I've heard rumors that your mother stole it. Well, I've come back and I want my bat," Mudine said, waving a string in the air. "She was the best bat I've ever owned."

Zoë's already pale skin grew whiter. Her voice was shaking as she said, "You can't have her back. She has a life and a family now."

"She had a life with me," said Mudine.

"She was your prisoner!" cried Zoë. "You can't call that a life!"

Mudine narrowed her eyes and peered at Zoë. "Why do you care so much about a bat?"

"Because she's my mother!" Zoë said, holding her head higher when she heard Maybelle's gasp behind her.

"Well, I'll be!" cackled Mudine. "Don't that just beat all?"

"I'm sorry," Dyspepsia whispered to Millie. "We didn't know she'd act like this."

Oculura frowned and reached up to her face, taking out one eye and sticking another in its place. She glanced from Millie to Zoë to Francis, then sighed and said, "Drat! I was hoping I was seeing all these long faces 'cause I'd put in the wrong eye again. You're supposed to be smiling. We came here for a party, didn't we? Let's get this shindig started!"

Suddenly, the room was a whirl of activity. The air was so rich with magic that it sparkled as witches sent their brooms to sweep the last of the dust from the floor, put up the rest of the garlands with a gesture, and carried the food from the kitchen on a mouthwatering breeze. And then the fairies were there, strewing flowers on the tables and floors, passing out nosegays, and filling the air with laughter. Grassina had followed the fairies into the room and soon the rest of Millie's relatives appeared in the doorway.

Watching Maybelle and Eduardo run off to join Bradston, Zoë said, "I need some fresh air. If I don't go out now I'm going to bite one of those idiots and that would only make matters worse."

"I'll go with her to make sure she's all right," said Francis. "You stay with your guests, Millie. It's your party and you should be here."

Millie was still watching Zoë and Francis work their way through the crowd when Grassina approached her. "I'm sorry your party won't be quite the way you'd planned, but I hope you enjoy it. This is your special day, after all."

"Thank you, Aunt Grassina. I just—"

"Grassina! You haven't changed at all since the last time I saw you," said Mudine, jostling Millie aside. "Except you do have a few gray hairs, and some wrinkles next to your eyes, and—"

"Have we met?" Grassina asked the old witch.

"It's me, Mudine! Don't tell me your memory is going, too."

"Mudine! It's been a long time."

"Sure has. So, I heard that you're no longer the Green Witch. Did you lose your magic, or what?"

Grassina sighed. "It's a long story, but no, I still have my magic." She glanced at Millie, saying, "Mudine and I knew each other years ago. She was one of the smartest witches I'd ever met and knew more about magic than any other ten witches put together. I'm curious though,

61

Mudine. We thought you were dead. What happened to you?"

"Dead? Ha!" said the old witch. "Though I *was* at death's door for years. I spent my money on one healer after another, but they were all a bunch of fakes. Then I heard about the witch doctor Ting-Tang. I went to see him and he cured me. See, good as new," she said, thumping her chest with her fist. "He was a smart one, all right. Not like the addlepated fools I saw before him. I'd recommend old Ting-Tang to anyone. He can cure just about any affliction. Say, is that girl really Li'l Stinker's daughter?"

"She met Zoë," Millie told her aunt.

Grassina nodded. "Li'l married a prince. They have three boys and two girls. Zoë is the eldest."

"What a shame," said Mudine. "Li'l was the best bat I ever knew. I was counting on her to live with me again. That husband of hers must be something special. What is he, a shape-shifter or a vampire?"

"Actually—," Grassina began.

"Time for presents!" shouted the Swamp Fairy. "Come over here, Millie, and see what we brought you!"

Millie smiled apologetically at Mudine and Grassina before crossing the Hall to the raised platform where the musicians were to perform. The fairies had taken it over, covering the floor with rose petals and decorating a chair with rosebuds. As she passed her family, Millie heard her grandmother Queen Frazzela muttering under her breath,

"Nothing is ready yet. The party wasn't supposed to start for hours."

"You have to expect this kind of thing when you invite witches and fairies, Mother," said Eadric.

Millie caught the angry look her father was giving his mother, which made her wonder just what was going on. And then Millie was at the platform and the fairies were showing her their gifts. They gave her gowns—a few made of fabric, but most made of materials like spiders' silk or moth wings. She received a cape made of violet petals and one made of mouse fur. Three flower fairies gave her two pairs of glass slippers for summer and one pair of heavy glass boots for winter. The Pumpkin Fairy gave her a bag of seeds, each one guaranteed to grow into a full-sized carriage good for one evening's ride. It was the Swamp Fairy who gave her the mice in the wicker cage and the directions for how to turn them into coachmen.

Then it was the witches' turn. Oculura and Dyspepsia gave her a crow that could speak seventeen languages and say the alphabet backward in each. Klorine gave her a magic mirror that would reveal whether a young man she liked was actually her true love. Ratinki gave her a covered basket filled with miniature witches' lights in all the colors of the rainbow. Other witches gave her ingredients to use in potions: fly feet, chicken ears, the eyes of blind cave fish, and the sweat of a left-handed man collected on the second Tuesday of a month starting with the letter *J*.

When her family approached carrying their gifts, Millie already had so many presents that she didn't know what to do with them all. Queen Chartreuse and King Limelyn gave her a new crown decorated with emeralds. Grassina and Haywood brought her books on plants and magic. Millie sighed when her parents gave her a collection of potions, lotions, and perfumes meant to soothe, calm, and relieve tension or bad moods. Of course they *would* give her a practical gift. Then Zoë handed her a necklace of bloodred stones from her family, and Francis gave her a pouch filled with coins from the Magic Marketplace that could be spent only *at* the Magic Marketplace.

"They're worth twice their face value on certain days," whispered Francis.

"What days are those?" asked Millie.

Francis shrugged. "They don't tell you that."

And then Queen Frazzela and King Bodamin were there, saying, "Our special gift for you is in the courtyard. Come along and see what it is."

Millie tried to find her parents in the crowd, thinking they would like to see the present, too, since it was part of the reason they had traveled so far. They were busy listening to a new arrival, however, a witch who was waving her arms as she talked. At Frazzela's urging, Millie left her parents where they were and accompanied her grandmother to the door leading to the courtyard. Until now, she'd forgotten all about her grandparents' promise and wondered what they could possibly give her that would be special, especially since she usually got magical presents and . . . Millie stopped dead at the top of the stairs. The special present was right there in the courtyard with a big pink bow on its neck. It was a small white pony, the very last thing Millie wanted.

"Don't you love it?" asked her grandmother, breathing into her ear.

Millie didn't know what to say. She thought horses were beautiful, but they hated her. If she went near the pony, it would behave like every other horse did when she got too close. It would rear and kick and try to run off and she'd have to pretend not to know why it acted that way.

"It's very nice," Millie said. Crossing her fingers inside the long sleeve of her gown, she added, "but I already have dozens of horses at home." It was a lie. Her parents had horses, but Millie couldn't even go into the stable.

"Really?" her grandmother said, a smile frozen on her face.

Millie couldn't approach the pony without attracting the kind of attention she wanted to avoid. Even so, she felt awful as she turned and walked back into the Great Hall. She just hoped she hadn't hurt her grandmother's feelings.

Francis and Zoë had followed her to the courtyard and they hurried to catch up now. "That was some special gift," said Francis. "I heard your grandparents talking while you were opening your presents from the fairies. They hadn't

65

even decided what to give you. I was there when a page suggested a pony and they sent him to the stable to pick one out."

Millie could feel the heat creeping up her neck. Her grandmother had insisted that Millie come to get a special gift, yet she hadn't even had a gift in mind. Worse, the pony was the most unsuitable gift anyone could have given her. *Calm down,* Millie thought. *Grandmother had no way of knowing.* Remembering her conversation with her parents, Millie took deep breaths until her heart rate returned to normal and her face was no longer hot. "I'm not going to get upset," she told her friends. "I'm sure my grandmother meant well."

The three friends had just walked into the Great Hall when they heard a commotion in the far corner. The witch who had been talking to her parents now had a wider audience as other witches crowded around her. "There were a dozen of them," said the old witch Millie knew was named Burtha. "They were crawling over the river walls and attacking the people in the town. I never heard such screaming in all my born days."

Emma and Eadric looked worried when they found Millie in the crowd. Taking her aside, her mother kissed her on the cheek and said, "I'm sorry, darling, but this is an emergency. Your father and I have to go. The sea monsters are swarming at Chancewold. We've been dealing with them for years, but there have never been this many at one time before."

"But it's my birthday party!" said Millie.

"It can't be helped," said her father. "We have to go. Those people are counting on us."

Millie could feel the pressure building behind her eyes and in her chest, but she was determined not to lose her temper. *It's all right,* she told herself. *They were here for most of the party. At least the rest of my family will be with me.*

"Haywood and I are going, too," said Grassina. "Some of those monsters sound familiar. I feel responsible for this."

"If they are the monsters you created, Aunt Grassina," said Emma, "then it's my fault they're there. I banished them from the moat without thinking about where they would go." She gave her daughter a hug. "Happy birthday, darling. Remember what we talked about in the carriage."

"I'll remember," Millie said through gritted teeth.

No one else seemed to notice when her parents and great-aunt and great-uncle left, because by then everyone was eating. Millie was wandering among her guests, thanking them for their gifts, when she came across Frazzela and Maybelle. She would have continued on if she hadn't heard Maybelle say, "When you told me last week that you could get the fairies to come to a party, I must admit that I didn't think it was possible. Nobody can get more than three fairies at a social event anymore. Here are the coins I owe you. I was sure this was a bet I couldn't lose."

"I told you that the fairies and I are great friends," said Frazzela, taking the coins.

Millie frowned. If this was all about a bet . . . She stepped in front of the two women and turned to face her grandmother. "When did you invite the fairies?"

"Last week," said Frazzela.

"Before you invited us?" said Millie. "How did you know we would be here? I was supposed to have my party at home."

Queen Frazzela shrugged. "I knew your parents would come once I told them that the fairies were expecting you to be here for a birthday party. If you didn't come, the fairies would have been angry and everyone knows you don't want to make fairies mad."

"But you would have made them mad if we hadn't come," said Millie.

Frazzela sniffed. "I knew your parents would never let that happen."

Millie could feel her face growing warm, but this time she couldn't have stopped it if she'd wanted to. "You mean you tricked us into coming? You insisted that we have my party here because you wanted the fairies to come and you knew they always came to my parties?"

Maybelle laughed and said, "Whatever works!"

"Don't act so indignant," Queen Frazzela snapped at Millie. "It's about time you came to see me."

Millie didn't want to lose her temper, but learning that her grandmother had manipulated her family to win a bet made her angrier than she'd been in a long time. Even then, she might have been able to stop the change if she hadn't seen the smug expression on Maybelle's face and the unrepentant look on her grandmother's. This time Millie's whole body grew hot as her heart rate went up and her skin began to prickle. Her eyesight grew sharper, too, until she could see a hair quivering on Queen Frazzela's chin and flakes of powder on Maybelle's nose.

Even in the throes of the change, Millie had enough sense to turn on her heel and start for the door. "Don't you walk away from me again, young lady!" shrilled her grandmother.

And then the change happened between one heartbeat and the next, and a dragon stood where the human girl had been. The last thing Millie heard before she flew through a window was the sound of her grandmother screaming.

Seven

illie had been flying for hours, unable to decide where to go. She'd considered going to Chancewold to help her parents, but she couldn't bear to face them after having done exactly what they'd asked her not to do. It was almost dark when she started toward home, but she knew she couldn't leave her friends to face the mess she'd left behind, so she turned around again. Finally, when she was calm enough that she knew she could turn back into a human if she wanted to, Millie returned to the castle in Upper Montevista.

The moon lit her way as she circled the castle, trying to find the window to her chamber. Because she couldn't tell which window was hers, she landed in the courtyard when the guards weren't looking. She had scarcely turned into a human when a bat settled on the ground beside her. There was a puff of dank air and Zoë was a human as well.

"I knew you'd come back!" said Zoë.

"I hate to ask, but what happened after I left?"

Zoë sighed. "It was awful. Your grandmother didn't stop screaming for the longest time. She said awful things about you and your mother and your mother's whole family. Oh, one good thing did come out of all this. Maybelle and Eduardo left. I know you don't want to hear what *they* had to say."

"Where's Francis?"

"In bed, I guess. Queen Chartreuse and King Limelyn are planning to leave as soon as you come back. They stuck up for you when Frazzela couldn't say anything nice."

They had been walking toward the door to the castle keep, but Millie stopped now and sat on the lowest step. "I don't know what to do," she said, resting her chin on her knees. "I knew I shouldn't get so angry, but I couldn't help myself. I wish I could learn how to control my temper."

Zoë sat down beside her and put her arm around Millie's shoulders. "And I wish I had some wise advice to give you, but I don't. I've seen what happens when you try to fix this with a potion or a spell."

"I think I can help," said Mudine as she walked out of the shadows.

"We don't want your help," said Zoë. "Millie doesn't need *you* to put a spell on her."

"I wasn't talking about a spell. I know someone who might be able to teach you how to control your temper. She's an old friend of mine. Have you ever heard of the Blue Witch?"

71

Zoë groaned and said, "What is it with witches and colors?"

Millie shrugged. "They're hereditary titles that the fairies give out. At least, my mother says a fairy gave the title to the first Green Witch."

"Are you interested or not?" asked Mudine. "Because if you aren't, I have better things to do than—"

"I'm interested!" Millie told the old witch before turning to Zoë. "Aunt Grassina told me that Mudine knows more about magic than most witches and that she's really smart. If she has any suggestion that can help me, I'd be a fool *not* to listen. I don't know what else to do, Zoë. I've tried everything I can think of and nothing has worked!"

"I'm not so sure about this . . . ," said Zoë.

Millie looked to Mudine. "Tell me where I can find this Blue Witch. I can't live this way any longer—having to pretend that I'm normal, and frightening people when I don't mean to."

"She lives in the mountains of the Icy North," said Mudine. "She went up there about twenty years ago and as far as I know she's still there. If anyone can teach you how to cool a hot temper, it's the Blue Witch."

"You aren't seriously thinking of going, are you, Millie?" Zoë asked her friend. "For all we know, this might be some sort of trap."

"What do you think I'm going to do to her—tie a string around her toe and hang her from my rafters?"

72

Mudine slapped her leg and snorted. "That's a good one, what with her turning into a dragon and all!"

"You know about that, too?" asked Millie.

"Everybody in the castle knows about it. Heck, everybody in five kingdoms knows about it now that that chatterbox Maybelle is out spreading the word."

Millie groaned and covered her face with her hands. "What am I going to do? The whole world is going to know that I have a bad temper and turn into a dragon at the drop of a pin. Did you know that my mother fell in love with my father when she was fourteen? If I can't control my temper, I'll never have anyone. I'll spend my whole life not knowing what it's like to fall in love."

"Go see the Blue Witch!" said Mudine. "She should be easy to find. Just cross the Bullrush River and head north past the swamp. You'll come to the foothills after that, and then the mountains. An eagle I know told me that she lives in an ice castle. Shouldn't take you long if you fly, 'specially if you're a dragon."

Millie stood up and straightened her gown. "Then I'd better get started. I want to be back before my parents are, and it takes them only about a week to make sure a sea monster stays subdued, then another few days to let the town thank them."

"Maybe you should wait and talk to your parents about this," Zoë said. "The Icy North is an awfully long way from here. I bet they'd go with you if you asked."

"No, they wouldn't," said Millie. "They'd just give me all sorts of reasons why I couldn't go, and then I never would go and I'd scare away any suitor who came around and end up old and lonely like Mudine."

"Hey!" said the old witch.

"How are you going to get there?" asked Zoë.

"Fly, of course."

Zoë hopped to her feet. "Then you'll have to wait until you're angry again. That should give me enough time to get ready. I have to change my clothes."

"You're not coming!" said Millie.

"Oh, yes, I am!" said Zoë. "You don't think I'd let you go on an adventure like this without me, do you? My mother would never forgive me if anything happened to you because I wasn't there to keep you safe. I am supposed to stay with you, remember?"

"Your parents didn't know I was going on a trip like this. I'm sure if they had known—"

"They wouldn't let you go. Just like Queen Chartreuse and King Limelyn won't once they find out what you have in mind."

"You wouldn't tell them, would you, Zoë?"

"How could I tell them if I was with you?"

"I can't believe you'd stoop to blackmail," grumbled Millie. "Fine, I guess you can come along."

"Maybe we should say something to Francis. He'll never forgive us if we don't tell him what we're doing."

"And how long will that take?"

"Not long," said Zoë. "Any chance you know the way to his room?"

Millie didn't, but a squire flirting with a maid in the Great Hall did. Although the girls expected to find Francis asleep in bed, he was bent over a book on fighting tactics with a witch's light bobbing by his shoulder. When they told him about their plan, Francis put down the book and stood up to stretch. "You can count me in. I have everything I need right here," he said, tapping the acorn he wore on a chain around his neck.

"Why do you need an acorn?" asked Zoë.

"It's like a magical trunk," said Millie. "He got it at the Magic Marketplace. He has all his stuff in it."

"I don't care if it is magical," said Zoë. "How much can you fit inside a . . . Oh, my!"

Francis had unscrewed the cap on the acorn and reached inside with the tip of his thumb and index finger. He pulled out what appeared to be a red thread, but as it emerged from the acorn, the thread became the corner of a red and blue carpet, worn in places but still sturdy enough to carry two people.

Millie was delighted. "You brought your magic carpet! You are so clever, Francis! It's not very big, though, is it?"

"It's perfect," said Zoë. "Now you can go without turning into a dragon first. You two can ride and I can fly."

"But I didn't even say that Francis could come," said Millie.

Zoë grinned at Francis. "Just do like I did and say you'll tell Queen Chartreuse and King Limelyn what she has in mind if she doesn't let you come."

"Zoë!" exclaimed Millie.

"Good idea," said Francis. "But I was going to suggest that she might like to have me along because of my fighting prowess and because I have this." Reaching into his acorn again, Francis pulled out a black dragon scale. "It belonged to my mother, but she gave it to me last year. It can help you find just about anything because dragons are so good at finding things and . . . Oh, yeah. I guess you wouldn't need this."

"Not really," said Millie, smiling in a most dragonlike way. "But you can come with us. Zoë and I would enjoy having your company."

"And my carpet," said Francis.

The royal castle of Upper Montevista was located in the southern end of the mountain range that covered the western half of the kingdom. The mountains were tall, with deep passes between them. A river ran at the bottom of the widest pass, covering a winding trail that had once bordered it.

High above the river, the winds that whipped the

76

mountainsides were treacherous even at their calmest. Millie hadn't given them much thought before she and her friends started out, but she soon realized that the trip was probably harder at night when they couldn't really see where they were going. While Zoë couldn't fly because of the wind, her bat senses worked just fine, so she clung to the frayed edge of the carpet in front of Francis, telling him when to turn and how far.

The wind continued to buffet them, nearly smashing the carpet against the rocks at times. They tried to fly lower and trace the course of the river, but at the first cry of a hunting griffin, Francis made the carpet rise until it was too high for even griffins to reach. Millie reveled in the excitement of dipping and soaring, of plummeting so that she felt as if she'd left her stomach behind or turning abruptly to avoid an outcropping that suddenly appeared in front of them. She laughed out loud at the thrill of it, the sound of her laughter lost in the roar of the wind.

Although it seemed to take forever to reach the end of the mountain range, it was only just past midnight when they left the mountains behind and entered the foothills. With the winds behind them, Zoë was able to fly on her own and took off from the little carpet. Millie glanced at Francis and it occurred to her from the rigid line of his back and the way he gripped the edge of the carpet that he hadn't enjoyed the ride the way she had.

"Are you all right?" she asked Francis.

"Just dandy," he replied, his voice still a little shaky.

"Thanks for going with me," she said, patting him on the back.

"I couldn't very well let you go without me," said Francis. "You're like my little sister. I couldn't live with myself if anything happened to you."

"Thank you," Millie said, her voice so soft that she wasn't sure Francis had heard it. She understood what he meant, because she felt just as close to him. It occurred to her that she hadn't really been thinking about either her cousin or her friend when she said that they could come. She wasn't worried about her own safety; even though she couldn't turn into a dragon whenever she wanted to, the fact that she was a dragon at times had made her feel almost invincible. And while her cousin had magic, and her friend could be a bat or a vampire at will, Millie didn't feel that either of them was as strong as she was. She glanced at Francis once more, then at the little bat, feeling responsible for them. They may have come to keep her safe, but it would be up to her to protect them.

Now that they were out of the mountains' shadows, the moonlight lit up the night, allowing them to see for miles. Millie was looking at the ribbon of silver that had to be the distant river when Francis said, "What's that?" and pointed at the ground below.

Millie peered into the darkness, trying to see what he was talking about. And then she saw it. A troll was charging across the uneven ground, waving an ax in one hand and a spear in the other. She could hear the faint sound of shouting. "Can you go lower?" she asked Francis, and leaned over the edge to watch the troll as the carpet descended.

At first she had to strain to make out what the troll said, but the lower the carpet went, the better she could hear it. The troll had three heads, one of which was shouting, "I'll flay him alive!" The other two heads roared in agreement.

"Maybe we should see who they're chasing," said Francis. "It might be some poor, innocent human who needs a brave knight like me to protect him."

"I don't know," Millie said. "We can't stop for every little thing. Besides, there's no telling what might be out there. What if it's a harpy or an ogre?"

"We won't know unless we look," said Francis. "As a knight, I'm sworn to protect the innocent. It won't take us too far out of our way. And you don't need to worry. You know I'll keep you safe."

"I'm not afraid," Millie said indignantly. "Oh, all right. Go ahead. See what it is. I just hope we don't regret this."

They found the intended victim stumbling down the far side of the next hill. Rocky outcroppings blocked the moonlight, casting a deep shadow over the fleeing figure.

"I'm taking us lower," said Francis. "I can't tell what he—"

Suddenly, the figure launched itself into the air and

grabbed hold of the carpet, dragging it down to the ground. Millie fell off with an *oof!* while Francis rolled a few yards and hopped to his feet, brandishing his sword.

"Get back, you knave!" Francis shouted. "Or I'll slit your gullet from . . . Oh, it's Simon-Leo," he said, sounding disgusted. Lowering his sword, he reached down to help Millie to her feet.

Millie stood up, rubbing her shoulder. "That figures. What are you doing here, Simon-Leo? Why is that other troll chasing you?"

The troll head with the neatly combed hair scowled. "It was Leo's fault," he said, jerking his chin at the shaggier head. "But then, it always is."

"Can you give us a ride?" asked Leo. "We need to get out of here before old Gnarlybones-Hothead-Rumpkin gets his enormous butt over that hill." One of the two-headed troll's big, coarse hands gestured behind them while the other began to smooth Simon's hair.

"Why did you drag us down?" Francis asked, as the troll bent over to straighten the carpet.

"Simon said you wouldn't stop if I didn't," said Leo. "Hurry up. We've got to go."

"He was right," Francis grumbled under his breath so only Millie could hear him. "Simon-Leo is the last person I would have helped."

"I know," Millie whispered back. "He's always so

awful. Listen, we'll just give him a ride somewhere and drop him off. Then we can be on our way again."

"Are you coming?" asked Simon. "Or should we go without you?" The troll plunked himself in the middle of the carpet, leaving little room for anyone else. Everything about Simon-Leo was wide, from his shoulders to his belly to his feet. He was taller than most trolls, too, a trait he'd probably gotten from his human father.

Grumbling, Francis took a seat in front while Millie tried to find a place big enough to hold her. "I think my mother told me that Gnarlybones-Hothead-Rumpkin is the commander of your mother's army. So why is he chasing you?" she asked, squeezing between Francis and the troll as Francis shot Simon-Leo a dirty look.

"Tell them what you did to him," Simon said to his other head.

"He's making a big fuss over nothing," said Leo.

"The carpet won't go up," said Francis. "You weigh too much," he told the troll.

Simon curled his lip in a sneer. "It's your cheap carpet."

"Or your lousy magic," said Leo. "Try again."

Francis waved his hand over the front fringe of the carpet, muttering to himself. He kept at it until perspiration beaded his forehead. The fringe fluttered, then rose into the air, pulling the rest of the carpet with it. Francis gestured again and the carpet lurched upward, then, with a terrible ripping sound, tore down the middle, dumping everyone on the ground.

"Ow!" Simon squealed.

"My carpet!" Francis exclaimed in an anguished voice.

Zoë zipped down and fluttered around her friends. "Millie, the other troll is coming. He says he's going to rip off their heads," she said, circling Simon-Leo, "and stuff them in—"

"We know," snapped Simon. "He's been saying that ever since Leo played a trick on him. Who's the bat?"

Millie was the first one on her feet. "That's Zoë. We can talk later. We're going to have to outrun the commander."

"He's not after us," said Francis. "I don't see why we have to run." He bent down to pick up the pieces of his carpet, and then dropped them when he saw how they lay limp in his hands. "It's no good anymore. The magic is gone." He glared at Simon-Leo. "You have to buy me a new magic carpet."

Simon snorted. "Like that's ever going to happen."

The three-headed troll was closer now, its heads shouting threats that were becoming all too clear. "When I get my hands on that half-baked . . . ," said one voice.

"I'm going to beat him to a pulp and spread him on my toast!" said another.

"You hate toast," shouted a third.

"You'd better run," Simon told Millie. He was still

talking when Leo, who was controlling the legs, lumbered away. "That dunderhead general won't like that you tried to help us," Simon called over his shoulder. "He could turn your brains to jelly with one solid thump."

"But we didn't try to help you," Francis called. "We'll tell him that you pulled us out of the sky and—"

"You're talking about a troll, Francis," said Millie. "Do you really think he'll care?"

Millie and Francis exchanged a look, and they took off after Simon-Leo. "We have to . . . do something," panted Millie as they started up another hill. "Trolls can run . . . for days, but . . . we can't!"

"What do you . . . suggest? We could . . . go in a different direction . . . from Simon-Leo," Francis said.

"And then what if . . . the commander follows us . . . instead of Simon-Leo? I meant that . . . we should distract them . . . somehow to get . . . them off our trail. I could . . . call a dragon . . . but it might take . . . a while for it . . . to get here."

Francis shook his head. "Don't bother. I have . . . a spell I . . . can use. My father . . . made me learn it . . . in case I ever . . . got into trouble."

Cresting the hill, they had started down the other side when Francis began to recite his spell.

A dragon roar . . . is just like thunder
As it rips . . . apart the sky.

Now make it loud . . . so that they'll wonder
If a dragon . . . is nearby.

There was a feeble cough, then a low rumbling sound. The shouting behind them didn't even pause. "Can't you run any faster?" shouted a voice.

"Not with this toe. It hurts!"

"It's our toe, too, you big baby!"

Millie and Francis had caught up with Simon-Leo and were already passing him when Simon said, "That's it? You're using magic to make sounds? A real wizard would have called up a real dragon!"

The rumbling was getting louder, as if a herd of horses was running across hard-packed ground.

Francis frowned. "Give it . . . a minute," he said before glancing at Millie. "Why isn't he . . . short of breath?"

"Bigger lungs," said Millie. "My mother said . . . that's why their chests . . . are so broad."

"I thought it was . . . to hold up . . . their fat heads," Francis panted.

"What did you say?" said Simon.

The first roar sounded like a dragon with asthma, but the next was much louder. It hit them just as they reached the bottom of the hill, knocking them flat on their backs. Zoë tumbled from the sky and lay there, twitching. Everyone covered their ears as best they could, waiting for the roaring to end. When it did, abruptly and without warning,

Zoë shook herself and took off, flying back the way they'd come. Francis and Millie were helping Simon-Leo to his feet when she returned, shouting, "He's gone!"

"Did she say something?" Francis asked Millie.

"Huh?" she replied.

The noise had been so loud that all they could hear was the ringing in their ears. Zoë couldn't hear them either, so she kept talking. "I saw him running the other way. Did you know that he has a stone toe? It shines in the moonlight. I thought it was pretty, for a troll."

Millie's hearing was just starting to come back. "What's that about a toe?"

Zoë, whose hearing had recovered faster than anyone else's, repeated what she'd already told them.

Francis snorted. "What did you do to the commander, Leo?"

The shoulder on Leo's side shrugged. "It was nothing really. I told him that I'd found a leprechaun's pot of gold and let him think he'd bullied me into telling him where it was. When he went to look for it, I locked the door into the mountain so he couldn't come back in. He dug and dug, but never found the gold."

"Because there wasn't any," said Simon.

"And then the sun came up and he couldn't get inside the tunnel so he hid in the hole he'd dug."

"For an entire day," said Simon. "The only part of him that wouldn't fit was his toe."

"Trolls turn into stone if sunlight touches their skin," Millie explained to Francis.

"I know," he said.

"It was his own fault," said Leo. "He should have dug a bigger hole."

"Wasn't your mother mad when she heard what you did?" asked Millie.

"She's off looking for Father again," said Simon. "She told old Gnarlybones-Hothead-Rumpkin to watch us. Gnarlybones told her he would; he likes it when she goes away. It gives him time to plan his revolution. He's been trying to overthrow her for years."

"Simon-Leo's mother is the troll queen," Millie explained to Zoë.

"I know," said the bat.

"Shouldn't you tell your mother what he's planning?" asked Millie.

"She knows all about it. Tizzy says that it's nice he has a hobby to keep him busy."

"Tizzy is one of his mother's heads," Millie explained to Francis.

"I know!" he snapped.

"So, why are you here?" said Simon. "Isn't this a little far north for you?"

"We're on a quest," said Francis. "Millie wants to learn how to control her temper."

"Why don't you just announce it to the world?" said Millie.

"Can I come, too?" asked Leo. "I can't go home now until Mother comes back and that could be weeks."

"Or months," Simon said, sounding sad. "I don't know why Father keeps running away. We miss him so much when he's gone. He has to know that Mother will always go after him. Last year she took us with her. She called it our family vacation."

"Simon-Leo's father is Prince Jorge," said Millie. "That's why his speech is so much better than most trolls'."

Simon nodded. "Our father used to lock us in an old chest and sit on it if we messed up our words."

"Give me a minute," Millie told him. "I have to talk to my friends." Zoë landed on Francis's shoulder and he and Millie walked to the other side of a nearly dead shrub. "I don't think we should let him go with us," whispered Millie. "You know he'll do something to get us in trouble. He always does."

"We can't trust him," said Francis. "Leo thinks it's funny to play nasty tricks on people, and Simon is just nasty."

"I've never met him before," said Zoë, "but he makes me uncomfortable."

Millie nodded. "Then it's settled. He can't go with us. Just don't be mean when you tell him," she said to Francis.

"Why do I have to tell him?"

"Because I'll probably feel bad if I do it, and then he'll talk me into letting him go," said Millie.

"That's true," said Zoë. "You'd better do it, Francis."

"This isn't fair," he grumbled as they headed back to where Simon-Leo waited.

"Why can't I go?" asked Simon when Francis told him of their decision.

"Because we don't have time to waste and you can't travel in the daylight," said Francis.

"But you're traveling now and it's night," said Simon-Leo. "Are you sure it isn't because you don't like me? Most people don't. That's why no one ever invites me to go anywhere."

Francis looked embarrassed. "Well, that's not . . . I mean, we didn't . . ."

"Never mind," said Simon. "You can go without me. I'll find somewhere to hide. Gnarlybones-Hothead-Rumpkin will come back once he thinks the dragon has gone. He'll want to see if it really ate me or something."

"Are you sure you're going to be all right?" said Millie. "I mean, I don't want to leave you in danger."

"Oh, no, I'll be fine," moaned Simon. "You continue on your quest, leaving me here, alone, to face the commander's wrath."

"Maybe we should—," Millie began.

Francis took hold of Millie's arm. "See you later," he told the troll, and began to hustle his cousin toward the distant river. "Good luck with what's-his-name," he called over his shoulder.

"I feel awful," Millie said, glancing back at the forlorn figure watching them go. "We should have let him come with us. I'm going to go back and tell him—"

"That's exactly what he wants you to do," said Francis. "Just keep walking. Simon-Leo will be fine. He always is. That troll gets into more scrapes than a tumbler's knee and he always comes out laughing."

"I suppose," said Millie.

Eight

*M*illie and Francis were closer to the river than they'd expected. After climbing one more hill, they spotted the water gleaming in the moonlight only a half mile away. Dawn was hours off as they approached the Bullrush River and began to discuss how they would get across.

"If only we had a boat," said Millie.

Francis looked thoughtful. "I don't know about a boat, but I think I can manage a raft."

With Zoë's help, Millie and Francis searched the riverbank until they found a suitable log, which had probably washed ashore during a recent storm. Francis was holding his hands over the log, preparing to use his magic, when something crashed through the underbrush and Simon-Leo appeared.

"What are you doing here?" asked Francis, sounding annoyed.

"The same thing you are," said Leo. "I'm going to cross the river. What are you doing with that log?"

"We told you that you couldn't come with us."

"Is that supposed to make a difference?" Simon said. "My father always says that, too, but it hasn't stopped me yet. Don't tell me you're not strong enough to lift that puny log! A baby troll could toss that from one side of a cave to the other."

Leo grunted. "Step aside, weakling, and let a real troll carry that for you."

He was bending down to pick it up when Simon said, "You can count me out if you're going to lug that thing around. I don't do manual labor." The head closed its eyes and pretended to go to sleep.

"I could lift it if I really wanted to," Francis muttered, as Leo hefted the log into his arms.

"Where do you want this thing?" Leo asked Francis, turning to face him. Millie had to duck as the log swung around, and when Francis pointed out where he wanted the log to go, she scrambled to get out of the troll's way. With Francis in the lead, Leo carried the log three hundred yards to a small protected beach. The log landed with a crash when he dropped it, scaring a flock of sparrows out of the shrubs nearby. While Francis bent over the log once again, Leo went off to rummage in the underbrush for something to eat and Zoë went in the opposite direction in search of tasty bugs.

Millie was sitting on a large rock well out of Francis's way when he glanced at her and said, "Have you ever tried to make a raft?"

"My magic isn't strong enough for that," she replied.

"Your magic would get better if you'd practice," said Francis.

"I do practice," said Millie. "It doesn't make any difference. My mother says it's because so much of my magic is tied up in my dragon side."

"Maybe when you're able to control when you can change, all your magic will get stronger."

"I hadn't thought of that," said Millie. "I hope it's true. So, what are you going to do with that log?"

"Watch," Francis said. Muttering under his breath, he pointed at the log and twiddled his fingers. A moment later, the log shuddered and split in two, lengthwise. Each half then split into thirds. Before the last pieces touched the ground, Francis had made a vine inch across the dirt and wrap itself around the lengths of wood, tying them together into a raft.

"Very nice," said Millie. "You're good, you know, maybe even better than your father."

"My father is great at what he does. He can't help it if his magic isn't as showy as my mother's."

"What's going on?" asked Leo, stomping along the shoreline with a dripping honeycomb in his hand. When he bit into his treat, he didn't seem to notice the swarm of bees crawling on his head as they tried to stab their stingers through his tough skin. Simon was awake again and was eyeing the other head's trophy. Although the food ended up in the same stomach, the head that ate it was the only one that got to taste it.

"Oh, aren't you clever," Simon said in a sarcastic voice as he studied Francis's handiwork. "You made yourself a little raft."

"It's not so little," said Francis. "It will carry Millie and me just fine."

"Here, you want a taste?" Leo said, offering his sticky fingers to his other head.

"From that filthy hand?" said Simon. "It would be like licking dirt."

"Your loss," said Leo, sticking all of his fingers into his mouth at once.

Simons shuddered and looked away. "The things I have to put up with."

"Say," said Francis, "I've been wondering, why do you have normal names like Simon-Leo when most trolls have names like Stinkybreath?"

"You know our cousin?" asked Leo.

"We were named after our mother's great-grandmother," Simon said. "She had two heads, like us. Our real names are Salmonella and Leotuckus. We prefer the shorter versions."

Francis grinned. "I would, too, if I were you."

"What are you doing now?" Zoë asked, landing on Millie's shoulder.

"We're about to launch the raft," said Francis.

"Say," said Leo, studying the raft as he licked the last of the honey from his fingers, "shouldn't that be in the water?"

"That is where it belongs," said Francis.

"I thought so," said Leo. Simon ducked out of the way as Leo bent down and hoisted the raft over his head. "Last one in the water's a bucket of slime!" Leo shouted as he started to run.

Millie and Francis glanced at each other and smiled. A moment later they were racing down to the shoreline. This time they let Leo win.

"Here!" he said, tossing the raft onto the water. It bobbed on the surface, threatening to drift away, until Francis waded in and grabbed it.

"Climb on," he told Millie.

"This looks like fun," said Zoë, and she flew down to perch on the raft.

Millie had one foot on the planks when Leo ran past her and lunged for the raft, landing on the edge.

The raft upended and sank with Simon-Leo facedown in the water. The backwash hit Millie, knocking her onto the shore and leaving her drenched and shivering. Zoë fell into the water and was floundering until Francis fished her out. "Are you all right?" he asked as the little bat gasped and choked.

"I think so, no thanks to him," she said, glaring at Simon-Leo. Francis turned his head away while the little bat shook her wings, sending droplets flying. "Why don't I meet you on the other side?" she said, and took off into the night sky.

"Thanks for asking about me," said Millie as she wrung out the hem of her tunic.

"I knew you were fine," Francis replied. "It wasn't like *you* were drowning."

"Mumph!" said Simon, as the troll stood up, spluttering.

Relieved of its burden, the raft shot to the surface. Once again, Francis had to wade into the water to get it.

"You are such a nincompoop!" Simon shouted at Leo as he ran his fingers through his hair. "Why do you have to ruin everything? I hate the days when it's your turn to control our legs!"

"Sorry," mumbled Leo.

"You take turns?" asked Francis.

"Yes, we do, as if it's any of your business!" snapped Simon. "We each have a hand to use, but have you ever tried to walk when you control one leg and someone else controls the other? It does not work, believe me! We decided when we were young that we would take turns. Today was his turn. Tomorrow will be mine and believe me, things will be very different!"

"I said I was sorry," said Leo.

The shoulder next to Simon shrugged. "Whatever. I suppose we have to walk," he said, and sighed.

"I didn't know there was a bridge from Upper Montevista to the kingdom of Bullrush," said Francis.

"There isn't one. We're going to walk along the riverbed. I don't like doing it because it ruins my clothes, but since brainless boy has already taken care of that, we might as well go in."

"I like walking under the water," said Leo. "The fish are so pretty and so easy to catch!"

Millie looked puzzled. "I thought trolls were afraid of water."

Simon looked scornful. "Most trolls are, but when we were little our father used to throw us in the river and hold us under with a stick. After the sixth or seventh time we stopped being afraid of the water. We learned how to hold our breath for a really long time, too. So," he said, turning to his other head, "do you think you can stay out of trouble this time?"

"I don't know why you're always mad at me," Leo said as the troll waded deeper into the river. "I don't get mad when you do dumb things."

"I never do dumb things," Simon began just before both heads slipped under the surface.

Millie stepped onto the raft, but this time she was able to get to the middle and sit down. "Hold on!" Francis said as he hopped on behind her. It didn't take a lot of magic to steer the raft, so they were both able to look around as they sped across the water.

Millie leaned over the edge and tried to peer into the depths but she couldn't see much. "This water is too brown to see through. Where do you suppose Simon-Leo is?"

"Does it matter?" Francis said, sounding glum. "We're never going to be able to get rid of him."

The raft stopped with a sudden jerk so that they both had to clutch at the sides to keep from falling in. "I have a bad feeling about this," said Millie.

Francis looked worried. "We must have hit a rock or something, but whatever it is, it must be awfully big. This is the deepest part of the river."

Suddenly, two hands reached out of the water and slapped the edge of the raft beside Millie. A moment later, a head appeared as well. The river nymph glared at them with her algae-green eyes while her long green hair floated around her. "You can't possibly think you're going to get away with that!" she said.

"With what?" asked Francis. "We haven't done any-thing wrong."

"You dumped your smelly garbage in my water, that's what!"

"We did not!" said Millie. "The only thing we put in the water was this raft, and it was made from a log that we took out of this very same river."

"I beg your pardon, but I have it on good authority from three trout and a whole school of minnows that you threw a foul, stinky piece of trash in this river and then started across on your spindly little raft."

"We didn't throw any . . . Oh, wait a minute," said Francis, beginning to smile. "Maybe we did, although we don't usually call him trash. His name is Simon-Leo and he's a troll."

"Francis!" said Millie.

"You put a troll in my river?" cried the nymph.

Millie shook her head. "Actually, he put himself in your river. We were as surprised as you are that he wanted to walk across."

"On the bottom," Francis added.

"No!" wailed the nymph even as she dove back into the river, sending a wave of cold water over Millie.

The raft started to move again, drifting downriver until Francis's magic steered it back the way they wanted to go. "That was fun!" he said as they neared the riverbank.

"Maybe for you," said Millie.

Zoë was waiting for them when they finally stepped ashore. She had turned back into her human form and looked like a pretty, pale, young woman. "You're all wet," she told Millie, whose hair was hanging down around her face in a dripping tangle.

"I noticed," Millie said. She sat down under the branches of a tree and arranged her skirts around her. "Just give me a minute to dry off." Leaning back against the tree trunk, she closed her eyes and thought warm thoughts. Her magic flowed through her, warming her from the inside out. When she opened her eyes again, her clothes were dry and her hair was soft and fluffy. She yawned and glanced up at her friends. "I have to take a nap before I can go any farther."

Francis echoed her yawn with one of his own. "We should all get some rest," he said, sitting down beside Zoë.

The sound of splashing water drew their eyes to the river, where Simon-Leo was emerging from the water with an eel wrapped around Simon's neck and a gnawed fish in Leo's hand. "Ugh!" said Simon as he pulled the eel free and tossed it back into the water. Leo grinned and stuffed the last of the fish into his mouth.

The water seemed to boil and the enraged nymph burst out of the river behind Simon-Leo, shouting, "That was the most disgusting thing I've ever seen. Don't you dare come back! That goes for all of you! What that monster did to my poor fish! I don't know if they'll ever be the same again. I'm coming, babies," she cried, and she sank back under the water's surface.

"Who's that?" Simon asked, staring at Zoë as if he'd never seen her before.

It occurred to Millie that he hadn't, at least not the way she was now. "This is Zoë," she said.

Simon scowled at her. "What are you talking about? Zoë is a bat."

"Sometimes," said Zoë. "Sometimes I'm a vampire. You

have two heads. Why can't I have two shapes?" Turning back to Millie and Francis, she said, "I'm going to take a nap, too. You took so long that I did some exploring. I found a cave off that way." Zoë pointed toward the east where the first hint of daylight was graying the sky. "I don't like sleeping out in the open if I can help it."

Both Simon and Leo looked interested. "Good!" said Simon. "I was wondering if I'd have to cover myself with leaves or dig a pit before the sun came up. How far away is this cave?"

"Not very," said Zoë. "But it's kind of small."

"I'll make it work," said Simon.

"See you tonight!" Zoë told her friends.

"Tonight," murmured Millie, and then she was asleep.

Nine

It was late afternoon when Millie woke to the smell of sizzling fish and campfire smoke. Francis was squatting beside the fire, turning the stick on which he'd skewered a medium-sized trout. She watched him for a minute, thinking about how nice it was that he had come. She could have made the trip by herself, but having friends along made it more of an adventure and less of a chore.

Francis turned his head and caught her looking at him. "You're awake. Good. Breakfast is almost ready. Are you hungry?"

"I'm starving," she said. "I feel like I haven't eaten for days."

"Zoë said the cave was in that direction," said Francis, pointing to the east. "I thought we'd eat, then try to find it. We can get an earlier start that way. I was kind of hoping that if we left early enough, we might be able to lose Simon-Leo. If that cave isn't very far from here, we could get a good head start before the sun sets."

"That isn't very nice," said Millie. "He really does want to go with us, but having a troll along..."

"I knew you'd agree," said Francis. "Telling him we didn't want him with us didn't work. Maybe this will. And I've been thinking... I know you want to be back at your grandparents' castle before your parents return and, well, so do I. My parents are going to be mad when they hear that we went off without telling anyone, but it won't be so bad if we're already back when they hear about it."

"We'll do our best," said Millie. "If you want, we can eat while we walk."

"Good idea," he said, handing her one of the sticks. "Now, do you want to figure out which way they went or should I get my dragon scale?"

"I'll do it," said Millie. "All I have to do is think about it really hard, and it is easier if I'm looking for a place rather than an object. But don't ask me to find people yet. I'm still not very good at that. And don't talk to me while I'm doing this. I've never seen this cave, so it might be a little tricky."

"You sure have a lot of restrictions," said her cousin.

"Francis!"

"Sorry."

Closing her eyes, Millie turned to the east and thought about a cave. Because she couldn't picture a cave she hadn't seen, she imagined something cool and dark with stone and dirt all around it. She cast her thoughts out and down, because it was sure to be underground. Ah, there was something. Keeping the image of a cave in her mind, Millie opened her eyes and began to walk. "You'd better keep up," she told Francis. "This isn't easy, you know."

"I should have used that scale," Francis muttered.

Although it was sunny when they started out, clouds soon turned the sky dark. Millie lost track of time, but they had been walking for at least half an hour when they reached the edge of a bog.

"Are you sure we're going the right way?" asked Francis. "This doesn't look like the kind of place you'd find a cave."

"This is it," said Millie, sounding more confident than she felt. "Just a little bit farther."

As they entered the bog, the ground grew softer beneath their feet and they had to pay more attention to where they walked. Although some people might have been hesitant to enter a bog when night was approaching, the land reminded Millie of the swamp behind her family's castle and she wasn't the least bit afraid. The sun set while they were walking, and with the clouds blocking the moon and stars, they had little light to see by. Millie let her dragon sense take over and continued on without slowing. She heard Francis murmur something under his breath and knew that he was using a spell to help him see.

Soon Millie saw a light flickering in the distance. It drew closer, but she ignored it, for she had a good idea what it might be. It wasn't long before Francis saw it as well. Touching her arm, he pointed to the light, saying, "It looks like we have company."

"Will-of-the-wisp," said Millie. "Don't pay it any attention and it will go away. All they want to do is lead us astray and abandon us in some perilous situation."

"I know," said Francis. "They've been banished from Greater Greensward for years."

Millie kept following her dragon sense, forging a path through the bog, but the will-of-the-wisp began to zigzag in front of them, trying to attract their attention. Eventually, it came so close that Millie could almost see the shadow figure carrying the light.

"Where's this cave, anyway?" asked Francis. "It's a lot farther than I expected it to be."

"We should be right on top of it," said Millie. "It feels like it's under us now. Look around and see if you can find an opening."

When they finally found the cave, it was more like a hole than the image Millie had carried in her mind. Its sole entrance was at the base of a small swell in the ground and it went down and back from there. The space inside was only about three feet high and four feet deep, not nearly big enough for a troll.

"There must be another cave somewhere around here," said Millie. "No troll as big as Simon-Leo could have fit in this."

"Why don't you try finding Zoë?" said Francis.

"I told you that my dragon sense doesn't work very well when I look for people."

"So?" said Francis. "I don't think this worked all that well, either."

"But I can't just . . . I mean, I might . . . Oh, all right. I'll give it a try." This time, when Millie closed her eyes, she pictured her friend Zoë as a bat. Her dragon sense was a little hazy at first, but after a minute or so she began to feel as if she *might* know where to find her.

"I think she's in that direction," she said.

"You mean where the will-of-the-wisp lights are headed?" asked Francis.

"No . . . Oh, wait . . . Yes, I guess so. I'm sure it's just a coincidence," she said, watching the lights float across the bog. There were more of them now and they all seemed to be heading in the same general direction, which just happened to be the way Millie wanted to go.

They fell in line behind the lights, following them around sinkholes and puddles that looked shallow, but that Millie could sense were treacherously deep. Then another set of lights appeared, angling across the bog to intersect the lights that she and Francis were following. Millie had a feeling of foreboding as the second set approached, as if some real danger was coming to meet them. She had just caught the sound of something large stomping through the muck when suddenly all the lights flared, showing them an angry two-headed troll and a bat only yards away. For a moment Millie could hear the shadow figures laughing, then the lights went out all at the same time and she and her friends were left in the dark.

"It's about time you showed up!" exclaimed Simon. "Those little nits have been leading us all over this quagmire, doing their best to get us lost."

"I told you not to follow them," said Zoë. "It doesn't matter how much you threaten them; will-of-the-wisps are never going to take you where you want to go."

"When I get my hands on them, I'm going to rip their heads off and stuff them down their necks!" growled Leo.

"I don't know if they have necks," said Francis. "Or heads, for that matter."

"Watch it, pipsqueak," said Leo. "I'm not in the mood for jokes."

"What happened, did you wake up on the wrong side of the rock?" Francis asked.

"Uh, gentlemen," said Millie.

"He's just in a bad mood 'cause the cave was kind of small," said Zoë.

"I've seen rat holes bigger than that," said Leo. "I had to spend an entire day rolled up in a ball so the sun couldn't reach any of my valuable body parts and turn them to stone. My back is killing me."

"It's my back, too," said Simon. "But my neck hurts worse than my back."

"I bet my neck hurts worse than yours does," Leo said.

The grass rustled. Millie could sense the presence of the will-of-the-wisps, watching and waiting for something bad to happen. She had heard that they enjoyed witnessing other people's pain and suffering, which is why they liked to lead people astray. They couldn't have known that she and Francis knew Simon-Leo and had been looking for him all along. Because the will-of-the-wisps were probably expecting some sort of fight, it was the last thing she wanted to give them, so it irritated her that her friends wouldn't stop arguing.

The pressure was starting to build up behind her eyes when Millie tried again, "Everybody, this isn't getting us—"

"Simon and Leo have been whining like that all day," said Zoë.

"I'd hold my tongue if I were you, bug breath," said Leo. "You should have told me how far it was to that cave."

"And how small," added Simon.

Leo grumbled, "I have half a mind to . . ."

"You have half a mind, period," said his other head.

"I tried to tell you—," Zoë began.

"Please stop arguing," said Millie. "This isn't—"

"Don't you try to tell us what to do," said Simon, with an edge to his voice. "You soft skins think you're so much better than trolls, but let me tell you—"

The pressure behind her eyes was getting worse, but Millie was trying not to give in to it. "I never said we were better than—"

"You don't have to say it," said Leo. "We've seen the way you look at us. That goes for you, too, baby wizard. You think you're something special, but your magic is no match for my strength!"

Francis muttered and a ball of fire flared to life on his palm. Although it was small, the ball was big enough to light up the bog around them. Simon-Leo was crouched on the other side of a puddle, all four eyes reflecting red in the firelight. Zoë darted back and forth between her friends, too agitated to land.

"Care to test that theory?" asked Francis.

"That's enough!" Millie roared, the transformation already begun. She felt her scaled feet sink into the squishy ground and the cool night breeze ruffle the edges of her wings as she rose up on her hind legs to tower above her friends. The will-of-the-wisps' whispers of fear were so soft that she almost didn't hear them.

Although Leo's eyes never left Francis, Simon glanced at Millie and froze. "Leo," he said, "I think you should look over here."

"Why? Francis is just . . . Whoa!" Leo said. "Did you do that, wizard boy? 'Cause if you did, you're better than I thought. Last time you just made dragon sounds. This looks like a real dragon!"

"I am a real dragon," Millie said, shaking out her wings. "I'm also Millie and I did this to myself. I wouldn't be so quick to disparage soft skins, Simon."

Lights flickered back to life as the will-of-the-wisps edged away from the dragon that Millie had become. She turned and looked out into the dark, seeing all the shadow figures, including the ones that weren't carrying lights. Taking a deep breath, Millie exhaled a long tongue of flame that sent them scurrying across the bog.

"Now," she said, turning back to her friends, "maybe we can get going before someone else tries to use us against one another."

Ten

With Millie guiding them, the four were soon out of the bog and headed in the right direction. She waited until she was sure they were safe, then told the others that she wanted to see what lay ahead, and took off into the night sky. After circling over them once... twice... she flew over the countryside, exulting in the sense of freedom it gave her.

The land beyond the bog was lightly forested, with enough rolling hills to make it interesting. Here and there a village nestled among the trees, giving proof that humans could scratch out a living even this close to the Icy North. As the rolling land became the foothills of the next mountain range, Millie turned around, intent on rejoining her friends. The sun was already warming the ground when she landed and turned back into a human; her solo flight had given her the peace of mind she needed to return to her human form.

"Where's Simon-Leo?" she asked Francis and Zoë,

who were resting sprawl-legged and weary beside a narrow stream. Zoë was a human again and had dark circles under her eyes.

"I found him a cave to sleep in," Zoë said, yawning.

"Don't *you* want to sleep in a cave?" asked Millie.

Zoë shook her head. "I'm staying with you this time. Simon and Leo snore like giants grinding rocks into sand. I hardly got any sleep yesterday."

"We're going to rest for a while and then get started again. Maybe we can lose the troll this time," Francis murmured as he closed his eyes.

Millie sighed. She would already be talking to the Blue Witch if she'd gone alone as a dragon. Having her friends along was great and she appreciated that they wanted to help her, but it also meant that her trip was taking a lot longer than she'd intended.

The rumbling of her stomach reminded Millie just how long it had been since she'd eaten. She remembered how Francis had caught and cooked fish for their breakfast the day before, and not feeling as tired as her friends, she decided to return the favor. She'd watched boys fishing in the river back home, and she knew that they used long sticks with strings on the end. It seemed easy enough, so she went in search of a stick while her friends rested. After tying a thread from the hem of her skirt onto the stick, she made herself comfortable on the bank of the stream. Millie dipped the string into the water and waited. When a dragonfly darted close to inspect her, she remained perfectly still. She watched a squirrel jump from one tree to another, sending a leaf spiraling down to settle on the surface of the water. Then something small and furtive rustled in the underbrush on the other side of the stream.

"Caught anything yet?" Zoë asked, suddenly appearing at her side. Even though Millie was used to how silently her friend could move, it was still a little unnerving.

"Not yet," Millie said, glancing up.

Zoë sat down beside her. "I've never fished before. Is it fun?"

"Want to try it?" asked Millie, and handed her the stick.

They sat there in companionable silence for a few minutes, waiting for something to happen. Millie was getting bored by the time Francis came to join them, yawning until his jaw made a cracking sound. They still hadn't had a nibble.

"I wanted to catch breakfast, but I don't think there are any fish in this stream," said Millie as Francis sat down between her and Zoë.

"What are you using for bait?" he asked. Taking the stick from Zoë's hand, Francis lifted the string out of the water. "What the . . . You don't even have a hook. How do you think you're going to catch a fish on a string?"

Millie didn't like the way he was looking at her. "You did," she said, and tried to snatch the stick back from him.

112

Francis held it out of reach and laughed. "I had a hook and bait. You don't know anything about fishing, do you?"

"We were just trying to do something nice," said Zoë.

"That's what I get for traveling with two princesses. Neither of you knows how to do anything practical."

"All right, Lord Smarty, since you know everything, why don't you catch our breakfast?" said Millie.

"You won't have to do that," said a voice from the other side of the stream, and then two boys stepped out of the underbrush. "I'm Seth," said the older boy, who couldn't have been more than ten years old. With his blond hair and high cheekbones, he reminded Millie of Zoë's brother Vlad. If the boy hadn't had such rosy cheeks, she would have wondered if he was a vampire as well. "This here is my brother, Johnny," he said, pointing to the other boy, who appeared to be a few years younger. "Our village isn't far from here. If you come with us, we can get you a good hot meal."

"And why would you want to invite three strangers to your village like that?" said Francis. "For all you know, we could be cutthroats."

"Or witches," said Zoë.

"Or vampires," said Millie.

"Naw," said Seth. "We saw you sleeping. You didn't take turns keeping watch, and any cutthroat worth his salt would have known to do that."

"And witches would have used magic to make their

113

breakfast," said Johnny. "And vampires would want to drink blood, not eat fish."

"I suppose you're right," Francis said, looking solemn. "But you still haven't explained why you would invite us to a meal."

Seth glanced at his brother, then back at Francis. "We don't get many strangers around here. We like to hear news from the rest of the kingdom."

Johnny nodded. "Do you know any stories about brave knights? Or wizards with real magic?"

"I know a few," said Francis, looking more than a little smug.

"Then you've got to come with us!" said Seth. "Our pa would be mad if we didn't bring you back."

"The whole village will want to hear your stories," added Johnny.

"In that case, we won't want to disappoint them," Francis said, dropping the stick on the ground.

Seth crowed with delight. The two boys crashed through the underbrush, then crossed the stream, hopping from stone to stone.

"I'm not so sure that this is a good idea," Millie whispered to Zoë. "We don't know anything about these people."

"I'm too tired to worry about it," replied Zoë. "They're ordinary boys, Millie. They don't have bushy eyebrows like werewolves or the lingering smell of vampires; I would recognize that right away. I really don't think two witches and a vampire need to be afraid of ordinary people. What could they possibly do to us? You and Francis will have a nice meal and we'll be on our way. I'm sure there's nothing to worry about."

The boys hadn't been exaggerating when they said that their village wasn't far. After only a ten-minute walk, they came across a footpath that soon widened into a narrow lane. They passed an abandoned farmer's hut with weeds growing waist-high in the doorway and no sign of any animals. Although they smelled wood burning, they didn't see any other dwellings until they reached the village itself. The houses were made of sticks, with mud filling the chinks in between, and thatched roofs that needed to be repaired.

As they approached the first of the huts, they passed a man armed with a rusted bell and an old, battered sword. He was peering into the woods, but he looked away long enough to nod at the boys and give Millie and her friends a cursory glance before turning back to the trees.

"What's he looking for?" Francis asked Seth, but the boy had seen someone else and was already waving and shouting.

"Pa!" called Seth. "Come see who we found!"

A group of men gathered in front of one of the huts

turned around. One of the men spoke to the rest, then hobbled toward the children like an old man, using a knobbed stick to help him walk. "Who've you got there, son?" asked the man.

"We found them by the stream, Pa. We offered them a meal."

Their father frowned. "Which stream are you talking about?" he asked. "You went into the forest again, didn't you? How many times have I told you not to go—"

"These two are princesses, Pa! We heard the fella say it!"

"Princesses?" the father said in disbelief. "I'm sure he didn't mean real princesses. You didn't, did you?" he asked, turning to Francis.

"As a matter of fact . . . ," Francis began.

The look in his eyes must have been all the affirmation the boys' father needed. Years seemed to melt away from his face and his voice became more animated as he said, "They're real? Who would have believed it? Boys, go tell your mother to add the last of that goat meat to the pot. We got ourselves two real princesses for guests! We're going to have us a party tonight!"

"If you don't have enough food—," said Millie.

"No, no, we'd be honored to have you stay, Your Highness," the man said, his head nodding like a toy on a string. "It isn't every day such fine young people as yourselves come to our village. My name's Jacob," he said as he escorted them into one of the huts. "And you've met my boys, Seth and John. That's my wife, Bernia, there by the fireplace." A matronly woman smiled and nodded, but it was Jacob who said, "So, what brings you to our part of the kingdom?"

"We're on a quest to the Icy North," said Francis.

"Well, then, a good hot meal is just what you need. You won't be getting many of them up there. Now, you have a seat right here," said Jacob, indicating the only bench in the poorly lit room, "and I'll see about getting you something to eat."

There was barely space on the bench for all three of them to sit, but Millie, Zoë, and Francis squeezed together as villagers piled into the room. Men and women, young and old had come to see the strangers. The young men greeted Francis politely enough, but then turned their attention to Millie and Zoë, smiling at them and trying to talk over the din as more and more people arrived. Millie noticed that she and Zoë were the only girls there more than five or six years old. There were adult women, of course, but no other girls close in age. She thought it was odd and was about to mention it to her friends when an old man with an ancient lute appeared in the doorway. Working his way through the crowd, he took a spot on the hearth and soon lively music joined the noisy conversation.

Millie was flattered by all the attention the young men were paying her and was sorry that it was impossible to hear what they were saying. They seemed nice, however,

117

passing a mug of cider from hand to hand until it reached her, and doing the same with a bowl of stew when it was ready. After that, Millie's mug was rarely empty. Although Zoë didn't eat anything, even she couldn't refuse the full mug they pressed on her.

As everyone around them ate, or at least drank, the evening wore on in a haze of good food and better music. It wasn't until Millie had turned down a third helping of stew that Jacob raised his hand in the air and called for quiet. "Now that you've had a chance to sample our hospitality, we're anxious to know what news you might have to share. What can you tell us about the Kingdom of Bullrush?"

"We haven't seen much of Bullrush," said Francis. "Just the will-of-the-wisps and the river."

"I've heard tell of those will-of-the-wisps," said the old man with the lute. "They take you places no man wants to go and leave you there till your bones rot."

"They can't harm you if you don't follow them," said Millie. "Just stay out of the bog or take a serviceable torch with you if you have to go in."

"You don't say?" said Jacob. "And what about the kingdoms beyond?"

"Sea serpents are attacking Chancewold," said Francis. "There's never before been so many plaguing them at once."

"Ah," said one of the young men, "that would be by the sea, then?"

"It's beside the Yaloo River," said Francis. "Chancewold is in southern Upper Montevista."

"I've been there," said the old man. "I went with my pa when I was just a boy."

"What else can you tell us?" asked Bernia.

Zoë cleared her throat. "The giants are building a boat so they can explore the Eastern Sea and what lies beyond."

"Giants are curious folk, always poking their noses into the strangest things," said the old man.

"And the people of Upper Montevista are more accepting of witches now than they used to be," said Millie. "They have some helping their army."

"Those Upper Montevistans always were smart people," said Jacob. "I remember a few years back when . . ."

As individual conversations started around the room, parents with younger children began to gather their families and take them down the lane to their own huts. One couple with a little girl about five years old stopped in front of Millie and Zoë. "Thank you," said the woman. "You don't know how much it means to us to have you here. I'm just sorry that—"

"Now, Ebba," said her husband, taking her by the arm, "we mustn't bother the princesses with your chatter. It's time we got Maite to bed."

Ebba nodded. "I'm sorry, that's all I wanted to say."

"What do you think that was about?" Millie whispered as the woman's husband hustled her out the door.

"I don't know," said Zoë. "Maybe she was sorry because they couldn't stay longer."

"I suppose," Millie said, but the woman had made her uneasy.

Over a dozen people had gone home, leaving more room in the hut. The young men gathered closer now and sat on the floor in front of the bench. "I hear you like to fish," said one.

"I don't know if I do or not," Millie replied. "Today was the first time I've ever tried it. I wasn't sure how to do it, so I'm afraid I made a mess of things." He was a good-looking young man and talking to him made Millie wonder what it would have been like if she hadn't been born a princess and had lived in a village like this one.

"I'd be happy to show you how," he said, his eyes smiling into hers.

"Gib!" said his friend, elbowing him in the side. "She's a princess, remember!"

The young man blushed and looked away. "My apologies," he said. "I shouldn't be making offers I can't keep."

"We have to go," Francis said, getting to his feet. "It's already dark."

Millie glanced out the door as she stood up beside him.

120

The room had been so dark inside that she hadn't noticed that the sun had set or that their hosts had lit candles. "I didn't realize it was so late," she said. "We never should have stayed so long."

"You don't have to go!" said Jacob. "I was planning to offer you a place to spend the night. I know we can't offer you anything like you're accustomed to, but we can give you a warm place to sleep and breakfast in the morning."

"We really must go," said Millie. "We need to reach the Icy North as soon as possible."

"Surely you can stay for one more drink!" said Jacob.

"I don't think we—," Francis began.

"Here you go!" said Bernia, refilling their mugs with her pitcher. "You have to have a drink in your hand so we can wish you well."

Jacob raised his mug, saying, "To a safe journey!" Still watching Millie and her friends, he drank deeply and smacked his lips when he'd finished.

Millie, Zoë, and Francis looked at one another. Francis shrugged, and all three friends drank from their mugs.

"To friendly faces and good food," Francis said, prompting them all to drink again.

"I need to sit down," Millie said after taking another sip. The room had started to sway and her head was feeling a little funny. "Just for a minute or two." Sitting heavily on the bench, she bumped into Zoë, who had sprawled across half the seat. With her eyes closed for just a moment, Millie didn't notice Francis slump to the floor, seemingly boneless.

Eleven

illie decided that her mouth tasted the way her shoes might after a trip through the stable yard. Her eyelids were so heavy that she wasn't sure she could open them, or even if she wanted to. Her mind was blurry, her thoughts fleeting and hard to hold on to as she tried to remember where she was and why she was there. Wherever it was, it wasn't very comfortable. Her back hurt, her ribs and arms were sore, and her neck was so stiff that it hurt to move it even the tiniest bit.

It was a few minutes before she remembered the party the night before and the nice villagers she'd met. They'd offered her and her friends beds for the night. She couldn't recall if she'd accepted their offer, but she must have fallen asleep at some point.

"Psst, Millie!" It was Zoë's voice, sounding rough and scratchy. "Are you all right?" she asked.

Millie shook her head, wincing at the pain in her neck. She was too muzzy-headed to focus on anything for long and had to fight to open her eyes; when she finally got them open, nothing made any sense. While she'd expected to see a wall if she was in a villager's hut or leaves if she was lying under a tree, all she could see were rocks, dirt, and a pair of filthy feet in scuffed shoes. She were wondering who the shoes might belong to when she realized that they were hers.

"Millie!" Zoë said again, her voice louder. "Wake up! We have to talk."

Millie groaned and raised her head, which she hadn't realized was hanging limp until that very moment. It was so bright out that her eyes began to water. She blinked to clear her vision, but her lids felt grainy and rough, making her eyes water all the more. It wasn't until she tried to rub her eyelids that she realized her wrists were tied and she couldn't move them. A rope had been wrapped around her waist and another around her ankles, securing her to something cold and hard behind her.

"I'm over here," said Zoë. Millie turned her head in her friend's direction. Zoë was tied just like she was and secured to a stone pillar. "I think the villagers did it. They must have put something in that cider. I didn't eat anything and the cider was the only thing I drank."

"But why would they do that?" asked Millie. "They seemed so nice."

"I don't know," said Zoë, "but it can't be for anything good. Do you think you can free yourself? Maybe your magic . . ."

Millie shook her head and winced. The movement had made her dizzy and made her head ache. "I can try, but I doubt it will work. My head feels funny. I don't think I can concentrate enough to do my magic yet."

"Why don't you try while I go see if I can find Francis? I shouldn't be gone long."

"But how are you going to . . . Oh, yeah," Millie said, having forgotten for a moment that Zoë could turn into a bat. Things were getting fuzzier, almost as if she . . . A moment later, Millie's head sagged again.

Millie came around the next time to the sound of crunching gravel and the *swoosh, swoosh* of rubbing scales. Her head was a little clearer this time, her mind not quite so muzzy. Zoë was gone—Millie remembered that she had been there—and no one else could have made the noise, unless . . . What Millie had thought was a rock suddenly swung around and looked in her direction. It was a head, covered in dull red scales and attached to a long, snakelike body that stretched nearly twenty-five feet behind it. Millie thought it might *be* a snake until she saw that it had two legs and wings so tiny that it couldn't possibly fly.

Seeing that Millie was awake, the beast studied her in silence, almost as if expecting her to do something. Nearly a minute went by while they watched each other before the creature said, "Why aren't you screaming? The others always screamed, most of them quite loudly."

"Why would I scream?" asked Millie.

The creature snorted. "Perhaps you don't know enough to be afraid. Don't you know what I am? I'm a dragon and I'm here to eat you. Someone tied you up so you could be my dinner. I'm going to bite you and my venom will make you writhe in pain before it kills you. Are you going to scream now?"

Millie shook her head. She wasn't afraid. After all, she was much more powerful than this creature—when she was a dragon. She was wary, however, because she wasn't a dragon now. As a human, she was as vulnerable to this creature's bite as anyone else. If she could hold it off for just a few minutes, she might be able to *make* herself get angry.

"You're not really a dragon, so I don't know why you call yourself one. I know a good number of dragons. They all have real wings and can fly. I've heard about creatures like you. You're a knucker."

"My, aren't we the expert?" said the knucker. "It doesn't matter what you call me, I can still kill you with one bite."

"I thought knuckers ate rabbits and deer."

"Or stray children. I ate a few, then got a real taste for them. When the villagers kept them at home, I destroyed a few of their hovels and told them they had to give me a girl a week or I'd destroy their village and kill them all. The silly things begged and groveled until I couldn't take it anymore. I'm a kindhearted beast under this scaly exterior, so I made a deal with them. I told them I'd eat their children until they gave me a princess or two. I've heard that princesses are sweet and very tender. But I'm sure that will never happen. There hasn't been a princess around here in years."

The knucker began to scratch at the ground with his talons and it took Millie a moment to realize that he was toying with old bones, all with deep grooves that could only be the marks of knucker teeth. Millie tried to get mad by thinking about the villagers and how they had betrayed her and her friends. But she couldn't get too angry with them. The bones scattered around the pillars showed just how many loved ones the villagers had already lost.

"I tried eating the younger ones, but now I eat only the girls of a certain age," said the knucker. "Too young and they don't have enough meat on their bones. Too old and they're tough and stringy. You look to be just about right," he said, eyeing Millie with appreciation. "Are you ready to scream yet? I'd enjoy eating you more if you screamed. You'd get your juices flowing then. I really like that in my food."

"I'm not afraid of you," said Millie. "I would be if you were a dragon. Of course, if you were a dragon, you could fly away from here and find your own princesses."

"Pha! Flying is overrated."

"You're just saying that because you can't do it. Why, I've seen dragons at the Dragon Olympics who could do the most beautiful loops and spins. And the flames! Why, Flame Snorter can breathe a flame nearly a hundred feet long."

"Aha!" shouted the knucker. "I thought there was something about you! Your smell alone would give you away. You wear their stench like a bad perfume. If you've gone to the Olympics, you must be friends with the big dragons. They're soft-brained fools to befriend humans like you. They couldn't be any dumber if they tried!"

"How can you say such things?" said Millie, not noticing her skin beginning to prickle and the pressure growing behind her eyes. "They are the smartest, most bighearted creatures in all the kingdoms. Compared to them, you're nothing but a newt!"

"A newt!" shrilled the knucker. "How dare you? I get sick to my stomach just thinking about those high-and-mighty dragons giving themselves airs when everybody knows that they crawl out of their shell one leg at a time, just like everybody else. And I've heard talk about your friend Flame Snorter. She eats gunga beans and hot flami-peppers to stoke up her fire. If that isn't cheating, I'd like to know what is!"

"Flame Snorter is not a cheater," Millie growled as the pressure filled her head and made her spine feel like it was burning. "All the dragons at the Olympics eat gunga beans and hot flami-peppers. If you had ever gone, you would know that."

Millie's skull was already changing shape as the knucker cried, "Are you calling me a liar? I've changed my mind. I'm not going to wait for you to scream. One bite and you'll scream, anyway. What are you doing? No, you can't . . . That's not possible!"

The ropes broke with a loud *snap* as Millie's muscles grew. She stretched her neck, arching it over the knucker. Knowing that her wings were impressive, she opened them behind her and fanned the air. "You were wrong," she breathed, letting a trickle of smoke escape from between her teeth. "I'm not a Dragon Friend. I'm *one* of those soft-brained fools. And guess what? I eat gunga beans and hot flami-peppers, too. That must mean I'm a cheater. Want to see how far I can breathe my flame?"

"I never s-said . . . I-I mean, I didn't know . . . H-how could you . . . ?" stuttered the knucker.

Millie narrowed her eyes and bent down so that her nose was almost touching his. "I would run if I were you," she whispered in a menacing voice. "And never come back here again. If I ever hear that you or any of your kind are hurting these people, I will hunt you down. I might even get my friends to help me. Maybe we can make a contest out of it. You'd better go now. I'm giving you to the count of three and not one second longer."

The knucker ran so fast that by the time Millie had counted to three all she could see of him was the dust he'd stirred up. Inhaling deeply, Millie shot her flame down the path he'd taken. The stream of fire turned the bones on the ground to ash, crisped the grass, and licked the ground fifty feet away. Millie thought she heard a pained yelp, but she decided that it was probably just wishful thinking.

Beating her wings, Millie rose into the air. She could see the knucker now, tearing across the countryside as it headed toward the bog in the distance. Millie wondered who would suffer more if the knucker were to meet the will-of-the-wisps. She was still feeling good when she dipped one wing and turned in the direction of the only village she could see. It looked tiny from a distance and not much bigger as she got closer.

Millie was looking for her friends, but she wasn't surprised when a villager spotted her first. The sentry at the end of the lane near where they'd entered the village the day before saw her and began to ring the bell. Dragons have excellent eyesight and Millie could see the look of terror on his face. While she couldn't be angry with the villagers for what they'd done, she didn't have to like them and it gave her a certain sense of satisfaction to have gotten her revenge against them, no matter how small.

She was circling over the village, watching everyone run for cover, when she saw Zoë flying out to meet her. Certain that her friend would follow, Millie flew just far enough from the village that no one could see her and landed on the ground with a sigh.

"Did you use your magic to get free?" asked Zoë, settling on Millie's shoulder.

"I guess you could say that," said Millie. "Have you found Francis? They didn't hurt him, did they?" Although she hadn't been seeking revenge against the villagers, the thought that they might have hurt her cousin made her consider changing her mind.

"He's fine," Zoë said. "They tied him up and left him in a cowshed. He told me that they told him they were going to let him out tonight."

"After they were sure we'd both been eaten," said Millie.

"Probably," said Zoë. "Francis feels just awful that you and I were taken. He was still unconscious when I found him and he felt sick when I told him what the villagers had done. I told him that we were all right, but he feels like such a failure. You know how much he wanted to be our protector. To top it off, he wants to be an invincible knight, but now he's sure that everyone is going to know how easy it was to trick him."

"I have an idea," said Millie. "Francis has his armor in the acorn. Tell him to put it on and go to the center of town. I'll meet him there when he's ready. He'll know what to do after that."

Millie waited until she was sure that Francis had gotten ready before she returned to the village. No one else was outside when she saw him standing in the middle of the lane, brandishing his sword. Cupping her wings, she landed ten yards away and roared, fluttering the thatch on the nearby roofs and knocking over a pitchfork and a scythe left leaning against a wall. Doors that had been open a crack slammed shut. Somewhere a small child whimpered.

Francis's helmet clanked when he nodded at her in salute. Raising his sword, he took two steps and shouted, "Have at it, foul beast. You'll torment these kind people no longer!"

Determined to put on a good show, Millie took a deep breath and exhaled flame at Francis, being careful to keep her fire away from the too-flammable huts. Her cousin danced aside easily. Holding up his shield, he advanced on Millie with his sword aimed at her heart. Millie flamed again. The fire hit the center of the shield, flowed to the edges, and shot off the sides in every direction. Francis kept coming. When he was almost close enough to touch, Millie whirled around, lashing at him with her powerful tail. Francis leaped over her tail and somersaulted out of the way. Someone cheered in one of the houses behind her, stopping abruptly when Millie turned to look.

On his feet again, Francis aimed his sword at Millie's neck. "Come closer that I can separate your head from the rest of your body," he commanded.

"Come and get me, if you can," rumbled Millie. Taking another deep breath, she waited until he was in position, then blew a tongue of flame that she let grow feeble and die.

"The dragon's losing its fire," a villager said from a partially opened door. "The knight might have a chance after all!"

Francis may have heard the man, because he lunged at Millie and continued to chase her when she darted out of the way. "I have you now!" he shouted as they ran through the village and out the other side. Once the forest hid them from sight, they slowed to a walk. Francis called out and slapped the flat of his sword against his armor to make the sounds of battle, while Millie roared and puffed smoke into the air so it could be seen above the trees.

"I'm getting tired," Francis finally said. "Do you mind if we end this now? A little bit of blood would be really convincing."

"Forget it, Francis," said Millie. "There's no way I'm going to let you poke me with your sword. Why don't we try this instead?" With a final roar of anguish and a great puff of smoke, she rose into the air and flew in the direction of the village, letting one leg dangle limply and doing her best to make her flying look ragged and uneven. Hearing the villagers cheer below her, she let her head droop and flew off even more slowly, landing when she saw Zoë.

Her friend was a human once again when Millie found her. "Francis said he'd meet us here," Zoë said.

"I hope he appreciates this," grumbled Millie as she sat down with a sigh. "This is the last time I'm going out of my way to make anyone look like a hero."

Twelve

They made good time by walking most of the day and well into the night and didn't stop until they had reached the foothills at the base of the snow-cloaked mountains. Francis was delighted that they had lost Simon-Leo, although Millie kept expecting the troll to reappear.

Even from a distance the mountains exuded a bone-chilling cold that only got worse as the night wore on. Although they didn't want to attract attention, they decided to build a fire to chase away the cold.

"You should have seen their faces when they came out of their huts," said Francis as he tossed another log onto the fire. "I've never seen happier or more surprised people."

Seated on the other side of the fire, Millie nodded. "And you didn't even need my blood to prove to them that you were a hero."

"I didn't want your blood," Francis said. "*Any* blood would have done just fine."

"He wanted to stab me with his sword just so he'd be more convincing," Millie said, turning to Zoë.

"I did not!"

"You were telling us about the villagers?" prompted Zoë. She shivered and pulled her cloak closer around her. She didn't like the cold and this was more intense than anything they'd felt before.

Francis pulled a blanket out of his acorn and draped it around her shoulders and then sat beside Zoë and took her hands in his to warm them. "They cheered for me," he said. "I'm surprised you didn't hear them. Some of them slapped me on my back until they hurt their hands on my armor. They wanted me to stay to celebrate, but I told them I couldn't."

"We know what happens when you celebrate with them," muttered Millie.

Francis shook his head. "They promised me that they aren't going to do that anymore. They won't need to since they think I killed the dragon."

"And I chased off the real human-killer," said Millie. "It wasn't a dragon, it was a knucker."

"The villagers believed it was a dragon and that's what counts. Say, I thought knuckers ate things like vermin and farm animals," said Francis.

Millie shrugged. "This one had acquired a taste for humans, too."

"The villagers made me promise that I'd go back and visit them someday," Francis added.

"That's fine," Millie said, "as long as you understand that Zoë and I will not be going with you. As far as the villagers know, that knucker ate us, bones and all."

"They said they felt bad about that, especially since they thought I'd killed the beast."

"Shh!" said Zoë. "Did you hear something?"

"Just my stomach growling," Francis said.

"No, it was over there in those trees."

"I don't see anything," said Millie.

"I don't, either," Zoë said, "but I could have sworn . . ."

"What's that?" Millie squeaked.

An enormous shape had appeared seemingly out of nowhere, breathing heavily and waving its arms over its huge head. Francis dropped Zoë's hands and reached for his sword.

"There you are!" rumbled a voice.

Millie was the first to realize who it was. "Simon-Leo! You found us," she said.

"Not again!" muttered Francis.

"My mother taught us how to track people," Leo said. "Sometimes she'd let our father go just so we could practice. You didn't think I was gone for good, did you?"

Millie sighed. "Of course not," she said, darting a glance at Francis, who was mumbling to himself. "But we've had a very eventful time since we saw you last. We were tricked . . ."

Zoë nodded. "And drugged . . ."

"And tied up," said Francis.

"Good," said Simon. "I was hoping it was something like that."

"You said they'd run off and left us on purpose!" said Leo. The hand closest to him reached up and wiped a tear from his eye. "You said they didn't want us around, just like everybody else."

One shoulder shrugged. "I wasn't sure," Simon said.

"Then you shouldn't have said it!" said Leo.

"Sit down and tell us how you found us," Millie said before the heads could really start to fight.

"We followed your footprints for a time," said Simon as the troll plopped down on the ground between Millie and Zoë.

"You mean I followed their footprints!" Leo exclaimed. "You fell asleep again."

"It was boring," said Simon. "So, what do you have to eat? I haven't eaten in days. Leo devoured every toad we found last night and our stomach has been sour ever since."

Francis didn't want to share his food with the troll, but he looked into his acorn when Millie insisted. He was still rooting around when Millie felt a prickling on the back of her neck. She looked up and saw that Zoë was peering over her shoulder, and looking just as uneasy as she felt. "Do you feel it, too?" Millie whispered.

Zoë nodded. "Someone is watching us. I noticed it before, but then when Simon-Leo came I thought it had been him."

"Here's an apple," said Francis as he handed the fruit to Simon.

"Is it poisonous?" asked Leo. "They give us indigestion. Our father used to give them to us before we went to bed at night. He said our stomachaches were all in our heads."

"As far as I know, the apples are fine," said Francis.

"It might be the villagers," Zoë whispered. "Maybe they followed Francis."

"Maybe," said Millie.

"I'm going to take a nap," said Leo. "Simon, it's your turn to stay awake."

"Thanks a lot," Simon grumbled. A few minutes passed before he spoke again. Glancing from one huddled figure to the next he said, "Why are we sitting here wasting the dark when we could be walking?"

The only response was the crackling of the wood in the fire.

When Millie woke, snow was hissing softly as it fell from the sky. Zoë was curled up next to her as close as she could get, with Francis just as close on the other side. Snow had accumulated on them, making them look like a lumpy snowdrift in the all-white landscape.

Because it was already daylight, Millie half expected to find that Simon-Leo had gone to seek shelter from the sun, but he was there, feeding the fire and sitting exactly where he had been when she fell asleep.

"Why are you still here?" she asked as she wriggled out of her blanket.

"There's a snowstorm, if you haven't noticed," said Simon. "I can't see the sun, can you? We'll be fine as long as the snow keeps falling. Wake up, Leo," he shouted at his other head. "You like the snow. You're going to love this."

"Wha . . . ," said Leo, his eyes popping open. "Did you say there's snow?"

Simon smiled. Tilting his head back, he closed his eyes and stuck out his tongue. Leo copied him, smacking his lips as the melting snow trickled down his throat. "You know what I want to do?" he asked his other head. "Snow trolls!"

"Don't be such a baby!" said Simon. "We haven't made snow trolls in years. Next you'll want to have a snowball fight."

"Good idea!" Leo said as he reached out and grabbed a handful of snow. Simon's mouth formed an O of surprise when the snowball whacked him full in the face. He sputtered and coughed, then reached for some snow himself. Millie kept well away from the troll as the two heads pelted each other.

The sound of the troll shouting soon had Francis and Zoë up off the ground, although they kept their blankets wrapped around them.

Francis stomped his feet. "I'm freezing and we're not even in the mountains yet! It's only going to get colder," he said, glancing at Zoë and Millie.

"You could use your magic to get warm," said Zoë.

"So can Millie," he said.

"I can warm myself," said Millie, "but it's not going to do you any good. Why don't you make everyone some warm clothes? Zoë's lips are turning blue."

"I'm a knight, not a seamstress! I don't know anything about sewing."

"You don't need to," said Millie. "Your magic will do it all for you. Just try coming up with a spell that includes everything you want your magic to do."

"I guess I don't have any choice since no one else can do it," he grumbled to himself.

Simon shouted and Millie glanced at the troll. Leo was shoving his other head's face into the snow while trying to get rid of a mouthful of snow himself. Both troll faces were bright red and couldn't have looked happier.

"I have a spell ready," Francis said. "Now, don't talk while I do this."

A hat of fur, and gloves that will
Keep us from the winter chill.
Thick boots to make our toes stay warm
A cloak to block a winter storm.
Leggings make our legs stay cozy
Scarves to turn our faces rosy.
To keep us warm in this fierce breeze,
Bundle us in all of these.

Suddenly, they were all dressed in the warmest of clothes and no one was shivering. Francis turned a satisfied smile on his companions and said, "What would you have done if I hadn't come with you?"

"Mmph!" Leo muttered from behind the thick red scarf that now covered his nose and mouth.

Simon looked at his other head with disdain. "Did the hats have to have tassels? And what's that on my shoes?"

Millie glanced down at her own feet. The boots were made of some brown animal hide and were laced shut with a white cord that ended in fluffy white balls. Glancing at her friends, she saw that they were dressed in the same clothes in different colors.

"I like them!" said Zoë.

Millie thought Francis might have blushed, but she couldn't be sure because most of his face was hidden behind a bright green scarf.

"Well, I feel ridiculous!" said Simon. "I don't need these clothes and I'm not going to wear them!" He started to undo the fastenings on the cloak, but Leo slapped his hand away.

Pulling the scarf down from his mouth, Leo glared at his other head and said, "I don't care if you like them or not. We're keeping the cloak and the boots. These are the nicest clothes we've ever had and the first ones that weren't handed down to us from cousin Wartlips-Stinkybreath."

"I didn't think you cared about clothes," said Simon.

Leo turned his head away. "There's a lot of things you don't know about me."

Simon shrugged. "So, we'll keep them on. Are you people ready to go yet?" he asked, turning to frown at the others. "This storm doesn't look like it's going to let up anytime soon."

The snow had been falling steadily the whole time they'd been talking. Even the depressions left by their bodies had filled in.

Francis turned to Millie. "Which way do we go now?"

Although she already knew the answer, Millie checked her dragon sense one more time. "Through that pass," she said, pointing to where two mountains met high above them.

"I'll go first," said Francis, pulling his tasseled hat down more firmly over his ears. "Who knows what we'll find in those mountains."

Thirteen

Millie and her mother both suspected that Millie's limited magic was somehow bound to her dragon side. Like a dragon, she could perform simple magic without using spells or potions. Although she was hopeless when it came to changing objects or living creatures, Millie could make herself warm enough to dry her clothes or to stay cozy on a blustery day; she didn't need the warm clothes Francis had created. She liked them, though, and appreciated his efforts so much that she wouldn't have dreamed of turning them down.

Millie had other abilities as well, things that she'd never told her mother or her aunt or anyone else in her family. Just like Zoë could smell other vampires, Millie could sense the presence of magic. So when their hike through the foothills seemed to be taking an unusually long time, and they seemed to be climbing the same hill over and over again, Millie closed her eyes and listened. Under the whisper of the falling snow and the breathing of her companions there was

143

a soft murmuring sound that she couldn't identify except to say that there was definitely magic at work.

Focusing on the magic, she decided after a time that it was old and had been in place for many years. It wasn't strong, but it didn't need to be since all it was supposed to do was discourage people from going into the mountains. It would be easy to turn it aside for the short time they would need to pass it. While her friends complained about their aching legs and rumbling stomachs, Millie walked in silence, suppressing the magic of the hills while letting her own personal magic guide her footsteps.

It was midafternoon before she no longer sensed the magic. When she opened her eyes she was surprised to see that they had reached the middle of a large mountain. The snow was deeper here, the air colder. Although her body remained warm and comfortable, she could see that her friends' eyes were watering and their cheeks were red. Ice was forming on the outside of their scarves. Millie was thinking about offering her scarf to Zoë when Francis stopped suddenly and exclaimed, "Will you look at that!"

Millie stepped out of the footprints her companions had made and peered through the still falling snow. At first she thought the figures were men. They were tall but rounded in odd ways. She had to go closer to see them clearly. They weren't real men at all, but snowmen formed from large balls of snow. Each one was holding a sign. DANGER! said one sign. GO BACK! said another. COME NO

144

CLOSER! DO NOT ENTER! LEAVE NOW OR FOREVER BE A FROZEN BALL OF ICE! The signs were large and written in bright colors meant to stand out in a world of white.

"What do you suppose this is all about?" asked Francis.

"I guess somebody doesn't want us to go up the mountain," Zoë said.

"The signs aren't just for us," said Millie. "Somebody doesn't want *anyone* to go up the mountain. You can stay here or go back now, but I'm not going to let a few signs stop me."

"Me neither," said Zoë.

"Of course not," said Francis.

"I think I should scout ahead," said Zoë. "You can keep walking and I'll meet you up there."

"Do you really think that's a good . . . ," Millie began, but Zoë had already turned into a bat and fluttered up the mountain.

"May I make a suggestion?" said Leo. "Simon and I should go first. Our feet are bigger and we can make bigger footprints for you to walk in."

"I think that's a very nice offer, Leo," said Millie.

With snow more than knee-deep, having Simon-Leo in the lead to break a trail for them made all the difference. They climbed the mountain more quickly now, despite their growing fatigue. Millie's dragon sense told her where the ice castle was located. What she didn't know was whether or not the Blue Witch was in it. While she and her friends

145

slogged through the ever-deepening snow, she listened for magic again. It was there, right where she could feel the castle was located, but it seemed to be centered on a thing rather than a person. *How odd,* she thought.

Simon-Leo was plowing through a snowdrift when Zoë returned. The little bat came fluttering weakly toward them, her wings so stiff from the cold that they could no longer bend. "Help!" she cried, and tried to land at their feet but ended up in the snowdrift instead.

Francis plunged his hand into the snow, scooping it out until he reached the little bat. "Zoë, say something!" he said, sounding desperate, but all she could do was moan.

"Give her to me!" Millie said as Francis tried to warm Zoë with his breath. "I can get her warm faster than you can."

"Here," he said, handing the bat to Millie. A thin layer of ice had formed on Zoë's body and wings. A thicker layer glistened on her ears and chin. Zoë's mouth was moving, but no sounds were coming out as Millie took her friend from Francis.

Cradling the little bat in her hands, Millie thought about getting warmer. The temperature of her hands rose until they glowed. As the ice on Zoë melted, the water trickled between Millie's fingers, refreezing even before it reached the snow.

Francis hovered by Millie's side, peering down at Zoë. "How is she?" he asked.

"Give me a minute," said Millie. Zoë was shivering so hard that Millie's hands shook, but even that ceased as the bat grew warmer.

"I'm all right now!" Zoë finally called, pushing aside Millie's thumb to look up at her friends.

"What did you see?" Millie asked as she set Zoë on the ground.

"More snow," Zoë said, once she had returned to her human form. Pulling her scarf higher around her neck, she looked up at the mountain and said, "That's the last time I become a bat until we get to where it's warmer. I didn't think I was going to make it back this time."

Francis threw his arms around her in a hug, saying, "Then don't even think about doing it again. And don't you dare ask her to!" he added, turning to Millie.

"But I . . . It was her . . . ," Millie said, astonished. "It really was her idea," she told Simon-Leo as Francis adjusted Zoë's hat.

"I know," said Simon.

They continued on with Simon-Leo in the lead and Francis walking behind Zoë so he could help her over the rougher patches. Millie came last, smiling to herself each time her cousin showed his concern for her friend. She had never realized how much they liked each other.

After a time they reached a part of the mountain where rock jutting higher than their heads sheltered them from wind and snow.

"Look at that," said Francis.

Millie turned to follow Francis's gaze and gasped. A trio of snowmen stood frozen in the shelter of the towering rock just ahead. Unlike the first snowmen they'd seen, these weren't made from balls of snow, and looked amazingly real, as if they'd been sculpted in midstep.

Simon sighed. "I'll see about this."

The troll had just started to lumber toward the snowmen when Millie cried out, "No! Don't go any farther! They aren't snowmen, they're real. Look at the face of the last man!"

Just like Millie and her friends, the men were lined up in a row following in the footsteps of the person in the lead. Although his companions were facing forward, the figure at the end of the line was looking back. The expression on his face showed fatigue and worry the way a real, ordinary man's might. While her companions discussed what they should do next, Millie closed her eyes and listened for magic. It was there, a rough hum that made her feel edgy.

"Stay close together," she said, interrupting whatever Francis had been saying. "It'll be easier if we go through this all at once, so we're going to have to walk side by side."

"What are you talking about?" asked Francis.

Millie nodded in the direction of the pass. "There's magic at work there. I can feel it. I can keep it from hurting us if we hurry, but we have to stay together and we have to be fast."

"I don't understand," said Francis. "What do you mean you can sense magic? I didn't know anyone could do that."

"Well, I can," Millie snapped. "And if you'll listen to me I might even be able to do something about it."

"I think we should do what she says," said Zoë.

Grateful that at least one of her friends trusted her enough to listen, Millie said, "We're going to walk past those men without stopping. I don't think we have to go far to get past the magic, but stay together until I tell you we're safe."

Millie shut out everything except the magic. It lay thick on the ground in front of them, waiting to make each step harder until they could no longer move at all. She pushed against it with her mind, picturing it as a big unwieldy mattress that she was trying to prop up on its end, leaving enough space for them to walk by. It took all her concentration to keep the magic away, because it sagged in places and leaned toward them in others. She walked on, trusting in her personal magic to keep her on the right path, and had to fight to block out everything else when her friends started shouting. It wasn't until she knew they were past the magic that she let down her guard and looked around.

A snow leopard was crouched on a rocky outcropping about head-high just a dozen yards away. Seeing its eyes fixed on them, its back hunched, and its tail twitching, Millie knew that it was getting ready to pounce.

Francis had his sword unsheathed and ready when the

big cat leaped, but Leo was there first, grabbing the leopard around its middle and squeezing. While the leopard shrieked and spat, clawing at the troll's leather-hard skin, Simon tried to stay out of the way, ducking when a paw came too close. "What should I do with it?" Leo asked, clutching the writhing cat to his chest.

"Let me run it through!" said Francis as he closed in with his sword.

"No," said Millie. "Toss it!" And she pointed back the way they had come.

Leo glanced at her, nodded, and tossed the leopard toward the snowmen. The cat landed in a great puff of white as snow exploded from under it. Shaking its head, the cat turned back toward the troll. With its victim in sight, the cat took one slinking step, its belly brushing the snow. Its next step was slower, and the third never quite happened; the animal's front paw extended but was never set down. Even from where she stood, Millie could hear the sound of crackling as ice formed and the leopard froze, turning completely white from nose to tail.

"Are you all right?" Millie asked Leo.

"Uh-huh," he replied.

Simon scowled at him and said, "Well, I'm not. I don't care what you want to do, but I don't like to fight. I'd appreciate it if next time you'd consult with me before snatching up some ravaging animal who wants to shred us into table scraps."

"Sorry," said Leo. "It couldn't have hurt us, not really."

"That isn't the point," Simon said.

They continued on, catching glimpses of the top of the pass as they climbed. The wind picked up, whirling the snow around them as they fought to put one foot in front of the other. Hunching into the wind meant that they could stagger a few feet, but it would take them hours to go the short distance to the top of the pass that way, provided they weren't blown off the side of the mountain first.

"Maybe we can find a cave?" Simon said, turning to Zoë.

"Don't look at me," she replied. "Unless I'm a bat, I can't find a cave any better than you can and I'd freeze solid and be blown to the next kingdom if I turned into a bat now. What about you, Francis? Do you have any spells that could help us?"

"I've been trying to think of one. I suppose I could build a shelter out of ice, but there isn't much else I can—"

A roar shook the ground as a massive white-furred body slammed into Francis, knocking him into a snowdrift. Zoë screamed as another figure emerged from the blinding snow to pick up Simon-Leo and toss him aside as if the troll weighed nothing at all.

Millie glimpsed the face of one of the creatures when it suddenly loomed in front of her, standing taller than the tallest knight in her father's army. Its small, red-rimmed eyes were nearly lost in the shaggy white fur that covered its face. When it opened its mouth to roar, its yellow fangs were almost as sharp as a dragon's. Her ears still ringing, Millie ducked and rolled out of the way, trying to evade the beast's grasp, but then it had her and in the next instant she was flying through the air only to hit the rock and ice with a horrible thud. She thought she might be dead until she realized that she wouldn't hurt so much if she were. Struggling to sit, she didn't see the beast before it picked her up and threw her again. A moment later she heard Zoë scream and Simon's bellow cut short.

Suddenly, Millie was mad. It wasn't a gradual thing that took time to build, but a real, uncontrollable fury that snapped her from human to dragon in a heartbeat. Her wings opened with a crack like thunder and when she roared the mountain shook so hard that sheets of packed snow slipped free, causing an avalanche.

Using her dragon sense, Millie looked for her friends. She found Zoë, curled up in a ball of snow, bouncing down the side of the mountain. Millie scooped her up with her talons and held her close to her body, raising the temperature so that her friend could get warm. She saw Francis sliding feetfirst as he struggled to get hold of something to stop his fall. Millie caught him just as he catapulted off the side of the mountain into empty air, snatching him in midfall and holding him the way she was holding Zoë. Simon-Leo was harder to find, having been caught in the avalanche and buried under the rushing snow. Millie's scaled body was glowing with heat as she cradled Zoë and Francis closer to her and dove into the snow to pluck the troll from its depths with one of her hind feet. He thrashed and squawked as she flew into the air again, screaming as she rose higher.

"Be quiet," she said, curling her neck around to look at him. When the heads continued to bellow she shook her foot and added, "Stop that right now or I'll drop you."

Each head closed its mouth with a snap. The next time she looked back, Simon had his eyes squeezed shut, but Leo was looking with awe at the mountainside below.

With her friends safe, Millie flew toward the pass, circling when she saw the place where they'd been ambushed. The wind and snow had died away, yet no matter how hard she looked she couldn't find any sign of the creatures that had attacked them. She would have continued to look, but Francis groaned, bringing Millie's thoughts back to her friends. It was time to take care of them now. She'd take care of the white-furred monsters later.

Fourteen

illie wasn't sure what to do. She had rescued her friends from certain death, but she had no idea what shape Zoë and Francis were in. For all she knew, they could die. When she tried to land, the ice beneath her began to melt and she had to flounder out of the pooling water, afraid that her charges might drown if she stayed on the ice for long.

Simon-Leo seemed fine, but neither Zoë nor Francis had said anything, which really had her worried. She supposed she could take them to the flatlands, but they were so far away. Even the foothills were too far.

It was nearly dusk when Millie saw the other dragon. She had flown over the pass in search of the ice castle, where she hoped to ask the Blue Witch for help, but before she could reach it, Francis had groaned again and Millie knew she had to set them down right away. She was looking for a flat rock big enough to land on when something flew so close that the wind of its passing knocked her off her stride.

Startled, Millie looked up from her study of the mountainside and saw a dragon unlike any she'd seen before. His scales were white tinged with blue, his wings were well shaped, and his body was long and sleek. When he turned and flew back to join her, she saw that his deep blue eyes looked kind and had the spark of intelligence common to the larger dragons.

"Are you lost?" he asked as he matched his speed to hers. He was about the same size as Millie, and his voice had yet to deepen into that of an adult male.

"I guess you could say that," she replied. "My friends are hurt. I need to land so I can help them."

"Follow me," he said. Tilting his wings, he turned and swooped across the face of the mountain to a ledge swept clear of ice and snow. "This is my home," he told Millie as he landed. "Or, at least, it is now." Glancing at her friends, he pointed at Simon-Leo. "I can understand being friends with humans, but that one's a troll, isn't it?"

"Unfortunately," Millie said as she dropped Simon-Leo on the ledge. The other dragon backed out of the way as Millie landed and very carefully laid Zoë and Francis beside the troll. She nudged Francis with her talon and was relieved when he turned his head.

"I think somebody hit me with a sack of bricks," he

said. Opening his eyes, he looked up and saw his cousin. "Oh, it was you."

"I didn't hit you with anything," Millie said, feeling indignant. "I caught you when you were falling to your death."

"Did you have to be so rough? I think you cracked one of my ribs."

Millie frowned at him. "You could say thank you," she said, and turned to Zoë.

"How is she?" Francis asked, and groaned as he tried to sit up.

"I don't know," said Millie, and nudged Zoë with a talon. When her friend didn't respond, Millie looked up at the other dragon with her brow ridges creased in worry. "I think she's unconscious."

"I have something you could try," said the white dragon, and headed to the back of the ledge.

Francis looked worried. He rolled over and got to his feet, even though it was obvious that he was stiff and sore. Kneeling by Zoë's side, he turned to Millie and said, "Will she be all right?"

"She will be if I can help it," said Millie.

Francis was watching over Zoë when Millie turned to see what the other dragon was doing. The ledge went farther back than she had thought, and opened into a cave. From what she could see, it was big enough to hold a dozen dragons and had another opening at the rear. Sacks and trunks were stacked against the cave walls and it was one of these trunks that the white dragon opened. He was returning to her when something in the cave moved and Millie realized that Simon-Leo was rooting through the sacks.

The white dragon must have seen the troll at the same time, because he glanced at him and said, "I wouldn't go to the back of the cave if I were you."

"Why not?' Simon asked. "Is that where you keep your treasure?"

The dragon snorted. "I wish I had a treasure. There's nothing there except poison gas."

"Poison gas?" Millie asked when he returned to the ledge.

"I sleep in that room. I've been so mad lately that I exhale poison gas in my sleep. Even a troll wouldn't last long if he breathed enough of it. Here, give your friend one drop of this. Two, if one isn't enough."

Francis hovered by her side as Millie took a small bottle of tonic from the white dragon's talons, pulled out the glass stopper, and let one drop fall between Zoë's parted lips. When nothing happened, she gave her friend another drop, then sat back to watch. Millie felt helpless with Zoë lying there with skin even paler than normal and her chest barely moving as she breathed. She wanted to do something . . . anything, but there was nothing, unless . . . Millie turned to the white dragon. "Can I give her some more?"

The dragon shook his head. "Another drop would kill her. Either this will work soon or—"

"Ooh, my head," moaned Zoë.

Francis sighed with relief. "Thank goodness," he said. "You had us worried."

"What happened?" asked Zoë. "The last thing I remember, those monsters were chasing us. One tossed you into the air, Millie. I thought I'd never see you again." Her voice was gaining strength as she spoke and the barest hint of color had come back into her cheeks. Suddenly, she looked like herself again.

"I saw it all," said Francis. "A monster rolled you around in the snow and tossed you down the side of the mountain, Zoë. I tried to stop him, but he knocked my sword out of my hand and threw me after you."

Zoë shivered. "I had the nicest dream, though. I was all warm and toasty. The air smelled good—not like here. What is that smell?" she asked, wrinkling her nose.

"I smell it, too," said Francis. "It's sour, with a real bite to it."

"I don't smell anything," Leo said.

Simon smirked. "You never do."

"That's the poison gas," said the white dragon. "It won't hurt you unless you breathe it in when it's concentrated. That's why I said you shouldn't go to the back of the cave."

When Zoë shivered again, Millie turned to the white

dragon. "Would it be all right if I started a fire? I'm Millie, by the way, and this is my friend Zoë, and my cousin Francis, and that," she said, pointing at the troll, "is Simon-Leo."

The dragon grinned and his whole face lit up. Millie's heart gave a funny lurch. *What's wrong with me?* she thought. *He's a dragon, not a human.*

"My name is Audun," he said. "You could start a fire, except I don't have any wood. I can get some if you want. I'll be back in a couple of hours. There are some trees on the south side of the last mountain in the range and I—"

"You don't have to go to all that trouble," said Millie.

"I don't mind," said the dragon.

"Why don't you just use coal?" said Leo. "I found some in a sack back there."

"What's coal?" asked Audun.

"I'll show you," said Leo.

Everyone waited while Simon-Leo trotted into the cave and returned lugging a bulging sack. "This is coal," Leo said, dumping the sack on the ground. "It burns like wood, only it doesn't smell so good, so I wouldn't do it inside the cave. We have a whole lot of it in our mountain."

"We'll do it out here," said Millie. "Maybe the fire will block the cold air from blowing into the cave."

Audun looked on while Leo piled the coal on the ledge. A puff of coal dust reached Audun, smudging his pure white scales. "My grandfather brought that with him. He was going to take it with us to our new home."

"What happened?" asked Millie. "Where is your grandfather now?"

"He's with my grandmother and my parents, locked away in a castle," said Audun.

"There," said Leo, "you can start the fire."

"I'll get two rocks," Audun said, glancing back into his cave. "We can smack them together and get a spark."

"There's no need," said Millie. "I can handle this part myself."

Taking a short breath, she exhaled a trickle of flame onto the coal, turning it a warm, glowing red. At the same moment, a line of fire raced from Millie's flame across the cave and into the room beyond. *Whoom!* Fire exploded in the back chamber, burning with great intensity for a moment and going out just as quickly.

"I guess your poison gas was flammable," she said, giving Audun an apologetic look. "I hope I didn't burn up something important."

"There wasn't much back there," he said, his eyes wide in disbelief. "How did you do that? I've never seen anything like it. That was amazing!"

Millie felt her face get hot. "All the dragons where I come from can do that."

"No one around here can. All we can do is breathe poison gas."

"That sounds pretty impressive to me!" said Simon.

"I guess it makes sense," Millie said, watching the water

160

from melted ice trickle out of the cave. "If you breathed fire, you would melt half the mountain."

"What else have you got back there?" asked Simon.

"Just stuff my grandfather collected," said Audun. "We were on our way to a new home when we stopped to rest. We were planning to stay here only a day or so."

The troll was already edging back into the cave when Audun glanced in his direction. "Mind if we look around?" Leo asked.

"I don't care," said Audun. "I already told you, there isn't much there."

Millie was using her talons to rearrange the coals in the fire when Audun turned back to her. "You can touch fire?" he asked, sounding amazed.

Millie glanced up. "Can't you?"

Audun shook his head. "Frost dragons can get burned just like most creatures."

Francis and Zoë got up to follow Simon-Leo, leaving Millie alone with Audun. "How did your family get locked away in a castle?" she asked.

"The day after we arrived, an eagle told us that a witch had built a castle near here," he said, his eyes growing fierce. "My grandparents went to see her. When they didn't come back, my parents flew off to look for them. I wanted to go, too, but my father made me stay here in case my grandparents came back. He said it was so they wouldn't think we'd left without them, but I really think it was to protect me.

The next morning I went to the castle and saw their claw markings on the ice. The witch had blocked the door so I couldn't get in and my family couldn't get out. It's been three weeks and nobody's returned yet."

"Where is this castle?" asked Millie.

"On the far side of that mountain," Audun said, pointing at the next mountain over.

"She wouldn't happen to be the Blue Witch, would she?"

Audun nodded. "That's what the eagle called her. How do you know her name?"

"She's the reason we're here," said Millie. "I came to learn something from her and my friends came to help me."

"If you're smart you won't go anywhere near her," Audun said.

"I have to see her," Millie replied. "It's why we've come so far and gone through so much."

"Do you know a way in?" asked Francis. He had come up behind Millie, but his eyes were on the white dragon.

Millie glanced at her cousin. "Audun says that we shouldn't try to see the Blue Witch."

"If we listened every time someone told us not to do something, we'd have turned back long ago." Francis held up a sword so the white dragon could see it. "I wanted to ask if I could borrow this. I lost my sword today and I don't want to go into that castle without one. You have a lot of them back there."

"Sure," said Audun. "You can keep it if you want to. It doesn't have any jewels on it, so it isn't worth much to me."

"Thanks!" said Francis, running his fingers the length of the scabbard. "This is perfect!"

"*Do* you know a way in?" Millie asked the white dragon.

"Yes, but you won't be able to use it. After the witch captured my family, she filled in the entrance so nothing bigger than a human or a troll," he said, glancing at Simon-Leo, "can fit through the door."

"Then I guess we'll have to wait until Millie is in a good mood," said Francis.

Audun looked puzzled. "What does that have to do with going to see the witch?"

Millie sighed. "I'm not always a dragon. I turn into one only when I'm angry. Usually I'm a human girl and could fit through that door."

"Did an evil witch cast a curse on you?" asked Audun.

"Nothing that simple," Millie said. "My mother is a witch who likes being a dragon. She was a dragon too often when she was expecting me, and I'm the one who has to pay the price."

Audun looked confused. "Do you really think that being a dragon is so awful?"

"It's not awful at all!" she exclaimed. "I love being a dragon! The only time I feel free and at peace is when I'm a dragon. It's just that I wasn't born to be one, not like you."

"So, about that door," said Francis.

"I don't like this," said Audun, "but if you have to go see her, I'll show you the door on one condition. Once you get inside, you have to try to find my family. I need to know if they're alive and if there's some way I can get them out."

"That's it? Go into a castle made of ice, get an evil old witch to reveal her secrets to Millie, then free some dragons who will probably spout poison gas at us?" Francis was practically sputtering as he looked from Audun to Millie and back again. "You can't be serious. It's bad enough that we have to go in there at all!"

"I don't know what else to do!" Audun told Millie.

"Of course, we'll do it," said Millie.

"Millie!" said Francis.

"We're going in, anyway, aren't we?" she asked her cousin. "It won't be that hard to look around. Between your magic and Simon-Leo's strength, it shouldn't be any problem to free a few dragons."

Audun's gaze traveled up and down Francis. "You have magic?" he asked.

"Yes, I do. So you'd better watch your step!"

Millie ground her teeth and glared at her cousin. "Francis, you're being rude!"

"Somebody around here needs to set this dragon straight," he snapped. "And I know *you're* not going to do it."

"How do you turn into a human?" asked Audun. "I wish I could."

164

"I have to relax," Millie said, "which isn't easy when I have such an infuriating cousin around." She glared at Francis again, but he pretended not to see it.

"And then what?" asked Audun.

"Then it just...happens," Millie said. "When I'm relaxed enough I think about being a human again, and I am."

"Can you do it now?"

Millie closed her eyes and tried, but nothing changed. "I guess not. I must still be too wound up inside."

"Can you hurry up, Millie?" said Francis. "I want to get this whole thing over with and get home before my parents do."

"You didn't get your parents' permission, did you? How old are you, anyway?" Audun asked him.

"That's none of your business," said Francis.

"Stop it, both of you!" Millie roared. "I'm going to go lie down and try to relax, which isn't going to happen if you two are fighting."

"I take deep breaths when I want to relax," said Audun. "If that doesn't work, I think about a place that I really like—one that makes me happy. That's what my mother told me to do when I was just a hatchling."

Millie found a comfortable spot against the wall of the cave and curled up so that her nose was resting on her tail. Although she didn't think she could fall asleep, she was so exhausted that she was soon snoring gently. When she woke a short time later, she saw Audun only a few feet away, watching her.

"That was amazing," he said. "One moment you were the most beautiful dragoness I've ever seen and the next you were the most beautiful human. You must have really powerful magic to transform that easily."

Millie sat up and brushed the hair out of her eyes. "I don't know. I can't control it yet."

"But you will. Someday you'll be able to do all sorts of things. I've never met anyone like you before."

"I don't think there are too many people like me around," she said, and glanced past the dragon to the cave opening. "It's time for us to go."

"If you're ready."

"I am," she said, taking the talon he offered to help her up. "I guess it's now or never."

Fifteen

$\mathcal{M}$illie and her friends stood at the lip of Audun's ledge, looking down. A small cloud floated past beneath them and when it was gone there was nothing to see for a very long way. The ground was so far below that only a dragon could have seen a human on its surface.

"How are we supposed to get down there?" Francis asked. "I don't think even Simon-Leo could jump from here and live."

"You don't have to jump," said Audun. "I'll carry you to the castle. Millie, would you like to ride on my back?"

Francis glanced at the dragon's back and shrugged. "I suppose if it's the only way. I'll go first, and give you a hand up, Millie—"

Audun snarled and lowered his massive head so he was face-to-face with Francis. "I offered Millie a ride, not you. I'll carry you the same way you came here—in dragon claws."

"I don't think that's fair," said Francis, turning a little pale.

"Dragons don't have to be fair. It's the only way I'll carry you, but if you don't like it you can stay up here—forever. My lady," Audun said, lowering his neck so that Millie might climb onto it.

"Isn't there any way—," Millie began.

"No," said Audun. "I will not have that boy on my back."

"I'm sorry, Francis," Millie said as she took hold of one of Audun's ridges. "There isn't room for all of us up here, anyway. And you'll be perfectly safe in Audun's claws. I carried you that way myself."

"Where should I go?" Zoë asked in a small voice.

Millie glanced back and saw real fear on her friend's face. "Audun, do you think perhaps . . ."

The white dragon sighed. "I suppose I can carry her, but I'm not letting that troll climb up, so don't ask!"

"I wouldn't want to sit up there, anyway," grumbled Leo. "I'd probably get blown off!"

"The wind . . . ," said Zoë.

"You'll be safe," Audun replied. "Just hold on to my ridges and I'll fly slowly."

The dragon held still while Zoë climbed up behind Millie. When he reached for the troll, Simon closed his eyes while Leo watched everything with great interest.

"Uh-uh," said Francis. "You're not picking me up like that. Hold your foot still and I'll climb on."

"I'll have to tighten my grip so you don't fall," warned Audun.

"I know," Francis said, positioning himself so he could reach his scabbard. He tensed up, waiting for the pressure, and relaxed when the dragon didn't squeeze him.

"Hold tight," said Audun.

As the dragon's muscles bunched under her, Millie felt Zoë lean against her back. The great wings began a slow and steady beat, and suddenly they were in the air, soaring out over the vast emptiness that had opened beneath them.

"Wow!" Zoë breathed into Millie's ear. "I've never flown this high before. This is incredible."

"It is," Millie said, gazing around her in awe. Although she had flown alongside this same mountain only hours before, she had been too worried about her friends to appreciate the scenery. She gasped as the sun caught the snow on the mountains in a sparkling sheen of purest white. The deeper snow showed hints of blue, the same shade as the streaks on the white dragon. Tightening her grip, Millie glanced down. They were up so high that the river that ran between the mountains was the slimmest of lines. Riding a dragon was almost as exhilarating as *being* a dragon, although she would never have dreamed of trading one for the other.

They were approaching the next mountain in the range when Audun said, "Watch out. We're going up," and then they were climbing. Millie leaned forward so that she was hugging the dragon's neck, with her body pressed against the side of his ridge. Zoë bent over as well, holding her face against Millie's back as they arrowed nearly straight up. Even after Audun leveled off, Millie stayed where she was and was glad she had when he began his descent and the wind whistled past them.

She saw the ice castle right away; it would have been impossible to miss. The light reflecting off its surface would have been blinding if the sun hadn't been setting. The castle had been constructed in the cleft formed by three mountains. Like the surface of the mountains around them, the walls of the castle were white and blue. With tall, slender turrets and pinnacles, and lacelike arches that reached to the mountains themselves, the castle could only have been built with magic.

Millie's muscles were beginning to tremble from the effort it took to hold on when Audun finally set down Francis and Simon-Leo before landing at the foot of the castle. Zoë groaned as she slid into Francis's arms; Millie soon followed, her fingers still bent and stiff.

"The door's inside that archway," said Audun. "It's the only door in the entire castle. There are no windows or other openings. I know, because I've spent weeks trying to find a way in."

"How are we supposed to do this?" asked Francis. "Do we bang on the door or sneak in? I think we should sneak in."

"I say we barge in screaming and swinging axes," said Leo.

"You would," said Simon. "I think we should knock."

"For once I agree with Francis," Audun said. "The only way you'll be able to enter that castle is to sneak in."

"How will we get inside?" asked Zoë.

"That's easy," said Francis. "The door is made of ice. I could open that in my sleep."

"Then I guess this is good-bye," Millie said, turning to Audun.

"Be careful," said the dragon. "I know we've only just met, but I don't want to lose you, too. If you're not back in a few hours, I'm coming in after you. I can use that coal to melt the door."

"You won't need to do that," said Millie. "We'll be back before you know it." Standing on tiptoe, she kissed the dragon on the cheek and turned to join her friends.

"I can't believe you just kissed a dragon," Francis told her as they started toward the door.

"My mother kissed a frog," said Millie, "and look where they are now."

"That's different," Francis grumbled.

"Francis, half of the time I *am* a dragon. Do you really hate *me* so much?"

"No, of course not," said Francis. "But that doesn't mean I have to like the dragon who has his eye on you."

"Do you think he really likes me?" Millie asked.

"I don't get it," said Francis. "You'd have to be deaf, blind, and stupid not to see it, and I know you're not any of those. He looked like you'd cracked a lance over his head when you kissed him, he was that stunned."

Millie stopped and looked for the dragon, but he had already moved out of sight. When she turned back to Francis, he had reached the door and she had to run to catch up.

The door was only about five feet high, but from the depression around the frame it was obvious that there had once been a much bigger opening that had been filled in with more ice. With his friends huddled around him, Francis placed his hands on the door and muttered,

> Door of ice so white and clean,
> Open up for me.
> Let us pass within your halls.
> Listen to my plea.

The door shivered and opened, letting a cool draft wash over them.

"That was it?" asked Simon. "That was the spell? I always thought spells were supposed to be long and complicated with all sorts of mumbo jumbo tossed in to make them sound important."

"I could do that," Francis said, "but that kind of spell takes a whole lot longer to make up. It's easier to make a mistake when you say them, too. I've found that if I keep my spells short and to the point, I get better, faster results. Did you see how fast that door opened?"

"If you don't mind, could you talk about this later?" said Millie. "The door is open and we can go in. That's all we need to know."

"Some people can be so grumpy," Francis said as he waited for his friends to go past. When they were all inside, he pulled the door closed behind him.

"Don't lock it," Millie whispered. "We might have to leave in a hurry."

The walls of the corridor were blue, as were the ceiling and the floor. Candles burned in sconces with a flame as cold as the walls. The corridor was bright from the light reflecting off the ice, but the walls were oddly shaped, with bumps here, dips there, deeper patches of blue in some places, and fanciful swirls in others.

At first Simon-Leo took the lead simply because he blocked the hallway with his broad shoulders and big stomach and wouldn't let anyone get past him. With his ax in his hand, he opened every door and peered inside, then shut it before anyone else could look. Francis was getting increasingly frustrated with this and kept trying to get past the troll, but he wasn't able to until they turned a corner and entered a wider corridor with even more misshapen walls. With so many bumps and bulges, it was nearly impossible to see more than a dozen feet in front of them.

Millie was beginning to wonder if they'd ever see a

living creature, when something stepped out from behind a bulge in the wall and almost ran into Francis. Millie gasped and Francis pulled his sword from its scabbard. It was one of the furry white monsters that had tried to kill them.

"Get back," Francis said, shoving Millie and Zoë behind him. "I'll take care of this."

"You and me both," said Leo, while Simon squeezed his eyes shut.

The beast opened its mouth as if to roar, then seemed to think better of it and closed its jaws with a snap. It watched warily as Francis and Leo approached it from opposite sides. After eyeing them both, it turned to Francis and knocked his sword away with one swift blow. The creature looked like he was about to tackle Francis when a cheery voice said, "Why, hello there!" Jerking its head as if it had been punched, the beast disappeared back around the bulge in the wall.

While Francis made as if to follow the beast, Millie turned in the direction of the voice. A little old woman dressed in a blue gown and a darker blue over-tunic was framed in an open doorway. She was smaller than Zoë and could easily have been mistaken for someone much younger if it hadn't been for the wrinkles etching the skin around her eyes. Her white hair had been done up in bows and curls that wobbled and bounced against her cheeks every time she spoke. Her clothes were clean and looked new, her shoes old and battered.

"I have guests!" she said, clapping her hands. "I haven't had guests in . . . Let me see now . . . five, no, seven . . . nineteen . . . No, no, that wasn't it. I know!" Her face lit up as she looked at each one in turn. "I've never had guests before. You four are the very first ones! Isn't this delightful?"

"Delightful," Zoë echoed as the old woman took her hand and started pulling her into the room behind her. It was a Great Hall, far bigger and more elegant than the bright and open Hall in Greater Greensward or the dark and dreary one in Upper Montevista. Zoë cast a pleading look at Millie and Simon-Leo, who were already following her to the door. They were about to enter the room when Francis returned, looking cross.

"What are you doing?" he asked from the doorway.

"You don't know how nice it is to hear another voice! My invisible servants are wonderful, but they never speak and I have been pining for someone to talk to. I talk to them, of course, but it's difficult to hold a conversation when you never know if the other party is in the room or not. Come in, come in! Supper should be ready soon."

The old woman pulled Zoë out of the way, then stepped back and waited for the others to enter. A creature much like the first snowman was about to follow them into the Great Hall when the old woman grabbed the door and slammed it in his face.

While the old woman chattered about how good it was

to see them, Millie looked around the Hall. There was one long table in the center of the room with dozens of chairs on either side. Nine of the creatures, or snowmen, as she was beginning to think of them, stood with their backs to the wall, watching the woman. One of them curled its lip in a silent snarl when it caught Millie looking at it, but it neither moved nor acknowledged her presence in any other way.

"I'm sure my servants will have plenty of food," said the old woman. "They always anticipate my needs and just now I need to take care of my guests."

Millie almost giggled when one of the creatures scowled and plodded from the room, taking great care to open and close the door silently.

A bell chimed softly somewhere in the castle and the little woman clapped her hands. "Dinner is ready!" she said, smiling brightly. "Now, my sweetlings, take your seats at the table. You can tell me all about yourselves while we eat. My name is Azuria. I'm the Blue Witch, of course. Oh, my, I have so many things to tell you. I've told my servants all my stories and I'm sure they're sick of hearing them, but now you're here and you haven't heard any of them. We could stay up all night talking and it would all be new to you! This is so exciting. Come along now! There we go. You take that seat, young man, and you sit there, sweetling. You'll sit beside me, young lady. And you, you're a troll, aren't you? You'll sit across from me so I can talk to both of your heads at once. Isn't this fun?"

At first Millie found the woman's ceaseless chatter annoying, but she soon realized that as long as the woman was talking she didn't need to say anything, which gave her plenty of time to look around. The chairs were wooden, as was the chest at the side of the room. There was a fireplace at the far end, but no logs inside or charring on the walls that would have shown that it had been used. The walls were blue and weren't completely straight, bulging in some places and bowing at others. A heavy wooden chandelier hung from an oddly shaped hook in the center of the room and the ceiling above it was blue in irregular splotches. The only source of light in the room was the candles in the chandelier and those set on the chest, but the light of the flames reflected off the walls of ice so many times that the room was as bright as daylight.

As Azuria rang a little bell the snowmen came and went, bringing in platters and refilling mugs. Their big, fur-covered hands were awkward, but they tried hard to do whatever the old woman seemed to want. Whenever the witch was talking to someone else or occupied with her food, Francis made faces at the snowmen, who made the most gruesome faces back. The game ended, however, when Azuria noticed a particularly awful face that Francis was making and asked him if he had a twitching disorder.

The food was wonderful, the flavors delicate or robust depending on the dish. It was so good, in fact, that Millie decided it must have been prepared with magic. Her mother had served food made with magic when they were on family trips. It was always delicious and served at exactly the right temperature, just like the Blue Witch's food. There wasn't anything wrong with a magical meal, in fact, Millie often preferred it, but it was interesting that the witch's food wasn't cooked in the normal way.

Millie looked up when Francis kicked her under the table. "Well, my dear," the old woman said, "is it a secret?"

"I'm sorry," said Millie. "Did you ask me something?"

"Your name," said the Blue Witch. "I've already told you mine, and your friends have told me theirs."

"I'm Millie," she replied.

The old woman smiled. "What a nice name! And what brings you here, Millie?"

"Actually, a friend of yours recommended that I come to see you. I don't know if you'd remember her, but her name is Mudine and she—"

"Mudine! Why, of course I remember her! She and I were best friends when we were children. We lived in town just blocks from the Magic Marketplace. My mother sold sweetmeats that enabled a person to speak any language she chose. Mudine's parents had a stand right across the way. They sold poultry. You know—geese that lay golden eggs, chickens that lay copper . . . When we were small,

Mudine and I spent our days playing beneath the stalls, watching for dropped coins and listening to the older witches talk about their magic. We learned a lot that way. Why, I remember, there was an old wizard who sold shoes . . . Here, would you like more soup?"

One of the servants hovering beside the table reached for Millie's bowl just as the old woman held up the ladle. Reaching across the table, she poured the hot, beet-red soup on the creature's hand so that it trickled off into Millie's bowl. The snowman didn't make a sound, but its mouth opened wide and Millie could have sworn she saw tears well up in its eyes.

"Everything is delicious," Zoë said from the other side of the table. She winked as Millie fished long white hairs out of her soup with her spoon and dropped them on the floor.

"If you grew up in the city, how did you end up here?" Millie asked Azuria.

"Oh, that's a long, sad story, but I'd be delighted to tell it to you," said the old witch. "I was madly in love, you see, but my beau was an unfaithful brute. When I learned what he had done, I packed my things and headed north, proclaiming that I was going as far from him as I could get. I ended up here in the midst of the most dreadful blizzard. I wandered for days and would have perished if my invisible servants hadn't found me and nursed me back to health. While I was regaining my strength, I told them about this marvelous castle I had visited when I was a girl. And wouldn't you know—they built this castle for me, which is just like the one I described. They've been adding onto it ever since. In fact, they built a whole new addition just a few weeks ago."

"It's beautiful," said Millie. "When Mudine said that you lived in the Icy North, I never imagined that your home would be as lovely as this. She said that you would be able to help me with a problem that's been troubling me my whole life. Every time I get angry I—"

"That sounds fascinating, my dear, and I'd love to hear all about it tomorrow. I know I mentioned staying up all night and talking," she said, stifling a yawn, "but I'm just too tired to do it tonight. It's time we all got some rest. But I must tell you that once I go to bed my servants blow out all the candles and the castle gets dismally dark. I wouldn't go anywhere after that if I were you. An ice castle can be very dangerous at night."

"But we weren't planning to stay long and—"

"Of course you're staying! As my very first guests, you can't just leave! You'll spend the night and tomorrow we'll have another opportunity to get to know each other. Now, if you'll excuse me . . ." Pushing back her chair abruptly, the old woman didn't seem to notice that she had shoved it into the stomach of one of her servants, who had been standing behind her. She tried to shove the chair back again and again, but the servant was doubled over in pain and the chair kept battering him, smashing his toes and pounding his shins. "Something's wrong with this chair," the old woman muttered. It wasn't until another servant helped the first one stagger out of the way that Azuria was able to put her chair where she wanted it to go.

The Blue Witch was already headed for the door when Millie and her friends realized that she was leaving. They stood, pushing back their chairs as the servants jumped out of the way. Millie was wondering what she should do, when Azuria turned back and said in a loud voice, "My guests need beds for the night. The girls should sleep in one room, the boys in another."

Her invisible servants stood poised to run as soon as she left, but Azuria no longer seemed to be in a hurry. "Sleep well, sweetlings," she told the four friends. "And remember what I said about staying in your rooms."

Millie nodded and said, "We will." She had no intention of wandering the halls in the dark with those abominable snowmen everywhere.

"Then good night," said the Blue Witch, blowing them each a kiss. "Sleep tight and don't let the ice bugs bite."

"Are there really such things as ice bugs?" Simon asked as Azuria left the room.

"I don't think so," said Francis. "But even if there were, they'd be the least of our worries."

Leo nodded. "Especially with those monsters lurking everywhere."

"I was thinking of the fact that I have to share a room with you," said Francis.

The room that Millie and Zoë shared was an odd shape, with a big bulge on one wall and a dip in the ceiling that brought the ice low enough to graze Millie's hair. It made Millie uncomfortable, although Zoë didn't seem to mind it. "My family spends a lot of time in caves, and they're usually pretty uneven," she said as she plumped up the heavy blanket she'd found folded on one of the two beds. "I've been meaning to ask, why do you suppose Azuria stopped you when you were trying to tell her why we came to see her?"

"I don't know, unless she really was tired. Maybe it's better this way. Audun thought she was evil and we don't know her well enough yet to say if she is or not. Are you sure you checked the room?"

"Yes, and so did you, at least a dozen times," said Zoë. "There's nothing here. Do you think I'd go to sleep in a room with those monsters in it?"

"I know. You're right. I just can't shake the feeling that we're being watched."

"That's not surprising, considering we have been ever since we met Azuria. I think it's a good thing she can't see them. Can you imagine what it would feel like to know they were watching every move you made all day, every day?"

"I'd hate it," said Millie. "And you're probably right.

Having them watching us for just a few hours has already gotten to me."

"I know we don't really know Azuria," said Zoë, "but she seems pretty nice if you ignore her craziness. Do you think she *really* can't see those monsters, or is that all pretense?"

Millie shrugged. "I guess she could have a form of snow blindness and can't see anything that's white. Otherwise the I-can't-see-them thing would be too hard to make believable."

Zoë stuck her head under the blanket and poked around inside it. "I suppose. And what about the evil part? I know the Green Witch is supposed to be the nicest, most powerful witch in Greater Greensward, but are all witches with color names supposed to be like that?"

"I think they're powerful, but I don't know about nice," said Millie.

Zoë's hair was a tangled mess when she came out from under the blanket. "Do you think she did something to Audun's family?"

"I have no idea. I haven't seen her do any magic yet, so I don't know what she's capable of doing. However, we'll find a way to explore the castle tomorrow. If there are dragons hidden here, we're going to find them. What are you doing? Are you going to sleep under that blanket or what?"

"I have to," said Zoë. "Just not like this."

Millie watched as Zoë climbed onto the bed and stood on the pillow. The air shimmered around her as she turned into a bat. The cool, dank puff almost made Millie sneeze.

"It's too cold in here to hang on to that ceiling," Zoë said as she shuffled off the pillow. "There are no bugs here, so I'm famished as a bat, but I can't stay a vampire with you sleeping this close to me. The temptation to bite you would keep me awake all night. It's bad enough that I can't sleep during the day without worrying that I might sleepwalk and bite you at night. Well, good night. To sort of quote Azuria, 'sleep tight and don't let the vampires bite.'"

"Very funny," said Millie, pulling her blanket up around her neck. While Zoë burrowed under the covers, Millie glanced around the room one last time. Although they'd both checked the room repeatedly, she wanted to make absolutely certain that there were no snowmen hiding anywhere, waiting for her to fall asleep. She hadn't seen any, but she still couldn't shake the feeling she'd had since the moment they entered the room that someone was watching her.

Sixteen

illie woke the next morning to Zoë shaking her arm and saying, "Get up, sleepyhead. We have a lot to do today."

"You're up awfully early," Millie said, yawning. She glanced at her friend, then sat up to get a better look. "What's that on your cloak? It looks like white fur. That wasn't there yesterday."

Zoë looked down and began picking off the fur. "Let's just say I'm no longer hungry."

"You didn't!" said Millie. "And after we promised we wouldn't leave the room."

"I never promised any such thing. I woke up in the middle of the night because the castle shook and I heard this awful rumbling sound. I'm surprised you didn't hear it, too. By the time the noise stopped I was wide awake and starving. And since there aren't any bugs here . . . I'd never bite a friend or someone I really care about, but I don't like those fuzzy, white monsters. They aren't so bad, though, once you get to taste . . . I mean, know them." Zoë tilted her head and gave Millie an irritated look. "You should be grateful I did go out. Now there are fewer monsters to follow us around today."

"I'm surprised one of them didn't try to stop you," Millie said as she threw off the covers and reached for her cloak. "They seem to run in packs."

Zoë shrugged. "Actually, a few of them did try. I told you I was really hungry. I was mad, too. They attacked us when we were cold and unprepared. I thought it was time someone did the same to them."

"I doubt it will make a difference," said Millie. "But you never know. Want to go to breakfast with me? I'd like your company."

Zoë smiled, showing off her vampire fangs. "I'll go, even if it's just to see how many monsters are left."

❧

There were four snowmen in the Great Hall when Millie and Zoë arrived. One of them, standing by the door, flared his nostrils and sniffed when Zoë walked past. She smiled at him and licked her lips. Instead of scowling at her like he might have done the day before, the snowman looked afraid and shifted uneasily from foot to foot until Zoë had walked away.

Millie was glad to see that Simon-Leo and Francis were already there, sitting at the long table in the center of the

Hall. She could see the steam rising off the porridge they were eating even before she sat down. "Did you sleep well?" she asked, noticing that Francis and Leo both had black eyes.

"No," Leo and Francis said at the same time.

"He snored," said Francis, pointing at Simon.

"I couldn't help it," Simon said. "I'm coming down with a head cold."

"We were talking last night," said Francis.

"Before or after your fight?" Millie asked.

"Both," said Francis. "We think you should ask Azuria the question you came to ask."

"Or get the magic doodad you came to get," added Simon.

"So we can go home," Leo said.

Zoë shuddered. "You're scaring me. You're starting to finish each other's sentences. Millie, I have to agree with them—I think we should go home as soon as possible before it gets any worse."

"Very funny," said Francis.

"I tried to ask her my question last night," Millie told them. "I'll try again as soon as I see her."

When one of the snowmen brought two more bowls, Millie noticed that he was careful to keep his distance from Zoë. He served them quickly, then scurried back to his place by the wall. Zoë handed her bowl to Simon-Leo, who was happy to eat her porridge. Millie noticed that the snowmen drew together after that to whisper behind their hands.

"I don't like the way the monsters are looking at Zoë," Francis said.

"She went out for a bite last night," said Millie.

"There you are!" sang Azuria as she breezed into the room. "Did you sleep well? I know I did. I like to sleep snuggled down under warm blankets in a cold room. Make sure to tell me if my servants don't take good care of you. I'm holding them responsible for your well-being, so let me know if everything isn't perfect."

"Everything is fine," Millie hurried to say when Simon opened his mouth. "We would like to look around your castle today, if you don't mind. And I really do need to ask you about my problem, so—"

"Millie, I'd love to continue our little chat about Mudine," Azuria interrupted. "Why don't you come with me? Your friends can explore the castle to their hearts' content. You can rejoin them later."

"I'll be right there," said Millie. Turning back to her friends, she said in as soft a voice as she could manage, "See if you can find the dragons. We have to take care of that before we can go home."

Zoë nodded and patted her hand. "Just be careful," she whispered back. "We don't know how far we can trust her."

❧

188

The three snowmen who had followed Azuria into the room stayed with them as Millie and the old witch walked side by side down the corridor. When they reached the stairs, instead of going up as Millie had expected, the old woman led her down to the dungeon. "Follow me," she said, taking a candle from the wall before crossing to another door and another set of stairs.

They'd gone partway down when Millie glanced back. This time only two snowmen were following them, the third having stayed at the top. The stairwell was dark except for the light of Azuria's candle, but as they continued on, Millie was surprised to see that it was lighter ahead. It was warmer, too, and became increasingly hotter the lower they went, until the stairs ended and they stood in a cave glowing with a reddish light. Steam rose from the floor, and pools of water bubbled on either side of a narrow path. Someone had taken the time to encircle the pools with low stone walls just high enough to make comfortable seats.

Millie was still looking around when Azuria slipped off her shoes and lowered herself onto the edge of one of the pools. She sighed with relief as she dipped her feet into the water.

"Well, don't just stand there," said Azuria. "Sit down and take off your shoes. The water feels great, see!" Leaning back, the old woman kicked her feet in the water, splashing the path all the way to the bottom of the stairs.

Millie tried not to stare as the two snowmen scurried up the stairs and out of sight. "I dearly love a good, long soak," Azuria proclaimed in a loud voice as she continued to splash. Millie was wondering if the old woman had gone completely crazy when she finally pulled her feet out of the water and whispered, "Are they gone yet?"

"They just left," Millie said, and gasped when she realized what the woman had asked. "You mean you knew I could see them?"

"Of course, my dear. I've known for a long time that they aren't really invisible. It's just that my eyesight was damaged when I was lost in that blizzard. I couldn't see anything at first, but it's come back bit by bit and I can make out bright colors now."

"Is that why all the walls are blue—so you can see them?"

Azuria laughed. "I told my servants that I wanted them blue because I'm the Blue Witch, but that wasn't the real reason. I may not be able to see something that's white, but I can see the shape of it when it stands in front of a wall and blocks my lovely blue. They give themselves away in other ways, too. I can see their red-rimmed eyes and their fur when it gets dirty or stained. I can hear them when they walk, although they try very hard to be quiet. And I can smell them. I have a very good sniffer," she said, patting her nose with one finger. "If you ask me, they smell like wet dogs, which I never could abide. Now, tell me, my dear, why did you come to see me? You're having a problem with your magic, aren't you?"

"How did you know I have magic?" asked Millie. She sat down on the ledge and turned to face the old woman.

"Because Mudine would never send you to see me for anything less. I've been collecting every bit of information I can find about magic since I was a little girl. If I can't help you with a magical problem, no one can. So, what's wrong? I didn't want you to tell me while they were around," Azuria said, indicating the stairwell where the snowmen were waiting. "But you can tell me now."

"I need to learn how to control my anger. Every time I get angry I turn into . . . something."

"Ah, I see. Can you give me some examples of when this has happened?"

"It's been like this all my life, but lately I've tried to control it and I just can't. I lost my temper when I'd made plans for my birthday party and we had to drop everything and go to my grandmother's instead. And I really lost my temper when I learned that my grandmother had tricked and manipulated my parents into having the party where she lives just so she could show off for someone she wanted to impress. And then I lost it again when someone insulted a person whom I really care about. And then—"

"It sounds to me as if anger isn't your real problem. You've gotten angry over things that would have made anyone angry. I think your real problem is your magic. You

191

don't need to learn to control your anger as much as you need to learn to control how and when you turn into a dragon."

"How did you know I turn into a dragon?" asked Millie.

Azuria tapped the side of her nose with her finger again. "I told you I have a very good sniffer. I can smell the dragon in you even when you're human, which means that your dragon side is always present. It isn't a bad smell. I'd describe it as hot and spicy, which is much better than wet dog."

"So what can I do to control *when* I turn into a dragon?"

"Do you have difficulty turning into a dragon at other times?"

"I can't do it unless I'm angry."

"And how about turning back into a human? Do you have to be angry then, too?"

"No, actually, I have to be calm and happy."

"I see. Come closer, child, and let me look at you." Putting both hands on the sides of Millie's face, Azuria drew her so close that their noses were almost touching. After peering into the girl's eyes for a moment, the old woman sat back and nodded. "Just as I thought. In order to turn into a dragon, you have to tap into your dragon magic. You must reach into yourself, find the fire that lies dormant within you, and coax it into flame. So far you've let your anger do this for you, perhaps out of an unconscious fear that your fire might hurt your fragile human self. That's why you've had to be calm to return to your human form. Don't worry; finding your fire *won't* hurt you. It will only make you stronger, because once you are able to consciously tap into your fire, you'll have much greater control over all your magic."

"I think I understand what you're saying, although I'm not sure how to do it," Millie said.

Azuria patted Millie's knee. "You will learn, my dear. Just give yourself a chance."

"I will." Millie stood and took a step away from the water. "Tell me something. Why did you want to come down here? Did you know your servants wouldn't stay long?"

"My servants!" said Azuria. "Ha! My *jailers* is more like it. I just call them my servants because I think it's what they want me to believe. You have to understand, they were kind at first and really did save my life in that blizzard. I was delirious for days afterward. I'd lost my sight and the feeling in my hands and feet. They cured me as best they could. In fact, it surprised me how well they did. I think it surprised them, too. Then they started to do other things for me, like build me the castle and cook food better than any I'd eaten in years. It was magic, that much was obvious, and it didn't take long before I figured out it was *my* magic. I'd brought an object of power with me, you see, and they had found a way to tap into it without actually touching it. After a time I got enough of my eyesight back that I could get around on my own, and I realized that they were watching me. Everywhere I'd go, they'd be there, watching what I did every minute of the day. Even the most attentive servants aren't that thorough, so I knew that something was up. They were after something, and it didn't take a genius to know it was my object of power. As long as they had me around, they could tap into the magic. But just think what they could do if they had the object themselves! They wouldn't need me, and they could go anywhere they wanted. So I tested them just to see what they would do." Azuria rubbed her hands together and chuckled. "I made a fake crystal ball and gave it a real polish. I treated that thing like it was the biggest treasure anyone had ever had and never let it out of my sight. Why, I slept with the darned thing and took baths with it and even sang to it at night. I must have had twenty of my *servants* following me around, hoping to get their hands on it."

"What happened?" asked Millie.

"One day when I knew they were all watching, I smashed it on the floor. You would have thought I'd killed their mothers! Some of them forgot themselves enough to howl! I had to come down here to be by myself so I could laugh till my sides hurt. They don't like the heat, you see, and they especially don't like hot water."

"When you splashed the water earlier and poured hot soup on that one's hand yesterday . . ."

"I splashed the water in case one of them was brave

enough to follow us down here. They stay near the top of the stairs when I get in a splashing mood. I wanted some privacy so we could have this conversation. And as for the soup . . . Oh, I do all sorts of things to those poor creatures just to see if they'll let down their guard and make a noise. I figure they deserve it. They've been driving me crazy with their snooping and their silence for years."

"Then why do you stay? Couldn't you leave and go live somewhere else?"

"And just where would I go? As old as I am and with half my eyesight gone, I'd have a hard time fending for myself anywhere else."

"I don't mean to be rude, but I don't think that's true. Mudine told me about a wonderful witch doctor who cured her of some terrible sickness. She's looking for someone to live with her. I know she's really lonely and would love to see you again."

"Mudine? You mean she didn't marry that old scalawag Olebald Wizard?"

Millie shook her head. "As far as I know, Mudine never got married at all."

"You don't say? Well, then, I might follow your suggestion and go see my old friend. Yes, indeed, that sounds like just what I should do." The old witch pulled her feet out of the water and turned so she could set them on the ground. Using Millie's arm to steady herself, she stood, saying, "So, now that you've got your problem solved and

I might have mine solved as well, maybe it's time we go back to civilization."

"That sounds good to me, except . . . What do you think your invisible servants will do when we try to leave the castle? If they haven't found your object of power, they aren't going to stand back and let you go. I know you said that they were kind to you, but they were horrible to us. They attacked us on the mountainside when we were on our way here. They tried to kill us!"

Azuria sighed and shook her head. "I was afraid they were doing something to make people stay away, but I didn't know it had gotten that bad. When I first came here I noticed a low-level magic working to discourage people from reaching the mountains. I thought they were shy and just wanted their privacy. But they must have taken stronger steps after they learned about my object of power, because no one has come this far for twenty years. It makes sense if you think about it. If they wanted to keep me until they found my object of power, they wouldn't want anyone coming to take me away or get the object before they could. If they tried to kill you . . . I shudder to think what they might have done if someone had actually reached the castle."

"But somebody did. Some dragons came to see you, and they haven't been seen since. You don't know if there are any dragons in your castle, do you?"

Azuria shook her head. "I haven't seen a dragon in years."

"Could your servants have used your object of power to lock dragons in your castle without you knowing it?"

"Anything is possible. The object is very powerful. Why? Were these dragons friends of yours?"

"They're members of a friend's family," said Millie. "Audun has been waiting for them to come home; he thought you were keeping them prisoner here."

"As far as I know, I'm the only prisoner in this castle, but you go right ahead and look for your dragons. When you've found them I'll have us out of here in two shakes of a dragon's tail. I know a lot more about how to use my object of power than my jailers ever did."

The snowmen were waiting at the top of the stairs just as the Blue Witch had predicted. They pressed themselves against the wall to let Millie and Azuria pass, but Millie didn't like the way they looked at her, and she began to wonder just how private her conversation with Azuria had been.

Shortly after she returned to the Great Hall, Millie's friends came in, talking about what they'd seen. For once there weren't any snowmen in the Hall, so she asked them how their day had gone. While Simon-Leo had explored the dungeon, Francis and Zoë had climbed the stairs to each of the towers and had come down shivering, saying that there was a snowstorm raging outside, but that they hadn't seen any dragons.

"I could find them in a minute if I had a farseeing ball like your mother's," Francis told Millie.

"Magic could help, if only . . ." Millie broke off as something occurred to her. It might work, but it would be easier if she were alone. "Please excuse me. There's something I want to try."

On the way to the room she shared with Zoë, Millie looked for snowmen, but they all seemed to have vanished. She wondered about that as she shut the door and inspected the room to make sure there weren't any lurking behind a hidden panel or hiding under a bed. What would make them change their habits so suddenly? Even if they had overheard her conversation with Azuria, why would they disappear like that?

Having made sure that she was alone, Millie sat on the bed and closed her eyes. Although she didn't have a farseeing ball and probably wouldn't be able to use one if she did, she had another kind of magic that just might help. Listening for magic on her way into the mountains had been easy. She doubted that listening for dragon magic would be very different. All dragons had magic of some sort, even after they died. She hoped to find Audun's family alive and healthy, but if she didn't, at least she'd be able to tell him what had happened to them.

Clearing her mind, Millie shut out the sounds of the ice creaking under the onslaught of the storm, the scrape of a bench in another room, and the beating of her own heart—and listened. At first there was nothing to hear aside from the background hum of magic left over from when the castle was built, but as she concentrated she began to hear another sound, a thrum *thrum*, thrum *thrum* that was amazingly strong once she knew what to listen for. Millie opened her eyes. The source had to be close by. In fact . . .

Fetching a candle from the hallway outside her room, Millie climbed onto her bed and held it up to the wall. There was something back there, something pale against the blue. Moving the candle flame closer to the wall, she followed the shape of the thing, trying to decipher just what it might be until she saw something nearly round and about as big as her fist, blue against the white—and it blinked.

Millie had found the dragons.

Seventeen

illie found it hard to control her excitement as she went in search of Azuria. She had wanted to shout the news as soon as she saw the dragon, but she didn't want the snowmen to hear, although now they seemed to have gone somewhere and not come back. Although Millie knew she wasn't very good at finding people with her magic, she tried to focus on the Blue Witch. When that didn't work, she thought about the magic Azuria must have around her. This time, she found the old woman in less than a minute. Leery of alerting the snowmen, Millie didn't knock, but just opened the door and slipped through, shutting it behind her. The old woman was there, brushing her hair in front of a mirror.

"Good!" said Azuria. "You can help me with my hair. My servants usually do this, but they seem to have deserted me. I can feel my hair, I just can't see it. How does it look?"

"Here, let me," said Millie, taking the brush from the old woman's hand.

"Now, tell me why you came looking for me," said Azuria. "I can see by the expression on your face that you have news."

"I found the dragons!" said Millie. "They're frozen in the walls of this castle! That's probably why the walls are so oddly shaped."

"I've wondered why the servants add on to the castle when I'm the only one who lives here. They did it again last night. Did you feel the castle shake?" Azuria squinted at Millie. "Why are you standing there with a brush in your hand? Let's go free the poor creatures! This isn't going to be easy, so I need to take . . ." The old woman crossed to a chest and knelt down beside it. She muttered to herself as she rooted around, and finally sat back on her heels, saying, "This should do the trick." The vial that she held had a gold filigreed stopper that seemed to glow with a light of its own. After draping its golden cord around her neck, she shoved her hand at Millie. "Here, help me stand up. All this ice makes my joints stiff. Now, where exactly are the dragons?"

Millie braced herself and hauled the witch to her feet. "I saw one in the wall of the room where I slept."

"Then that's where we'll start," the old woman said as she opened the door.

They stepped into the hall so intent on their errand that Millie didn't notice the snowmen at first. When she realized that they were appearing one by one out of thin air, she stopped and put her hand on Azuria's shoulder. "They're back," she said. "They must have done something to make themselves truly invisible."

"Really?" said the old woman, placing her hand on her chest so that her fingers covered the vial. "Then they've learned how to draw more power from my object than I'd realized!"

The snowman closest to the witch smirked and reached out his hand. Millie noticed that his fur was smudged with a deep, dull black. *Just like Audun's scales when the coal dust blew on him,* she thought, and gasped when it occurred to her what that might mean. *Audun must have brought coal to melt the door like he said he would. If he'd gotten in, surely I would have seen him by now. But I haven't, which might explain why the snowmen were adding on to the castle last night: Audun is trapped in a wall, too.*

Millie was hoping that she was wrong when the snowman took hold of the vial and yanked so hard that the cord snapped.

"Ow!" cried Azuria. "That hurt, you buffoon!" The old woman struck out, but it seemed that she still couldn't see the snowmen because her blow merely grazed the creature's ear. Raising her hand to point in his general direction, she said, "You won't get away with this," and had just started to chant when another snowman knocked her to the ground.

"No!" Millie shouted. She was bending down to help

Azuria when a blow landed on the back of her head and everything went dark.

❧

The first thing Millie noticed was the cold. She'd never really felt cold before because her metabolism was somewhere between that of a dragon and that of a human. But she was shivering now, which was a new sensation and one she didn't particularly like. Her natural reaction was to wrap her arms around herself, but when she tried, she found that she couldn't move. She wasn't quite awake yet, so it just seemed odd to her, certainly nothing to worry about. However, when she tried again and still couldn't budge, it bothered her enough that she finally came fully awake.

Something isn't right, Millie thought, and tried to open her eyes. They were as cold as the rest of her and felt as if they were frozen shut. She worked on her eyelids for a while, squeezing her eyes tightly shut, then trying to open them wide. When she got one partly open, she wondered if she really had because all she could see was a sea of blue. It wasn't until she had both eyes open that she saw something that wasn't blue, off to her right. She focused both eyes in that direction and realized that she was looking at a face. It was a large face and belonged to a white dragon. And then it all came back to her—how she'd found the dragon in the wall and gone to tell the Blue Witch and then been hit on the back of her head.

Millie felt another new sensation then—fear. Of course, she'd felt some kinds of fear before—fear for her friends' safety, fear that she might never meet the person who was right for her, fear that her parents would be angry—but she'd never felt fear for her life. Now, trapped in a wall of ice, she feared she'd never get out and would die there without anyone ever knowing what had happened to her.

It occurred to her that she wouldn't have to stay trapped in the ice if only she could turn into a dragon. The other dragons couldn't free themselves because they breathed poison gas instead of flames. If she were a dragon, however, she could free them all and then she'd teach those snowmen a lesson so they'd never harm anyone again! She was getting worked up over the prospect, but she just couldn't seem to make the transition. The problem was, she wasn't angry as much as afraid and worried.

Millie took a deep breath and tried to calm herself. She thought about what Azuria had said about tapping into her dragon fire. It sounded simple enough, if only she knew how to do it. The most she could manage was to adjust her own temperature and . . . Perhaps the two things were related. Could she have been tapping into her fire every time she adjusted the warmth of her hands or body? Maybe this wouldn't be so hard after all.

Millie closed her eyes and turned her thoughts inward,

searching for the source of the heat. There it was, deep inside her, a fire reverberating with so much power that she couldn't understand why she hadn't heard it every time she'd listened for magic. As she reached toward the fire she found that she could draw enough warmth from it to stop her shivering, but she could go only so far before the heat became a palpable force that pounded with the rhythm of her own heart, pushing her away with each beat. Azuria had been wrong about one thing: this was no ember waiting to be coaxed into a flame—this was a fire waiting to engulf Millie.

Reluctant to go any closer, she tried to think of something else she could do. If only she could get angry enough to tap into the fire the way she usually did. But she wasn't angry and trying to make herself mad hadn't worked. What if nothing worked? What if she couldn't change? What if she was trapped in the ice forever? Her parents would be furious that she had gone and worried that she hadn't come back. She was sure they would come looking for her, but unless they talked to Mudine, which seemed extremely unlikely, they wouldn't know where to look. There was always her mother's farseeing ball, but what if the snowmen could block it? She was going to be stuck in this castle forever, she just knew it!

If only she had never left Upper Montevista and come on this hopeless quest. Except . . . it hadn't really been hopeless because she had found her answer. But now, even though Azuria had assured her that the fire wouldn't hurt, Millie was looking for a way to avoid it. It wasn't the Blue Witch's fault that the fire was so big or that Millie was too scared to follow her advice. She could breathe fire, she could swim in fire, so why was she afraid of the fire inside her?

The thought that her own timidity might be holding her back was more than Millie could bear. She took a deep breath and looked toward the fire, resolved to do whatever she had to. Having traveled so far seeking the witch's advice, it would be foolish to ignore the witch now.

Determined, Millie started toward the fire. This time she didn't let herself think about what she was doing, but instead forced her way past the battering waves of ever-growing heat. Then, suddenly, she was through. To her surprise, the fire *didn't* hurt. The heat pulsing around her was invigorating and made her feel invincible—powerful, unafraid, and ready to take on anything.

This time, when Millie opened her eyes, she was delighted to see that although she was still locked in the ice, she was a dragon. The ice around her splintered as she shifted her weight, but she was still trapped and the pressure of fitting into a space that was too small for her dragon body was making it hard to breathe. The deepest breath she could take as a dragon wasn't very deep, but it was enough to allow a tongue of flame to melt the ice in front of her mouth. She struggled to take another breath; this time the narrow flame shot long and true, melting the ice all the way to the outside edge of the wall. She had fresh air now, although little space in which to breathe, so she took her breaths carefully, melting more of the ice around her with each exhalation. Water trickled out the hole in the wall, turning into a small river as the hole widened.

Once Millie had melted enough ice that she could take a truly deep breath, she began to work in earnest. She melted the ice behind the dragon to her right and was relieved to hear the creature free itself and scramble out of the wall. Knowing that at least one was alive gave her hope that the rest were as well, so she blew flames until she grew dizzy and light-headed. She rested for a moment, peering through the blue around her, hoping to locate another dragon. Instead, she saw Azuria and Zoë, shivering together in the sea of blue. Moving with great care, she melted the ice around them, then used her talons to break the rest of the ice and free them. Neither one was conscious. Millie laid them on the floor and went back into the wall to look around for others.

She found an elderly dragon and freed him, then continued on until all of her friends and the rest of Audun's family were either lying on the floor as they came around, or up and helping the others. Tired but happy, Millie went from dragon to human making sure that they were all right. When she reached Azuria, the old witch looked up and smiled. "I thought it was you. Glad to see you got that whole dragon thing under control. Did you get everyone out?" she asked, nodding at the dragons.

"I think there might be one more, but he wasn't near the others. Do you know where the snowmen went?"

"Ran off with their tails between their legs, if they have tails, that is. I've blocked them so they can't tap into my magic again. Should have done it long before this, but they were using it to take such good care of me that I didn't really want to."

"How could you block them? I thought they took your object of power with them. That vial . . ."

"That vial wasn't my object of power! My left shoe is," she said, lifting her foot and twisting her ankle back and forth so Millie could admire it.

Closing her eyes for a moment, Millie listened for the object's magic. It was there, a steady background noise that was so constant and pervasive that it was hard to notice unless she was specifically looking for it.

"They never did guess it was a stinky old shoe," Azuria continued. "That vial had some mighty tasty syrup in it, though. That stuff is great if you ever get a sore throat. I figured I'd need it once I started my incantations to free all the dragons. I wish I still had it. Sitting on this cold floor has made my throat hurt something awful."

"It's time you got out of here," said Millie. "Take everyone out of the castle and get them to safety while I look for Audun. I don't know if he's here or not, but I have to make sure."

"I want to get some things from my room," said Azuria. "That troll boy can come with me. He looks like he's strong enough to be of some use. Simon-Leo, come give me a hand! And before you go," she said, turning back to Millie, "see how that girl's doing. She looks awfully pale to me."

While Simon-Leo helped the old woman to her feet and supported her as they walked down the hall, Millie sat beside Zoë. Her friend was shivering in her sodden cloak, so Millie hugged her until both Zoë and the cloak were dry. "Are you all right?" she asked as Zoë pulled away.

"I'm fine," the girl replied. "Although I've never been so cold in my life."

"Where's Francis?"

"I told him I was all right so he went to talk to Audun's grandfather. They're comparing notes about the dragons from the different parts of the world."

Millie nodded, but her mind was already on something else. "I owe you an apology. I never should have let you and Francis come with me. I've put you both in danger throughout this whole trip."

"Don't apologize for something that wasn't your fault," said Zoë. "You didn't make me come with you. It was my decision, just like it was Francis's. And I'm glad we came. After hearing about our parents' adventures for so many years, it was time we had one of our own!"

Millie grinned. "I'm happy you feel that way, because it isn't over yet. You and Francis need to go with Azuria. I think Audun came looking for us and may still be trapped in the walls."

"Don't worry about us," said Zoë. "Go look for Audun. Just be careful. We started this trip with you and we want to end it the same way."

Millie had already listened for Audun while she'd been freeing the others but hadn't sensed any other dragon magic close by. While her friends made their way out of the castle, Millie paced the hallways, her head cocked to the side as she listened with more than just her ears. When she finally sensed something, it was so faint that she almost passed it by. It was less of a sound than a tickling, like the tip of a feather traced along her cheek, but it was enough to make her curious.

She studied the wall separating her from the source of the sensation. It was thicker than the rest, with a blue so deep in places that it was almost black. Try as she might, she couldn't see the curve of a sleek tail or the angle of the ridge down a back. Millie searched for the sensation again, trying to pinpoint it in the depths of the blue ice. When she believed she had it, she melted the wall in front of her a few inches at a time. Taking a deeper breath, she let out a bigger flame, but still the ice melted ever so slowly. She kept at it, however, until she thought she saw the outline of something. . . . It was Audun, she was sure of it, but a dark cloud swirled around him, making his figure indistinct.

As hard as she had worked before, Millie worked even harder now. She took deep breaths, melting the ice until she had almost reached the cloud. Audun hung suspended in the shifting vapors with his eyes half-closed. Millie listened again; his magic was fainter than before, as if he were fading away. Unsure of what the vapor might be, Millie stopped melting the ice when only a few inches were left and began scraping at it with her talons. When she finally broke through, she cautiously sniffed the air. Just as she had feared, it was the same smell that she and her friends had noticed in Audun's cave. It was poison gas, and from the look of the cloud swirling around the white dragon, it was very concentrated.

Millie knew that she had two choices, neither of which appealed to her. She could either melt the rest of the ice around him, probably igniting the gas, or chip away at the ice with her talons while breathing it herself.

It didn't take Millie long to make her decision. Breathing in the poison gas might kill her and then she wouldn't be able to help anyone. However, if she were to melt the ice and the gas did ignite . . . She'd just have to be quick, that was all.

This time, when Millie filled her lungs with air, she started moving before she exhaled. The ice melted in a blast of heat and she launched herself through it just as the gas inside turned into a ball of fire. An instant before the flames engulfed Audun, Millie wrapped her limbs and tail around him. She adjusted her body temperature so that she could absorb the heat of the fire with her back while chilling the side closest to him. The fire was fierce and hot, but it didn't last long. By the time it died away, the entire wall had melted, leaving a gaping hole in the side of the castle.

Audun was stirring in her grasp when she laid him on the ground and vaulted into the air. Although she hadn't been sure that she could take the fire into herself, now that she had, she knew that she had to release it before it consumed her. Choosing a gap between two mountains, she plunged into its depths and let her heat dissipate, melting the ice around her and creating a clear mountain pool.

Carrying the heat of the fire had left Millie feeling tired and weak. She floated in the pool, scarcely able to keep her head above the surface, and was on the verge of losing consciousness when she felt herself lifted from the water and carried into the air. "Are you all right?" Audun asked, gazing down into her eyes.

"I am now," Millie said with a certainty that surprised her. "How are you?"

"I couldn't be better," he replied, despite the singed scales that darkened his cheek. "Thank you for everything. You rescued my family and then you rescued me. I was coming for you when those beasts froze me with some sort of magic and covered me with ice. I would have been there forever if you hadn't come along. I can't believe you soaked up the fire like that. You have to be the bravest dragon I've ever met. Look, here are my parents. I want you to meet them."

Millie turned her head to look as Audun landed beside the ruins of the Blue Witch's castle, where his family had gathered. Like Audun, his family's scales were white, tinged with blue. They all thanked her effusively, but only his grandmother seemed to notice the tender way Audun set her on the ground when Millie swore that she was strong enough to stand, and how he wrapped his tail around hers in a proprietary sort of way.

The old dragoness frowned, but before she could say anything, Audun's mother stepped forward. "While we were trapped in the walls we saw everything that went on in that castle. You were very brave, my dear, especially for a human."

"Thank you," Millie said, smiling at the dragons. The only one who didn't smile back was Audun's grandmother.

"There you are!" Azuria shouted as she hobbled across the snow. Simon-Leo was weighted down with a huge leather sack and a rolled-up rug so long that the end dragged on the ground as he followed her. Millie recalled having seen the rug on the floor of the Blue Witch's chamber, but she wondered how the old woman thought she could possibly take it with them.

"That was fantastic!" shouted Francis. "I didn't know dragons could carry fire the way you did."

"Neither did I," Millie said.

Zoë looked anxious as she drew close to peer at Millie. "How do you feel? You don't look like you usually do. Your scales are still green, but they're kind of pink around the edges."

"I'm fine, Zoë. I just—," Millie began.

"First this streak of fire shot out of the castle and then it hit the ice with a *whoosh*!" Francis said, more excited than Millie had seen him in a long time. "We didn't know it was you until Audun brought you back. That ball of flames was you, wasn't it?"

"Yes, it was. I was just—"

The snowdrifts behind the Blue Witch exploded and a horde of snowmen tumbled out, roaring so loudly that Millie's heart skipped a beat. Azuria began to fumble at the sack Simon-Leo was carrying. Seeing that the old woman wouldn't be ready before the snowmen reached her, Millie leaned toward Audun and said, "Why don't we take care of this?"

Audun nodded and the two dragons took to the air.

While most of the snowmen watched them with wary eyes, some of their companions made great sweeping gestures with their arms and looked confused when nothing happened.

"I think they just learned that their magic no longer

works," Millie told Audun. The dragons swooped lower, making the snowmen duck. When Audun breathed poison gas in their direction, the snowmen grabbed their noses and pinched them shut. Although they had been prepared for a frost dragon's poison gas, they looked startled when Millie lit the gas with her flame. Howling, the snowmen threw themselves into snowdrifts, then ran away with their charred fur still smoking. When they were certain that the snowmen were gone, Millie and Audun landed, standing so close that their tails touched.

"I don't know about you," said the Blue Witch, "but I'm ready to get out of here. Anyone want a ride? Simon-Leo, you can put the carpet down now."

Simon-Leo grunted and dropped the sack so he could unroll the carpet on the snow.

"That can't be a magic carpet," said Francis. "It's huge."

"You bet it's huge," agreed Azuria. "I've had this thing for over fifty years and I spent a fortune for it. It can hold all of you, even the troll, although I draw the line at dragons."

Millie laughed. "I think I can get home on my own," she said, and turned to Audun. "I have to go now. I'm glad I got to meet you. Thank you for helping us. You saved Zoë's life with your tonic and you helped us find the Blue Witch."

"You don't need to thank me," said Audun. "You saved my entire family. You're a very special dragon, Millie. Are you sure you have to go?"

Millie nodded. "My parents are going to be worried sick about me if I don't get back before they do. Take care of yourself, Audun." Millie could have sworn that he blushed when she kissed him on the cheek. Simon-Leo chortled, but Millie didn't care. She felt as if she'd known Audun for years.

❧

Although the carpet sagged under Simon-Leo, Azuria didn't have any trouble getting it to rise. "Now you take over," she told Francis, who was sitting beside her, his hand almost holding Zoë's. "The way my eyesight is, I'll have us crashing into mountains before you know it."

Francis looked delighted and didn't even glance back at Millie as he guided the carpet down the valley. Millie sighed and spread her wings. She took off, rising into the air to circle over the castle, then came back to fly low over Audun. "Will I ever see you again?" she called.

"You couldn't keep me away if you tried," he shouted into the wind, and waved until she was out of sight.

Magic carpets are very fast, but even the best magic carpet is no match for a flying dragon. Millie could have been back at her grandparents' castle within a few hours, but she slowed her pace to match that of the carpet. However, every now and then she flew ahead, lost in her thoughts, and then had to fly back to look for her friends.

The last time this happened was right before she spotted the mountains of Upper Montevista. It was late in the day and she would have preferred to go on, but she turned around to tell the others that they were almost there. Not everyone was happy to hear the news.

"I hope my parents aren't back yet," said Francis.

"What will you do if they are?" Zoë asked.

"Tell them about how I used my magic, I guess," Francis replied after a moment's thought. "That should make them happy."

"What are you going to tell your grandparents?" Zoë asked Millie.

"I don't know," Millie replied. "My father's parents probably won't want to see me. My mother's parents will probably be mad that I left the way I did."

"Are you going to tell your parents what happened?" asked Francis.

"Eventually," said Millie. "I've never kept secrets from them before. I don't see any reason to start now."

"We'll, *I'm* going to look up my old friend Mudine," said Azuria as her carpet skimmed above the top of the tallest mountain in the range. "We have a lot of catching up to do and I want to know if she's really looking for someone to share a cottage. While I'm at it, I'm going to ask her about that witch doctor friend of hers. Maybe she'd like to show me where to find him."

"I'm going to stay at your grandparents' castle for a few weeks until my parents are back from their trip," said Simon-Leo. "You don't think they'll mind, do you, Millie?"

"Oh, they'll mind, all right," Millie said, laughing.

Francis turned around to glance back at Simon-Leo, a guilty expression on his face. "You've been so quiet, I forgot you were there," he told the troll. "I guess I should turn around and take you back to where we found you."

"You don't need to do that," said Millie. "I think Simon-Leo *should* stay with Queen Frazzela and King Bodamin. Maybe after they've had a troll living with them for a few weeks, they'll appreciate a granddaughter who's a dragon only part of the time."

Francis snorted. "That's a great idea, but who's going to suggest it?"

"I will," said Millie. "And this time I think I can talk to my grandmother without worrying that I might lose my temper."

"Because she already knows that you turn into a dragon?" Francis asked.

Millie shook her head. "Because I don't think I'll turn into one unless I want to. You can't imagine what a relief it is to know that I might finally have a choice."

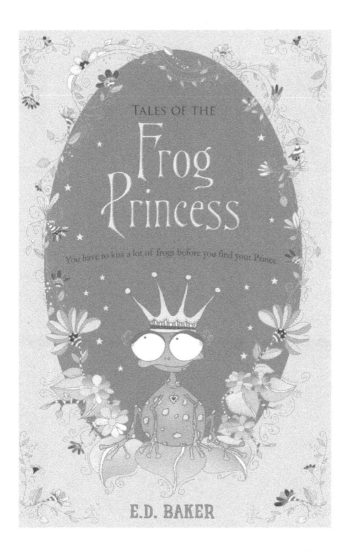